Thick Chicks

a novel

K.L. GILCHRIST

ALSO BY K.L. GILCHRIST

Broken Together

Holding On

Hallway Lights

THICK CHICKS

A NOVEL

K.L. GILCHRIST

Thick Chicks is a work of fiction. Names, characters, places, and incidents are either a product of the author's imagination or are used fictitiously. Any resemblance to actual persons, living or dead, business establishments, events, or locales is entirely coincidental.

Cover design by Rocío Martín Osuna

Published in the United States by ISG Press.

Scripture quotations taken from the *Holy Bible, English Standard Version*.

Library of Congress Control Number: 2019916652

ISBN 9781734170597

Ebook ISBN 9781734170573

This novel is presented solely for entertainment purposes. The author and publisher are not offering it as mental health, physical health or medical advice. While best efforts have been used in researching and preparing this story, the author and publisher make no recommendations or warranties of any kind and assume no liabilities of any kind with respect to the accuracy and completeness of the contents and specifically disclaim any implied use for a particular purpose.

For my mother, Sharon E. Gilchrist

SCRIPTURE

"A person standing alone can be attacked or defeated, but two can stand back-to-back and conquer. Three are even better for a triple-braided cord is not easily broken." (*Ecclesiastes 4:12*, English Standard Version Bible)

∽

"A friend loves at all times, and a brother is born for adversity." (*Proverbs 17:17*, English Standard Version Bible)

∽

"For you are still of the flesh. For while there is jealousy and strife among you, are you not of the flesh and behaving only in a human way?" (*1 Corinthians 3:3*, English Standard Version Bible)

PART I

FALL

1

CHABLIS

I f anyone asked me how I feel right now, I'd say blessed.

Being joyful? That's how I roll.

So, I've got a smile on my face right now, even though I'm sitting in my doctor's office waiting to be examined. Today is my yearly physical. I'm happy about that because I get to talk and laugh with Dr. Houtman. She likes me, and I adore her, but I don't see her that often. I'll probably be here for like fifteen minutes before she tells me to get my flu shot and get out of here.

"Is all that hair yours?" The nurse asks when she approaches me with a blood pressure cuff in her hands.

"Definitely. I have the receipt for all twenty inches of it."

"What type?"

"Brazilian virgin. You can curl and dye it. Make it wavy. Straighten it. Everything."

"Well, it looks great on you." She smiles at me while fastening the cuff to my arm and then pumps the bulb to inflate it. It deflates. Her smile fades. "Your file says you're twenty-five years old?"

"That's right."

"I'm going to do this again." She readjusts the cuff.

"Okay."

She measures my blood pressure twice more, then flashes me a tight smile before she says, "The doctor will be in to see you shortly."

She shuts the door and I gaze down at my toenails. They've grown long, and the red polish has chipped off. I'm off work today. I can stop by Modern Nails for a mani/pedi. Can't wait to get over there after my doc tells me the usual. *Blood tests are good. Try to lose a little weight if you can. Have the nurse give you a flu shot. I'll see you next year.*

Five minutes later, a salt-and-pepper-haired, glasses-wearing Dr. Felice Houtman walks through the door.

"Chablis Shields, love the hair."

"Dr. Houtman, love the lab coat."

We've greeted each other in the same way for the past three years. I love having an older black female doctor. There's nothing like it. I can talk to her about anything.

She checks my ears, nose, and throat. Makes me breathe in and out a few times with the stethoscope pressed against my back. Then she sits on her little round stool and pulls up my test results from the computer.

"Hmm," she says, leaning closer to the screen.

"I know, I know, take a few pounds off and get my flu shot, right?" I swing my legs back and forth as I push a long lock of dark brown hair out of my face.

She wheels around on the stool. Now she's frowning. "I'm afraid I have a few more directions for you this year."

I stop swinging my legs.

Dr. Houtman takes off her reading glasses. "I'm going to be straight with you. I'm not happy with your blood pressure or your blood test results."

"What's wrong?"

"We measured your pressure three times this morning. It's definitely elevated. The last reading has it at 140 over 90. Your cholesterol numbers were better last year, and so was your blood sugar. You didn't forget and eat something the morning of the blood test, did you?"

I'm thinking. Last Thursday morning? Breakfast? No. I only drank water on my way to Quest Diagnostics. They drew my blood and then I drove to work.

"No," I say.

"Any late night eating?"

"I'm dead to the world at night. The results are that bad?"

"I've seen worse blood sugar numbers, but yours was higher than last year."

These results make no sense. Physically, I feel good. Mentally? Well, I've only had one panic attack this year. And that was because Mariah insisted on making me wait on a street corner while she got the car from the parking garage in Chinatown. Some man rushed up way too close behind me on the sidewalk, the world in front of my eyeballs narrowed and I felt as if I was about to have a heart attack. If not for Mariah finally bringing the car around and nudging me into the back seat, I might have fallen down right on the curb.

Yes, I have issues, but none of them have to do with my internal organs.

"So, what do I do?" I say, snapping out of my trance.

"You know."

"Take off some weight?"

"For a start."

"I don't do diets. Can I stop by an exercise class a few times a week? Will that help?"

"You should absolutely exercise. You should adjust your eating habits, too, but those changes may not be enough to make a major difference. I'm writing you a prescription for blood pressure medication. We'll monitor you while you're on it."

Dr. Houtman stands up and sifts through a stack of pamphlets on the shelf above the computer desk.

"I'm giving you information on how to choose a good nutrition program. And listen, I never believed that crap about everyone needing to have a certain BMI. I see a lot of patients. Some people have bigger bodies, and they are just fine. It's not the number on the scale or your clothing size that's a problem. If you're living a clean life, taking care of yourself, and your numbers are good, I could care less what you weigh."

"So—"

"Your pressure is up. Now I care what you weigh. Oh, and you've gained another ten pounds since last year."

"Fantastic," I mumble, staring at my overgrown toenails again.

She scribbles something on her pad. "Take this." She passes me the pamphlet and prescription.

I sigh as I take them and stare at the pink slip of paper. The scribble is too hard for me to read. Something starting with an M. I have no idea what it is and no clue how it will affect my mental state. I'll have to mention it to my therapist, Dr. Jerrica, next week.

Dr. Houtman stares me down. "There's a reason they call hypertension the silent killer. Heart disease will sneak up on you."

"Serious?"

"As a heart attack."

"That's not funny."

"It shouldn't be."

The rest of my appointment takes about ten minutes. I thank my doctor before she leaves, then slide on my underwear, jeans, and shirt. The pamphlet and prescription I shove into my bag. Those pieces of paper weigh almost nothing, but seeing them in there makes me tired so I sit down to slip on my heels. A minute passes and I'm still sitting here. Just thinking.

This is where I am today.

And this is how I got here.

Six years ago, I got beat up. Bad. Baseball bat. Ringing sound. Blood on the ground. That's what I remember. It happened right after I left the dance studio and walked down the alley to the main street. My attacker struck me from behind, punched and slapped me and then tried to choke me out, but that's when two guys passed the alley opening. When they turned inside, the attacker ran off. One guy stayed by my side while his friend called for and flagged down the ambulance. If those men hadn't walked past at that exact moment, I'd have died that night — no more Chablis Charmaine Shields.

Anyway, when I woke up at the hospital, I saw my mom pacing in front of the bed. She kept patting my body and mumbling about keeping me warm because the stupid blankets were thin and cheesy and not worth spit and Charlene Shields' daughter deserved better. Then she stalked out to the hallway to calm down my dad, Sonny. I heard his voice bouncing off the walls when he called his brothers Fred and Buzzy, and his twin nephews Aaron and Adrian—the terror squad he assembled to drive through Wilmington and get that fool, Tony. Because of course it was him. Who else knew I'd be alone in the alley right after Friday night modern dance class?

Tony. My boyfriend turned ex-boyfriend. I loved him before he ambushed me. Maybe I deserved it. I don't know. Someone's loose lips told him I'd cheated with two different guys, and he came after me.

When the cops scanned the crime scene, they found the bat lying on the side of the alley. The boys in blue checked it for fingerprints and matched those to Tony when his mom, Ms. Gloria, made him turn himself in.

That bat blow delivered one nasty concussion, and Tony's hands did the rest. Two black eyes. A cut down my right cheek. Fractured nose. Bruised body.

Assault and battery. Tony pleaded guilty. The judge gave him five years in prison.

My dad dismissed the sentence as some fraganackle bull.

At home, my mom chain-smoked every day while she took care of me. She also arranged for me to transfer from Wilmington University in Delaware to Temple University the following fall. I would live with my cousin, Mariah, and her family in Philly.

The healing year.

Ten full months of rest at my parents' house. The doctor's office and the rehab center were the only places I visited. My concussion didn't heal well at first and specialists told me to avoid stimulation.

The headaches, blurred vision and the fact that my world had come to a complete stop made me depressed. My mom tried to help by bringing me my favorite foods and letting me drift in and out of sleep most days.

No TV. No friends. No life.

Eventually, my concussion healed. Black eyes. Fractured nose. Bruised body. All of it returned to normal. That cut on my right cheek?

It morphed into a thin, dark scar. MAC Studio Fix concealer covers it pretty well now. My long sew-in helps hide it, too.

The seventy pounds of excess weight which grew on my body while I lay around eating and trying not to lose my mind after the attack?

I still have them.

Only now I have ten more.

But I refuse to sit here feeling sorry for myself. I need to get on up out of this chair and keep right on living my best life.

I've got a lot going for me. I'm cute and I have a good job and, considering what happened to me, thank God I don't have major problems with men. I still date, but I proceed with caution for a few reasons. Firstly, I'm not about to fall for a man with anger issues. Secondly, I've been a born again Christian since I turned twenty-one, so I prefer Godly men. Thirdly, I'm prone to panic attacks. So, if I ever meet a dope single brother who's got love for a thick chick, a heart for Jesus *and* he can handle the fact that I have a therapist on speed-dial, I shall embrace him and be his queen forever.

When I finally come out of the exam room, I step into the tiny side office to get my flu shot and then I'm down the hall and out of the building.

Outside, the air carries the scent of Philadelphia morning commuter traffic. It's really warm for a mid-September morning and I sweat a little when I start walking, listening to the sound of my heels as they click on the pavement.

Lose weight, huh? What if I don't want to take off 80 pounds? I need to start praying to the Lord right now. Just go on and drop to my knees and pray about my body and a bunch of other stuff I don't really feel like dwelling on.

I cross the street to the parking lot. When the wind kicks up, it takes my store-bought hair skyward and slams a gust of air against the back of my neck. I stand stock still because I'm starting to feel dizzy and my vision is narrowing. Clenching my fists inside my pockets, I breathe in for four seconds. Then I hold the air in my lungs for seven seconds, then exhale for eight seconds. I do this a few more times until the dizziness fades. After I blink twice and then once more, I focus on a crack in the gray sidewalk until my vision clears.

"I sought the Lord, and he answered me," I whisper, lifting my face to the sky. "He delivered me from all my fears."

Nothing's wrong. Nothing's wrong. Nothing's wrong.

No one is here.

2

MARIAH

"Mom, Gianna's mother is coming to pick her up from practice." Mariah Shields-Rodriguez's daughter, Benita, told her over the phone. "They drive past our house. They can drop me off at home."

"Binky, I said I'd come get you."

Mariah rushed through the downstairs hallway of their home, holding the phone to her ear and peering at the empty wooden hook where her keyring should rest. Now, where were her keys?

"But you don't have to," Binky said.

"Oh, but I will."

"Mom, this is crazy. It's only dance team practice. Don't rush over here."

"Maybe I want to see you and talk to you about your new routine? And I'd love to speak to Coach Letts for a minute." Mariah planted her hand on her hip.

"I can show you our new routine at home."

"Benita, I'm picking you up. That's final!"

"Fine. Whatever."

Mariah found herself listening to silence when her daughter ended the call. *Binky.* Perfect nickname for her. Sometimes it seemed as if she'd never grow up. She'd always be a big-eyed infant crawling through the house with a binky in her mouth, even though she was now a teenager.

The name typed on her birth certificate read Benita Valentina Rodriguez. Beautiful girl. Beautiful name. Her attitude, however, needed some work.

Sighing, Mariah rounded the corner into the kitchen.

Keys.

Yes. Right next to the fruit bowl.

She put the phone down and wiped a bead of sweat from her brow before picking them up. The time on the wall clock read four p.m. Binky's dance team practice ended at five. Mariah could make it to the high school gym with enough time to see at least the last few minutes, and then talk to the coach about her daughter's attitude on the team.

Darn it! She'd been sitting too long that afternoon, paying their household bills online. Her right foot still had pins and needles in it. A stabbing pain shot across her sole and up her leg.

Maybe it would have been better to let Binky take that ride home with Gianna? On second thought, no. The last time she'd let Binky do that, Binky decided it would be fine to go out for dinner with Gianna's family, then shopping, and then she'd come home and collapsed onto her bed. No homework or studying at all. Her semester wasn't starting out great, and Mariah's threats to make her quit the dance team had fallen on deaf ears.

So yes, Mariah definitely needed to do the bathroom shuffle, then leave the house in time to pick up her daughter. Since the late September air was warm, she didn't need to stop and grab a jacket. She made it to the bathroom, then out of the house and into the car in less than ten minutes.

Turning the key in the ignition, she ignored the dinging sound meant to remind her to strap on a seatbelt she had no intention of using. She pulled her phone from her bag to check it one last time before leaving home.

Nothing else from Binky. One text from her best friend, Towanda, just to say *hey*. One from her older sister Tamron asking if she'd received the packet about their summer family reunion. A whopping total of ten texts from her cousin Chablis, but Mariah didn't have to answer those because Chablis didn't require a response. She always forwarded every picture and link she found interesting.

Not one message or voicemail from her husband Oscar.

Mariah tapped his name in her favorites. She backed out of the driveway and into the street while waiting for the call to connect.

"Hey, honey," she said after he answered. "Just wanted to check on you. How's your day so far?"

"Are you calling from the car?"

"Yes."

"I've told you time and time again not to do that."

"I'm on speakerphone."

"You're still distracted. You know, you don't listen to me at all."

"Oscar, I'm fine." She gripped the steering wheel with one hand. "How's your day?"

"Busy. And yours?"

"It's the house, nothing exciting. I did get in touch with the contractors for the upstairs windows. They can install them next month. Is that okay?"

"That's fine."

"And I'm still deciding if we should go ahead and do the downstairs as well. What do you think?"

"Whatever you decide will be fine." Oscar's voice dipped lower. "Listen, did you look into what we talked about this morning? That Lifesum health app thing? I've heard good things about it."

"I'll get around to it."

"When?"

"When what?"

"When are you going to review it? If you like, we can look at it together tonight. What do you say?"

"We'll see."

"No, we should make time for this. After dinner, you shouldn't be doing anything, right?"

"Os, listen—"

"See, you're brushing me off like you always do. You know, I'm trying to help you, but sometimes, you make things hard."

"Oscar—"

"I have to go. Talk to you at home."

After he ended the call, Mariah threw the phone onto the passenger seat so hard it bounced to the car floor. She bit her lip and kept on driving.

Lately, whenever she interacted with her husband, disappointment flowed from him like ocean waves onto the beach. And whenever they had a conversation, he always seemed to find a way to make her body a talking point. It was like he woke up each morning hoping to find the version of her from their first year of marriage.

The fun-loving, free-spirited, one-hundred-and-thirty pounds lighter version of her, to be exact.

But people change.

Giving birth to Binky had placed Mariah's body in a tailspin. Her weight had increased dramatically after that pregnancy. As she'd raised their daughter and settled into home life, she'd placed her body and life goals on the back burner and, all right, maybe she enjoyed food and drink a little more than she should have.

Sure, she was all for creating better habits in her life. But every year, her family required more of her. She always wanted to push herself to reclaim old life dreams and minimize her body issues, but *later* became her favorite word. *Later*, she'd take off the pounds for good. *Later*, she'd return to college, finish her degree and start a small business.

Later.

Somewhere along the way to later, her hormones got out of whack. She wasn't sure which one arrived first—diabetes or polycystic ovarian syndrome. The hormone trouble messed with her fertility, further straining her marriage. From the beginning, they'd talked about on having at least four kids, but Binky was all they had so far.

Mariah could practically touch Oscar's disappointment about that, but what could she do?

Pray for him. Love him. And maybe later she'd consider his latest opinion on how she should address her health.

But right now, she needed to pick up his daughter.

· · ·

Already outside, Binky stood beside a car in the parking lot with two other girls from the dance team. Practice must have ended a little early. Mariah still intended to speak to the team coach before taking Binky home. She needed to ask how Binky's behavior had been with the dance team, since two weeks earlier, Coach Letts said Binky liked to make sarcastic comments behind her back.

Mariah parked in the lot and headed toward the school building. Binky rushed over before Mariah even reached the curb. "Mom!"

"Benita!" Mariah kept moving.

"Where are you going?"

"I'm here, so I'd like to talk to the coach for a second. Where is she?"

"Still in the gym."

"Hop in the car while I talk to her."

"Mom, you don't have to do that."

Mariah stopped talking as she entered the side door to the gym. Binky trailed her. A couple of girls and a boy lounged on the bleachers inside. Dressed in school colors, they looked adorable and bubbly and perfect and resembled Disney kids. Coach Letts stood off to the side, unplugging the sound system.

Mariah smiled as she walked over. "Coach! So, how is Benita doing? Giving you any problems?"

Coach Letts frowned, holding an extension cord in her hands. "I'm glad you stopped by. And for the record, most days Benita is just fine."

"And the rest of them?" Mariah felt footsteps behind her as Binky paced in the background.

"I'll be honest with you." The coach lowered her voice. "She's far from being the easiest young lady to work with on this team. It's not her technique, it's her attitude. If things go well, she's pleased. If they don't, she mumbles under her breath and blames her teammates. And I asked to see some of her test grades today…"

"Bad?"

"Below average." Coach Letts pushed the stereo cart toward the equipment room and gestured for Mariah to follow. "It's early in the semester, and I'd like her to start off with good grades so she won't have any problems staying on the dance team when the semester ends.

It would be great for you to talk to her about her study habits. The other girls admire her dance skills and rhythm, but I'd like her to set an example academically, as well."

Mariah nodded. "You've got my support. I'll talk to her."

Again, she thought.

Binky had slipped away, but Mariah spied her by the gym door. Her daughter was slim, but with curves in all the right places and growing taller each year. Her thick curly hair was dark and wild, framing her face. She resembled a young Mariah.

Unfortunately, somewhere around age twelve, her smile had gone AWOL, replaced by the same permanent scowl she had no problem showing her mother as she approached.

"Mom, we need to go."

"First of all, fix your tone."

"Sorry. Can we go?"

"Why are you rushing me?"

Binky didn't answer right away. Mariah watched as her daughter shifted her weight from foot to foot, looking around nervously.

"Benita, what's wrong?"

"Just...Mom, please come on." Binky said, walking away fast.

Mariah followed, moving out of the gym quick to catch up with her pretty daughter with the gorgeous hair and the thin frame. A girl who didn't carry an ounce of excess weight on her body.

Binky walked way too fast for her mother nowadays, and she probably wished she was the daughter of an equally thin woman.

And the embarrassment of that thought stung Mariah so much it accompanied them as a silent passenger in the car all the way home.

3

TOWANDA

Towanda Mathis gazed into blank faces, not that it mattered. She would still finish her pitch with a flourish and leave them wanting more. Remote in hand, she pressed the button that returned the projector screen to its hiding place in the ceiling. She unfastened the front of her navy-blue Calvin Klein blazer as she took long strides to the wall to turn the lights back on, then walked back to the front of the room.

Time for Q&A.

"Ladies and gentlemen, that completes my presentation today. And remember, in today's world it won't be enough for MEGANDA to simply advertise a new style of watches. You aren't only selling a product. MEGANDA is a brand. My firm will help you cultivate that brand and build trust with new and existing clients. We will help you set well-defined business goals, track key metrics for your success and help you expand into new markets."

She stepped forward and gestured to the marketing materials on the conference table. "In your booklets, you'll find information that breaks down the finer points of what my firm offers regarding inbound marketing, digital branding and building your business. ThinkLARGE wants to help your customers come to you. Does anyone have any questions?"

A tanned man in a short-sleeved blue shirt raised his hand. "I have a question."

"Yes, how can I help?" Towanda asked.

The man dropped his booklet to the table. "No offense to your company, but do we really need all this? I mean, we make watches. Watches. I don't get all this branding stuff."

A hard question but a good question. Towanda moved closer to the end of the conference room table, but instead of sitting down, she planted her feet wider and leaned forward. "May I have your name, please?"

"Patrick."

"Patrick, I understand what you're asking. And I'm sure you'll understand if I mention Accurist, Apache, Apple, Armand Nicolet, ASUAG and American Waltham Watch Company. Do you know these names?"

"I know some of them."

"Some?"

"Everyone knows Apple."

"Absolutely everyone knows Apple." Towanda raised her left arm and pointed to her wrist. "And on my arm right now is an ASOON smartwatch. You may not have known this watch existed." She lowered her arms and leaned in a little closer to Patrick. "But I'll bet you knew Apple had a smartwatch, and you know at least a little about their brand and the story of their company."

Patrick nodded. "Yes, I do."

Towanda backed off and stood up tall once again. "Patrick, your company is worth much more than a logo, a name and good watches. There are many watch companies. How will MEGANDA stand out from the competition? How about the fact that your watch parts are all manufactured in the United States? For a certain type of buyer, that information could make the difference in a sale. We want to target that buyer and make MEGANDA their preferred watch company." Her eyes scanned the room once more. "Are there any more questions?"

She searched the crowd. No questioning looks and no raised hands. She could close out now.

"Thank you so much for your time."

Those around the table applauded. From the back of the conference room, Nelson Anders, the MEGANDA company CEO, rose from his chair. He offered his hand as he walked toward her. "Thank you for your presentation, Ms. Mathis."

"Towanda, please," She shook his hand. "Think of me as a friend you called in to help you out."

"Well, thanks, Towanda." Nelson had a long face and even longer brown hair pulled back with a rubber band. He wore faded blue jeans and a button-down blue plaid shirt. "I guess you can tell our team here is all about the hardware and tech side of things."

"Serving companies like yours is my specialty. You start small, but you'll build up soon enough." She rubbed her sweaty palms against her slacks. "By the way, is there a place in this building where I can buy a bottle of water?"

"Sorry about that. We should've had water here for you." Nelson turned and pointed toward the door. "Just down the hall and to your right you'll find the vending machines."

"No worries." Towanda retrieved her black purse from the office chair in the corner. "Your team can take a moment to look over the numbers I've outlined for you."

She headed out of the conference room and down the hallway. On the way to the vending area, she pulled a tissue from her purse, dabbed at her forehead and wiped off her hands. She hoped no one had seen she was sweating.

Even if they did, so what? She was there to pitch marketing and branding services, not win a modeling contest.

Nelson had emailed her a week earlier, asking her to meet with his small startup company. He told her he used to work with the CEO of Zoumi, a small tech outfit out of Horsham, PA. The way she obtained most work for her consulting company, thinkLARGE, was through word of mouth, the name of the game in the LinkedIn era.

In the vending area, Towanda bought a bottle of Aquafina, taking several long sips while she leaned against the drink machine. At least

MEGANDA rented shared office space while they worked to expand their business beyond their watchmaking shop. Last month, she'd met with a four person, all-natural cosmetics company. Those ladies worked from a dining room.

Did Towanda take the account?

Of course, she did.

And with thinkLARGE's help, soon enough, more women would clamor for GiveGoodFace bronzing powders, lipsticks and mascaras.

Towanda took her time walking back to the conference room. She was only halfway down the hallway when she heard the voices. Patrick was talking to Nelson. She shook her head as she listened. Every work team seemed to include one loudmouth skeptic who thought he could save the company money by avoiding marketing and brand development. She decided to wait until their conversation ended before walking back in.

"Building our company brand. That's it?" Towanda overheard Patrick say. "That's what she wants us to pay for?"

"She had a point with that watch example," a woman responded.

"She was way too overbearing in her approach. Really, I got a little scared at the end," a different man spoke up.

"Me too," another woman said. "I think Patrick wanted to run."

"Guys, I need you to pull yourselves together," Nelson said, his voice serious. "We are here to evaluate her proposal. You all told me you wanted the same type of marketing that got Zoumi noticed. I brought you the woman who provides it. We are professionals here. May I remind you the walls are thin?"

Maybe Towanda shouldn't have pushed so hard? But she couldn't resist. She'd done the research. Why not show it off, even if it made people uncomfortable?

She couldn't wait to leave and call Mariah to tell her about today's presentation. Mariah would probably laugh and then tease her about falling asleep in the back pew at the church service last week, missing Pastor Downes preaching on the topic of compassion.

Towanda pulled herself up to her full six-foot height, closed her water bottle, then placed it and the tissues into her purse as she marched toward the conference room door.

Authenticity. Large and in charge. Emphasis on *in charge*.

"Ladies and gentlemen, I see you are reading the booklets," she announced. "I'm sure I have a package which will meet your needs."

She scanned the room. Again, blank faces. No mouths moving.

Nelson nodded toward her. "We'd like to take a week to consider the marketing and branding packages your company offers. Can we get back to you on Monday?"

"Certainly. It was wonderful meeting all of you. Have a pleasant afternoon."

She held her head high, clutching the extra booklets in her hand. With her black Dooney & Bourke bag hanging from her shoulder, Towanda moved from the conference room to the hallway, from the hall to the front vestibule and from there out the door to the parking lot. She finished her water on the way down the sidewalk to her car, tossing the bottle in the recycling receptacle before crossing the parking lot.

So what if some MEGANDA team members thought she was intimidating? She'd long been used to having a voice and personality that matched her imposing frame.

While swimming with the sharks in the business world, a super-sized presence had become her asset.

In any company setting, she could lean in hard enough to break a conference room table.

Towanda gazed around the half-empty parking lot as she dug her keys from her bag and clicked the fob to open the door to her gray Range Rover. The comfortably warm September weather made her feel optimistic, despite what she'd just heard in the conference room.

It would be good to secure this account so late in the third quarter. For now, she'd drive back to the thinkLARGE office, send out follow-up communication and check on the status of two other accounts. Then she'd sit and talk with her assistant Jackie, who was also the office manager for thinkLARGE, about the possibility of hiring an intern from one of the local colleges. Later tonight, she'd compose her recommendations for the thinkLARGE website updates and email those to the web designer.

Laser sharp focus on tasks? Towanda's specialty.

Those poor young employees in the conference room? They didn't know any better. She should thank them. That conversation she'd heard while she'd stood in the hallway? When MEGANDA hired her, that verbal exchange would cost them about a grand in extra hourly fees padded into the invoice.

Towanda smiled.

Silly folks.

They'd just bought a brand new set of tires for her Range Rover.

4

CHABLIS

S omeone just sent me a text, because I see my phone vibrating on my desk next to my keyboard. Usually, I try not to send messages while I'm working, but I pick up the device anyway when I see it's a message from Mariah.

Hey! R u there?

I text back, *Hey, beautiful!*

I'm serious about getting pounds off this year. Need u to buddy up with me.

Wonderful. For more than a week I kicked Dr. Houtman and her pamphlets out of my head. Now Mariah's coming for me. I roll my eyes as I tap my phone screen.

Me on a diet?

Diet, exercise, better nutrition. We can lean on each other.

U ask Towanda?

I will l8r. She's in boss mode right now. I want to get us all together to talk about it. U free this Thursday?

Get back to me after you talk to T. No matter what happens, I'll be there for you.

Thx. Love u!

Bless u. TTYL.

I put my phone down and just stare at it. I didn't want to start a diet when Dr. Houtman lectured me, and I don't want to start one now, either.

Lose ten pounds. Gain ten pounds.

Besides, I've seen too many women crash land with their weight loss adventures on social media.

Take my friends. Every January, Simone, Felicia and Nikki go crazy over some new super-vegan/green-algae/drop twenty-pounds-overnight eating plan. Then they spend the next two months getting skinny while smothering their faces with MAC and Urban Decay and snapping pics of themselves in every conceivable place, including the bathroom, before posting the shots to Instagram. When April rolls around, they go to their Big Mama's Easter dinner and they all fall off the diet wagon like bales of hay.

But Mariah just asked me for support. Mariah. She practically adopted me after I left Wilmington. She didn't have to open her home and let me live there while I finished college, but she did. I can't forget that. She wouldn't ask me to partner up with her if she didn't need me. She has the most weight to lose. I'm a thick chick, but I can still shop in stores that aren't exclusively for plus size for the most part.

So, while I'm not happy about dieting, I'll do it for a little while to support Mariah. If I can drop twenty pounds, it should lower my blood pressure. I do know high blood pressure is dangerous.

Last week I talked to Simone about it. She's thin, but her pressure shot up during her pregnancy and she had to be monitored through her last two trimesters. Her son turned out fine, though. He's a beautiful boy with a head full of jet-black curls. His dad is some guy named Thomas who works as a lighting engineer on movie sets. Simone plans to take baby Najee and move to southern California next month so they can get married. I'll help her pack. Another friend moving on.

Someone rattles my cubicle wall. I hate that.

"Yeah?" I pull off my headphones.

It's my co-worker Josh. "Meeting in Conference Room G in fifteen minutes. 'Kay?"

"Got it."

Josh is a sweetheart. I don't know why he didn't send us all a group chat, but okay. Fifteen minutes? That's enough time for me to be proactive and take a peek at what WW online has to offer for diet options. But before I do that, just for fun, I pick up my phone again and fire off a text to Mariah's best friend Towanda.

Hey girl boss! Mariah text you about supporting her for weight loss?

Ten minutes later, I'm studying online eating plan options and Towanda's text arrives.

Are you serious? Leave me alone. I'm busy!

Whatever.

Towanda could hang up on me in the middle of a phone call, call me munchkin or tell me to leave her alone seventy times in a day and I'd never take it personally.

She's a grouch sometimes.

Maybe people expect her to be mean since she never smiles at you with her teeth showing unless you're tight with her. She has a soft heart, though. In January, my job switched health insurance providers. I didn't pay any attention to the fine print in the new plan and this March a $700 therapist bill hit my mailbox. I mentioned it around Towanda after church one Sunday. A few days later, when I called to set up a payment plan at CCS Counseling Associates, they told me the balance had been paid in full. I know Towanda took care of it.

My coworkers shift around in their cubicles. Sounds like they're getting ready for the meeting. I only have a few minutes to look at WW options. I squint to stare at the asterisks next to each offering and see there is a weekly fee. My budget only has room for essentials. I'm single with no kids and no house, which means nothing is deductible on my taxes except for tithes, student loan interest and the money I donate to buy farm animals twice a year through Heifer International. Forget ditching giving. My therapist gets a monthly co-pay I have to keep paying if I want to manage walking down dark streets without feeling as if I'm about to have a heart attack. Weave maintenance costs me eighty a month and I'm not changing my hairstyle. Not much room for weight loss program fees.

Time to stop searching for expensive diet plans and go to the conference room for the meeting. When I get there, I see my manager, Christopher, and eleven of the fifteen workers in my department.

Christopher glances at me as I take a seat around the table. "Did you pass Harry on the way down here?"

"No," I say, wheeling myself closer to the table.

Christopher reaches over to the conference room phone and presses the buttons for Harry's extension. "Harry, let's go!"

Two minutes later, Harry comes huffing into the room out of breath. With his gray-streaked sandy brown hair and lean features, he looks more like a college basketball coach than a software test engineer like the rest of us. He shuts the door behind him and finds a seat.

Christopher looks around the table. "I don't want to waste time, so let me tell you why I called you all in here. Some of you asked me about the team lead position for automated test. Those of you who applied, thank you. I appreciate you for the work you've done here. You're all winners in my book."

This promotion seemed like a great way to grow, so I applied for it last month. I'll get this. I know I will. No company wants to recruit from the outside because it costs too much.

Christopher continues. "We've made a decision, and it was approved by upper management today. I'm happy to say your new test team lead is sitting here right now."

This sounds good. This could be it.

Christopher sits back with a grin. "Congratulations to Joshua Smalls. He's your new team lead!"

Applause and shouts of congratulations go around the room. I look up and see Josh turn beet red from the tips of his ears to the center of his face. My eyes shift down at the floor, then back at Josh, over at the painting on the wall and finally around the table at my cheering coworkers. Aleksey's ice blue eyes catch mine, and that's when I remember to clap.

Josh is a great worker. I should know. I trained him last year.

Typically, by five-thirty, I'd be out of the office and zooming away from the company campus in my Focus. This afternoon, I stay in my cubicle seething and pretending to work while the cubicle farm empties. Around six, I walk down the aisle. The only person still around is Anant. He sits turned around wearing his noise cancellation headphones.

The light is on in Christopher's glass-doored office. I lean into the doorway and knock a little too hard on the doorframe. "Got a second?"

His smile is welcoming but his eyes say he expected this.

"Certainly. Come on in."

I glide in, shut the door behind me and plop down in the gray office chair in front of his massive desk. He has two computers and four screens placed around the U-shaped structure. Data scrolls down all the screens. It looks like God gave him the task of monitoring all the prayers ascending to heaven.

"Christopher? What happened?"

"This is about the Josh decision?"

"Yes."

Christopher rubs the brown beard growth on his chin. "For what it's worth, you are hands down our best team member. I can always count on you. Five people applied internally for the team lead. The decision came down to you and Josh."

"I trained him on all our test processes."

"I'm aware of that. You're both great candidates. You both have the right certifications and dedication to the company."

"So, what happened?"

"It was a tough call. But when we isolated the leader tasks alone, Josh was the best choice."

"You just said you can count on me."

"Absolutely, but the committee thought you might be too tentative when coaching your fellow team members to be accountable for the quality of their work. That could be a detriment when someone gives you a hard time about meeting our test deliverables."

What else can I say?

"Thanks for your time." I stand up.

"Chablis, there will be other opportunities in the future. I'm sure of it," he says.

I'm not sure of anything, so I just shut his office door and walk away.

· · ·

IT'S TUESDAY NIGHT, AND MY CHURCH LIFE GROUP STARTS AT SEVEN SHARP. The Jones family hosts it in their Chestnut Hill home. Ever notice how every place of worship seems to have one Ken and Barbie couple who live in a perfect house with an athletic son, an adorable daughter, and a yellow Labrador? Well dip Ken and Barbie in a cocoa fountain and erase the furry animal from the picture and you'd have Dr. Brian Jones and his lovely homemaker wife, Tracey. I love them to death, though. Relationship goals all the way.

Their front door is open when I arrive, so I walk in, kick off my shoes on the mat and direct myself to the dining room. My whole life group family sits in there, chowing down and talking. I'm not in the best mood, so I keep quiet and wave at everyone. I grab a plate and fill it with chicken and vegetable stir-fry with brown rice.

Dr. Jones calls to me. "How was work, Chablis?"

I grimace. "Don't ask. Pray for me."

Although this would be the best place for me to vent, I don't want to talk about being passed over for team lead. Or my elevated blood pressure. Or my friends moving on in life. I keep my eyes centered on my plate until it's time to sing and pray.

When dinner is over, we all troop to the living room. I raise my hand to volunteer to teach the youth Bible lesson, but Tracey stops me.

"Oh no, you don't," she says. "You've taught the youth lesson three times in a row. Stay with us tonight."

Across the room, Jesse and Kim Chase, who have two young sons, are already herding the kids into the family room.

I stuff myself into a corner of the huge sofa and scan the adult lesson sheet. And before I can say *boo*, here comes the Reverend Alex Robinson, sitting down so close to my left hip I think I can feel the Samsung in his right pocket. He's single. Nice man. Full of love for the Lord. He's not much older than me. Around thirty. We get along fine and if we'd met years ago, we might have started seeing each other. About six months after he joined our life group, Tracey Jones scheduled a Saturday evening group outing to Pennsylvania 6. I was supposed to attend as Rev. Robinson's "date." I refused to go. Firstly, because he's in my church life group, so doesn't that make him family or something? Secondly, I've listened to his prayer requests. If I hear him ask one more time for prayer for his former fiancée D'Londa, and her gospel singing career and his attempts to keep their friendship, I'm going to find out where D'Londa lives and force her to marry the man and put him out of his misery.

I check my phone and fire off a few quick texts to Simone about my job situation. When I glance up and see Tracey giving me the side eye, I flash a smile and drop my phone in my purse at my feet. I then volunteer to read our theme verse, which is Romans 12:2.

Life group has officially started.

My head floats among the clouds the whole time. An hour passes, and before I know it, everyone kneels to pray for one another. I close my eyes, but I have a feeling my prayers don't reach past the ceiling.

When prayer time ends, we stand up and walk to the family room and cheer for the kids as they recite their verses. We stand in a circle, hold hands, Dr. Jones delivers the closing prayer and then we break out. In the front hallway, I slip on my shoes and jacket and then we head out the front door to our cars.

Job over. Life group over. Let me get to the store so I can shop and go home already.

At the GIANT, there's nothing close to low-calorie in my cart. Why?

Because I don't want it.

Maybe later, but not now.

I pick up a two-liter bottle of Coke, three plastic-wrapped pizzas, some frozen meals for work lunches, Colgate, Listerine and Lottabody hair mousse. I'm in the checkout line texting Simone back because she finally answered my message.

The checkout girl waves her hand to get my attention. "Miss?"

"Yes?" I look up from my phone.

"You must not have seen it. We have Diet Cokes. They're on sale too. Not just regular."

"I saw them. Thank you," I say, gripping my phone while I force my expression to remain blank.

She cracks her gum and rings me up.

Its clear her parents never taught her not to be rude, so I just pay and leave.

When I'm in my car, it takes me a minute to put the keys in the ignition.

Right now? I just feel heavy.

And I don't think it has anything to do with the weight on my body.

5

MARIAH

Mariah placed white serving bowls full of salad and grilled chicken in the middle of the dining room table, then walked back to the kitchen to get a pitcher full of iced tea. After she carried that to the dining room, she found herself back in the kitchen alone. She might as well wash the pots and pans. Towanda and Chablis were supposed be there for dinner at 6:30 p.m., but it was almost seven and neither of them had arrived yet.

As Mariah turned on the sink's hot water tap, she heard heavy footsteps approach from behind. Oscar wandered into the kitchen. He scanned the table and counters. "I knew I smelled something delicious coming from this room. Where's the food?"

"In there," Mariah said over her shoulder before turning back to the sink. "You staying down here? Hanging with us women tonight?"

"Uh-uh." He peered inside the doorway leading to the dining room. "I have a date with SportsCenter."

"Fine, fine," she said, rinsing an aluminum pan. "You know I asked Chablis and Towanda to hold me accountable for my weight loss goals. I'm serious this time. I'll do whatever it takes."

"I'm here to support you, too. Remember that. But, uh, do you think…"

"What?"

"Is this the best way for you to start? I mean, do you need them here just to start? Aren't you making it harder on yourself?"

Mariah whipped around, one hand dripping water and suds on the kitchen tiles. "Are you saying I can't do it?"

"All I am saying is if you're trying to lose weight, inviting Towanda and Chablis over here may not be the best way to start. When are you going to see your doctor? I don't want you doing this without the right guidance. You need someone official to help you. No offense, but you know Towanda gets wrapped up in all her business stuff. And Chablis has major issues of her own."

Oscar hadn't said anything Mariah hadn't thought about before. Yes, she should call her doctor to talk about her plans, but she'd have to summon up the courage first. Doctor visits had become so humiliating and she had to endure them several times a year because of her diabetes. She couldn't even hold a decent patient-to-doctor discussion about anything else bothering her, like her seasonal allergies. Anything from itchy skin to a hangnail seemed to be caused by her weight, to the point where she felt depressed as soon as she walked into the office. But if she could manage to shed some pounds on her own, she'd feel more empowered.

"I'll get to the doctor, but please, let me do this tonight," Mariah said. "I just want to hang out and talk and get ready for major changes. I know it's going to be a fight and I don't want to be alone in it."

Oscar hesitated at first, but then he smiled at her. "Well, I'm proud of you then. Just promise me you'll call and set up an appointment?"

Mariah relaxed her tense shoulders as she sized him up. His gaze appeared as it had fourteen years ago — full of love and hope. She'd been drawn to him since the day they'd met, and those feelings had never really disappeared, despite their current issues. From day one in their relationship, she'd loved his confidence, his concern for her and the moments with him when all she felt was warm and loved and pleased.

That delightful first year when they'd bonded and conceived Binky?

Like heaven.

Nowadays, she clung to those precious memories as if they were a security blanket. How they used to care for each other and make one another smile. How she brought beauty to his apartment when it became their love nest.

This transformation Mariah planned might be more for Oscar and Benita than it was for her. She loved them so much. Her heart swelled, thinking about them.

They would see. She'd be successful, and she and Oscar wouldn't just turn back the clock on their relationship, they'd take their union to a whole other level.

But she'd keep all those thoughts inside for now.

"I will," she told him.

"Well, it sounds like you've got it all under control, so let me get something to eat and get back upstairs before Towanda comes in bossing everybody around."

"You know you ain't right."

Mariah heard a knock at the back door and didn't even bother to look through the glass before letting in Chablis, who had her eyes glued to her phone screen. She used her hip to push the door shut, then walked over and had a seat on a kitchen chair, her fingers still tapping away.

Oscar traveled back through with his plate filled. "What up, Chardonnay!" He leaned over and kissed Chablis on the forehead.

"Ya got jokes, huh?" Chablis said to Oscar's back as he headed upstairs. She rested her phone on her lap as she finally moved her gaze to Mariah. "Where's T?"

"She should be here soon. Who are you texting?"

"Nobody. I'm on Facebook. Sending out some happy birthdays and happy anniversaries and stuff like that."

"How many friends do you have now?"

"Almost a thousand."

"You can't possibly know all those people."

"I don't. I friend people I meet from everywhere."

"You have that many followers on Instagram?"

"No. Only like five hundred." Chablis lifted her eyes from the phone screen.

"So, are you posting more on Instagram now? Because I can show you how to post to Facebook and Instagram at the same time and—"

Mariah took a dishrag and wiped the counter. "I don't need to do all that."

"Speaking of Instagram, where's Binky?"

"Upstairs studying. Said she didn't want dinner tonight. She has a big science test on Friday."

"She's not eating? You sure she's not turning anorexic on you?"

"No. She ate some leftover pastelon a few hours ago. She's upstairs studying because I talked to Oscar about how bad of a start she's gotten this semester and he had a discussion with her."

"Daddy put his foot down, huh?"

"Yep."

Abrupt as always, Towanda swung through the back door, slammed the door shut, and hung up her leather laptop bag, which looked more like a sleek purse, on the row of wooden hooks on the wall. She wore a baggy gray sweatshirt, bulky white Adidas sneakers and gray leggings revealing five inches of calf and ankle.

"Chablis! Smooches!" Towanda leaned over and pecked Chablis's cheek.

Chablis pointed to Towanda's laptop bag hanging on the wall. "That bag is nice, girl. I'm gonna steal it."

"You'd have to be able to reach it to steal it." Towanda made her way over to Mariah and gave her a hug.

Chablis stuck her tongue out at Towanda and then flashed her an exaggerated smile.

"Ladies. Dinner. Let's go." Mariah gestured toward the dining room.

In the dining room, they ate together and talked about work, home, memories and everything else. When the light coming through the windows dimmed for dusk, Mariah pushed away her plate, her eyes darting back and forth between her friend and cousin.

"I want to get down to business. I texted both of you about support for weight loss, and I'm serious about it." Mariah sighed. "I'm really trying to change this year."

Mariah looked at Towanda.

Towanda looked at Chablis.

Chablis looked at her thighs.

"I'm joining you." Chablis moved her gaze from her lap. "I've gotta drop a few pounds myself. My doctor has me on meds for high blood pressure, and I'm sorry, but I'm too darned young and cute to take a pill every day."

Mariah sat up straight. "I know I'll need to have at least two people beside me, and I don't want it to be Oscar because he'll just bug me to death. Ever since Binky turned nine, he's suggested everything. Weight Watchers. L.A. Weight Loss. Hydroxycut."

"And a partridge in a pear tree?" Towanda joked.

Mariah kept going. "Biggest Loser, South Beach, Atkins—"

"We hear you," Chablis interrupted with a groan.

"Eat This, Not That. Eat Right for Your Blood Type, SparkPeople..." Mariah rattled off more.

Chablis reached across the table and patted Mariah's hand. "Enough. Okay, beautiful, we understand."

"Some of those programs I didn't take seriously, but some of them I started and lost interest in or I ended up starving and just quit. This time I'm going for a whole new me. Oscar and Binky, I have to do this for them and for me." Mariah's voice broke. "And I can't fail this time."

Chablis reassured her with a smile. "We won't let you fail. Right T?"

Towanda looked up from her phone. "Uh. Um hmm. Yeah."

"Can we have a no phone zone for like ten minutes?" Mariah tapped her foot on the carpet. "I promise to return you to your device-filled lives as soon as we're done here."

Towanda placed her phone face down on the dining room table.

Mariah leaned forward. "Ladies, please keep me accountable. Make sure I track what I'm eating, and any exercises I do, make sure I tell you about them. If you don't hear from me, bug me. Just keep me on course."

"Which means?" Chablis asked.

Towanda pushed her glasses up on her nose. "She means to make sure she does everything she just mentioned, every single day."

Mariah nodded. "Exactly."

"All right." Chablis shrugged. "Anything else?"

"I'll start a private Facebook page where I'll log my weekly weight and goals. Follow my lead." Mariah said. "I think I have a great name for the page, too. Check your email in the morning."

"Anything else?" Towanda asked.

"Nope. This is it for now," Mariah announced. "Time to send you both back home."

"All right, bestie." Towanda turned toward Chablis, who was getting up from her chair. "Come on, munchkin, it's dark. I'll walk you to your car."

"Mariah, you need any help cleaning up?" Chablis offered.

"No." Mariah stood up. "But I'll need lots of help from tomorrow on."

6

TOWANDA

Towanda listened to Mariah's disappointed voice over the phone. "T! I thought you were in this with me. How come you haven't you posted anything in the Facebook group? It's been a week already."

Towanda sighed and ran her fingers through her light brown curls. She glanced at the chrome clock on her home office wall. 6:30 a.m. Early morning work time.

"Mariah, you named the group the *Thick Chick Clique*. What are we? Fourteen?"

"You want a different name?"

"The name isn't the problem. The problem is I don't know what to post on that page."

"Post your goals for your health and weight loss journey."

"Oh, well, then, my lack of posts is appropriate."

"Huh?"

"I have no weight loss journey."

"Then just post what your goals will be when you start."

"I have no goals for this. I love the way I am. Ain't nobody bad like me." Towanda pressed the button to turn on her computer monitor, then stood up and padded out of the office and down the hall to the kitchen. She needed strong coffee.

As she'd predicted, she'd secured the MEGANDA account. Now she needed to work her magic on their company branding. And despite her experience when she'd stood outside of their conference room, she looked forward to doing a phenomenal job for them.

Now, if she could finesse Mariah off the phone so she could get started.

"Think of it as a lifestyle change. Don't you want to take better care of yourself through better eating and exercise?" Mariah insisted.

Towanda dumped two scoopfuls of French roast in the paper filter, shut the top of the coffee maker, and pressed the *Brew* button. "Haven't put any thought into it, to be honest."

"You want to start thinking?"

Towanda sighed again, louder this time. "You want to get off my phone? It's early. Don't you need to take Binky to school?"

"I'm getting ready to jump in the shower right now."

"Good. Go jump then."

"You shut up," Mariah laughed.

"You shut up. You called me." Towanda poured skim milk into her bright red *EVERY DAY I'M HUSTLING* mug. "How are you so darn chipper this morning?"

"I just finished my early morning walk."

"Peachy."

"Okay bestie, can you at least look at what we've posted so far on Facebook. Even if you don't need to make any changes for yourself, at least be there for Chablis and me. Be interested in us two keeping up with our goals."

Looking at Facebook and commenting on her friends' posts? That wasn't so hard. Towanda could check in each morning before starting her work and appointments. "Now that I can do."

"Good. Love you. Have a great day, T!"

"Yeah…yeah…I love you too, have a good one." Towanda tapped the phone to end the call. She filled her cup with hot coffee, then headed back down to her office. She logged into Facebook and entered the Thick Chick Clique page. At five that morning, Mariah had posted a picture of her feet on the scale. Her silver anklet was pretty. She'd posted that her weight wasn't budging.

Towanda scrolled down the page. She saw that Chablis posted multiple times a day. But she tended to post pics of her daily make-up/hairstyle/jewelry combinations, which made no sense for a weight loss accountability page. Towanda had to admit though, Chablis had looked like a page out of *Essence* yesterday with her pink/purple lipstick and her fake pink reading glasses.

Towanda pushed herself several feet back in her office chair. She gazed around the room. Neat and clean, with not a folder out of place. Just as she liked it. The Philadelphia skyline served as the view from her condo window. She loved waking early and entering her home office to witness the sunshine illuminating the city as it woke up. Her office at the thinkLARGE headquarters was exceptional, but it didn't give her this view.

She took another glance at Facebook and considered taking a snap-shot of herself and posting it to the group page.

No, wait.

No need for her to do that right away. She'd come up with some-thing to post later on.

Time to think about a lead nurturing campaign for MEGANDA.

"HEY, WONDER WOMAN, HAPPY FRIDAY!" TOWANDA LEANED DOWN AND hugged Nana hard around the shoulders. "You need a chaperone out here on these mean streets, looking good and all!"

Nana grinned as she pushed Towanda away. "Hush with all that."

Towanda kissed Nana's cheek, then used her thumb to rub away the moist smudge of magenta lipstick she'd left there.

Madeline "Maddie" Mathis. Towanda's Nana. Her favorite person in life. That Friday, Nana had on a natural-looking lace-front wig, one with loose black waves and streaks of gray throughout. Her long-sleeved gray jersey dress and black heels were sophisticated and smart-looking.

With barely a wrinkle in her face, only a few lines around her mouth and her eyes bright and curious, she didn't look like your average grandmother. Nana's husband, Towanda's grandfather Miller, had died in 1978, before Towanda's birth. Nana used his insurance money to start the family bakery and cafe, Nana Cakes, which she'd run with delight for decades. But after Auntie Dawn passed away and Auntie Reecie retired from baking, Nana had closed her business and started traveling the world. Every six months, she visited a new state or country.

Towanda and Nana were meeting for dinner at South Kitchen and Jazz Bar in North Philly because Nana craved low country food and wanted to hear the music. Towanda had offered to pick her up on the way to the restaurant, but because Nana refused to act as if she was aging, she used her smartphone and hired an Uber.

"Wanda...sit...sit..." Nana never called her by her full name. "How are you doing?"

"Well, I have a new client. Another startup company, but this one produces watches."

"I want to hear about your life, Wanda, not your work."

"My work is my life."

"That's plain foolishness."

"It's the truth." Towanda glanced at the waiter approaching their table. She held up a hand when he reached them. "Can you please bring us water and iced tea with lemon?"

The waiter nodded and passed them two menus before stepping away.

"I want to know about everything other than work, granddaughter," Nana said.

"Yes, ma'am. While you were in Toronto, I had my kitchen floor redone. Oh, and I finished my Christmas shopping early. And brace yourself, woman, I wrapped all the presents with my own two hands. Imagine that."

"You and that smart mouth of yours. When will you stop?"

"Maybe never."

"I raised you better."

"You raised me well, and I appreciate you, lady. Wait 'til you see your gifts this year, you'll fall over on those heels."

"Wanda?"

"My life, right. I'm still going to Rise Church, but mostly so I can hang out with Mariah, listen to the choir, and laugh during Pastor Downes' sermons."

"All right now. Have you met anyone there?"

"No."

"There are no single men in that church?"

"Oh, they've got them. Some of them have potential, but most aren't looking for a six-foot, glasses-wearing woman with enough money and business interests to make their male egos feel threatened."

"That's how you see yourself?"

"That's how I am. If a man can't appreciate it, that's his loss."

Towanda stared down at her menu.

Single men. Hmm. She'd love to date one. Trouble was, she had a hard time meeting the right person. He'd have to be tall because she was tall. He also needed to be smart because she hated dumb men who couldn't hold a conversation. Towanda actually wasn't hung up on facial features. As long as he didn't scare her, he didn't have to be pretty. It would be great to meet a tall, clean, talented business owner, but she'd only met two of those at Rise, and both of them were sitting next to their wives.

What she *really* wanted was to open more businesses and continue building her empire. And she'd love to own property in Philly. Sure, she wanted a husband and kids too, but she'd have to wait until she met the right person. In the meantime, when she wanted to relax and enjoy family time, Mariah and her relatives were always there for her.

Towanda looked up when she heard feet approaching.

"Wonder Woman," Towanda said in a stage whisper, "we need to order, because I think our waiter is about to stalk us again. Choose something quick."

On cue, the waiter returned with ice-cold beverages. Nana ordered the lobster bisque and the wood-grilled salmon. Towanda requested the lamb shank with sautéed vegetables.

Nana sipped her iced tea. "How is Ms. Mariah doing?"

"She's on some life and health kick this season. She asked me to join in. I don't know. Something where we try to encourage her to lose weight. As far as I can see, she hasn't lost a thing. Chablis is doing this too. Now she could drop ten pounds in a heartbeat if she just cut the weave out of her hair."

"Oh, Chablis. Is my cutie still having issues?"

"She's holding on."

"Not having dizzy spells in the street anymore, is she?"

"We haven't seen anything like that in a long time. I think therapy helps."

"I see." Nana nodded and reached for a slice of bread to butter. "So, you and Mariah are wellness buddies? That's something new."

"If you want to call it that." Towanda took a sip of water. "So, Wonder Woman, where are you traveling next? I know you plan your trips in advance. Am I buying you a bathing suit and cover-up, or snow boots and a new down jacket?"

"I've been thinking about that Alaskan cruise commercial I saw when I watched Charles Stanley last week. You know the one. I called you about it. Seven days in Alaska. I'll see the mountains and glaciers."

Towanda took another a sip of water. "Good idea. Better see them now, because I heard they're melting, and neither one of us are getting any younger."

Nana remained silent for a moment as she looked Towanda in the eyes. She reached out her hand to squeeze her fingers. "I love you."

"I know you do. I love you too."

Nana gripped her hand tighter. "I want you to be happy. You work so hard, Wanda."

"I'm happy."

"Really? Because you can hide behind jokes about the world and your friends, but I'm your Nana."

Towanda gazed around the restaurant. She heard musicians setting up their instruments in the jazz parlor. Why couldn't the musicians already be playing? At least then Nana could concentrate on the gorgeous sounds instead of questioning Towanda about her private life.

The truth was, there *was* something else she wanted. She'd love to connect with her mother somehow. The woman was out there somewhere in the world, but Towanda was never able to summon enough courage to go find her.

Towanda's strength was apparent in all her business dealings.

But with the one thing that would mean the most to her?

She was weak.

"ThinkLARGE keeps me centered. I'm valuable to my clients," Towanda told Nana, abandoning her thoughts about her mother. "My condo is amazing, my assistant keeps me on track and my contractors are on point, but I'd like to hire more full-time staff. Church is okay when I manage to get there. I love things just the way they are, and honestly, I don't think I can ask for much more. It is what it is."

Nana sat back in her chair as a server set her lobster bisque in front of her. "It is what it is?"

Towanda paused until the server moved away from their table.

"When we buried daddy, I sat next to you at his funeral and you told me to keep moving forward. So, I moved forward. Now I'm here, I'm educated and I love my career. I don't want for anything, and yes, Nana, I'm happy."

"Then why'd Mariah ask you to join her for weight loss?"

"She wants people to be there for her. It's a support thing."

Nana picked up her spoon and stirred her bisque. "You know what, you don't need to change anything, but she needs you, so be there for your friend, honey."

Towanda placed her napkin in her lap and murmured thank you to the waiter as he slid her meal in front of her.

She probably shouldn't have mentioned Mariah and the whole support thing in front of her grandmother. Nana probably thought Towanda was a being self-centered, selfish frenemy instead of a loving, supportive friend.

That couldn't be further from the truth.

Towanda was the one who had planned Mariah's combination bridal shower/baby shower fifteen years ago. After Mariah gave birth to Binky, Towanda would babysit whenever Mariah called needing a break. In the past few years, she'd listened every single time Mariah wanted to talk about her frustrations with Oscar. Towanda had even followed Mariah and Oscar and became a member of Rise Community

Church. Towanda was a loyal friend, and she'd make sure Nana understood that.

"Come on. Mariah's like a sister to me. Of course, if she needs me, I'm going to be right there for her."

"Now that's the Wanda I know and love. And you know, if you start working out with her, and start showing people your smile more instead of frowning at people all the time, that would be great. Seems like a win-win to me."

"Could you at least spare my feelings a little?"

Nana swallowed a spoonful of her bisque and shrugged. "Why should I do that? You can take it." She put her spoon down and reached over to pat Towanda's arm, winking as she did it. "I should know. I raised you."

7

CHABLIS

This Sunday I sit with fifteen Help Squad ministry workers in the big conference room on the second floor at Rise Community Church. We all wear dark blue jeans, white sneakers and white t-shirts with *NEED HELP? Ask Me!* across the front in black letters. Name tags hang from our necks on lanyards. About once a month or so an older church lady will pull me to the side of the sanctuary to ask if I might want a nickname written on my name tag instead of CHABLIS. Because, you know, sometimes people struggle with alcoholism.

These ladies mean well. Whenever they say this, I hug them, kiss their soft cheeks and tell them the Lord might be using me to inform people temptation will always exist and they need to overcome through faith.

Then I walk away and forget their suggestions. Chablis is the name on my birth certificate. If God wanted anything different, He would've told Sonny and Charlene Shields.

Twenty of us serve in this ministry. Five are out helping in different areas of the building right now. That leaves the rest of us to attend the Sunday morning check-in meeting with Pastor David Downes.

Unless he's sick or traveling, he meets with us. He's pretty energetic for a sixty-year-old man. He coaches us to walk our talk at all times. Like the time he told us if a visitor came in looking as if they hadn't eaten in days and we didn't reach in our pocket and give them what they needed to buy food, we should quit ministry immediately. We're here to serve selflessly, not just stand around wearing CustomInk t-shirts.

"Good morning, ladies and gentlemen." Pastor Downes' southern drawl enters the room before his stocky body. "Are we ready to serve today?"

Most of us say yes, but some of us are barely awake. I elbow Michael Seay, who's slumped in the chair next to me. He nods his head and pulls up his body. He's the first seven-foot tall man I've ever met. Our ministry leader, Aja Jansen, tried to persuade him to serve on the Security ministry, but he told her he enjoyed meeting people and providing assistance. So, he roams the building with the Help Squad. We try to make sure he doesn't trample any of the kids.

Pastor Downes bows his head. "Let's pray. Father, guide us in our service today. May we offer our heads, hands and hearts as we seek to serve those who have made their way here to worship. Lord, allow us to learn their needs, and through our care, may they see the hand of God extended to them. This we pray in Jesus' name. Amen."

"Amen," we all repeat.

Sliding on his reading glasses, Pastor Downes scans a page in his folder. "Aja, you're still in the supervisory position this month. Is your team supporting you and is there anything you need?"

Aja Jansen glances over to the pastor. "My team is supportive. My only issue is our teens. We keep finding them lying across the couches and on the carpet in the Visitor's Lounge."

He makes a note in his folder. "I see. In other words, avoiding the regular worship or youth service and treating the lounge like their own family room?"

"Can you make an announcement during the service? I've tried redirects a million times."

Pastor Downes rubs a hand over his bald head. "I know what would be better. Next time you see them avoiding the service, take out your phone and take pictures of them. Tell them you're texting those pictures to me and I'm going to post them on Powerpoint slides along with a WANTED sign."

We laugh.

"No, seriously," he says. "Assign Michael Seay to the Visitor's Lounge. Michael, when you see teenagers in there, gently offer to escort them over to the sanctuary. They'll get the point after a while."

"Got it, Pastor." Michael chuckles.

Pastor glances around the table and smiles. "I've heard great things about this ministry. You all love God and you're passing that love on to others. People feel cared for when they step in these doors. That's the whole point. So, keep doing what you do."

I love serving in this ministry. My regular post is the Information Desk. Underneath the desktop, two locked cabinets hold supplies. Supplies are anything someone might need when they visit Rise Church, and it ranges from tissues and cough drops to baby wipes and diapers, or information about our church. Help Squad works together with the Usher ministry, but while the ushers greet our congregation and control the crowd, Help Squad members travel to get something a person might need or match someone to a prayer partner.

Aja assigned me to the desk because I'm tech-savvy and a people person. I use a laptop to look up information for people or direct them to church resources. Our church has created its own database of local counseling providers, day care centers, senior centers, men's and women's shelters, food reclamation projects, food pantries, temporary job services, addiction help and so on. Sure, we could tell people to use Google, but Pastor Downes has asked us to work within the community to keep a list of current local resources in case someone requires immediate help.

Provide support as soon as possible and with love and prayer. That's our ministry.

"All hearts and minds prepared to serve?" Pastor asks us.

We all nod.

"Thank you for your service." He closes his folder, hands it to his assistant and leaves.

I stay seated because we still have fifteen minutes before the service begins at ten. Nikki comes over and gives me a quick hug. She's assigned to serve in the balcony today.

"Meet me in the atrium after?" She asks. "A group of us are going to IHOP when service is over."

Now, I have no business going to IHOP or any other place where I can drown buttery pancakes in thick maple syrup. It's embarrassing to think about, but I haven't done a single thing to help myself or support Mariah as far as weight loss is concerned. Instead, I swallow blood pressure medication every morning. Even if I hate the idea of doing an organized weight loss program, something or someone needs to help me start this health initiative or meds may become a way of life for me.

"No IHOP for me," I tell her.

"Why?"

I stare at her short platinum blonde curls. She looks good blonde. One day I need to go bold with my hair color. "There's a thing with my blood pressure. I've gotta take off a few pounds. I can start by kicking IHOP out of my life."

"You need some help losing weight?"

"I wouldn't mind. Beats doing Weight Watchers."

She leans down and whispers to me as she points toward the other side of the conference room. "Did you ask John Gerald?"

"Ask him what?"

"For help."

"Why would I do that?"

"I heard he eats like he's training for the Olympics. He does Cross-Fit, and I know he tried out for American Ninja Warrior."

The entire time we're whispering, John sits at the far end of the table. I feel stupid murmuring about someone I can see thirty feet away from me. He looks over at Nikki and me but doesn't say anything. He's served on Help Squad for the last six months, and I think I've heard him speak a total of seventeen words.

Most of those were *Amen*.

He's twenty-seven, athletic with tattoos on both biceps, and he's always chewing gum. Not that I've been paying much attention to him.

When he first joined the Help Squad, my friend Felicia and about three other single women were, in my opinion, chasing him around the church. Rumor has it they spied on him changing his t-shirt after shooting hoops at the church summer barbecue, and he has six-pack abs and a v-cut. Guys like that don't pay a lot of attention to ladies like me. They tend to put smart, bubbly, cute chicks in the friend zone while they search for a supermodel to date. But I don't care about that anyway because I've got bigger concerns than trying to get a man. What do I have to lose by asking for John's help?

"Hey, John!" I call over to him. "Can I holla at ya for a second?"

I stand up and travel down to the end of the table. Nikki hangs behind me, all smiles and eye movements.

Is this high school?

I turn around and shoot her a *stay back* look as I sit in the abandoned chair next to John. He turns toward me and offers a shy smile.

I'll have to start the conversation. "I hear you do CrossFit."

"Yeah."

"And um...you know something about good diets?"

"Little bit."

I need to get to the point because Nikki is silently leaning against the wall, watching us both.

I go for it. "My doctor told me my blood pressure is elevated and I'm on medication right now but I don't want to stay on it. She told me to take off some weight and I'd like to do it as soon as possible. My cousin started an accountability group, but we aren't motivating each other at all. I'm not desperate yet, but I'll take any help I can get. And did you try out for American Ninja Warrior?"

"Yeah."

"So?"

"What are you asking me?"

"Would you train me, please? Help me with nutrition and exercise? If you can just show me how to do it and help me become consistent, I promise, I'll take it from there."

"No."

"Really?"

"No."

"Like, for real? You won't even think about it?"

"No," he tells me, in a gentle tone. "No offense, but about a dozen people here at Rise have asked me to train them. I say no because most people won't do the work to transform themselves. My diet is strict. My exercises are tough. And aren't you in a church life group with Dr. Jones?"

"Yeah," I say, wondering how he knows that.

"How come you didn't you ask him for food and fitness advice?"

Why didn't I ask Dr. Jones? Firstly, the last time I saw him, I was ticked off about my job and not talking to anyone about anything. Secondly, Dr. Jones is married and I don't feel comfortable asking some woman's husband for help with my body. If I have a choice, and it seems like I do right now, I want help from a CrossFit guy who tried out for American Ninja Warrior.

"You really want to know?" I ask.

"Yeah."

I repeat my thoughts out loud. "I didn't think about it last week in life group meeting because I was ticked off about being passed over for a promotion. Second, Dr. Jones is a cool brother, but he's very married, and I don't need his wife calling me up tripping like some jealous spouse. If I have a choice, I'd rather get help from an unmarried American Ninja Warrior who also does CrossFit."

John's laughs and the sound is deep and rich. "I hear you. Sorry about the job situation, by the way."

"Thanks. So, what do you say? You'll help me?"

"Tell you what, I'll think about it and I'll let you know."

"Okay, well, all my contact information's in the ministry directory."

"All right. See you later," he says, grabbing his keys.

"See ya," I say.

When he's left the room, I turn my chair around.

"Nikki?"

"I'm here."

"Did I just ask an American Ninja Warrior to be my trainer?"

"*Aspiring* ninja warrior. He didn't make it past tryouts."

"Whatever."

"Yeah, you asked him."

"Lord," I sigh. "Have mercy on me."

8

MARIAH

G etting started meant getting started.
No more excuses.
The morning after Mariah declared to Towanda and Chablis that she would transform herself, she put herself in motion. But first, she needed to get rid of any food that would tempt her.

"You need to see your doctor first. Seriously."

That came from Oscar, who stood on the deck watching as Mariah lugged a Hefty bag to the steel can behind their house.

"Os, I will, I promise, but I can't get an appointment until next Friday. I need to start today."

Mariah's black sweat-suit with pink stripes running down the sides defined snug. She kept tugging up the front of her pants to stop the waistband from folding down beneath her muffin top. She slammed the trash bag into the can, then pulled herself upright, wiping away a small trickle of sweat from her forehead. Forcing a smile, she trudged back to the house.

"See, now? No more junk in the kitchen. What time is it?"

Oscar held the back door open. "Just 6:30."

"Good. I'm gonna walk around the block for a half hour."

"Wait. I can throw on some sweats and walk with you." He started toward the staircase.

Mariah paused, one hand resting on the front door. She didn't know what to say. Oscar appeared excited. She smiled, warmth washing over her.

But no. Her body, her fight.

Besides, she didn't need him watching her huffing and puffing around the block.

"No," she told him. "I have to get used to making exercise a habit. If I start relying on you to walk with me, the first day you get busy it might mess up my habit."

"All right. Well, then, I'm going to take my shower."

"Before you do that, make sure you—"

"I know. Wake up Benita and tell her she's not wearing ripped tights under her school uniform today."

"Thanks. Back in thirty."

On the sidewalk, Mariah paused to put in her earbuds, tap the Pandora app on her phone and set it to the Workout station. The leaves on the trees were beginning to transform from green to gold, orange and cinnamon colors. It was their neighborhood, but no neighbors were out.

And that's exactly how she wanted it as she moved down the street.

The first trip around the block was easy, even relaxing, as she listened to music and breathed in the fresh air. She also learned to ignore the feeling of her tight sweatpants rubbing against her thighs.

The second trip?

She'd had to walk uphill on the return to their house, and now her heart thumped a little. Nothing too bad. She could handle it. She would get in the second lap with her face toward the sun.

On the third lap, she neared twenty-five minutes of walking and wanted to stop because her feet hurt.

She rounded the bottom of the hill when she saw them.

Two women, each of them wearing black running tights and brightly-colored running shoes. One wore a hot pink tank top, and the other had chosen a lime green running bra to cover her chest. Both of them boasted high ponytails flapping in the breeze. Mariah stepped to the right to let them pass, her head held high. She kept pumping her arms in her exaggerated walking style.

The women made eye contact and smiled as they approached on their way down. Mariah grinned back. As they passed, lime green running bra nodded and called to Mariah. "Keep going! You've got this!"

Encouragement.

The woman's statement was probably meant to inspire Mariah, but instead, it made her smile fade. She turned around to watch the speed racers continue down the block. Then she returned her gaze to the sidewalk in front of her. Hard pavement curving uphill teased her.

How long would it take for her to be able to run down the block wearing nothing but Nikes, tights and a glow-in-the-dark exercise bra?

The answer arrived in her brain in a split second.

A long time.

"WHY DO DOCTOR'S OFFICES ALWAYS SMELL LIKE ALCOHOL AND OLD rubber? Nobody invented a Febreze anti-hospital scent by now?" Towanda joked.

They were waiting together at Mariah's doctor's office on the Main Line. Mariah hadn't planned to take her bestie along, but a few days earlier, Towanda had called and announced she would support her at her doctor's appointment.

True to her word, Towanda had arrived at the house on time to pick Mariah up and drive her to Dr. Drew's office on Friday afternoon.

The nurse called from the hallway. "Mariah Shields-Rodriguez?"

Mariah pushed herself up out of the chair and followed the nurse to the examination room, with Towanda trailing her. In the exam room, the nurse measured Mariah's blood pressure, then told them the doctor would arrive shortly.

Mariah scooted herself up on the exam table. "You don't wanna sit?"

"No, I'm good."

"You look like my bodyguard with your arms crossed like that."

A grin appeared on Towanda's face. "It's not like I haven't served as your security before. Remember the party on Penn campus, sophomore year? The DJ played reggae all night and people complained."

"Girl, don't remind me." Mariah put a hand over her eyes. "I left the downstairs for like ten minutes to go to the bathroom, and how many barking Qs surrounded the door when I tried to come out?"

"All I know is it was a sea of purple and gold. I pushed down the hall and yelled at those fools to back up off my friend."

"I'm so glad you came up there. Remember, you were downstairs dancing hard with some dreadlocked brother in the corner. I didn't know I'd need security just to go pee."

"Those brothas saw a new girl in white denim booty shorts walk upstairs, and they went on the hunt. I saw one of them pull your water bottle right out of your hand and start kissing it. It was crazy."

Mariah chuckled and looked down. "Seems like a lifetime ago."

"It was." Towanda removed her glasses and wiped the lenses on the edge of her shirt. "But hey, thirty is the new twenty."

"I'm thirty-four."

"Add a few years."

"And too big to wear booty shorts now."

"So what? Daisy Dukes are out of style, anyway."

Someone tapped on the door and then pushed it open. Dr. Drew stepped in.

"Good morning," he said.

"Dr. Drew, this is my best friend, Towanda. She's with me today for moral support."

Towanda extended her hand. "Good to meet you, doctor."

"Same here." He shook Towanda's hand, then sat down in the desk chair across the tiny room. He looked at the computer screen in front of him. "Mrs. Rodriguez, we saw you about…six months ago?"

"That's right."

Dr. Drew turned his head and coughed. It sounded harsh, sharp and painful. When he finally stopped, he directed his words to her. "You're obese."

Mariah crossed her arms over her chest. "I know. I'm dedicated to making a change right now. That's why I'm here."

"It's going to be tough."

"I know that, too."

"According to your records, you've failed all of your previous weight loss attempts in the past four years."

Mariah rolled her eyes. "Thank you for your trip down memory lane, doctor. I'm here today and I'm ready. What do I do?"

Dr. Drew coughed again.

Towanda stepped over and offered him a lozenge. "Halls?"

"No, thank you," Dr. Drew said. "You're still on Metformin for your blood sugar control. And your blood pressure is borderline today. It's something we want to keep an eye on because you are so incredibly obese."

Mariah bit her bottom lip and glanced at Towanda. Towanda looked as if she was trying to restrain herself.

"I can say you are down five pounds." Dr. Drew continued.

"Good." Mariah nodded.

"But that's not enough, especially with your diabetes," Dr. Drew insisted.

Mariah sat up straighter. "How much do I need to lose to start reversing these issues?"

Dr. Drew swiveled around and looked her in the eye. "I'd like to see you start by losing a hundred pounds in the next year or so."

"A *hundred*?"

"On a healthy eating plan and with exercise, yes. But, optimally, you should consider weight loss surgery."

"Gastric bypass?"

"There are other options. Sleeve gastrectomy has shown to be a good option for some of my patients."

Mariah stayed silent for a moment.

Surgery?

Even with diabetes and tight clothing, she'd only considered herself someone who'd grown overweight. But here was Dr. Drew pointing her toward an operation. She'd heard once you cut your body for weight loss, you'd used your final option.

Was it time to use her final option?

"Surgery, huh?"

"Mrs. Rodriguez, bariatric surgery may save you from future health problems. As your primary care professional, I wouldn't be doing my job if I didn't refer you for a consultation."

Towanda spoke up. "Aren't there major risks with those procedures?"

"Yes." Dr. Drew leaned in toward them. "Weight loss surgery is major surgery. I'm referring you because of your metabolic disorders. After the consultation, you can discuss the risk factors and benefits with your family."

Mariah snapped out of her daze. "How much weight will I lose?"

"Depending on your course of action, you could lose 50% of your body weight in the first year."

"Where do I go for the consultation?"

Dr. Drew pulled a thick pamphlet and a typed sheet from the shelf over his desk. "PMHU Bariatric offers four types of intervention options. Read the information thoroughly, then call the 800 number for your consultation."

"YEAH, MOM!" BINKY JUMPED FROM HER SEAT AT THE DINING ROOM table. She ran around the table to give Mariah a bear hug. "You're gonna look amazing. I'm so happy for you!"

Oscar frowned. "Surgery?"

Mariah's rubbed Binky's thin arms around her neck. "Think of it as an intervention for weight loss. You know, get back to the old me."

"Like in those old pictures! Mom, you looked like me. OMG, you're gonna get back to that. WHOO HOOO!" Binky danced behind her mother's chair.

Mariah stared at her silent husband. "Os, come with me to the consultation."

Oscar stared straight ahead, his arms crossed tight against his chest.

She turned to speak to her dancing daughter. "Benita, leave the room."

"But shouldn't we celebrate? This is gonna help you, right?"

"I don't know if this is for sure yet, and maybe I shouldn't have told you before I talked about it with your dad. Now, I need you to leave. Thank you."

Binky snatched her pink sweatshirt from the floor. It had fallen from her waist when she'd jumped up. She took her glass of iced tea from the table and stalked off.

Mariah waited until she heard her daughter's feet ascending the staircase before she spoke again. "Os, what's the matter?"

"Bariatric surgery? People die from those operations. Weight loss surgery isn't like getting a pedicure, and you sat there with a smile on your face informing me you plan to make me a widower?"

"There's no guarantee I'll die from weight loss surgery."

"No guarantee you won't, either."

"Come on! You're overreacting. Think of the benefits. I can lose more than fifty percent of my weight inside of a year. How is that not a good thing? You've wanted me to take off this kind of weight for years. Admit it."

"Not by going under the knife! Honestly, all I wanted you to do is embrace a healthy lifestyle, reverse your diabetes and get your hormones under control so we could continue to grow our family."

"Don't start with the whole family thing, okay? If that's all you wanted, we could have visited a fertility specialist years ago."

"All right. You tell me. Why haven't you tried harder to improve yourself? I've been behind you every step of the way, and you've never taken any of my advice seriously. Now suddenly you want to go the surgical route? I'm disappointed."

"Excuse me?"

"You've gotten bigger every year for the past ten years. You spent—what? Maybe two weeks cutting down on your food and prancing around the block in the morning? Of course, it's not enough." He fixed his eyes on hers. "Now you want surgery before you try a trainer and nutritionist?"

She pushed herself back in her chair. It rocked beneath her weight. "Prancing around the block? That's what you think?"

"Yes, that's what I think. And another thing. I don't know what you eat while I'm at work. Just because I see you eating a salad tonight doesn't mean you're not inhaling junk you hide. I've seen fast food bags in our bedroom trash before."

Mariah clenched her fists on her lap. She turned her gaze toward the ceiling as she blinked back tears from her eyes.

"I'm not trying, huh? All those crazy diets since Binky was little and I'm not trying?"

He softened his tone. "Honey, I'm here for you, but I'm just not on board with this whole surgery thing. Maybe we can see a nutritionist together or visit the gym every evening."

"Not trying?"

"Mariah—"

"I don't try? Okay. How 'bout I try this surgery and I try to forget what the heck you think about it? How about that?"

Standing up, she grabbed her phone off the table and left the dining room. On her way through the kitchen, she snatched her keys from the bowl on the kitchen table. She kept on walking right out the back door, then climbed into her car and slammed the door shut.

Oscar arrived at the back door but didn't move any further. He remained there, staring at her. She stared back at him as she placed two phone calls.

The first call?

PMHU Bariatric. She left a message to schedule a consultation and information session.

Her second call?

Towanda.

She answered on the third ring. "Mariah."

"T, come with me to the bariatric consultation. I've made my decision. I'm doing this."

"Let me know the date. I'll be there for you."

9

TOWANDA

Towanda squinted at a naked belly button bearing a shiny silver ring. It seemed the jewelry had searched for a perfectly smooth home and found it, right in the middle of Binky's body.

When Towanda looked up, she saw her goddaughter beaming. "Your mother's going to destroy you."

Binky sat down, tugging her mint green sweater back down over her midriff. "Auntie, you don't like it?"

"It doesn't matter if I like it. When your mom and dad find out, you'll need these new sneakers to start running like Usain Bolt."

Towanda and Binky were shopping at Bloomingdale's — their quarterly godmother/goddaughter date.

When Binky was little, Towanda used to take her to the local museums or to performances at the Walnut Street Children's Theatre. But ever since the Binky had grown from girl to teenager, it was all about the clothes.

Binky frowned as she pulled a pair of white Basket Heart Opulence Pumas from her feet, placed them to the side, then opened a box containing Fenty-x-Bow sneakers. "It's not that deep. It's jewelry. So what?"

"Then why are you telling me? And who gave you this piercing, sans parental consent?"

"Got it last month when I was spending the weekend with Grandma Joan. My cousin Andrea came by and we were hanging out. She has an artist friend who does piercings."

As Towanda watched Binky lips move, she tried to figure out the best time to tell Mariah about her daughter's navel ring.

Call or text her?

No.

Face-to-face would be better. How about when she dropped Binky off later? No. Towanda didn't want to see Mariah start yelling at Binky.

What about next week during Mariah's bariatric consultation?

No way. Mariah would be nervous enough already.

Darn it. Binky's navel ring was Binky's problem. Why did Towanda have to say anything? Binky should be the one to confess it.

Towanda groaned. "I'm telling you now, you better have a plan for how to let your parents know. Especially because you just told me."

Binky pulled a stray lock of hair away from her face and finger-combed it into the messy top knot on her head. "But you're not like them. You buy designer brands. You're generous. When you talk to me it's like cool, you know what I'm saying?"

"Your parents and I are in the same age group. If I'm not ancient, neither are they."

"Yeah, but they're always like, *Benita, no you can't stay out after ten o'clock. Benita, go to bed, it's a school night. Benita, no boys!*" She pouted. "They're so corny. Going to Rise only makes it worse. I get sick of it."

Towanda watched Binky frown and fuss. If she only knew. At the age of fourteen, Towanda had frizzy hair, wore thick-lensed glasses, and sported buck teeth. By then, her father had been dead for two years. Her mother? Long gone. Binky, on the other hand, was beautiful, loved, and blessed. She possessed two dedicated parents who cared about what she wore, whom she talked to and where she spent her time.

Mariah and Oscar raised her in a clean home, drove her to a phenomenal church every week and made sure she attended a successful high school. Braces had straightened her teeth. Every three weeks she went to the hair salon, so her long dark curls were practically flawless.

Fourteen years of round-the-clock nurturing and this kid was complaining?

There could only be one reason for this rant.

Towanda tapped Binky's elbow. "Who's the boy?"

"Oh, I'm just talking in general." Binky reached down to tie the bows on her shoes.

"I don't think so, darling. Try again." Towanda closed her eyes and rubbed her temples. "You have a secret navel ring. You can't decide on the right sneakers. Your parents raised you right, but now you hate their rules, which were fine for you until now. Who's the boy?"

"Idris."

"School or church?"

"Huh?"

"School or church. You don't go too many other places, girl."

"School. He's new this year."

"You like him a lot?"

"He's all right." Binky blushed.

"Let me guess, you told mama bear you have a crush, and mama bear said?"

"*No boys. Period.* He can only be my friend. She said I need to nurture good friendships, that it'll help me in life and whatever." Binky pulled off the Fenty-x-Bow sneakers, placed them in the box and held them on her lap. "But Auntie, I'm in high school now."

"I see."

"Can I meet him at your place?"

Towanda opened her eyes wide. "What?"

"Can I come to visit you, and then like Idris can come over and we can have pizza and watch a movie or something? I'm allowed to visit you whenever I want. What if I sleep over next Saturday and Idris stops by to hang out with us for a little bit. Please?"

Towanda reached over and held Binky's hand tight, leaning in close to her face. "Darling, I love you. Thanks for confiding in me. But please understand, I won't ever co-sign on some secret mess like that. I won't *ever* do anything like that to your mom. You got it?"

Binky's eyes met Towanda's. "Got it."

Towanda straightened up and gestured toward the shoe box. "I'm getting those sneakers for you, right?"

"Love you back, and yes. Thanks." Binky passed Towanda the box.

"You're welcome. Now think about a lunch spot that won't break the bank, okay?"

"Fogo De Chao."

"Yeah, right. As soon as you earn some Fogo De Chao money. Whatever happened to asking for McDonald's?" Towanda asked as she walked toward the register.

At the counter, the petite saleswoman smiled up at her. "Did you find everything you were searching for?"

Towanda pulled out her American Express card. "I think so. Teens are so flighty. This week she'll want these. At Christmas, it will be something else. I'm a sucker, though. Love that girl."

The cashier scanned the shoe box. "I saw you over there talking to her. Your daughter is gorgeous. She seems to love you a whole lot, too. You're a lucky woman."

Towanda turned her head to glance over at Binky, who was sitting down, texting on her phone. A feeling Towanda couldn't quite name washed over her. Even though Binky had two well-functioning parents, it could also be said the girl had been blessed with another woman who loved and cared for her regularly. Towanda had changed Binky's first diaper while Mariah recovered from her C-section. Towanda also bought Binky her tricycle and her first scooter and had taken her to see her first ballet.

One day Towanda hoped to have a daughter just like Binky — a girl so attractive, people often stared at her. And this cashier thought Towanda was Binky's mother?

"Thank you." Towanda said, looking back at Binky again. "She's a special young lady."

AT HOME THAT AFTERNOON, BAD NEWS ARRIVED IN THE FORM OF A SLACK notification. thinkLARGE's social media strategist, Jerome, would be unable to complete his plans for designing a social media strategy to reach MEGANDA's target market. Jerome's mother had suffered a stroke Friday night. He needed to drop everything and fly to Texas immediately.

Towanda cracked her knuckles as she read his message two more times. Of course, she understood. It was a family emergency for Jerome, but it would leave thinkLARGE in a major bind. The final draft of the plan was due next week. She'd been counting on him to pull that part through. thinkLARGE needed the MEGANDA account. Every deliverable for them had to be on point.

Sighing, she pushed her chair away from her office desk and stared out the window. This year, revenue for thinkLARGE had dipped nearly 20% from what the business had brought in the previous three years. Now they'd entered the fourth quarter of the year. Sure, the company had several ongoing accounts, but there had been fewer new clients this year. Towanda needed to double-down and drum up new business or invest in more direct advertising to attract new accounts early next year.

Returning to her computer, she answered Jerome's message, requesting a phone conference with him on Monday. Even if he couldn't finish the work himself, she could interview him and try to finish the initial plan on her own. If she had to, she would stay up late to complete it. But no matter what, thinkLARGE would deliver.

Towanda's mobile phone buzzed on the desktop. She leaned over and looked at the caller ID.

Mariah.

Towanda swiped the screen to answer it, then tapped for speaker mode and returned her attention to the computer.

"Yes, bestie?"

"Silver pink Puma Fenty-x-Bow sneakers? Really?"

"That's what she wanted."

"You spoil her."

"I'm her godmother. Spoiling is in my job description."

"You should know there's a little Rihanna wannabe here taking pictures of her sneakered feet propped up on the deck railing outside."

"You're kidding."

"No, I'm not. I'm about to take a pic of her and send it to you.

Chablis will probably see it on Binky's Instagram in about five seconds, so I don't need to send it to her."

Laughing, Towanda sat back in her chair. "Well, at least I know she's enjoying the footwear."

"Thanks for all you do. We appreciate you."

"I told you, that's my job. Now I'm putting you off my phone. I have to send a team message and handle a work issue. And it's Jackie's birthday next week, so I have to make sure I have a cake and flowers delivered so we can celebrate her."

"T, when you get done, take a look at the Thick Chicks Clique page. I posted something deep today."

"I'll take a look. I promise. Talk to you later."

Check the Facebook page. Check the Facebook page.

Towanda scanned the screen in front of her. She'd get to it in a minute. Right after she sent out a Slack message about Jerome's absence. Maybe she wouldn't have to take on all of his work on her own? Tonja, thinkLARGE's associate marketing consultant, should be able to assist. With teamwork and focus, they would not fumble the MEGANDA account.

After she exited Slack, Towanda pulled up Facebook and clicked to enter the Thick Chicks Clique page. She still hated that ridiculous name.

Chablis had posted something thirty minutes earlier. She'd uploaded a picture of herself at lunch, smiling and posing with her girlfriends from Rise. Towanda rolled her eyes. Did she actually think she'd lose weight chowing down at Applebee's every week?

Anyway—Mariah's posts. There were two of them. One was from six in the morning, and it showed her feet on the scale. She'd lost two more pounds. The other post, all text, she'd posted an hour earlier.

MARIAH SHIELDS-RODRIGUEZ

September 29 at 1:30 PM

I did some journaling and soul-searching today while my daughter was out with her super-cool godmother (wink). I wrote so much I need to buy a new journal book. I won't put all that here, so don't worry. I'll summarize.

In a week, I'll be sitting in a room talking about weight loss surgery. I'm excited and scared, but if this is the road God is putting me on, I accept it. Do you know what will make me really happy? If I can do all the things I'd always planned for myself. I wanted to be a business owner. I wanted to be on the cover of FORBES. I've spent years hiding from a dream that now seems so far away it hurts to think about it. I think if I can have some help, just a little assistance, and if the mirror starts to look a little like the old me, I'll have the confidence to finish my degree, take the graduate business courses and push on with my ideas. Today, I started brainstorming. None of these ideas are ready for primetime, but they gave me hope. Ladies, I am planning world domination!

WORLD DOMINATION? FROM SHEDDING SOME POUNDS?

This Mariah seemed so hopeful and full of life, a lot like the best friend Towanda remembered from high school. The model-looking girl who shocked her family by telling them she had no interest in walking down a runway, being someone's skinny canvas to display their art. The Mariah who majored in Business Administration, but then met Oscar in her Microeconomics class and soon after stopped talking with Towanda about getting her MBA.

But today, this post sounded like Mariah planned to move full-speed ahead and try to enter Towanda's domain.

In charge. All business. Take no prisoners.

"Sorry sweetie, but there's no room at the top of the hive for another queen bee," Towanda sighed and mumbled to the air before shutting off her computer. "Go ahead, lose all the weight you want. Go from big housewife to small housewife, but *I'm* the empire builder. Business is my domain."

10

CHABLIS

"**M**onday."

I glance up from my phone to see John standing in front of the Rise information desk.

"Um...what?" I stammer.

"Monday," he repeats.

This man must learn how to speak more than one word at a time to me.

"Once more, please," I say.

He rests his hands on the desktop. "Two Sundays ago, you asked me to help you lose weight. I thought about it. We start tomorrow."

I want to jump up and dance like David danced. However, the silence in the atrium keeps me in my seat. Everyone else in the building is attending the evening worship service except for me, the doormen, and a few roaming Help Squad members.

"Thanks," I say.

"You're welcome." He turns to walk away.

I call after him. "Wait a minute!" When he looks back, I blurt out, "Don't I need more information? Starting tomorrow is good, but what am I starting?"

"Training."

I motion with my hands moving like a Ferris wheel trying to pick up new riders. "Training?"

"For weight loss. How much do you want to lose?"

"I'd like to start with twenty pounds."

He steps back over to the desk, phone in hand. He taps the screen a few times and turns it to me. "This is your cell number?"

"Yes."

"Cool," he says, sliding his phone into his pocket. "I copied your address from the ministry directory, too. Pick you up tomorrow at five."

"I won't be home from work 'til after six. Can we do it then?"

"A.m., not p.m," John calls out as he walks toward the far hallway, giving me a goodbye wave as he disappears.

Five in the morning? I'd have to be up sometime after four to get washed and dressed. Can I even get myself out of the bed that early? It's still dark outside at five. Aren't flesh-eating zombies roaming around outside at five in the morning? What if he expects me to run fast? What did I just get myself into?

"Chablis," Stacey Robins steps to the desk. She's another Help Squad volunteer.

"Uh, yeah...um...what can I help you with?"

"You okay, sis?"

I'm serving. Gotta pull myself together. "I'm fine. How can I help?"

"There's a lady in the first-floor bathroom with her baby. Says she just ran out of wipes. Can you pass me some?"

"No problem." I get off the stool to unlock the cabinet and hand Stacey the wipes.

She thanks me and walks away.

Tomorrow is Monday. I sit back on my stool and lace my fingers together to keep from biting my nails. I'm nervous, but really, it's only a training session.

What's the worst that could happen?

MY PHONE RESTS SOMEWHERE INSIDE MY MESSY BED COVERS. AT FIRST, I ignore it buzzing and roll back over, but then adrenaline shocks my system.

It's Monday morning. Training day. I reach down beneath the blankets, pull out my device and answer the call.

"Hello," I say.

"Get up!" John has some crazy song blasting in the background. "You've got twenty minutes to get ready."

I roll over and glance at the glowing numbers on my nightstand clock. 4:30 a.m. This man is yelling at me at O-dark thirty in the morning? To a soundtrack. And I asked for this?

"John?" I struggle to sit up. "Listen, can I meet you there? It might take me a little time to get moving and, see my eyes aren't even open right now..."

"Now you have nineteen minutes," he says. "Put your phone on speaker, lay it on a table somewhere and get up now!"

I'm so delirious I actually do what he says. I tap the screen for speaker, slide the phone onto my nightstand, then push myself out of bed and stumble toward the bathroom. There are all kinds of drum and bell sounds coming from my phone. The beat sounds familiar, but before I can name it, I whack my toe on the bathroom door. I hop around for a few seconds, slam the door shut, brush my teeth, hit the shower, and in a few minutes I'm back in my bedroom with a towel wrapped around me. Confused and damp, I rummage around my dresser drawers searching for sweats. This isn't even the workout and I'm already huffing and puffing.

"Ten minutes!" John yells through the phone. "I hope you took your clothes out the night before. Preparation is half the battle."

The music slows to a smooth jazzy rhythm, so I calm down as I get dressed. No longer sluggish, I race to my tiny closet, pull out my black Skechers, and put those on.

When the music stops, John's voice takes over. "Five minutes left. Don't make me ring your doorbell, because I will wake your neighbors!"

I stop in the bathroom real quick to apply concealer to the scar on my cheek, then keep moving as I grab my phone and purse, leave my bedroom, snatch up my keys and head out of my apartment. Locking the door behind me, I turn and do a crazy silent sprint to the staircase, down the steps, and out the front door. I've never seen John's car before, but I figure it's him when I see a black Jeep pulling up to the front walkway.

He steps out of the driver's side, watching me as I rush over. He's wearing black shorts, a FAITH OVER FEAR sleeveless steel gray t-shirt, and black Nikes. Why, oh why didn't I take time to fill out a last will and testament before taking this journey?

He walks around and opens the passenger door for me but stops me before I climb into his ride. "What are you wearing?"

I gulp and look down. "Sweats?"

"On your feet?"

"Skechers."

"Here's your first lesson in fitness training--be ready. You need cross trainers and running sneakers, the good kind, and activewear shirts and pants."

"What's the best place where I can—"

"I'll text you a list later. Let's get going."

I climb into his Jeep, where I'm surprised to see a man and woman in the backseat. I nod to them.

"Hey there, how you doing?" This comes from the man, who is large and ginger-haired and has tattoos decorating his neck and arms.

"Hi. Good to meet you." That comes from the ultra-fit woman sitting next to him. Her head is clean shaven around the sides and back, and the top is coiled purple locs.

John takes his car out of park. "That's Travis and Sheena. They work out with me at LA Fitness."

"Hey," I say to them and turn back around fast. I'm sitting in a Jeep full of ninjas and we are headed to the gym. The clock on the dashboard reads 4:52. Please, Lord, help me get through this and I will never ask you for anything else in the history of my time on this planet. Lord you are gracious and good and your mercy—

"Why are your eyes closed?" John asks.

"I'm praying."

They all laugh as I open my eyes and keep praying until we reach the gym. We all climb out of the Jeep and head inside.

"You're my guest today, but you'll need to sign-up for your own membership," John tells me as we walk through the doors.

"Clothes, sneakers, gym membership." I tally costs in my head while watching Travis and Sheena unzip their hoodies as they walk around the round desk at the front and head straight down the middle toward the weights. "How much is this going to cost me?"

John leans down close to my ear. "Second lesson. Your health is priceless. Yes, you're going to have to spend money, but it's for a good reason. In this country, you either invest time and money in your health when you're young, or you pay for your illnesses and joint replacements later. I'll help you create a budget later today. Let's go over to the treadmills."

After he checks us in, we start moving over toward the right side of the room. There's a cool skylight right above us and a Juice Bar on the left side of the building, but something tells me I better not think about asking him if I can get a smoothie right now. John, Sheena and Travis must not be as crazy as I thought, because there are quite a few serious exercisers here, and most have on headphones. It's five in the morning.

Five. In. The. Morning.

We find two treadmills together. John steps onto his. I step onto mine, straighten myself up, press the Quick Start button and I'm walking.

Three minutes pass before John gets chatty. "How do you feel?"

"Fine."

"When's the last time you had a regular exercise routine?"

"Never."

"What about high school? Do any sports? Cheerleading? Field hockey?"

"I danced."

"Like around the house?"

"No, as in dance classes and recitals. Ballet. Jazz. Modern. Started with ballet when I was six. I even took some acro classes. I thought I'd always...never mind."

"No. Go on."

I feel a little dizzy, so I grip the bar in front of me and stare at my hands to center myself.

When I am afraid, I put my trust in You, I think. *Everything's fine. Everything's just fine.*

Deep breath in, to a count of four. Hold for seven beats. Exhale for eight.

Good.

I do this twice more and relax. I should've known better than to take that trip down memory lane.

"Never thought I'd be up at five in a gym," I say when I finally turn to glance at John. "Will I walk this whole time?"

John looks at me with his eyebrows raised for a moment, right before he reaches over to push up the pace of my treadmill until it reaches three miles per hour. "Keep on walking. When I come back, we'll talk about food, and then I'll drive you home."

"That's it?"

"For today," he says, stopping his machine. "Stay at this pace."

"Where are you going?"

"To do my own workout. It'll take about thirty minutes."

He walks away from the treadmills and elliptical machines and my eyes follow him. He goes into a corner for several minutes of rope jumping, and then he stretches.

When he walks away and I can't see him anymore, I leave the treadmill to creep over and spy on him. He's in the free weight area doing squats with a barbell on his shoulders. Pull-ups. Planks. Pulldowns. Sit-ups. More pull-ups. Knee raises. Jumps over a weight bench.

Then he starts over.

My stomach wraps itself into a tight ball as I dash back over to the treadmill so I can *stay in my lane.* I fear for my life if he thinks I'll ever do anything like that.

Twenty minutes later he's back on the treadmill beside me after his whole ninja warrior routine ends. And he has the nerve to smile at me.

"Hey, ninja! I mean, John," I say.

"Ha, ha, ha," he says, pointing at me. "Time to talk food."

"Sure. I like food."

"I'm not even going to ask you what you eat now, or if you've ever had an eating plan before."

"That's a relief—"

"Because today I'll text you your clean eating plan."

"I'm pretty sure that doesn't mean I eat off clean plates at all times."

"No, but it's the simplest way to help you without making you count points or calories. Think of your plan this way. If the food came from a lab or a factory, you don't eat it."

"Pizza would fit into this where?"

"Nowhere."

"It figures." I frown. "Should I weigh myself before I do all this?"

He shrugs. "You can if you want, but you should take time to create healthy habits before you obsess about numbers. I'll send you instructions for how to prep your food, and every time you eat, text me a picture of your meal. Sound good?"

The simple food talk seems natural for him to rattle off. I'm not so sure, but I nod at him anyway. I'm working out next to a guy who tried out for American Ninja Warrior. He knows my name and he picked me up at my apartment to train me. God let me come this far, so I'll keep going.

"What's the name of that song you blasted through my phone earlier?" I ask him.

He stops his treadmill and grins wider. "That song? Oh, that was "Take Me to the Mardi Gras." "

I HATE JOHN GERALD. I'D KICK HIM INTO THE SCHUYLKILL RIVER IF I could get away with it explaining myself to the police or having to meet with Pastor Downes for an intense discussion about all the commandments I'd broken. Right now, I'm sitting far away from him in the Rise Church conference room so I can keep my hate vibes to myself.

My body aches.

I'm starving.

My nerves are shot and I'm jittery. For real, my teeth are vibrating.

I can feel John's eyes on me from the other end of the table. I ignore him. I'd pick up my pen and notepad, but I can't, because my hands hurt.

How did I get this way? Monday was decent. I'll start with Tuesday.

Tuesday, John let me walk on the treadmill for five minutes before making me stretch every muscle in my body. He also made me test how much weight I could hold on a barbell. Then he led me through squats, chest presses, push-ups, dips, lunges, tricep extensions, bicep curls, and planks. After all that, I came back to the treadmill for walk/jog intervals for twenty minutes.

Wednesday, John invited himself to bring Travis and Sheena into my apartment kitchen. I stood back and watched, horrified when he told them to throw away anything containing sugar or starchy, carby goodness. While all this was going on, John went back to his Jeep, then came back upstairs with two grocery bags.

"What's that?" I asked him when he set the bags on the counter.

"This is what you'll eat." He pulled out containers of food, including spinach, which I hate.

He filled my refrigerator with salad greens, eggs, chicken breast, Greek yogurt, lemons and limes, peppers, berries and cottage cheese. My cabinets received oatmeal, cans of tuna, brown rice and boxes of green tea. Then we all left for the gym, where he proceeded to keep pushing up the pace on my treadmill until I was running.

Thursday was a repeat of Tuesday, only with burpees. Burpees are an exercise straight from the pit of hell.

Friday was like Wednesday, except on an elliptical machine.

Saturday morning was my choice, but John texted my workout options. He told me to walk for an hour, then find a good beginner yoga video on YouTube. I scowled after I read his texts, and I shoved the phone under my pillow before rolling over and going back to sleep.

When Felicia called me later, I asked her to make sure my hair-dresser, Quinsara, tightened my weave and my mom dressed me in a pink suit at my funeral.

Now it's Sunday and I'm here at Rise. I have no idea what the pastor told us, but I say Amen. As everyone else stands, I'm groaning to my feet, clutched onto the chair in front of me as John saunters over, grinning.

"Chablis. How ya doing?"

"Don't you talk to me," I whine. "Get thee behind me, Satan."

"Little sore?" He raises an eyebrow. "Did you not enjoy Mardi Gras week?"

I'd smack him if my arm could move faster than a snail.

"Listen, take some ibuprofen and have an Epsom salt bath later," he says. "I promise, your pain will subside."

"Get away from me before I call Michael Seay or security. Whoever I see first!"

He just laughs and pats me on the shoulder. "See you tomorrow morning."

As soon as my alarm clock buzzes Monday morning, I dash to the bathroom, where I strip and stand on my bathroom scale. There's no way I'm going to be in this much pain without seeing if it's working.

I look down at the red numbers glowing between my feet. I step down, then step back on again.

No mistake.

Four pounds. History.

Time for me to get ready. Ninja John will be here in twenty minutes!

11

MARIAH

Mariah rubbed her arms through her long-sleeve t-shirt as she sat on a cushioned folding chair inside the large gray room for the PMHU Bariatric information session. Nerves made her cross her feet at the ankles, uncross them and then cross them again.

She glanced around at the other people, some of them fidgeting with their clothing or toying with the information papers they'd all been given to read. Today, she had to get through this session and the wide world of bariatric surgery.

"They're late." Towanda stated the obvious as she swiped her iPad screen, then shut it off and slid it inside her bag. "We're waiting for them and they're late. Do they charge less money to the insurance company if they're late?"

Mariah shot her a look. "Stop, please."

"You sure you want an operation from people who can't look at a clock?"

"I asked you to stop. I'm anxious enough."

"Whatcha anxious for?"

"This is surgery, for one thing."

"You aren't having surgery today. This is an information session."

"And I'm not all that happy about Os right now."

"What's wrong with him now?"

"He stopped me on the way out of the house." Mariah leaned in, lowering her voice. "He told me again, as if I needed a reminder, that he's disappointed in me. He thinks this surgery is a mistake and he wants me to reconsider having it. I don't know. I think he's scared, but I don't want to back off this decision. T?"

"Yeah."

"Think I should change my mind for him?"

"No. Maybe he needs to think about your feelings and a few other things."

"Like what?"

"Seeking help for his control issues," Towanda said. "But don't you worry about that. The sooner you have the operation, the sooner you can return to being the number one mother and wife on the planet. Best stay-at-home mom on the main line, right?"

"Hey now, I don't plan to be just that for much longer. I only need fifteen credits to complete my degree, then I'm going straight into an MBA program. Oh, and I forgot to tell you all about my plans for the Quality Experience store. It's going to have an emphasis on customer service and cater to—"

Towanda put up her hand. "Um-hm. That's good. Real good. You just keep on scribbling down your little ideas. That's awesome." As the conference room door swung open, she leaned over and whispered to Mariah, "Right now, it's showtime."

A clean-shaven man in a white lab coat walked in and proceeded to the front of the conference room, accompanied by a smiling brunette woman. A few seconds later, a short, dark-haired man followed.

The woman addressed them. "Welcome everyone."

The medical team introduced themselves. Friendly nurse, Janet. Doug, a weight loss counselor. Dr. Seng himself. He greeted them all with a warm smile and a brief overview, then nurse Janet switched off the lights and he launched right into his PowerPoint presentation. Mariah tapped notes on her phone based on the talking points on the screen. Thirty minutes passed swiftly and then the presentation was over. When the lights were turned on, Dr. Seng addressed the small crowd. "Do you have any questions?"

Mariah kept her thoughts to herself, preferring to listen to the others go through Q&A on all things bariatric-surgery-related. So many things to consider, and Mariah had to admit, the faces in the room and the doctor's smooth, assured voice made it all sound so easy.

But in the end, she'd be the one who'd have to be tested, measured and finally, cut. Her body would be invaded by medical tools. Chills ran down her spine when she thought about it. PowerPoint slides and smiling faces couldn't explain how much pain she'd be in, and by then, everyone else would be gone, nowhere in sight as she recovered at home.

Mariah raised her hand, speaking up when Dr. Seng nodded at her.

"What about the pain of the surgery?" she asked him. "Discomfort. How much will it hurt?"

"That's difficult to say because we can't determine your tolerance for pain. What I can tell you is our team will do their best to keep you comfortable during and after surgery. We'll also give you a prescription for liquid painkillers."

Mariah glanced at Towanda, who just shrugged at her.

Doug stood up. "Your questions about pain and discomfort? When you visit our support group, those men and women will share their experiences with you. It can help with your decision."

Again, everything seemed so effortless. Even payment for the surgery would be covered through her insurance. White coats and helping hands and personal support to enable one procedure, after which, extra pounds would vanish from Mariah's body.

"Thank you," Mariah said, sitting back down on her chair.

"Everyone, this information session is step one," Dr. Seng told the group. "For those of you who choose to continue, you'll meet with Janet, who will review your preliminary information, and then you'll meet with me. I'll review your diet history and talk with you about your current habits and lifestyle. We'll also talk through the requirements for your pre-operation diet, which is the one-to-two week liquid diet you'll adhere to before surgery day. If you follow the pre-op diet well, you can expect to lose between five to fifteen pounds before your surgery. You'll also stop any current medications, even if you have to resume them after the surgery."

A woman with short blonde hair and a nose ring raised her hand. "I'm on meds to help manage my blood sugar. I'll discontinue that?"

"Yes."

Then a caramel-colored man wearing a Sixers shirt waved his hand before speaking. "Say I start this. What do I go home and tell my wife? How many days before I actually have the procedure?"

"It's different for each patient," Dr. Seng said. "But I can say we'll work hard to have you move toward your health goals as soon as possible."

As soon as possible?

What if Mariah had to start her pre-op diet a week before Thanksgiving? Instead of talking about gifts, she'd have to tell her family and friends she could barely eat anything during the holidays. But more than that, what about Oscar and Binky? What if something went wrong and she had to stay in the hospital at Christmastime?

"Everyone, I've heard many of your concerns before, and they're all valid," Dr. Seng said. "Here's what you need to take away today. Make sure you are making this decision for yourself, not for your husband, wife or parents. And here's what to share with your families—in the last decade, bariatric surgery technology has been perfected by leaps and bounds. It's as ordinary as performing a hip replacement. Your family should be more concerned about losing you to complications of diabetes, heart disease or stroke if we do not use this tool to help you move toward a healthy body weight."

"Can you say that again?" Towanda blurted out. "I need to record it so I can replay it for her husband."

"Towanda!"

"Sorry," Towanda said, sinking back into her chair.

Mariah glanced over at nurse Janet. Yes. As soon as the session ended, she'd go over and make the appointment.

MARIAH CLUTCHED HER PURSE ON HER LAP AS SHE SETTLED IN THE

passenger seat of Towanda's Range Rover. "Well, that's done. I'm on my way, I guess."

Towanda steered them out of the parking lot. "You're really ready to do this?"

"I have to."

"You mean *we* have to."

"What?"

"I'm joining you."

"Are you serious?"

"Why not? I can call my doctor and get a physical and approval. It should be a lot easier for you if you have me to partner with."

Towanda didn't say anything else as she steered them through traffic. Mariah half-expected her bestie to start giggling and say she was only kidding. Towanda had practically ignored posting anything on the Thick Chicks Clique page and now she was talking surgery? With her height, she carried her weight in a regal fashion.

Bariatric surgery? For Towanda?

Mariah pressed further. "You and me? Weight loss surgery at the same time?"

"Absolutely!"

"T, a hundred pounds off of you would make you a Twizzler."

"Oh, I'll still be large and in charge. Just without the thunder thighs."

Mariah stopped talking. Maybe the information session had provided a lot of food for thought? If that was true, Towanda had every right to think about surgery. Whether she would actually be recommended for the procedure was up to her doctor.

Mariah settled deeper into her seat. She'd pray for Towanda. Besides the comment about getting surgery for herself, what about that crack she'd made earlier about Mariah returning to being the best wife and mother? And she'd barely listened to her plans for school and business.

She glanced over at her best friend again.

Maybe Towanda was tired or flustered about business issues.

Yeah. That had to be it.

It had to be.

12

TOWANDA

Towanda's Monday morning started bright and early with a Tri-State Women in Business breakfast at the Marriott hotel. She arrived early to place free pens and notepads with the blue and white thinkLARGE logo, in front of each breakfast setting on the tables.

ThinkLARGE served as one of the sponsors for the networking event. Towanda learned early on these events were worth their weight in gold. People would first conduct business with others with whom they were familiar before trying a company from an advertisement.

When the breakfast ended at ten, she spent precisely thirty minutes networking and handing out business cards to new members of the organization before her phone alarm buzzed in her pocket. She turned the alarm off, then said goodbye to everyone. She needed to check a few emails on her iPhone and drive back to thinkLARGE.

In the Range Rover, Towanda placed her Fossil briefcase on the passenger seat and then pulled out her phone and tapped to open her messages. She grinned wide as she looked at the list. There were already three emails from women who had attended the breakfast, all of them asking for additional information about thinkLARGE services.

Good.

She scrolled down further. Nelson Anders, the MEGANDA CEO, had sent an email. She tapped the entry.

Dear Towanda,

I want to thank you and your team over at thinkLARGE. We already see increased interest in our products here at MEGANDA. Everyone here loves the #WhatsOnMyWrist Instagram campaign with the local Philly celebrities. Last week we were contacted by the both Metro and the Daily News for feature articles. People do want to know our story. They excited we have our headquarters right here in Northern Liberties. I would recommend your firm to anyone who needs a fresh style of marketing and brand development. Please feel free to add our endorsement to any promotional materials you create for thinkLARGE.

Sincerely,

Nelson Anders, CEO, MEGANDA Watches

"Yes!" Towanda cheered as she banged her fist on the steering wheel.

What a high!

A win for MEGANDA meant a victory for thinkLARGE. And with three new business leads, Monday was turning out to be an A+ day. Nothing could stop her now. She was on a roll. Should she email back and ask Nelson to sign a three-year contract for thinkLARGE services?

No. It might be too soon. She'd give it another month. But with the MEGANDA endorsement, thinkLARGE would attract more and bigger clients. Towanda could hire more staff just like she'd planned. Maybe even find a small multi-media company to acquire. Yes! She was moving forward steadily. Building her empire.

Since things were going so well, she could take the time to call her doctor about the chance for bariatric surgery. She'd call, request the approval, have it faxed to PMHU Bariatric or however those things worked and get the ball rolling.

When Mariah entered the fast track for weight loss, Towanda would be right there with her. They'd be super-skinny together.

Chablis might be taking a slower road, but that was fine, she'd catch up with them in time.

Towanda searched her contact list for Dr. Pat Rogers. Pat was so down to earth, for something like weight loss surgery, Towanda would call her for advice even if she weren't her primary care physician.

Dr. Pat's mobile rang until finally, it connected to her voice mail. Towanda left a message. "Hi Pat, it's Towanda Mathis calling. Hope you're having a great morning. I don't need to schedule an appointment, but I need your help for medical approval. When you have a break, please FaceTime me. Thanks."

With a smile on her face, Towanda placed her phone in the cupholder. She'd drive around for a while, that's what she'd do. Take a moment to bask in the glow of a winning morning. When Pat called back, she'd request what she needed, and then she would call Mariah and tell her they were all set.

Towanda cruised down Columbus Avenue and was passing Penn's Landing when her phone lit up. Luckily, she was close to a side street. She turned the corner, pulled over to the curb and then picked up the phone and tapped to accept FaceTime.

Dr. Pat's friendly face filled the screen. "Towanda. How's it going?"

Towanda mounted her phone on the dashboard. "Oh, I can't complain."

"Well, it's definitely not an emergency, otherwise you'd have skipped the waiting room and walked in here demanding an immediate appointment."

"Am I that bad?"

"Worse. But seriously, what do you need today?"

Towanda took a deep breath and then cleared her throat. "I want to talk to you about weight loss surgery. What would it take to get me an approval?"

When Dr. Pat let out a chuckle, Towanda frowned.

Dr. Pat eyes shifted to the side as she explained. "That's not for you."

"Why not? I'm not exactly Taylor Swift over here."

Dr. Pat raised an eyebrow. "For surgical weight loss at your height and weight, you'd have to have high blood pressure, diabetes or sleep apnea. You'd also need something else you don't have."

"What?"

"Multiple failed attempts to lose weight. Towanda, you don't have any of those issues. You're quite healthy and you know that, so why are you bugging me about this?"

Towanda shifted her own eyes away from the phone screen and mumbled, "My best friend."

"Your friend asked you to think about weight loss surgery?"

"No, she's getting the surgery."

"Oh." Dr. Pat sighed. "Well, I wish her the best, and it may be hard for you to tell her, but you'll have to inform her weight loss surgery isn't a buddy-system type of thing."

"But she's not the...okay...all right." Towanda returned her gaze to the screen. "Thanks for calling me back so quickly."

"No problem. How is your business doing these days?"

Waves of disappointment rippled through Towanda's body, but she managed to keep her eyes fixed to the phone and force a smile.

"Oh, you know me," she said. "I'm killing it."

FABRIC TEARS FAST WHEN YOU PULL AT IT HARD ENOUGH.

The first pillow, then the second, then the third. All of them, their fuzzy cotton outer shells ripped to shreds between Towanda's fingers. She pulled out their soft insides with her nails and scattered them over the living room floor like fake snow. Discarded and worthless.

She couldn't stop. Not until every single pillow on her sofa was turned inside out and tossed on the ground. If there had been a hidden camera perched in the high ceiling of her living room, the recorded footage wouldn't have made any sense. She towered above a shiny metal and glass table decorated with a silver bowl full of glittering round globes. Her hands snatched up pillow after pillow from the couch. She ripped each one apart, pulling the stuffing out before tossing it on the floor. The remainder of the room remained white, clean, contemporary and pristine.

Towanda reached for the last pillow and pulled it up to her face. She dug in and stopped.

What am I doing? Am I sad?

She shook her head.

Frustrated?

She shrugged.

Disappointed?

About what? There had never been room for disappointment in her world and she couldn't let it in now. So, she needed to stop ripping decorations to shreds. Why did she need to come back to her apartment anyway? Because she couldn't let Jackie and the others at the office see her as anything less than a pillar of strength, that's why.

She tossed the remaining pillow on the couch and then flopped down on top of it, stretching out to her full length, her feet dangling over the edge. She surveyed the scattered fabric on the floor and laughed. The scene looked like a bloodless polar bear had exploded.

Towanda stared at the stark white ceiling. Should she get a second opinion? No. This wasn't life or death. There was no reason for her to try to be thinner.

In Towanda's thirty-four years on earth, the one thing she'd been slammed with day after day was accepting the truth. No, her mother would not return for her. No, her father would never shake drugs and alcohol in time to survive.

No meant *NO*.

"Enough!" Towanda pulled her body erect, standing up from the couch. "I don't do pity parties. I don't like the appetizers!"

She shuffled through the white pillow remnants and headed straight down the hall to her home office. She plopped down in her office chair, pushing herself around to stare at the Philly skyline.

So what if doctors approved Mariah for weight loss surgery? The woman needed it for her health. Of course, the operation meant she would lose a ton of weight, with her face and body looking more like Binky's.

Towanda thought about the svelte, model-looking Mariah from fifteen years ago.

Towanda liked the heavier version better.

They'd bonded more throughout the years. When they went out together, no one pushed right past Towanda to talk to Mariah as they had when they were in high school.

If Mariah dropped the weight, the two of them might have less in common. Maybe Mariah would emerge from her shell and develop new friendships with other women who possessed runway model looks? What if the glamour lady also created a business which dwarfed thinkLARGE? If all that happened, would she still want Towanda as her BFF?

Why couldn't things just stay the same? Why did Mariah need to change anything? She could lose weight, sure, by why did it need to be this extreme? Things were fine the way they were. So Mariah and Oscar had a few rough patches because of Mariah's weight. It was nothing marriage counseling couldn't solve.

Towanda wheeled over to her laptop, opened it up, launched Safari and entered Facebook land. Inside the Thick Chicks Clique page, Chablis had posted a picture of herself leaving LA Fitness. She looked a hot mess in the photo, her weave tied up in a knot on top of her head and sweat running down her temples. Mariah had posted a prayer for all of them. She also asked for prayer for her bariatric surgery journey.

Towanda was the only one missing from the page. The only one sitting back reviewing everyone else's progress.

The only one still trying to figure out where she belonged.

13

CHABLIS

I t's cold this mid-November Saturday morning, but I don't feel chilled because my body feels warm, the sun shines bright and all is right with the world. I'm race-walking down the pavement like a champ. What am I wearing? Black running tights, a long-sleeved dry-weave t-shirt under my pink and black running jacket, and pink Nike Air Zoom Pegasus running shoes. Tim Bowman, Jr. sings to me through my Beats headphones, telling me, "I'm Good."

Never mind the fact that my trainer, Ninja John, runs like a mile ahead of me somewhere. Dozens of runners, walkers and bikers move around me, so I don't feel alone or anxious on this path beside the Art Museum. Years ago in therapy, I learned extreme avoidance can be a trap, increasing my panic attacks. So even though I'll never hang out in a dark alley again, I'm okay outside unless someone rushes up and surprises me from behind. Right now, I'm flowing along with everyone else. Thank God for the ability to move.

I'm supposed to be running right now. I ran for the first ten minutes, but when I saw John disappear around the first curve, I cranked up my music and slowed down. He'll probably catch me at some point. I don't mind if he fusses a little, though. During the past few weeks, I've learned he has a loud bark, but his bite doesn't exist. I show up every weekday morning at the gym. All I eat are baked chicken breasts, salads, and protein shakes. Pizza entered my body one time, and it was only one plain slice after a long work meeting ended. As of today, eleven pounds are gone, and that's enough to keep John from dropping me as his fitness charity case.

I reach the curve and race-walk myself around it, this time singing along to Tye Tribett, who tells me everything's fresh and it's time for me to move forward. As soon as I spot the Rocky statue, I see John has turned around and is now jogging toward me.

I slow my pace when he reaches me.

"Hey, buddy!" I say, winking at him.

He stops and taps the button on his wireless/waterproof/made-for-athletes headphones, glaring at me. "The deal is, this is an outdoor running day for you. I asked if you were okay with me running ahead and doubling back for you. You said you'd be fine running at your pace."

"I ran."

"For how long? The first five minutes when I could still turn around and see you?"

"Longer than that." I move my Beats to my neck. "At least ten, maybe twelve minutes, I swear."

He takes his headphones off, folds them up and stuffs them in the pocket of his hoodie. "Uh-huh. Let's chat."

John turns to jog to the bottom of the Art Museum steps, where he sits and waits for me. I jog over to him but do not put my Beats back on my ears. I'm expecting a lecture, and I'll stand there and take it because, yes, I'm goofing off.

He pats the cement next to him. "Join me, please."

I drop down on the hard step and turn my gaze to the sidewalk. People walk along, enjoying this lovely fall day, which is crisp, crystal clear and gorgeous, and this brother will not bring me down.

He stretches his long legs out in front of him. "Do you know why I'm helping you?"

This surprises me, because his voice sounds more like a caring father and not like a drill sergeant.

"I'm cute?" I answer.

"No."

"I'm not cute?"

"Chablis—"

"I take it this has nothing to do with my cuteness?"

John wipes a hand over his face. "All right, look. Do you remember serving on Help Squad at the evening service? The night I said I'd train you."

I nod.

"Remember anything else about that night?"

"Not really."

"Before service started, you sat down at one of the benches with a woman. She looked new. Maybe a visitor?"

Oh, yeah. That lady. She had sat apart from the crowd moving toward the sanctuary. I spied her from the desk and thought she was waiting for someone. But then I saw her brush tears away from her cheeks. She was wearing enormous dark sunglasses covering half her face.

Inside the church building? In the evening?

When a woman comes to church alone, crying under super dark sunglasses she doesn't bother to take off, it can only mean one thing. I left the information desk, went straight to her and hugged her. She took the tissues I pressed into her trembling hands while I prayed for her, asking the Lord to provide healing for her struggle.

Someone had hurt her. I know too much about how that feels.

"She needed help. I helped," I say, keeping my eyes fixed on the sidewalk. "That's what Pastor trained us to do."

"What made you hold her, though?"

Ugh. I don't want to get into all that on this crisp, sunny, blue sky day, so I shrug and mumble. "She needed love and prayer. And these steps are hard, so can we walk?"

"Sure." John eases up off the steps. He restarts the conversation as we begin moving. "You rushed to hold and help a stranger."

"Yeah, I did."

"That's when I told myself to help you."

"Oh, I get it." I shove my hands in the pockets of my running jacket. "Thanks, I think."

He ignores my sarcasm. "Do you know I have bad eyesight?"

"No."

"Yeah. I've worn thick lenses since I was like two. Kids used to make fun of me in school, but I needed my glasses. Without them, I'm almost legally blind. When I got to high school, though, I begged my Mom to take me to get contacts, and the optometrist prescribed gas permeable lenses—hard contacts. As soon as I started wearing them, people treated me different, like I was another person."

I turn my head to stare at his eyes.

"Stop staring at me. I have them in now. I can see you just fine."

"Sorry."

"Anyway, after I got my contacts, that's when I started thinking, what else can I improve? I was kind of skinny too, so on the weekends I lifted weights with my cousins. At school, I joined the wrestling and cross-country teams. My body improved and I kept at it."

"Destined to be an American Ninja Warrior."

He snorts. "You think so, huh?"

"Definitely."

John looks straight ahead as he walks a little faster. "My eyes are my weakness. Back in May, at the qualifying rounds for the show, I was halfway through the course when I blinked hard, and my right contact shifted. Since I couldn't see well, my depth perception was off, my hand slipped when I tried to grab the bar for the third obstacle. I fell and didn't qualify."

"Couldn't you have a do-over? I mean, it wasn't your fault."

"My do-over is next year." He shrugs. "I'm here today. I'm healthy. I love how my career's going. I look at it like this, if I wasn't supposed to compete this year, God's still in control."

We move along the sidewalk, the sound of city traffic rushing past us. I've teased John for weeks, squawking Ninja this and Ninja that, and he never corrected me. He didn't have to tell me about his eyesight today. I need to stop being so guarded. We turn down the paved path that cuts through the garden area. I point to an empty wooden bench.

"Can we sit over there for a minute?" I swallow at the lump in my throat. "I gotta tell you something."

John looks at me and nods, so we cross the grass and take a seat together.

I stare at the ground in front of me while I speak. "A long time ago, a man physically beat me. That's why I needed to pray for that lady at church—"

"Wait. Are you serious?"

"Actually...it was...my ex-boyfriend. He jumped me one night after dance practice. He hit me in the head, punched me in the face a bunch of times and tried to strangle me. A couple of strangers passed by and saw him and he ran off."

I pause to take a few deep breaths, long enough to relax and finish my story. "I had to rest and recover from all the injuries, and on top of that, I had a concussion and that took a long time to heal, so I laid around for a year. That's when I gained this weight. I tried to go back to dancing months after I healed, but I felt uncoordinated, so I stopped and concentrated on my college classes. But I used to dance all the time. I had a dancer's body."

When I raise my head, I see a strange look on John's face. His jaws are tight and his fists are clenched.

"When did all this happen?" He asks me.

"Six years ago. I was nineteen."

"Last time you were fit, huh?"

I nod. Pat my weave. Look down and around. "Yeah."

He stands up and starts pacing back and forth.

Did I do the right thing, telling him all my personal business? The wind blows around us as the sun plays peekaboo behind some clouds. It feels colder now. I said too much. Now he knows I'm damaged and he knows why. And I didn't even tell him about the panic attacks or the scar I hide with concealer every day. Our run/walk session is probably over now. He no doubt thinks I'm an over-emotional mess and wishes he'd never started this fitness journey with me.

John finally stops pacing and sits down next to me. He takes my hands in his. I ignore the tears in my eyes that I pray he doesn't see.

"Sweetheart, let me tell you something. I'm so sorry that happened to you. I don't know the dude, but I'm glad I don't, 'cause I'd beat him down right now. And listen—you're gonna get back what he stole from you. I'm working with you now, and you're getting fit and you're gonna go dance like you used to. I promise you that."

I stare down at the Nikes on my feet. "How long?"

"How long for what?"

I lift my head and our gazes meet. He has gorgeous eyes. "How long to get fit like you and Travis and Sheena?"

"If you push it?"

"Yeah."

"I've seen people transform themselves totally in less than fifteen months. If you do the work, it'll happen for you. All you have to do is be consistent."

This is my trainer and my new friend. I'm safe with him. And I signed up for this. Eleven pounds disappeared in a month, so I'm more than halfway to my first goal of twenty pounds. But now he's telling me I can get warrior-level fit. This is serious for me. Now I've made it serious for him.

"I'm in it to win it. So, what do we do now?" I ask.

He stands up, zipping his hoodie. "We run. This time I'll stay with you."

I stand and slide my Beats back over my ears.

Because it's time for me to push it.

14

MARIAH

Mariah's surgery? The roux En-Y gastric bypass. Preparation started weeks before with the pre-op diet, just like the PMHU team said. For fourteen days, she drank protein shakes for breakfast and lunch and ate dinners consisting of a few ounces of chicken on a bed of lettuce or green beans.

The result? She shed twelve pounds.

Three days before surgery, she'd stopped taking her Metformin. Then, the evening before, after making a four days' worth of meals for Binky and Oscar, she dragged her tired body upstairs and showered with the special soap she'd been given for her skin. She'd followed all her instructions to the letter, even arriving at the hospital with her family, two full hours before her scheduled operation time.

Inside the tiny hospital room, Mariah took off the chain around her neck and zipped it into a small plastic baggie. She pushed it toward Binky, who glanced up from her phone screen looking annoyed.

"Binky, put this in your backpack," Mariah said. "When you get home, put it in the jewelry box in my room."

Binky rolled her eyes. "Mom, you could have left it home to begin with."

"I know that, Benita."

"You wanna sit down? You're sweating."

Mariah wiped her forehead with a tissue. "I'm always sweating."

"Yeah, but now it's more," Binky said, shoving the baggie inside her small brown backpack.

Mariah reached inside her shirt pocket for a five-dollar bill and passed it to her daughter. "Make yourself useful. Find a vending machine and get yourself something to drink. Buy your dad an iced tea or something."

Binky took the money, slid off the end of the bed and left the room.

Good. Now her nerve-wracking daughter would be gone for a few minutes. All Mariah needed to do was take her clothes off and put on the hospital gown the nurse had placed in the chair. The same chair where a silent Oscar now sat.

Mariah tried being lighthearted as she spoke to him. "Can you help me? My t-shirt's stuck to my back. I can't go into the operating room with it on."

Oscar didn't budge. "I can't get you to change your mind?"

"Not at this point." Mariah sighed, reaching down to pull her shirt over her head.

What was he thinking? She couldn't back out now. She was here and it was time.

Oscar hadn't said much all morning, but she understood his passive aggression. He was still against her having the procedure, but if he flat-out forbid her to have it and her health situation grew worse, he'd feel responsible.

She took a deep breath and continued to undress. As soon as she returned to her old self, Oscar would see. The operation would be worth it. They could fly to Puerto Rico the next summer to visit his family. No need to buy an extra seat or ask for a seatbelt extender from the flight attendant. It would be just like old times — before the kid, the house and the health issues.

"Os, can you at least hand me my gown? The doctor will be here soon."

He pulled the plastic package from the side of the chair and handed it to her. She finished putting on the gown and slid in the bed in time to hear fingers tapping on the door. When it swung open, Dr. Seng strolled in with a file folder in his hands and a smile on his face. He wore scrubs and one of those blue hair coverings.

"Good to see you, Mrs. Rodriguez."

"Good to be seen." Comfortable in her gown, Mariah gestured towards Oscar. "You remember my husband, Oscar."

"Yes, good morning," Dr. Seng said. The two men shook hands and then Oscar returned to his chair.

Her doctor patted her arm. "I've reviewed all your pre-operation information and you're all set. Your surgery will take about two hours. I know Doug and Janet covered your post-operative activities during your appointment last week, but do you have any other questions?"

"No," Mariah said as she glanced at Oscar.

Oscar met her gaze for a split second before he went back to his tablet.

I'm going through with this. My life will be better, and Oscar will thank me later.

Mariah rubbed her hands together and turned back toward Dr. Seng. "I'm ready."

"Nervous at all?"

"A little."

"You can relax. We're all dedicated to your safety and success. After surgery, just let us know your level of discomfort and we'll take care of you right away."

"Thanks."

"You're welcome. See you soon."

She lay back on the pillow and closed her eyes, praying silently.

Father, see me through this. I'm trusting you for a great outcome. Amen.

This time when she opened her eyes, two nurses walked through the door. They helped her cover her hair, put soft booties on her feet and set up an IV, taping the long plastic tubing to her arm. They also gave her a shot to prevent blood clots — which hurt bad. Then they stuck a patch behind her ear which they told her would prevent nausea. An anesthesiology team arrived, and they administered a happy cocktail of painkillers to flow through her bloodstream during and after the surgery. When they left, the door rattled once more and in walked a group of people so noisy it could only be her family.

Mariah's mother, Joan, leaned on the arm of her father, Fred. Then there was her older sister, Tamron, and her older brother, Troy. All of them strolled into the small room like a parade. Binky followed them, sipping a grape Fanta and handing her dad an Arizona iced tea.

Mariah peeked through all their bodies. Where was Towanda?

"Hey, sis," Tamron showed Mariah a ceramic smiley face mug holding a pretty arrangement of yellow roses and white and yellow daisies.

Mariah grimaced. "I'm not dying or giving birth. Flowers?"

Tamron placed the arrangement on the small table next to the hospital bed. "Thought it might be nice for you to see when you get out of the OR. Hey Os! Quiet over there."

Oscar got up and gave quick hugs to everyone, but then wordlessly returned to his seat. Mariah shook her head and turned her attention to her parents.

Her father leaned down and kissed her cheek. "How are you feeling?"

"I'm good so far. Anybody see T? In the hallway or parking her car or something?"

Joan pulled the blanket up over Mariah's torso. "No. We thought she'd be in here."

Strange. Maybe she was stuck in traffic. Mariah couldn't check her phone for messages. It was locked away in her purse, secured in the set of drawers by the bed. Besides, nurses would be coming in any minute to wheel her down the hall. Her bestie would probably be the first face she saw after she woke up, making her laugh with jokes and snarky comments.

Binky pushed her way to her mother's bedside. She adjusted Mariah's blue hair covering so it stretched over her hairline.

"So, after you get skinny, can I add some highlights to your hair?" Binky asked. "Please? I learned how from YouTube."

"Forget my hair and my future skinniness. When we get home, we need to have a talk about those grades again. Understand?"

Binky hugged her mother fast. "Praying for ya, Mom." She turned away for a moment, but then leaned down and gave her a longer hug and a kiss on the cheek. "Love you, Mom. I know you'll be all right when this is over."

After Binky moved, Mariah's brother Troy took her place. "Love you, sis."

She clutched his hand. "Love you back. And you know there's still bottles of wine in my kitchen collecting dust. The ones you left after the Labor Day barbecue. When are you gonna come pick them up?"

Troy chuckled. "Keep 'em. We'll pop 'em open in a few months when we celebrate your success."

Mariah scanned the room once more. If she could pick the best way to leave the earth, this would be it. Almost all her closest loved ones crowded the room.

But Towanda should be in the room too.

Where was she?

Something must have happened.

And where in the world was Chablis?

Another knock at the door, and then it swung open again. A nurse clad in blue scrubs and her assistant in green scrubs headed straight for Mariah's bedside.

"Mrs. Rodriguez, it's time."

Mariah craned her neck to peek through the doorway. "Are you sure? We have to start now?"

"Yes, we're right on time. Are you having any trouble?"

Mariah wiped away another trickle of sweat. "No. My best friend. I was hoping she'd get here before I went to the OR." She dropped her head back onto the pillow. "Forget it. Let's do this."

"Not yet," Oscar stood up and walked to her bedside. "We have to pray. Can everyone please gather around my wife? Benita, put that phone down before I make it a paperweight!"

The nurses took a step back while Oscar grasped Mariah's hands and bowed his head. "Father, please cover my wife while she undergoes this procedure. Lord, as you promised in Psalm 41:3, we are trusting Your word to restore Mariah to good health. Keep her safe and let no infection or harm come to her. Amen."

When the prayer ended, Mariah remained silent but still squeezed her husband's hands for a few more seconds.

The lead nurse returned to Mariah's side. "Mrs. Rodriguez, you have a lovely family."

"Thank you."

"We need to wheel you down now."

"Okay."

"Everyone, the patient is ready, so if you could give us a little room, we're going to transfer her to the OR. She'll return here in a few hours."

Mariah's family moved back as the nurses put up the bed rails and raised the bed. Less than a minute later, they wheeled her from the room and down the hallway.

"Wait!" a familiar voice sounded.

Mariah stopped staring at the lights in the ceiling and turned her head to see a breathless Chablis rush to her side. She bent down for a hug, then stepped back and waved as the bed continued to the operating room.

"Sorry, cousin. I got stuck at the hairdresser," Chablis called out. "I'm praying for you. You'll do just fine!"

Mariah waved a hand as she traveled around the corner. Just like that, she'd officially left her family behind.

A new journey.

And this one was hers alone.

15

TOWANDA

Towanda needed to make something up.

She had no reason, business or otherwise, for skipping a visit to Mariah's hospital room before her surgery. No speaking engagements. No meetings. She didn't even have any chores at home. And she would never invent a fake emergency with Nana as a way out.

Mariah's bariatric surgery day?

Towanda flat out didn't want to be there. So, she'd stayed at home, in bed with a comforter wrapped around her, her smart TV on with the volume cranked up high, playing episode after episode of *The Walking Dead*. She'd muted her phone but she could still see texts appear in the banner notifications.

From Chablis: *T, where are you? The parking garage is kind of full. Just go on and drive to the top. We're in Room 407.*

From Chablis an hour later: *If you're working through a business solution, it's cool. Just text me back. She's still in the operating room.*

From Mariah's sister Tamron: *Hey woman, u gonna make an appearance today? You're not traveling, are you?*

From Binky: *Auntie, I miss you. After you check on Mom, can I go to dinner with you? Can we go to Honey's Sit N' Eat?*

And one more from Chablis two hours later: *She's out of the operating room. Doc said everything went well. What happened to you? Something going on with Nana?*

Zombies, viruses and bloody flesh. It seemed more natural for Towanda to see carnage on the screen than dwell on the insecurities living in her heart. So, she laid there with her eyes glazed while her phone buzzed and danced on the bed. She ignored every text and notification and finally turned off the phone after Chablis' last text.

Mariah was fine. Because, of course, she would be.

By ten that evening, Towanda had finished her binge-watching session. Wide awake in the silent room, she lay on top the bed thinking.

Should she try to get work done?

Not tonight. No way would she be able to sit in her office chair and strategize well. She'd be better off taking a long shower and calling it a night.

She chewed her bottom lip as she climbed off her bed. If she stood under the hot water long enough, maybe she'd figure out how to face her best friend the next day.

For once, Chablis' constant texting actually helped Towanda. Instead of feeling awkward and out of place as she entered the hospital, she strolled into the building while focusing on her phone screen.

Chablis had messaged: *Nobody heard from you. Holla back if you aren't dead.*

Towanda texted back: *Holla!*

Surprise of all surprises, Chablis didn't return the text. Instead, she called. Towanda rolled her eyes as she swiped to answer.

"Where are you?" Chablis asked.

"At the hospital on my way up to see Mariah."

"Good. She missed you yesterday. She was looking around for you."

Towanda sighed. "Shouldn't you be serving right now, munchkin?"

"It's an off-ministry week for me. Besides, I need a break. I think I might be crushing."

"On who?"

"My trainer, John Gerald. He serves in my ministry, but he's stationed on the second floor."

"He has two first names?"

"Please don't make fun of that."

"Wait, he's that athletic guy from church. The one with the sword and shield tattoos on his arms? Him?"

"Yeah."

"You have a crush on your trainer?"

"I think. Yeah."

"We're on the phone instead of texting, so I'll use this moment to say LOL!"

"Goodbye, T. Have a good visit."

Towanda slid her phone back in her bag as she walked toward the elevator.

That's cute. Chablis might seriously like someone?

Towanda had heard the attack was brutal, not that Chablis had ever talked about it all that much. But anything involving an ex-boyfriend, a bat and a concussion would be enough to make any woman ditch dating for a while.

What could Towanda say when she walked into Mariah's room? Even as the elevator rose on its way to the fourth floor, she still hadn't figured out an excuse. Nothing came to mind. The only thing she could concentrate on was her own footsteps. She hesitated for a second before she tapped lightly on Mariah's room door and then poked her head inside.

Mariah was alone. Oscar and Binky were probably at Rise. White roses and yellow daisies stood in a pretty arrangement on Mariah's nightstand. Towanda spied her sitting up in bed, her dark curls piled high in a ponytail. An IV was attached to her arm. She was staring across the room at the television screen. Towanda hesitated for a moment, then she took a deep breath and pushed her body through the door. Momentum carried her to Mariah's bedside. Maybe humor would disguise her awkwardness for the moment.

"Did I miss all the fun?" Towanda asked, testing the waters, a half-smile on her face. She studied Mariah's demeanor, which was a mixed bag--surprised, joyful and annoyed.

"Where were you?" Mariah asked, her voice raspy.

Towanda gulped and looked down at her feet. She could forget any joking around. Mariah had delivered the opening line to the main event with her eyes narrowed and pupils directed straight at Towanda's face.

"Home," Towanda mumbled, picking at her dry cuticles.

Mariah coughed and struggled to sit up higher. Towanda grabbed a pillow from the empty bed next to her and placed it at her best friend's back.

"T?" Mariah settled back. "Why?"

Towanda's eyes drifted to the ceiling, down to her feet and then across the room to the beige wall. She should have found a way to extract herself from her bedroom and go see her sister-friend before she went under the knife.

She should have, but she hadn't.

"I wasn't ready," Towanda said.

"Really? What did you need to get ready for? Enlighten me."

Towanda sat on the end of the bed, still picking at the rough skin on her fingertips. Towanda and Mariah. Thick as thieves through the years, but especially as grown adults. Always connected but taking different roads through life. This path seemed more divergent than ever.

Minutes passed and the television provided the only sound in the room, an episode of *Black-ish* playing in the background. Towanda didn't possess the words to describe her feelings or behavior. All she could do now was be present, which was more than she'd been able to do the day before.

"T," Mariah said. "You're here now. It's okay."

"I should have—"

Mariah shook her head before looking away. "It's okay. Let's forget it. All right?"

Towanda studied the fuzzy white blanket covering Mariah's legs. One look at Mariah as she kept her eyes directed at the window told

Towanda their friendship had buckled like a concrete sidewalk under heat.

Time might restore it to normal.

Or maybe time would be the jackhammer which tore it up completely.

PART II

SPRING/SUMMER

16

CHABLIS

O f all the activewear I use now, my exercise bra gives me the most headaches. I have to stand naked every morning, pulling a resistant band of Lycra over my head and around my chest. The stupid straps never land where I want, and once the cloth-covered rubber band stretches around my shoulders, I have to grunt and pull for at least a minute until it cups my globes like it should.

This Friday, though?

No struggle.

I mean—none!

After I pull the bra down, I stare in my bedroom mirror and see smooth skin all across the top of my chest. My shoulders look slimmer. And wait. There are no rolls under my armpits. I touch my face and run my fingertips from my chin down to my collarbone. When I lean closer to the mirror, right beneath my neck, my collarbone is visible. I swear, it's winking at me.

For months I've seen pounds tick down on the scale, but for whatever reason, I couldn't see significant body changes.

Now I see them, and for a second I want to cry. But I don't, because

I'm an overcomer. So, I finish dressing, grab my gym bag and my keys and leave my apartment.

John doesn't have to pick me up anymore. My gym equals my routine. Sometimes I even get there before him because I like to walk the treadmill longer to clear my head.

I don't see John when I stroll in, so I go on and get to work. The treadmill awaits, but first, I'm thrilled about my body changes and I want to tell the world. I take my phone, hold it high over my head, and get ready to take a photo to post to Instagram with the hashtag #PoundsandInchesGoneBaby.

But this doesn't happen.

Why? Because John walks up to the front of my treadmill and motions for me to hand my phone to him.

After I pass it to him, he shakes his head as he slides the device into his shorts pocket.

"You know better," he tells me.

Four months ago, I would have argued with him. Today I don't even answer. I violated rule ten of John's unwritten guidelines to respect thy workout time — no phone interaction unless I'm listening to music.

I crank up the treadmill speed and start to run. John runs next to me. We have a decent pace going for five minutes.

"This is what you have today." John hands me my workout sheet when we slow the machines down. "And here's your phone back." He presses it into my palm. "For music. Not selfies."

"No problem, coach. I'll take a picture later."

He pauses, a hint of a smile on his lips. "Let me guess. You noticed all your body changes today?"

"Yes," I sing. "My face. My neck. All across my upper body."

John's grin spreads. "Congrats. I was waiting for you to say something. So, are you motivated to keep pushing hard?"

"Oh, no doubt."

"That's what I want to hear. Go on and break the selfie rule. You've earned it."

And I do just that, with a grin on my face so there's no mistaking I'm over the moon right now. I ask John to lean in and we take two selfies together. One smiling, the other mean mugging as if we're about to do some damage up in this joint.

After I launch the pics into the Instagram universe, I scan my workout sheet. Five supersets of exercises with one cleanup superset at the end. Barbell clean and press followed by straight arm pulldowns. Regular grip pull-ups and bench dips. Dumbbell lateral raises paired with dumbbell tricep press. Hanging knee raises and standing cable crunches. Saxon side bends and decline bench sit-ups. The cleanup superset lists preacher curls, medicine ball slams, and torso twist. There's a note at the bottom of the sheet to add twenty jumping jacks between each superset.

No problem. I will crush this.

John goes to do his own workout, but once he sees me start, he keeps an eye on me. He'll step in to help if it looks as if I'm struggling. More and more, though, I can do this all on my own. He taught me proper form on these exercises. Now I'm in my zone, music in my ears, and I execute while John does his sets. People watch him when he tuck-jumps over weight benches. That's his level. Everyone has a degree of fitness. People like John, Sheena and Travis, theirs is just a higher level than mine.

When I glance over after I set up my barbell, I catch John watching me. Shaking my head is the signal I give to let him know I don't need a spotter. He gives me two thumbs-up. As I deep squat to pick up the bar, my smile extends so far I'm sure my dimples are twinkling. Andy Mineo is in my ear yelling *you can't stop me* and I start rep one of three sets of twelve barbell clean and presses.

It's grind time, and I'm pushing it.

SOMETHING STRANGE IS GOING ON. I CAN'T PUT MY FINGER ON IT EXACTLY, but I sense something. It's Saturday night and I just walked into the Rise Church Talent Cafe. This is a singles event, but I don't attend just because I'm unattached. I like to see my brothers and sisters sing, play music, dance or display their artwork. Rise provides water, tea and coffee, and the rest of us bring food to eat.

Talent Cafe used to be my favorite time for eating finger foods, cookies and cake. That was before I started fitness training. I've since been reformed. Before I drove over tonight, I ate baked chicken and a green salad and drank a tall glass of lemon water. In the lounge at the beverage table, I fill a large cup with hot black coffee. The bitter taste of the drink will murder any cravings before I consider wrecking my diet. John taught me this trick.

Two of my friends sit at a table toward the far end of the room. I head there to give hugs and chat before the talent portion of the evening gets underway.

"Hey, ladies." I place my coffee on the table, then lean into Felicia for a hug.

She squeezes me back. "We weren't sure you would make it."

"Why wouldn't I? I'm here every month." I move to my other side to give Nikki a hug. She has a weird look on her face as she gives me a lukewarm side squeeze and mumbles her hello.

I pull over a stool to sit next to them and then I pick up my coffee and take a sip.

Everything is quiet.

Too quiet.

You know, like maybe you were the topic of conversation, but then you arrive so no one knows what to say anymore.

Well, I don't play that game.

Not in church.

Not when these women are supposed to be my sisters.

I set my coffee back down and rub my eyes for a second. When I open them, I am staring right in Nikki's face. She gazes at the gray tabletop.

"All right, what's going on?" I ask.

Felicia answers. "Nothing. We're waiting for the first act to start."

I shake my head. "That's not what I'm talking about. Nik, you want to stop staring at the table?"

She lifts her head and blinks at me.

"What's the matter, for real, y'all?" I shift my eyes from Nikki to Felicia, who has taken over the job of scrutinizing the Formica.

"It's nothing," Nikki says. "Like she said, we weren't sure you were coming."

"I might have missed a few texts. I haven't been that busy."

Felicia looks up. "You haven't called us much lately, either."

Then Nikki adds, "You know what? I'm just waiting for you to come out and say it."

"Say what?" I shift my weight on the stool. I hate these high seats. I can never get comfortable on them. "I'm drawing a blank here, ladies. Help me out."

Felicia straightens her posture and stares in the eyes this time. "John. He's your man now? You're together, right?"

I triple blink. "Together where?"

She looks as if she wants to push me off this stool for being so stupid. "You know what I mean. Y'all a couple now?"

I read their body language. Mouths tight and foreheads wrinkled. They're serious.

Now I get it. They think I'm in a relationship and I never said anything to them about it.

These women are my sister-friends. They aren't anonymous faces in a sea of other Jesus followers at a big city megachurch. Other people I go to church with care about me, but they wouldn't stare me down like this.

I lean in closer to them. "What gave you that idea?"

Nikki snatches her phone from the table, swipes for a moment and then turns the phone around. "This."

And right there on Instagram, my face nestles next to John's and we are grinning up a storm. I have to admit, my dimples look amazing next to his dark beard, and I like that our skin tones match.

We look healthy. We look happy.

Which of course, I was until I walked in here to face my scowling friends.

I keep my voice low when I explain the pic. "We're definitely not a couple. Peep the hashtag. That's a training photo, not a couple's photo."

"But you've never posted one of these before," Nikki says.

"One of John's gym rules is that I don't take selfies, post or text during a workout session. He gave me a pass yesterday because of my progress. He's my trainer, and you know that." I shift again. "You could have asked me."

Nikki shrugs. "I didn't know what to think. I saw the picture and thought we'd missed something."

"Yeah," Felicia chimes in.

I roll my eyes. This is the trouble two gym selfies got me into. But even if I John and I started dating, why couldn't they be happy for me? Four months ago, I was cute and fashionable but alone. This week I post one fitness selfie with a guy by my side and I get some shade?

For real?

I place my hands on the table. "If you think I'm dating someone, ask me. I don't need the drama."

Felicia picks up her own phone, and her eyes scan the screen as she speaks. "Personally, I'm glad you aren't seeing him."

My skin prickles. "What's that supposed to mean?"

She taps her screen. "Chablis, it's not about you. You're all right. But John? Whew, that brother loves him some flowers in this garden."

Nikki agrees. "Yeah, we didn't want you to be a part of all that."

"Part of all what?" I ask, curious to hear more.

Felicia shares first. "He romances women he meets here and then he ghosts them. Just drops 'em without a word. I can't say who, but somebody told me Pastor Downes talked to him twice about it."

Then Nikki butts in. "I heard he got friendly with too many females in the Health and Wellness ministry until Dr. Jones asked him to serve in a different ministry. That's how he ended up on the Help Squad, or at least that's the rumor."

Did I know John sometimes goes out with women he meets at Rise? Of course. I don't think he's with anyone right now, but I'm not trying to be in his business. He's only my trainer. Why'd he transfer ministries to serve on the Help Squad? I have no clue, and honestly, I don't care. Besides, I doubt Pastor Downes would let John serve on any ministry just so he could use it as his personal eHarmony app.

Felicia places a hand on my shoulder. "Look, we get it now. He's obviously a great trainer for you. Plus, you don't have anything to worry about him loving and leaving you. He wouldn't do that to you because you aren't his type, so forget we said anything."

They nod at each other right before the lights flash a few times, which is the signal for the talent to start soon. I scoot my body around to face the front of the room. My face feels hot.

And did this chick just tell me I wasn't his *type*?

From the corner of my eye, I see John as he strolls in the door. He carries a bottle of Vitamin Water because he doesn't eat after five in the afternoon. Something he called intermittent fasting, which is basically fasting every day, which I won't ever do. It must work, because he does possess visible abdominal muscles. Not that I'm studying him while he's working out — I'm just saying.

He waves to me. I wave back. He doesn't come over to our area, though. Instead, he walks over to a group of people close to the lounge entrance.

When piano music plays, everyone quiets down. I glance across the room and catch John's eye again. He smiles. A jolt of energy flows through me. I smile back.

Maybe I'm not his type.

Yet.

17

MARIAH

Back in early November, Mariah's weight loss team had tried to prepare her—some post-surgery experiences might be unpleasant.

When she woke up three hours after surgery groggy, bloated and with the worst gas pain she'd ever experienced in life, she'd been ready for it. Her first few hours were all about getting her pain under control, but she'd been prepared for that, too. Then, five hours after surgery, she managed to sit on the side of the bed and the nurses encouraged her to walk around, which helped relieve the gas. And when she showered, as she ran her fingertips across the incisions on her bloated stomach, she understood she would carry those marks for the rest of the life.

Technicians made her swallow a disgusting liquid, then showed her a small computer screen that displayed how the drink flowed through her esophagus to her now much smaller stomach pouch. As soon as they determined her gastrointestinal system was free of leaks, she started the clear liquids diet.

Sips of water. Gatorade. Clear chicken broth. A day later, when she was released to go home, Binky came to the hospital. She sat at the edge of the bed and pointed to the table full of bottles.

"Mom, how much can you drink a day?"

"As much as I need to," Mariah had said.

Clear liquids marked her first three days, then she moved on to strained liquids and protein shakes and finally to a soft foods diet. By that time, she'd already accepted how and what she ingested had changed forever.

The way her family acted *after* the operation?

Now *that* was stranger than knowing her stomach only held a few tablespoons of food at a time.

First, there was Oscar. As soon as Mariah left the hospital, he hovered around her like a hawk. He didn't need to worry, though. Her support group had shared horror stories of people who tried eating greasy food or drinking soda after their surgeries. She had no desire to take a trip to the emergency room courtesy of a junk food binge. As soon as she was able to eat solid food, she measured everything and stuck to healthy foods.

Then, there was Binky. "Yeah, Mom," Binky would say nearly every time Mariah weighed herself in the upstairs bathroom. She jumped around and cheered whenever she spied a lower number on the scale. "Whoo-hoo, you're doing it! I'm so proud of you. Bikini body for you."

Binky always wanted to take pictures, but Mariah shooed her away. She didn't want to Facebook or Instagram any of this. She'd get back to the Thick Chick Clique page later on.

But the craziest behavior came from Towanda. The last time Mariah had interacted with Towanda for more than a few minutes at a time happened the day she'd stopped by the hospital. After that, each time Mariah texted, she'd receive only a short, friendly response. Mariah would call her in the evenings, and sometimes they chatted for a while, but Towanda seemed distant. Mariah tried not to think negatively about it, but as the days passed, Towanda's attitude became harder to ignore.

The second Monday in March, Mariah lay alone in bed clutching her pillow and battling emotions.

"Why should I get up?" she moaned to herself, burrowing beneath the comforter. "What's the point?"

Birds chirped outside her bedroom window. Spring would arrive in a few weeks, but everything felt dark and weird instead of light and hopeful. So much of her life had changed in such a short time.

"Honey?" Oscar padded into their bedroom and over to the bed. "You've been in here too long. Benita's at school now."

"Why aren't you at work?" Mariah said with a groan.

The weight of Oscar's body shook the bed. He rested a hand on her shoulder. "Looked like you were having trouble today. I didn't want to leave you."

"I'll be fine."

"Prove that to me by sitting up. Come on, babe. Sit up for me."

His warm touch comforted her, so she let him guide her to a sitting position in the bed. He moved her hair away from her face. "Were you going to sleep all day?"

"Maybe."

"No, no, no. Talk to me now."

Oscar's voice sounded soothing and Mariah had no reason to hide her feelings, so why shouldn't she talk it out?

"Things are so strange now," she said. "My body's changing so fast. My hair's thinning around the edges now. And sometimes I get so tired."

"Do you need better vitamins? We can get some for you."

"Let's do that. But what's really bugging me is Towanda's still tripping." Mariah shook her head. "I don't get it. Since the surgery, we only have these short talks. I don't know what I said. I don't know what I did. She won't say anything."

"Well, I'm here. Want to pray about it?"

She nodded.

Oscar closed his eyes. "Lord, my wife needs You to intervene in her life. She feels tired, she's worried about her hair, and concerned about her friend. Please provide for her at this time and heal her friendship. Ease her mind about her physical concerns. We trust You in all things, Lord. Thank You for hearing our prayers. Amen."

Mariah opened her eyes and then closed them again as Oscar leaned in to kiss her cheek.

"It's going to be all right," he said.

"You sure?"

"Positive. Now, what did you plan to do today?"

Mariah pushed the comforter from her lap. "I need to head down to Temple today. Get the ball rolling to finish my degree. I know I could call, but I'd love to sit and talk about my plans in person."

"Sounds like a good idea. As a matter of fact, I'll take you. We can do it together."

"Thanks."

"I'll make us some coffee to go. The shower's all yours, but you have to get a move on."

"I will."

After Oscar left the room, Mariah reached for her smartphone on the nightstand. First, she looked up information for Temple University's Undergraduate Admissions. She would need to submit an undergraduate request to re-enroll and talk to an advisor. Fine. She could do that.

Next, she fired off a quick text to Towanda. *Hey T, let's get together this week. I am NOT taking no for an answer.*

Towanda's response arrived five seconds later. *I am not able to respond right now. I will get back to you soon.*

Mariah clutched her phone in her hand and tried not to take the message personally. Towanda probably had an early morning meeting.

Fifteen minutes later, dressed in new jeans and a loose white t-shirt, Mariah slid her loafers on, gathered items in her purse and prepared to leave. On her way out the door, she grabbed her phone again. She'd wait until they made it to Temple's campus, then recheck her messages.

When she reached her destination, she looked at the screen. Nothing at all from Towanda.

What else could she do? Stalk the woman?

As much as it hurt not to hear from her friend, Mariah would have to wait. Whatever was going on with Towanda was bound to come out sooner or later.

Further down in her message list, Mariah tapped a text from Kim Chase. Kim and her husband, Jesse, had joined Rise Church a few years back. The lady seemed determined to gather all the married women to have fellowship together regularly. Mariah had received text invites to Friday House Fellowship before but had ignored them for months.

This week she had time, so why not attend? At least it would get her out of the house. Of course, there would be food at the fellowship, but she could take a protein shake with her.

Food. Relationships. Mariah could treat them both the same.

She could adapt.

"COME ON COUSIN, YOU CAN DO BETTER THAN THAT!" CHABLIS LEANED over the treadmill handrail, peering at the screen in front of Mariah. "Two miles an hour? For real, though? And you're clutching the rail?"

Members of Mariah's support group had reminded her to join a gym so she could tone her body and boost her health while she continued to drop pounds. Right after the Wednesday night meeting, Mariah had texted Chablis and asked to meet her the next morning at LA Fitness.

Big mistake.

Mariah released the rails and frowned. "All right, so I don't know how fast I walked before, and never mind that. What do I do now, Ms. Fitness guru?"

"Crank up that pace. That all you got? You can do better than that!"

"Stop yelling at me. What's wrong with you?"

"Nothing."

"When did you start barking like a coach?"

"Since I started moving my butt for the last four months, that's when."

"I'm not training for an event, so don't scream at me."

"Fine, fine."

"Just tell me what I have to do."

"Okay." Chablis pointed to the treadmill screen. "When you get comfortable with your pace, increase the speed. But I'm telling you, unless you have one foot in the grave, you walk faster than two miles an hour, so at least start there."

Mariah mashed her lips together as she pushed the speed button.

Her speed increased and she moved her legs a little faster. "What else?"

"Chill here for the next ten minutes. If you feel like you can move faster, push your speed up."

Mariah placed one foot in front of the other. "What're you going to do?"

"Oh, I'm running." Chablis pushed up the speed on her machine. "Walking is for newbies. I gotta get in a mile for warmup."

Mariah watched as Chablis donned her headphones and started to run. She'd tied her weave up high and away from her face. A pink sweatband surrounded her hairline and she wore gray tights with *Blessed* scrawled down the sides. Her bright pink t-shirt told everyone *I Can Do All Things*. Chablis didn't just appear smaller, she moved differently. As if she could conquer the world. In four months, Mariah's cousin had dieted, pushed and sweated off thirty pounds.

One foot in front of the other. Mariah walked, letting her thoughts keep her company.

Did I take the easy way out?

Even if she had, it was too late to reverse her actions now. Her body was altered, and now her mind had to follow, remaining in the land of decreased food intake and constant vitamin supplements. Exercise would also have a place in her life.

"Cousin," Chablis slowed her treadmill to a stop. "I'm going to go stretch."

"You're done running?"

"It was only a mile."

"But how long did it take you?"

"Ten minutes."

"Wow."

Chablis nodded her head toward the front door. "John just came in. I should start my workout now."

"But you just ran."

"That was my warmup."

"Okay, well, you do you."

"You'll get here soon enough."

"Remember to come back and scrape me off this treadmill after you finish."

Chablis winked before she skipped away.

Mariah looked down at her phone. Towanda hadn't returned Mariah's text from earlier in the week. That stupid automated message didn't count.

All right. Enough of this mess. If she needed to leave back to back messages, send a million texts, or camp out in the lobby of Towanda's apartment building, then that's what she would do.

But no matter what, they would work this out.

18

TOWANDA

A crowd filled the Corner Bakery Cafe. Towanda guessed the Center City office workers must've been dying to exit their cubicle farms. Everyone used lunchtime as an excuse to escape and enjoy the breezy April day.

She'd arrived at the eatery a few minutes ahead of the mid-day rush. After she ordered, she picked up her food and found a table toward the back of the eatery. She was settling in her chair when she looked toward the door in time to see Mariah walk in. Towanda tracked her friend's movement through the food service area and finally toward seating.

Towanda crumpled a paper napkin in her hand, trying to will herself to stop staring. She lost that battle, struggling to open her mouth for a basic hello as her friend approached the table.

Mariah looked amazing.

Towanda couldn't remember Mariah appearing this well-dressed and pulled together in at least a decade. She wore strappy black heels with her dark blue trouser jeans, a crisp white button-down shirt and a sharp mustard-colored blazer. With her dark hair brushed into an updo, curls cascading down the side of her forehead, the hairstyle made her face appear thinner. Flawless makeup adorned her smooth skin and gold highlighter accented her cheekbones.

Towanda finally found her voice. "Binky got a hold of you, huh?"

"You can tell." Mariah placed her purse in the chair next to her. "Yes, my budding fashionista had her way with me."

"She did a great job."

"You should text her and tell her. She'd love that."

"That's all you're eating?" Towanda raised an eyebrow as she glanced at the steaming bowl of tomato soup on Mariah's tray.

Mariah paused, her spoon in midair. "This is easy for me to handle."

"Can't you eat solid food now?"

"Of course, but soup is warm and filling."

"I get it." Towanda peered down at her club sandwich with potato chips. Her appetite swerved. "Maybe I should have had the soup?"

"What you're eating is fine. You do you, girl."

"How much have you lost so far?"

"Forty-eight pounds at my weigh-in last week."

"That was fast."

"Maybe a little too fast. I have some loose skin now."

Towanda leaned in closer, her eyes narrowed. "I don't see any loose skin."

"It's here." Mariah brushed her hand from her rib cage downward. "My lower belly and thighs mostly. I use Spanx every day, so it holds everything in and makes me look solid in my clothes."

"But you're happy about the weight loss, right?"

"Sure."

"You're on the fast track to skinny. Hurray for you."

"You sound like Binky. I'm not in this for skinny."

"Really?" Towanda rolled her eyes. "You've managed to dress up good health so much you should be on a magazine cover. Golden makeup and everything. How much have you lost again?"

"You know what, just stop."

"Why?"

"Because how I look is not why I forced you out here today." Mariah caught Towanda's gaze. "Stop about asking me about food or weight loss. I haven't seen you in weeks. Had to track you down and pin you to a lunch date for today. You barely answer my texts or my calls. I thought we were cool."

"We are."

"We're not, and you know it. How'd we go from talking every day to barely talking at all? What's up with you?"

Towanda dropped several chips back onto her plate and brushed the crumbs from her fingers. The table squeezed her tummy, so she pushed her chair back a few inches. She'd added eight pounds during the winter, but no way would she discuss that with Mariah.

The truth was, the months had passed swiftly. When the year started, Towanda plowed full steam ahead into securing new clients for thinkLARGE. She'd also hired an intern and one new staff member. When February arrived, Towanda vacationed in Alaska with Nana. After that, she poured herself back into her work.

But those were all excuses. Which Mariah must have known because she recorded fifteen back-to-back voicemails practically ordering Towanda to meet her for lunch. Towanda had caved and set up the Monday lunch date.

It shouldn't have been this difficult for her to see Mariah change, but it was. Towanda removed her glasses and rubbed her eyes for a moment. She put them back on and viewed her friend with clear vision.

"This club sandwich is amazing, but I still think I should have gone with the soup," Towanda joked.

"T?"

Towanda glanced around the room. "Nothing's wrong, okay. I'm turning into a workaholic. If you want to be concerned about something, be concerned about that."

"Turning?"

"Yeah, well..."

"Girl, you've been a workaholic since Nana Cakes."

"Workaholic. Head female in charge. Boss lady." Towanda shrugged. "That's me."

Business work had always been easy for Towanda to manage. If she did the right research and sat down and focused, she could come up with a strategy. Too bad her emotions couldn't be manipulated like a business solution.

Why was it so hard to have this conversation with Mariah? Almost as if she didn't know the woman who sat in front of her eating tomato soup and sipping a small cup of hot tea.

No. More like she didn't want to get acquainted with the energetic butterfly about to emerge from the cocoon formerly known as frumpy housewife Mariah.

A pang of guilt pierced Towanda. She looked down at her half-eaten club sandwich as negative thoughts slid from her brain to her throat, preventing her from wanting to ingest anything else.

"T? You all right?"

Towanda picked up a napkin and wiped her mouth. "I'm fine."

"So, you're going to stop avoiding me now?"

"I wasn't avoiding you before. I told you—"

"I heard you. Workaholic Towanda."

"Exactly."

"Whatever. Listen, I've enrolled at Temple again. I start in the fall."

"I see. You're moving straight ahead with finishing your degree?"

"Absolutely, but I need your help."

"With what? Study tips?"

"No, I still have this idea for starting a customer service training academy for young people."

Towanda held up a hand. "Customer service academy? Where'd you get this idea?"

A smile creased Mariah's face. "I had some ideas about it in the fall. I thought about all the bad customer experiences I've had, then I talked to a local business owner and she told me how she has a hard time hiring help because the young people who apply don't know how to present themselves or communicate well with customers."

"And you want to train them?"

"Train them and certify them."

"So, what do you need me for?"

"I figured you could guide me through setting up my business as an LLC, getting my DBA, stuff like that. You know, all the business setup items."

Mariah certainly was moving full steam ahead. She'd pushed right on past researching the viability of her business.

Poor Mariah. She'd have to find out the hard way.

"Did you think of a name?" Towanda crumpled her napkin.

"Not yet. I wanted your help with that, too."

Towanda pushed her chair farther back and studied her friend. What if Mariah wasted her time on a business that was bound to fail? Or what if the new Mariah experienced wild success with it? Could Towanda actually handle living in her best friend's shadow? Again?

She should say something to change the subject.

But what?

She stared down at her hands, focusing on her rings.

Oh, yeah. There was that.

"Mariah, your desire to help young people with their careers is wonderful, but isn't there another kid you should be focused on right now? Did you know Binky has a navel ring?"

"What navel ring? W—what are you talking about?" Mariah's eyes widened as she stammered.

"It's been months since she got it. I never heard you say a thing about it, so I figured she'd kept it secret after all."

"You knew and you didn't tell me? T!"

"Hey, listen, when I found out, I told her to tell you and Oscar. She'll back me up on that. I wasn't keeping it a secret on purpose."

Towanda watched as Mariah shifted around in her seat with a tense look on her face.

"Now, don't be too hard on her," Towanda said. "You don't want a blow up over a piece of body jewelry."

"T, I don't want her piercing her eyelids, tongue and who-knows-what next. And I don't want her skin tattooed just because it's cool today. Bad decisions now make for a harder life later."

Towanda nodded. "You're right, but how 'bout you lay that out for her in a calm, cool tone and not the *I'm going to snatch the hair off your head* voice? That'll turn her off more."

"Good advice. I might need to hit the gym before that conversation —and after—but its good advice."

A double vision of Mariah and Binky sat opposite Towanda as she smiled and replied.

"Now remember, you love your daughter. No matter what she does, no matter what changes to her body she might make, you love her."

TOWANDA COULD HAVE SKIPPED WORSHIP SERVICE SUNDAY MORNING, BUT she didn't want to. She'd been absent from Rise practically all winter, even though she enjoyed hearing Pastor Downes speak. When she did attend, she chose the evening service because it was less crowded, shorter and the choir was livelier. This Sunday, she'd be present for morning service because Mariah had texted her all week long asking her to be there.

By ten-fifteen she was already late, but no matter. Mariah was saving a seat for her and the praise team would still be singing. After she parked and hustled up the stairs and into the atrium, she flowed to the sanctuary. From the doorway, she could see Mariah and Oscar. They sat close to the middle.

Towanda took one step into the sanctuary, then hesitated. This caused the young lady who walked behind her to crash right into her back.

"Sorry," Towanda mumbled.

"It's okay," the young lady replied, stepping quickly past.

Towanda stood still near the back wall. She let the crush of people push forward in front of her.

Walk forward. Go on.

No, wait. One of the Help Squad members walked toward her. She recognized this young woman. One of Chablis' friends. Felicia.

"Ms. Towanda, are you okay?"

Towanda must have looked flustered. She straightened up and shook off the awkward feeling. She even swallowed the urge to tell Felicia not to call her *Ms. Towanda* because she wasn't that old.

Instead, she forced a smile.

"I'm fine. Thank you. Just...ah...yes, I forgot my Bible in my car."

Towanda leaned down, keeping her voice low. "I stopped to turn around and go back for it, but all these people were behind me."

Felicia nodded. "Can I get you a Bible from the information desk?"

"No, thanks." Towanda kept her eyes focused on the door. "I like to make notes in mine."

"Okay. If you need anything, let us know."

"I will."

Towanda turned and moved fast. Out of the sanctuary. Across the atrium. Down the stairs to the parking lot. Inside her car, she dropped her purse on the floor in front of the passenger seat, which, of course, held no Bible.

She didn't feel like pretending to be happy for the new Mariah. The incredible shrinking woman and her, *surprise*, ecstatic and devoted husband.

She could text Mariah later to say she overslept.

Or she could just let things be.

19

CHABLIS

Promotion time again at WebAbsolute. It seems Josh used the automated test team lead position as a stepping-stone toward a better job with a new software company in Malvern. My department bid him adieu during a team lunch at Outback Steakhouse. The food didn't tempt me at all, though. Why should I care about juicy ribeye steaks or blooming onions when a new leadership position is up for grabs?

But Josh's goodbye lunch happened last week. Now it's Thursday, and Christopher still hasn't called me into his office to talk about the team lead position. I'm trying to be cool, since Josh hasn't been gone that long. Besides, the Senior VP of Research & Development has to sign off on all promotion requests, and he's been away for the past month. I need to exercise patience.

I push back my chair and read my gray cubicle wall. It's filled with motivational sayings and pictures I printed from Pinterest.

The Lord will Provide. He Works it All for Your Good. God's Got It All Under Control. I Can Do All Things Through Christ Who Strengthens Me. Be Still and Know I Am God. For We Walk by Faith and Not By Sight.

Maybe it's overkill. Whatever. It helps. I whisper a short prayer about my career, then I just sit still for a minute.

Behind me, a voice knocks me out of my trance.

"G'day, Chablis."

I turn around fast. "I'd know that voice anywhere! Good to see you."

I stand up, then reach higher and give Sue Ryan a quick hug. She's a tall Australian lady with a head full of light brown hair and chic black-rimmed glasses. She used to be Senior VP of Quality Assurance back when this company was a startup. Sue also helped found the company, but she sold her interest in the business to return to Sydney to help care for her dying father. She's an interesting mix of tough and caring at the same time, kind of like Towanda, but with more smiles and paler skin.

Sue hired me back when the company had less than fifty employees. At the end of my interview, while one of the execs told me Franny in HR would be in touch, Sue stood right up, walked over to me, pulled me in with a fierce handshake and welcomed me to the company.

No one challenged her.

Later, she told me the company had hired Anant a month before, and his resume was practically identical to mine. She'd informed the team she'd hire the first female with equal qualifications and she did.

"Where's the rest of ya?" Sue's eyes rake me up and down. "You've changed."

"Just a little weight loss. I've been doing things differently this year." I step closer to her and lower my voice. "I was so sorry to hear about your father. I followed your posts on Facebook. He seemed like a wonderful man. My condolences."

Sue ducks her head. "Thanks, friend. I appreciate your prayers for him. It was just his time." She glances up at the ceiling, then back down to me. "Anyway, my brother is selling my share of the family land and I'm back in the states for good."

"I see. Gonna come back to work with us at WebAbsolute?"

"I think leadership is moving in a different direction than I fit into now. I stopped by today to check in on my old friends. Are they treating you well here?"

I shrug. "Things are fine."

"You have the opportunities you need? To move up and all?"

Sue is a hardcore champion for women in the technology workforce, so her question isn't a throwaway. I think about the Josh situation and shrug again.

"You can contact me at any time. Talk to me. I don't mind mentoring you," she says.

I nod because I know all my coworkers are probably listening. Our office is so quiet I swear I can hear mice in sneakers running down the carpet. "I know. But things are going okay."

She straightens to her full height. "That's good to hear, because if anything changes—"

We both swivel our heads to the side when we hear Christopher's glass door swing open at the end of our cubicle farm. This is unspoken office language saying someone in my aisle sent an instant message to my boss that Sue Ryan is here stirring up trouble.

She winks at me. "I'd better stop through to talk with Christopher. I think he hears a foreigner over here. Good to see you again. Please don't be a stranger. Message me any time."

"Good to see you too, and I definitely will," I say, meaning it.

As soon as Sue walks into Christopher's office, I drop back down in my chair and pick up my phone, because it's been vibrating nonstop with notifications. For the bazillionth time, I tell myself to enter the settings and turn off those social media alerts. As soon as I swipe to unlock my phone, a call comes through, making the device buzz in my hand. The caller ID says John Gerald. Right then I forget all about the test plans I'm supposed to revise as I grin and stare at his name.

I'm crushing. I know it. I don't care.

I tap to accept the call. "Hey, buddy!"

"How're you doing? Busy?"

"Well, I kind of have this job that involves testing expensive web applications so they don't blow up for the clients...so..."

"You're funny, you know that? I'm calling to give you a heads up about something."

"What's up?"

"Big changes are happening with my workload. So, training you in the morning will get spotty."

"All right. How spotty?"

"There's trouble with two big projects. I just got word of six a.m. mandatory meetings coming up."

"How do you want to handle my workouts?"

"I'll text you those the night before."

"And what about your own training?"

"I'll start working out in the evenings."

I'm panicking a little inside. "But I'm accountable to you. What if I slack off?"

He laughs at this. "Travis and Sheena. Want me to sic them on you?"

Travis is almost twice my size and he lives for CrossFit. Sheena's scalp is clean-shaven except for the coiled mound of purple locs on top, and she sports fifteen different piercings. Three of them are in her nose. Both of them have tattoos decorating their rippling muscles. And they know where I live.

I gulp. "Um…no."

"Listen, you've been at this for months and you're already a champ. Just keep going, and I'll check in on you from time to time. All you have to do is follow my instructions and keep texting me your meal pictures. I gotta go. Talk to you later?"

"Wait, are we still running together Saturday morning?"

"Oh, yeah. Definitely."

"All right. Talk to you later," I say, and tap to end the call.

Now I don't want to read any of my other text messages, not even the ones from Mariah and Nikki.

No more morning training sessions, huh?

Of course, I can do this on my own now, but I'd rather keep seeing him at the gym. Honestly, I'd want to see him even if we didn't work out together. When I asked John to train me, I didn't think I'd like him this much, or that we'd get along so well.

I wheel my chair around and place my phone inside the drawer on the opposite side of my desk. When I come back, I put my headphones on and return to software test land. My fingers glide across my keyboard, Pandora plays on my computer, and I hear Travis Greene singing "He's Intentional."

A few hours of work should keep my mind off the fact that things are changing. John works as a cloud architect for a company called SynerCloud. I work in technology, too, so I understand how tech teams work and what happens when stuff breaks and the engineers have to scramble to fix everything or the clients start threatening to take their business elsewhere.

Besides, John is not my man. He's only my friend and my trainer.

What am I doing after work today?

Nothing.

I stop typing and ball my hands into fists. No. I won't open my desk drawer. I won't pull out my phone. I won't text Nikki and Felicia with an offer to hang out at Olive Garden tonight where we can chat and chew and dive deep into bowls of buttery, cheesy pasta. Then we could follow it with hot fudge brownie ice cream bowls. After eating all that, I'd drive home so full I'd crash onto my bed in a carboholic high.

No thoughts.

No feelings.

Just full.

CHRISTOPHER IS AVOIDING ME.

How do I know? He's the first one to dash out of the fishbowl after the Friday SCRUM meeting. All through the review, I couldn't catch his eye once, not even while we worked through all the major bugs. I kept my cool, but I must have crossed and uncrossed my legs a dozen times, and I sighed all through the functional walkthrough.

Impatient, I know. But back when Christopher was happy to promote Josh, he told me there would be more opportunities to move up.

So, when I get up from my chair to follow Christopher down the hall, I'm not doing anything other than chasing my opportunities.

That's my truth, and I'm sticking to it.

"Knock, knock." I push open the glass door to Christopher's office. "Before you jump into another project, can I speak with you?"

He's behind his desk, hovering in mid-air for a second before he finally sits all the way down. His eyebrows arch in surprise, but he pulls himself together and gestures for me to have a seat across from him.

I make sure I shut the door before I sit down.

"Hi."

"Hi."

"Do you remember the conversation we had in September?"

"We've talked a lot this past year. To which conversation are you referring?"

"From back when you promoted Josh to team lead?"

"Ah...yes..."

"So, you remember then?"

"To be honest, I don't remember all the details. You'll have to refresh me."

"All right. I came here to meet with you the day you announced Josh's promotion. I talked to you about my submission for the job, and you told me the reasons why management approved Josh over me."

"Okay. Yes, I remember."

"Josh is gone now. His position is empty. I want to move forward and submit myself for the team lead role."

"Ah...we can't have you do that," Christopher says. "Your work is exceptional. You are an asset to this team and the WebAbsolute family. And in all my years, I've never worked around a more pleasant person. Everyone here adores you."

I have no words. All oxygen left my lungs after Christopher said *can't*.

He keeps going. "When Josh left, a decision was made that his position would be eliminated and there's no need for a team lead. There is simply no lead role available. I'm sorry."

I close my eyes for five seconds and breathe deeply. I'm disappointed, but so what. This is life. There's no team lead role for me at WebAbsolute. That's clear.

"Christopher, thanks for letting me know. I appreciate it."

"Do you have any more questions? I can't provide an answer for everything the company decides, but I'll do my best."

"No, I'm good." I stand up and automatically reach back to tug down my black skirt but find I don't need to because all the fabric falls straight down. "Thanks again for your time. I'll see you later."

I sit down as soon as I reach my cubicle. I leave my phone in my desk drawer because I don't want to see any notifications. Right now, I have bug reports to review.

When it's time to leave for the day, I gather up my things, shut off the lights in my cubicle and head straight out of the building to my battered Focus. There's no workout clothing in my car, so I drive in the direction of Target, where I buy some cheap running pants, an exercise bra, socks, and a dry-weave shirt. I have a spare pair of Nikes in my trunk. I get back in my car and drive in silence until I reach LA Fitness, where it is crowded beyond belief on a Friday evening.

In the locker room, I change into my new gear and tie up my hair with a pink bandanna. When one of the treadmills frees up, I get on and walk for two minutes before I crank up the pace and run non-stop for three miles.

And why am I doing all this? Because I can't do jack about the games people play on jobs, especially when it comes to being curvy, black and female.

But God taught me how to do one thing this year.

He taught me how to move again.

20

MARIAH

"**B**enita!" Mariah called upstairs from the living room. Feet shuffled above her head before Binky answered. "Yeah."

"Girl, what did I tell you?"

"Sorry. Yes, ma'am."

"I want you and your phone downstairs."

"Right now?"

"Yes, now!"

Binky trudged down the stairs and over to her mother, thrusting the phone toward her. "Here."

Mariah took the device. "Sit."

Binky slumped in a chair with her lips pursed and her arms crossed while Mariah tapped the password and reviewed her daughter's apps and games. Instagram. Facebook. Snapchat. Messages. Every few days, Mariah orchestrated a phone raid on Binky.

Binky's navel ring? Only the tip of the iceberg.

A week and a half after Towanda mentioned Binky's piercing, her RiseUP Youth leader, Dr. Wilma Blackshear, called Mariah with another revelation. A young man in youth ministry had texted a digital pic of Binky that the girl had since removed from Instagram.

Thankfully, she wasn't naked, but she was suggestively posed on her bed with her tongue stuck out, her thumb holding down the top of her pajama shorts, and her navel ring gleaming in the light.

Mariah thanked Dr. Blackshear for intervening, hung up and called Oscar. After she told him about the picture, Oscar drove home from his office, marched straight to Binky's room, and all Mariah heard for a full hour was yelling, crying and a whole lot of *discipline*. When he finished, he came back downstairs, handed Binky's phone to Mariah and told her to lock it away for the rest of the month.

But the month ended, Binky got her phone back, and now Mariah had the full-time job of monitoring a teenage girl who seemed to have nothing better to do than to try different ways of showing off her face and body and sending chat messages to boys.

"What is this?" Mariah scanned the phone screen. "Who's Idris?"

Binky moved her skinny shoulders up and down in a weak shrug. "A guy."

"What guy?"

"From school, Mom. I do go to school."

"Watch your tone. Why is he asking if you found a place to meet yet?"

"How should I know? That message must have just come through. I haven't read it yet. I don't know what he's talking about."

"Oh, I think you do." Mariah shut the phone off and buried it in the bottom of her purse. "Until your memory returns, I've got your phone. You can go back upstairs now."

"Mom, he's one of my friends from school. Why you being all extra?"

During Mariah's teen years, if she'd raised her voice while talking to her mother, she probably wouldn't have lived long enough to graduate high school. At fourteen, Mariah and her brother and sister were expected to respect their mother and support her. They loved Joan, and they wouldn't challenge her or talk back to her. What was it with these young girls today?

Mariah took a deep breath, then exhaled. "Back upstairs. Now."

"But Mom—"

"Bye, Benita!"

With Binky back upstairs doing homework, Mariah left the house to drive to her support group. Thank the Lord, she could escape and think about something other than the trouble her daughter was getting into as she grew older. In the car, she rolled the windows down to let the air blow through.

Maybe Towanda was right. Should Mariah even bother thinking about school or a business career right now?

IN SUPPORT GROUP, MARIAH COULDN'T SHIFT HER HANDS AWAY FROM HER face as tears streamed down her face. She read the numbers again and again while peeking between the cracks between her fingers.

Someone needed to grab her a tissue or maybe a wet cloth to clean up all the happiness, but no one moved. Everyone stood in a semicircle behind her, applauding. Those three red digital numbers flashed on display in front of her, and the numbers didn't lie. She'd reached fifty-five pounds lost. That meant she'd officially moved beyond her mid-point goal for weight loss.

Mariah wept, gulping in air and waving her fingers at Grace, the support group leader, who ran to a side table, grabbed a wad of tissues and thrust them in her hands. The last time she'd seen herself at this weight, she'd been standing in the bathroom at home, about to wake up Binky for her first day of the third grade. She'd cried then as well, but for a different reason — the number on the scale kept climbing with no sign of stopping.

"Congratulations." Grace patted Mariah on the back. "It's all right. You deserve this."

She stepped away from the scale, wiping every last bit of tears and makeup from her face with the scratchy tissues. The scale confirmed it. Fifty-five pounds down and counting.

"Honey, why don't you sit down?" One of the other ladies, Alyssa, led her to a chair and fanned her. "Take a few deep breaths. My word, I don't think we've ever seen such an emotional reaction here."

Mariah eased into a seat. "Can someone please hand me my purse?" She sniffed and wiped. "I need my phone."

Alyssa moved fast, retrieving Mariah's bag from a chair across the room and handing it to her. Mariah reached in it and pulled out her phone. She FaceTimed Oscar.

"Os, can you see me? Can you see everything?"

Mariah watched as he stared back at her. "Yes, I can see you."

"Okay, I'm turning the phone around now."

She took her phone, returned to the digital scale, stood on it, and turned the phone screen around. She grinned when she heard her husband's voice.

"Is that right? Is it accurate?"

Mariah turned the phone screen back toward her. "It's accurate. I've already weighed in twice."

A broad grin creased Oscar's face. "Aww, honey. Congratulations!"

"Less than half the weight I needed to lose is gone."

"I know, and I'm so happy for you. You did so well after the procedure, I can't believe you're so far along so soon. You followed everything your doctors told you to do. Good job."

"Thanks. I'm holding up our group here, so I'll see you at home?"

"See you at home, honey!"

Mariah walked back to her seat. Congratulations from the group and Oscar made her feel good, but now what? Her body remained altered. He couldn't offer to take her to Red Lobster for a celebration dinner. Or he could, but other than having a few tablespoons of food, Mariah wouldn't be able to eat much. Right now, the weight loss occurred like Dr. Seng had promised, but the lost pounds had a steep price--hard and permanent lifestyle changes.

She wiped her eyes with the soggy ball of tissues one more time. When she looked down at her feet, she saw the tips of her purple-painted toenails. She wiggled her toes, her knees, her hips, then finally her shoulders, loosening herself up. Only forty-five more pounds to go.

When support group ended, Mariah walked over and tapped Grace on the shoulder. "Can I ask you a question?"

"Sure."

Mariah gestured downward, her fingertips brushing her thighs. "I'm starting to see loose hanging skin on my lower belly and inside my thighs. It's on the undersides of my arms too, but it's getting really bad under my belly button. I've heard other people talk about this in the group. So, I can't do anything about this?"

Grace cast a sober look. "Unfortunately, this is one of the uncomfortable realities of your weight loss. You're successful, but the loose skin is also a part of your journey."

Mariah looked down at her belly. What would she look like after she shed the full hundred pounds or more? A well-dressed raisin? A woman in a wrinkled suit that couldn't be zipped off?

And how come Chablis wasn't having this issue?

"My cousin lost weight recently," Mariah said, looking back up at Grace. "I don't see loose skin anywhere on her."

"How's she losing it?"

"Mostly through weight training and running. And she's on some clean eating plan her trainer gave her."

"And how long has she been at it?"

"Since October."

"I don't know your cousin's genetics, but if she started in October and May arrives in a few days, she lost that weight slow and steady. When you do that, your skin can keep up with your weight loss. Exercise helps, particularly resistance training, because she's toning her muscles as she loses."

Mariah sighed. "What can I do? This skin is already bugging me."

"Talk with Dr. Seng. After you reach your goal, he can refer you to specialists to help with your skin."

"More surgery?"

"Body contouring." Grace lowered her voice. "Think about staying healthy and reaching your goal weight. That's your real focus. You'll handle the skin later."

Grace sounded reassuring, but Mariah didn't know.

With every single body decision she made, there was always something else to consider.

"WHAT'S ALL THIS?" MARIAH SAID AS SHE HUNG HER PURSE ON HER bedroom doorknob and marched into her bedroom.

Three brand new dresses lay across her bed. On the floor sat three pairs of high-heeled open-toe shoes in black, white, and silver. New jewelry boxes rested atop her nightstand.

She stood in her tracks in the middle of the room, unsure of what to do next.

"Do you like everything?" Oscar's voice reached her ears.

Mariah turned around to see her husband standing in the doorway, looking sharp in a tailored navy-blue suit and designer tie, his thick, wavy black hair brushed back and shining.

"I don't know what to say. This is for me?"

Oscar nodded, a smile on his lips. "Of course. Pick a dress to wear and then let's get out of here, because it's time to celebrate you. This is long overdue."

"But where did you get all this? When did you find the time? And the size? Will they fit? And how did you know what to buy me? And where are we going?"

He grinned. "Your other dresses looked like they were sagging on you, so last week I asked Benita to help me. She took a look at the sizes of your newer outfits, then told me wrap dresses would work because you can adjust them. I wrote everything down, took the list to Nordstrom and let the salesgirls do everything else. All I did was wait for the right moment to present it all to you." He walked over to her and wrapped his arms around her waist. "Pick what you like. We have a date to listen to live music and I don't want to be late."

Her heart full to bursting, Mariah kissed him, then picked up the navy-blue dress and undergarments before she rushed into the bathroom. When she tugged on a pair of Spanx, she prayed it would hide the drooping skin on her lower abdomen. She smiled when she donned the dress and tied the fabric in a pretty bow around her waist.

She raked her fingers through her dark curls. A quick makeup application and she was ready.

Back in her bedroom, she slid into the silver sandals and then walked to the full-length mirror in the corner of the room. She glimpsed herself from the bottom up. Her bare legs didn't look too bad at all. The wrap dress looked marvelous, and the Spanx did its job, pulling everything in well. Her dress even gave her bosom a nice lift. Her hair hung wild and curly, but it matched the look.

Better. A little sexy, even.

Oscar's voice intruded into her thoughts. "I'm speechless."

Mariah turned to see her husband viewing her with eyes that showed he hadn't forgotten their early years together.

He took her hand. "My lady, there's live music waiting for us at Heritage. Thank you for being my date this evening."

There would be time later for thinking about Binky or considering other surgeries, or whatever might cross her path in the future. Tonight, she'd enjoy stepping back in time, holding Oscar's hand and being his wife.

At the restaurant, Mariah enjoyed her kale salad, feeling fully satisfied with music in her ears and her partner by her side.

Later that night, in the dark quiet of their bedroom, their lovemaking seemed deeper and more vibrant than it had in years. It became an intimate celebration, one which almost brought tears to her eyes. Afterward, she rested with her head on her husband's chest, still enjoying his warmth on her skin. If she could grab that loving feeling and bottle it, she'd keep it with her every single day of her life.

He reached for her hand and brought it to his lips. "Honey, this is our time. I can feel it. I'm so excited. I'd love us to try for more children as soon as possible."

She stiffened, opening her eyes wide.

More babies?

Now?

Her body remained a work in process, changing daily. What if another pregnancy reversed everything? And Binky's recent behavior disturbed her. Should she even consider adding new little ones to their family?

Mariah moved her body up and kissed her husband's lips. She squeezed him tight but didn't say anything about having more kids.

He'd have to accept her love.

That was all she could provide for now.

21

CHABLIS

C all me crazy.

I'm wearing six-inch black stilettos for the RiseUp Youth graduation celebration. I also have on dark skinny jeans and a soft black cold shoulder top with WALK IN FAITH bedazzled across the front. I bought it from Etsy. My hair is tight, my makeup is flawless and my stomach hasn't looked this flat in years. Okay, I faked the flatness with two pairs of Spanx, but who cares?

I look good.

Tonight, thirty of our young people will announce their post-graduation plans. It's only the first week of May, but when the RiseUp Youth event committee planned this, they said it was impossible to put a later date on the church calendar because of prom conflicts.

Enough said.

Help Squad has arrived, and we are making it spectacular for them. We're going all out. A drill team. Cheerleaders. Praise music and soloists. Pastor Downes and first lady Juanita will hand out book scholarship checks to the kids who applied. There's also a nice spread in the Visitors Lounge after the ceremony ends.

My job?

Help decorate with balloons, flowers and streamers and then pass out programs as the families arrive. I'm carrying two baskets of flowers to the front of the sanctuary. I'm sure any minute now, John will walk through the doors and he'll see me looking more sophisticated than I have since we met — and I won't mind a bit.

I haven't seen him all week. When he gets here, I plan to turn around and smile sweetly at him while holding a basket of pink and red carnations. He'll flag me down when the program starts and I'll go sit next to him. He will smell clean like three-in-one Nivea Men body wash, and minty because he's always chewing spearmint gum, and then I'll lean real close to him so he can place his arm around my chair. We'll watch the ceremony together like two super-cool best friends who could level up soon.

"Chablis!" Nikki waves from the area where she just finished attaching balloons to the stage.

"Yeah."

"Put those baskets down and come get these programs. Parents are walking in."

I turn around, and sure enough, three couples stand near the sanctuary entrance. Time to put my fantasy on hold and help with the programs.

Nikki drops a Staples box in my arms. "Don't break an ankle girl, please."

"I'll be fine. If Beyoncé can dance in heels, I'm fine walking around a stage in them."

"Yeah, but you ain't Beyoncé."

"You know, it's good to overlook an offense, or so I read in Scripture," I call over my shoulder before hustling across the stage, down the stairs and up the side aisle to the wooden table, where I put the box down. I grab two big piles of programs and thrust them into Jhaila's and Mark's waiting hands. They're our two teen volunteers assigned to help at the door for the evening.

Things are coming together well. More people are trickling in. As soon as the center aisle clears for a moment, I pull my phone from my jeans pocket and step back to take a clear picture of the decorated stage.

"What'd I tell you about that phone?"

I know that voice, and I pivot around slowly so my store-bought hair gently trails behind me and stops to frame my face when I look at John.

Only then do I speak.

"Oh. Hi."

Because even though I am crushing, I refuse to sound like it.

His eyes open wide. "Wooooow!"

This thrills me to the point where my stomach does a triple Lutz.

"So, what are you trying to say?" I flutter my mascaraed eyelashes at him.

He steps back and stares me down. "I'm saying...*wow!*"

"Why, thank you," I say, like a thirteen-year-old at her first school dance. "I wanted to go all out tonight."

"You sure did." John steps closer and pulls me in for a hug. "You look beautiful. But hey, no makeup with a messy ponytail and sweaty exercise gear? That works for you, too."

As I cling to his muscular shoulders, I forget all about the training, the new clothes and everything else.

Because this moment.

This right here.

This is the best thing I've felt in more than six years, and in less than ten seconds it's over.

Before I settle back down to earth, I glance over John's shoulder. Groups of people are walking through the doors. Too many for my teens to handle. I must go, like Cinderella fleeing the ball, but not before I make a move.

"You staying for the whole ceremony?" I ask him.

"Definitely."

"Cool. Save me a seat?"

"You got it."

"Thanks," I say before I stroll away, proud of myself for finessing my way into sitting with him.

With another stack of programs in my hands, I walk over and stand next to Jhaila.

She grins at me, the pink bands on her braces showing. "You and Mr. John look good together."

"What do you know about good? We're just friends."

"Yeah, okay," Jhaila says in a tone which communicates disbelief.

I keep grinning as I hand out programs and say good evening to everyone walking past me.

Because it's *all* good.

JOHN AND I DON'T RUN TOGETHER EVERY OTHER SATURDAY ANYMORE because his work schedule has gotten so crazy, sometimes he needs to sleep in and rest. So today I work out on my own at LA Fitness.

Later, I clean up my teeny apartment, do my laundry and run errands. By mid-afternoon, I've exhausted myself physically and there's nothing else for me to do. At three o'clock, I'm lying on my couch staring up at the ceiling. Usually, I'd call around and see what my girlfriends or Mariah and Towanda are up to today, but I don't want to do that right now.

John is on my mind.

I loved sitting next to him during the ceremony yesterday, and together we clapped and cheered for the Rise Church high school seniors. We had a great time.

But that hug, though.

Can I even consider it the embrace of a friend? He's never pulled me in for a long hug before.

I could call Nikki or Felicia and ask what they think, but that's out of the question. I don't want to hear any gossip about John and his dating experiences or how he supposedly ghosts women.

Because I don't care.

I still like him.

He eats healthy, exercises daily and he's easygoing. It's also hard to ignore that he's smart, loves the Lord and he works hard. I even like his bushy beard and the small gap between his two front teeth. And other than my first week at the gym when he tried to destroy me, he's kind to me. He barely knew me, but he trained me for free and gave me gifts — if I can consider bags of salad and cartons of Greek yogurt gifts.

And he's available.

I know this for two reasons. First, it occurred to me that I haven't seen any ladies hovering around him this year. Second, last night, I flat out asked him if he was dating anyone. He said no, because he's focused on other things, and his work responsibilities seem to be changing so fast at SynerCloud he might not try out for American Ninja Warrior this year. But a couple of minutes later, he nudged me, then leaned over and said, "As far as relationships go, if it feels right, I'm all in."

So now I'm here in my apartment alone, and the gears in my mind grind those words. *If it feels right, I'm all in. If it feels right, I'm all in. If it feels right...*

Back to the hug. Did that mean John *is* feeling me?

"Okay, Chablis, knock it off." I flip onto my belly and grab my phone off the coffee table.

Tons of social media notifications. On Facebook, Sue Ryan has a status update. She's making money moves with a new technology company in the Delaware Valley. Go Sue! I'll send her a congratulations message later.

I tap to open Instagram. John hasn't posted anything today, so maybe he's home doing nothing this afternoon. Hmm?

I text him. *Hey! U there?* Then I place my phone on my thigh and wait. A few minutes pass and the device buzzes. I snatch it and stare at the screen.

Hey, his message reads.

Whatcha doing?

At work right now.

On Saturday afternoon? 😳😳😳

Bubbles appear on the screen until his next message arrives.

Our overseas team screwed up a hybrid cloud solution so now all hell is breaking loose. Please pray, our director is talking about firing people.

They cannot fire you!

No, I'll be fine. Our overseas team...IDK.

Praying for you. I'm sure it will work out.

Thx. TTYL.

Okay, so his job stress is real. I clutch my phone in my hand as I sit up and place my feet on the floor. I gaze at the blue and beige stripes on my flat Ikea rug and then I put my phone back on the table.

John is working hard on a Saturday afternoon. I adore his integrity and I love that he talks tech stuff with me because he knows I understand. Later today, he may need to unwind.

What if I invited him over and cooked dinner for him?

No, that wouldn't work. He doesn't eat after five in the afternoon, and I have no business cooking anything for anyone. There's a reason I used to eat frozen pizzas all the time. Anyway, I've got him on text right now, and my heart is thumping harder because I'm thinking of him.

What if I asked him to stop by for Vitamin Water? He'd probably laugh and think it's cute if I serve it to him in a fancy glass. Except I don't own fancy glasses. I could light some candles and drop lavender, cedar wood and sandalwood essential oils in my aromatherapy diffuser. He can sit on my couch and breathe in the scent of pure relaxation.

He'd hug me for that. I know he would.

And if he kissed me, I wouldn't mind.

And if he touched me, I wouldn't stop him.

And if he held me, I'd wrap my arms around his broad shoulders and pull him so close he'd wonder where I've been his whole life.

I text: *I'm here for you. Stop by and see me after work. I can help you relax.*

But I don't send it. Instead, I stare at my words beneath his. When I close my eyes, I can see us together with candlelight all around and my skin tingles. I open my eyes and look at my words. Is this really me trying to start this text?

I can't do this.

This isn't me.

This isn't the woman I've become.

But there was a time in my past. When I was younger and lived in Wilmington, and I craved dancing, and the shape of my body made grown men cry. Where I once caused a traffic accident by walking out of the dance studio wearing a black catsuit displaying curve after curve after curve. I adored my perfect body and everything I could do with it.

Everything.

I didn't know the meaning of loyalty. My body was my temple and I worshiped at the altar whenever I wanted and with whomever I desired — until my boyfriend found out and tried to beat the life out of me.

My phone drops to the floor as my hands start to shake. My heart-beat races and I place a hand over my chest.

Who was I texting?

Why was I texting?

My vision narrows, and when I raise up my head the room spins. The floor becomes the ceiling. The ceiling becomes the floor.

And what was I doing?

Texting John.

I like John. But why can't I breathe?

Can he bring me more air?

My hands are trembling now. I can't get any air or pick up that stupid phone.

I hate that phone! It can't stop my racing heart or give me air.

I want more air!

Please God! Help me!

My legs won't move!

Run! I need to run!

Have to get away so no one can beat me. Have to jump or duck or run before I die.

"NO!" I scream, slapping my cheeks.

Because this isn't real. No one's coming to hurt me.

"NO!" I scream again.

What's real?

What four things can I see?

My pink Nikes on the floor. My blue coffee cup on the breakfast bar. My TV. My running jacket on the bedroom doorknob.

What three things can I feel? The textured rug beneath my feet. The soft blue jeans on my legs. The cold metal bracelets on my arms.

I'm safe. I'm safe. I'm safe.

I take a deep breath and then blow it out. The shaking slows.

Another deep breath and my vision clears. Then I breathe in for four counts, hold for seven and breathe out to eight. Air moves freely in and out of my lungs as I calm down.

Fifteen minutes pass before I snatch my phone from the floor, delete that dumb text and turn off the device. John doesn't need me sending him a stupid message like that, and I need to repent for my lust over my friend and pray instead of getting carried away.

Putting one foot in front of the other, I steady myself as I walk to the kitchen. I make myself a cup of green tea, add a few slices of lemon and sit on my stool as I drink it down.

For a moment there, since I lost some weight and I'm attracted to someone, I managed to forget the one lesson it took me five years to reinforce — a friendly, bouncy, chaste chick won't get beaten with a bat for acting like a ho.

In other words, the *chubby, Christian, nice girl stays alive.*

22

TOWANDA

Towanda's fingers traced the edge of a glass shelf that held mason jars full of sugar scrub and moisturizing cream. Body products with delectable names. She leaned closer to read the labels. *Lemon Meringue Miracle. Vanilla Brown Sugar Bae. Spicy Sweet Pumpkin Dumpling. Honey Chocolate Molasses. GiGi's Sugar Cookie. Strawberry Lemonade Smoothie. PeanutButterChocolateCakeWithKoolAid.*

She didn't know if she should pick up one to sniff the contents or ask for a spoon and dig in. Normally, she hated super smelly body product stores. On shopping trips, she'd deliberately steer clear of those places because their intrusive scents gave her headaches.

So, when Barbara Jean Brown, the founder of Mrs. Brown's Body, contacted thinkLARGE for a consultation, Towanda took her time calling the woman back. But Mrs. Brown's voice sounded so kind and inviting on the voicemail. And since Towanda had hustled all year for new business, she went ahead and scheduled an appointment to visit the Cheltenham store. Now she walked in circles as she surveyed the shop's merchandise. Thank God, nothing in the room smelled like flowers or perfume.

"This is quite a selection." Towanda moved from the sugar scrub shelves over to a black wooden table which displayed shiny metal tins of *Soft Like Butta* beard balm in a neat pyramid formation. "You make all this on your own?"

"Not anymore." Mrs. Brown wiped the dust away from a glass shelf with the edge of her white apron. "My husband helps because he's retired now. My sons and daughters have jobs, but my grandbabies help me, and I have part-time staff. As you can see, we produce quite a bit."

"Very impressive," Towanda said. "I could stand here all day smelling the air in here. But then we wouldn't start our consultation, would we?"

"No, indeed we wouldn't." Mrs. Brown chuckled, gesturing toward the back. "Come on back to my office. Do you like herbal tea?"

"I'm a black coffee drinker, but since you're offering tea, I'll give it a try."

"Good, because no offense, you were looking a little weary when you walked through the door. Tea might help perk you up."

"No offense taken. I'm a little tired, I guess." Uh-oh. Mrs. Brown noticed her mood. Towanda needed to smile wider and straighten her shoulders. Try to look alive.

It didn't help that she'd spent all her recent hours working. And except for some short texts and a few brief phone calls, she hadn't had much contact with Mariah or Chablis. She'd also skipped church completely. But she couldn't allow any of that to affect thinkLARGE's bottom line.

Business first. Personal life later.

Mrs. Brown led Towanda through a narrow hallway, past a small sitting area, then over to a tiny office with ocean blue paint on the walls. She offered her a seat and served her strong peppermint tea in an antique teacup.

Towanda took a few sips, then smiled toward Mrs. Brown. "This is wonderful. Thanks so much."

"You're welcome." Mrs. Brown sat back in her chair and clasped her hands together. "So, how do we start?"

Towanda put down her teacup, then reached inside her shoulder bag and pulled out her tablet. "We've actually already started. We researched your company last week, and today I surveyed your products, so I have a feel for what you offer." She turned on the tablet. "Now tell me the full background story of Mrs. Brown's Body."

Barbara Jean Brown had been an office worker with City Hall for thirty-five years. After battling eczema and skin allergies for decades, she researched how to create her own lotions, soaps and other bath and skin products in her kitchen. Her items didn't contain preservatives or harsh chemicals and she boasted they were so safe you could eat them.

They became a hit, first with her family and then throughout her neighborhood. Her popularity grew as word spread through Germantown, Mount Airy and other areas. She retired from the city, and with a little help from her husband Eugene, Mrs. Brown's Body was born.

Towanda tapped out notes. "This is a wonderful home-grown business. We're going to enjoy creating a strategy for you."

"Can you make us as big as SheaMoisture or Carol's Daughter?"

"We can try, but what our firm will do first is determine who else might desire your products and work to expand your client base. We'll also make sure all marketing strategies are married well to your company's mission." Towanda motioned her head toward the storefront. "And I have to ask, did I see an all-natural anti-hair growth cream on the shelf out there?"

"You sure did."

"Does that really work? Because I can tell you, I've seen quite a few ladies at my church who could use something for their renegade chin whiskers."

Mrs. Brown's long gray curls jiggled about her shoulders as she laughed. "You're too funny!"

"I'm honest. I should buy a few bottles and give them out as gifts. Their husbands would thank me, and you'd earn some new clientele."

Mrs. Brown laughed again. "I'm getting such a kick out of you. You must come back to visit soon."

Towanda stood up and extended her hand. "Oh, I'll be back. I can promise you that. Mrs. Brown, it's been a pleasure meeting you, and it's going to be great working with you. You'll hear from us in a few days."

Mrs. Brown frowned as she waved away Towanda's hand, then

stood up and pulled her in for an embrace. "Listen, you call me Barbara Jean from now on. And I know it's not professional, but I give hugs to all my new friends."

A hug from a client? Not typical for a business meeting, but Towanda gratefully returned the embrace. Barbara Jean smelled of orange blossoms and warm ginger. When Towanda straightened up, she felt energized.

"Oh, I almost forgot." Barbara Jean stepped over to a corner of the office and picked up a small, glossy brown bag. She turned and handed it to Towanda. "This is for you. A thank you for your visit."

Towanda peeked inside the bag. It held miniature containers of *OrangeLovesGinger* sugar scrub, hand lotion and bubbling bath oil. "Thanks so much. I'll have to share these with my grandmother. She'd love these."

"Next time you visit, bring her along with you. The more, the merrier, 'cause we're all about family here. In fact, bring your mother, too. I'd love to meet them both."

Somehow Towanda managed not to flinch. Instead, she nodded as she turned toward the door. "Now that would be something."

Towanda drove back to the thinkLARGE office in silence.

Mother.

Just hearing the word was enough to bring down Towanda's mood for the remainder of the afternoon. But that couldn't happen today. She gripped the steering wheel.

Stay focused. No time for melancholy.

She couldn't even remember what a hug from her own mother felt like. What if her skin felt as soft and warm as Barbara Jean Brown's? What if she displayed a mouth full of healthy white teeth when she laughed? Or served delicious herbal tea in antique cups? Or leaned in and listened as Towanda talked?

It had been at least four years since Towanda had even considered trying to locate her mom. As a kid, getting any information about her mother had been difficult. Nana, Auntie Reecie and Auntie Dawn — all her relatives really, acted so angry

Towanda had been abandoned that no one wanted to give her much information. Her father, Rodney, only provided a name. Now that Towanda was in her thirties, was she courageous enough to try to find the one person she'd wanted to see her whole life?

No. She shook her head as though the movement would erase those thoughts from her mind. Years ago, Towanda had passed through the whole *what if I've seen her on the street* nonsense. She used to spend hours studying websites claiming to locate missing parents. Some of the stories appeared encouraging, but she'd also seen several cases where the mother or father had no interest in connecting with their offspring.

Towanda's life? Too full to make room for the amount of psychiatric therapy she'd need if her mother told her, "Thanks, but no thanks. I don't need to know you. You go have a nice life."

Point blank, she'd be better off not trying to find the woman. And she definitely didn't have the strength to ask why her mother had never returned for her. She'd have to be satisfied with knowing her mother's name.

Miriam.

AT THE THINKLARGE OFFICE, TOWANDA BREEZED THROUGH THE reception area, chatting with her executive assistant, Jackie, for only a minute. Usually, she'd stick around for at least fifteen minutes talking, but she wanted to write up her notes and initial plans for Mrs. Brown's Body.

Barbara Jean exuded warmth, generosity and acceptance. Companies weren't just names, they were people. And for a company owned by someone like Barbara Jean Brown, the customers should feel like a precious family member was helping them with their skin and hair care needs.

Local. Warm. Family-owned and operated. This account would be a joy to work on.

Towanda kicked off her shoes beneath her desk as she pulled her laptop and tablet from her bag. Then she reached in and pulled her phone from the zippered pocket. She stared at the banner notifications on the screen.

The Rodriguez Home had called Towanda ten times.

Why so many calls? Something must have happened. Towanda sat down in her office chair, tapping her phone to return the call.

Binky answered. "Auntie!"

"What's the matter, Binky?"

"Mom won't give me my phone back."

"That's why you called from the house phone? What did you do?"

"Nothing. But I need your help."

"What did you do?"

"It's not important. But please Auntie, can you get me a temporary phone? Something I can use for like a month?"

The girl must have lost her mind. "I can't do that. So, no. And where are your parents?"

"Dad's still at work. Mom's at the gym, but she'll be back soon. Where have you been lately? I need you."

"I've been working, that's all. And you don't need me. You're just trying to get your own way."

"Can you at least come get me? I feel locked up here. I can't talk to anybody or anything."

"What happened to your laptop? You can Skype and get on Facebook and all that."

"Dad took it last week. He told me to use the house computer to finish my homework assignments from now on."

"That rickety thing? Is it still running Windows XP?"

"I'm saying though, it's like going back in time over here. Ya gotta help me."

Towanda sighed. Binky. A couple of changes in her life and she fell apart. The girl needed to learn patience and resilience. Only God could help her in a few years when she went to college. If she ever had an argument with a professor, she'd wilt like a day-old lettuce leaf. Someone needed to school her. Her request was self-centered, but still, she'd reached out to Towanda. Her godmother.

Emphasis on *mother*. Towanda could turn her back, or she could take the time to be there for her goddaughter.

Towanda leaned back in her chair, drumming her fingertips on her desktop.

"Auntie?"

"Give me a second."

Towanda didn't have any more meetings that day, but she did have an account on which to start working. There was nothing wrong with letting Binky hang out with her in the office while she worked. She could finish her homework. Maybe scan and shred old office paperwork. Later, they could leave for Towanda's place and have dinner and a long chat about resilience, self-control and parental appreciation.

"Auntie?"

"Binky, you have exactly fifteen minutes to get your stuff together and be out on your front doorstep when I come to pick you up. Get your homework and an overnight bag. I'm calling your mom in a few minutes. If she says no, I'll call you back and cancel. Otherwise, come on and stay with me today."

"Can I invite a friend over? And can we get me a new phone?"

"No!"

"Thought I'd give it a shot. Thank you. Love you."

"Love you, too."

Towanda ended the call. She put her phone down but stayed seated in the same position for a moment.

She'd run into Mariah when she picked up Binky. But Towanda's goddaughter had said she needed her. *She needed her.* If Towanda kept playing games with Mariah and her family, she'd eventually lose the one beautiful young lady she'd been given to love, mentor and enjoy.

Okay, so Mariah had lost weight and planned to make other changes for her life.

So what?

Towanda would have to push past her insecurities about that. Who did she really want to be in the end? Mariah's bestie and Binky's role model? Or a cold, small-thinking woman who let negative emotions get the best of her?

Towanda sniffed her hands. They still smelled of orange blossom and ginger. She touched her skin and it felt supple and moisturized from the hand cream she'd sampled. On her desk phone, she pressed the auto-dial button for Jackie.

"Yes, Towanda."

"Jackie, I'm running out in a minute to pick up my goddaughter. If anyone needs me, they can reach me on my mobile. I should be back in forty minutes or so."

"No problem."

"Thanks, Jackie."

23

MARIAH

Mariah placed her phone on the passenger seat and beamed with gratitude as she drove towards home. Towanda would stop by to pick up Binky for the evening. Praise the Lord for small miracles! It had been months since Towanda had taken Binky anywhere, and yes, she sure could whisk that girl away. *Take her. Keep her. Send her back home after she learns to behave.*

Mariah turned into the driveway and looked in her rearview mirror in time to see Towanda pull up to the curb in her Range Rover. She exhaled with relief. Just like she'd prayed for, whatever had been bugging Towanda seemed to have worked itself out, almost as if nothing had happened.

There she was, out of her car and walking up the driveway, a mischievous grin on her face. She called to Mariah, "I hear you have an inmate who wants to escape from Alcatraz. I'm here to take her off your hands."

Mariah climbed out, rolling her eyes as she shut her car door. "Seriously, you may have saved me from catching a child abuse case today."

"Yeah, well, she needs to get her behind out here." Towanda

reached Mariah and gave her a quick hug. "I have work to do and so does she. And look at you, you're still coming down."

Mariah ignored the comment about her body and glanced toward the front door. "You're giving her work to do?"

"Oh, yeah. Make no mistake, I love her to death, but her auntie has scanning and paper shredding she can do after her homework is done."

"Does she know that?"

"No, but she'll soon find out." Towanda winked. "She has to earn her keep. I don't give refuge free of charge."

Both women stopped talking and watched as Binky walked out the front door with a bulging backpack slung over her shoulder. She let the screen door slam behind her. She wore a sleeveless light green t-shirt, camouflage pants and black combat boots, her hair slicked into a ballet bun, and a blank expression on her made-up face. Mariah followed with her eyes as her daughter marched over to the Range Rover and climbed into the passenger seat. She pushed a pair of aviator-style sunglasses onto her face as she sat there silently waiting.

Mariah turned back to Towanda. "This is so funny, I forgot to laugh."

"Did she just get in my car without speaking to you?"

"Yeah, and I'm her MOM." Mariah shook her head and sighed. "All this because of a phone I'm holding on to. You talk to her. I can't with her right now."

"Don't worry. She'll mellow out and be a whole new kid by tomorrow."

"Really?"

Towanda leaned over and whispered, "After an afternoon of paper shredding, she'll run back to her comfy room tomorrow."

"Thanks. And listen, wanna go bowling next week? We haven't been out in a while. I can reserve a lane and make it a ladies' night. Next Saturday?"

Towanda jiggled her keys as she walked back toward her car. "I'm pretty sure I'm free. Let's do it. I'll drop this girl at her school in the morning. We'll call you later."

"All right." Mariah couldn't resist calling over her shoulder. "Bye, Benita. Have a good evening!"

INSIDE THE HOUSE, MARIAH RUSHED UP THE STAIRS AND INTO HER bedroom. She'd just received a day pass from jail. She and Oscar could do the town tonight. Maybe they'd go back to Heritage again. Anywhere with music would suit her.

Standing beside the bed, she peeled off her t-shirt, sweatpants, and undergarments and tossed them in the hamper in the corner. Lately, she dressed and undressed right next to her bedside. She avoided standing by the full-length mirror by the window, or over by the mirror attached to the dresser. The mirror never lied. With every pound she dropped, she noticed more skin hanging around her belly and thighs. This past week she'd shed another five pounds, taking her weight loss total to sixty pounds. The gym workouts helped tone her upper torso, arms, and legs. Her mid-section didn't seem to want to follow along, though.

Body contouring? Inevitable.

The warm shower water helped clear her mind, and by the time she wrapped towels around her body and hair, she'd stopped thinking about another operation. She pulled on her robe, sat on the edge of the bed and called Oscar.

"Baby, we're kid-free tonight," Mariah announced as soon as Oscar answered the phone.

"Kid-free, huh? How'd that happen? Did your mom drive over or is Benita at a friend's house?"

"Nope. Towanda came and picked her up."

"Get outta here. What brought this on?"

"Binky called her, and I am not mad about that. I'm grateful, and I have no plans tonight. Wanna go out?"

"Of course. As soon as I get home!"

"Do you want to do Heritage again, or someplace else?"

"Your choice. I'll go wherever you choose."

"Fine."

"And did you have the chance to talk to Dr. Seng today?"

"No. What for?"

"To find out when it's safe for you to get pregnant and give birth. You have to find out soon. We aren't getting any younger." He laughed. "I'm ready to start trying right away. Hey, maybe God will bless us with twins, to help us make up for the time we lost?"

"Os, I still have forty pounds left to lose, maybe more."

"This is all so fast."

"Mariah, honey, what are you saying?"

Suddenly she felt chilly. She reached around to pull the robe tighter around her body.

Absolutely no fighting with Oscar tonight.

She understood her husband's desires.

But what did *she* want now?

Right now, she wanted to stop this conversation and move on to something more pleasant. They'd enjoyed one another so much two weeks earlier at Heritage. They could have a night like that again. She should tell him something, anything, to move away from this topic.

Mariah cleared her throat. "Os, you're right, okay. It's too late to call today, but I'll get right on it tomorrow, and I'll tell you what Dr. Seng says. Deal?"

"It's a deal. Can you wear the red dress tonight? I'd love to see you in that."

"Sure, I'll put on the red dress. Anything for you."

"That's my baby."

MARIAH WORE THE RED DRESS, BUT SHE WANTED TO WALK AROUND AS THE sun set, so they drove to Penn's Landing, where they could walk along the waterfront until they reached The Chart House. She'd fidgeted in the car the whole way there, and as they walked from the parking lot to the front of the restaurant, she kept rubbing her hands together, twisting her wedding ring with her fingers.

On their way inside, Oscar reached out to hold her hand.

"You planning to leave me?" he asked with a half-smile.

"What? No."

"The way you're twisting your hands, I keep wondering if you're trying to get that ring off."

"Sorry I'll stop."

"I paid good money for that little band. Hold on to it so I can hold on to you."

"I will."

"Are you ready to eat something?"

At their table, Mariah looked out over the Delaware River and listened to Oscar talk about his day. When the waiter asked what she'd like to drink, she ordered a glass of Riesling. She wasn't a big drinker. She probably had a glass of wine once or twice a year, but what else could she do to stop feeling so strange around her husband?

This man had actually joked about having twins. Twins he wouldn't have to carry, and that wouldn't change his body in the least. But if she tried to explain it to him, they'd probably have an argument. She didn't want to end the night that way.

By the time she ordered Mahi topped with tropical fruit salsa, she'd already finished her first glass of Riesling and asked for another. This time she sipped slowly, enjoying the warm feeling spreading through her body. Twenty more minutes later, she was completely relaxed. Mellow and detached from her thoughts about family obligations, rebellious teenagers and future children.

Leaving The Chart House, Mariah clung to Oscar's arm, cracking jokes like old times. At home, they didn't even make it to their bedroom. They started kissing and caressing in the car, and by the time they entered the house, Oscar slammed the back door, twirled Mariah around and peeled her dress and undergarments off so fast she felt dizzy. With passion reminiscent of their early days, they made love on the living room floor, all loud and noisy and intense. After it ended, they laughed together, lying on their backs as they looked up at the ceiling.

"I'm sending Towanda a dozen long-stemmed roses in the morning," Oscar said, clutching Mariah's hand.

"What for?"

"Because she took our kid and I got to have all this."

Mariah woke first the next morning. As the sun rose outside their bedroom, she stared at Oscar's sleeping frame in the bed. Their night before had started tense but ended with such fire and passion. She reached out and ran her hand over his tan, bare shoulder.

Get pregnant now?

He wanted to start trying as soon as possible, and if she told him to wait another few years, they'd wind up where they were before she lost weight, with him disappointed every day.

Sure, she'd call Dr. Seng today. But it didn't matter what he said, because she'd fudge it. Find a study. Search for a negative report about pregnancy after bariatric surgery. She'd do whatever she had to do and ask God's forgiveness later. Eventually, they'd have more babies. It didn't have to be this year or even next year.

It had taken a decade for Mariah to return to feeling this magical. She would *not* give it up now.

24

CHABLIS

S tupid scale. Dumb device.

I step on it. I step off. On it. Off it. On. Off.

Finally, I wind up and kick it clear across the bathroom. It slides across the tile and whacks into the side of the tub, where it leaves a tiny dent on the white enamel. I'm naked and sweating, and I need to put my workout clothes on and head to the gym, but I can't get the math out of my head.

Forty pounds lost.

The scale hasn't budged in four weeks.

So, I'm on a weight-loss plateau.

How did this happen? I exercise six days a week, and I'm still living on my clean foods diet with the grilled chicken and eggs and leafy greens and Greek yogurt and berries and coffee and tea. And I don't cheat.

Well…not anymore.

"Ahhhhh! Why? Why?" I pull my robe back on, run, and launch myself onto my bed, which is ten baby steps away from the bathroom door, so I don't travel far. I turn over, snatch my phone from the night-stand, and stare at the screen. No texts from John. Seeing a message from him would be the only thing that would yank me up out of my bad mood. But nothing's there.

Weight is only a number. I need to take three calming breaths and chillax. It could just be water retention, or maybe I added some muscle. There's a reason somewhere, I'm sure of it. In the meantime, I need to get dressed and go work out.

HARDLY ANYONE IS HERE. IT'S JUNE. LOTS OF PEOPLE HAVE STARTED THEIR vacations, or they take Friday off.

Good. More space for me.

I have resistance training today, and it looks like I'll be able to use a weight bench without waiting for someone to move. The elliptical machine is my choice for a warm-up, so I put on my Beats and head over there. But first, I peek at my phone screen one more time.

No texts from John yet. Where's my exercise list?

On the elliptical machine, I press the buttons and start moving so fast the insides of my thighs begin to burn. Five minutes pass before I step down and gaze around. I pull my phone from my hoodie and check my messages one more time.

Nothing.

It's almost five-thirty. Guess I'm going it alone.

I drag myself to the free weight area where I load a barbell with twenty pounds on each side and start with the first set of four reps of squats. Now I'm chewing my gum hard, my muscles are warm, and my mind is on my workout. So much so, I get knocked out of my zone when Sheena walks past, waving at me before I start static lunges.

"Hey, girl." I pull my headphones from my ears and put them around my neck.

She sits on the bench next to me, adjusting her black and white weight gloves. "You're hitting it hard this morning."

"I'm trying," I say with a nod. "Have you heard from John today?"

"Nah. He supposed to meet you here?"

"No." I scratch an itch on my neck. "He sends my workouts each morning, but I didn't get a text from him today."

"Yeah, and if he's not here, he's at his office working."

"Right."

Sheena shrugs as she slides weight plates onto her bar. "Or maybe he decided to get a jump on his packing before work today."

"Packing?"

She stares at me as if I know what she's talking about. "His apartment? He's got a lot of stuff to stash over in his brother's garage, and his place has to be empty before he leaves Philly. Travis and I are going to head over tonight at seven to hang out and help him finish moving stuff into a U-Haul. You gonna be there?"

My skin feels as if I jumped from a hot spring into ice water in like two-seconds flat, which is to say my body is on cruise control. I don't even want to know what my expression looks like.

John is packing and moving.

He's going somewhere.

And he didn't tell me, which means he's *ghosting me*.

I ease down onto the bench behind me. My friends warned me, but I didn't listen.

John romances women then ghosts them.

I didn't even get the romance part. How come I didn't get any romance?

Never mind. Never mind. Never mind.

"You okay?" Sheena calls over to me.

I snap to attention. "Oh yeah, I'm good."

She lies back on the bench, pushing her bar high above her chest. Her purple locs tumble to the side as she does this. "Will we see you tonight?"

I clench my hands into fists, then unclench them. "You sure will. As a matter of fact, can you pick me up on your way over?"

"Sure."

"Thanks."

Perfect. Now I can ride shotgun to this packing soiree. I may not be John's girlfriend, but I'm also not a punk, so if he's leaving Philly, he's going to have to tell me to my face.

And this time, I'm not about to dress up or put on heels or anything.

. . .

It's a little after seven when Sheena, Travis and I drive over to John's place. When we get there, I let myself hang back a little as we walk up the sidewalk leading to the bottom floor of the duplex John rents. I've never been here. Never had a reason to be here—until now.

I hear him before I see him.

"Hey, man," John calls out when he opens the front door and spies Travis. "Appreciate the help, bro."

Travis gives him a pound. "No problem. We'll have you packed in no time."

I lurk behind Sheena so he can't quite see me as he greets her, but there's no mistaking the surprise on his face when she steps past him and he sees me standing on the bottom step in all my frowning glory.

John raises his eyebrows. "Chablis!"

"Hi," I say in a flat tone. "Heard you could use help packing?"

He says nothing as he stands there looking at me. He wears an Eagles jersey and faded jeans with paint splotches on them. His feet are bare. He needs to trim his toenails. And his toes are werewolf hairy.

I push my weave out of my face when I look up at him. "You know, you missed sending me my workout today."

"Sorry about that. I overslept."

"Lots on your mind?"

"Uh, yeah." Then it must dawn on him—he's standing in the doorway talking to me as if I'm some stranger, not the cute and scrappy chick he trained for months. "Come on in. I'll tell you what's going on."

I step into the living room. Travis and Sheena are already stacking boxes in a vacant corner of the room. There's a thin, brown-skinned guy by the staircase, taking books off a wooden shelf. John gestures to him.

"Chablis, that's my buddy, Terrance. Terry, this is Chablis Shields." We nod a quick hello to one another.

"How'd you do at the gym?" John asks me.

"I did great. Ask Sheena."

"Sheena, how did she do?"

"She's a pro now. You got any water here?"

"Bottles are in the blue cooler under the windowsill." He shuts the front door behind me.

The space I'm standing in is a plain white painted room with faux hardwood flooring. It's filled with boxes, containers and bags. No couch or television or sound system. No artwork on the walls.

Yep. This man is leaving.

"Where ya going?" I ask him.

"Berlin, Germany."

A sound like a combination hiccup/snort comes out of my throat, along with, "Really. Germany, huh?"

John waves me over to the kitchen. "Let's talk."

I follow him inside. This room is pretty empty as well, but he offers me a battered black stool and I take a seat.

He leans against the sink. "You know about the early morning meetings at SynerCloud. My Saturday work sessions and all that."

"Yeah."

"I helped identify and correct problems with a tricky cloud solution, and that got my name circulated on some high-profile emails in the company. Last week, our CTO invited me to the headquarters in Berlin to work with our overseas team."

I'm impressed. Not because he's done all this work, but because I think this is the most I've ever heard him say about himself at one time.

I'm still not smiling, however. "Wonderful."

"Kind of bittersweet, though. Half of our German team got canned."

I don't need to hear the rest. "So, let me guess. Now they want you over there?"

"Yeah, until they can build the team up again. But it might depend on how much I like living in Germany."

I hold my breath when our gazes meet.

John looks away. "If things go smoothly and I enjoy my living space and my team. If I earn a management role, this move may be permanent."

"But what about American Ninja Warrior? What about CrossFit training?"

"If it's in God's plan, I'll keep training in a foreign country."

It's growing hot and stuffy in this kitchen and I want him to crack open a window, but I can't find the words to ask him. I look down to my thighs, where I can see my brown skin showing through the rips in my jeans. Time to go on and ask the million-dollar question.

"How come you didn't tell me?"

"I wanted to, I just kept putting it off, you know. Trying to figure out the right way to say it," he says, with a worried look that gives way to a softness in his eyes. "If you didn't figure it out, I like you—a lot."

Why, why, *why* didn't I change my mind and dress better before I came over here? Then again, I'm thinking, who cares? Curvy body, ripped jeans, and a WRSHP t-shirt, and he still likes me.

So much for not being his type.

"I like you too," I tell him. "Please don't act like you don't know that."

He gives me a half-smile as he keeps talking. "Anyway, with my job changing like this, I can't start anything now. You've been through enough in your life. I can't play with your emotions that way. Plus, I have to be careful. Last time I dated a woman from Rise, it didn't end well. She expected more from me, but I knew she wasn't right for me. I broke it off fast, and then a week later I got called into the Pastor's office over some lies she started spreading."

This is all refreshing. So, John isn't a love 'em and leave 'em type of guy. And he likes me, at least enough to consider my feelings.

Wow. I had thought, maybe in time, we might turn out to be more than friends. But if God is airmailing this brother straight to Berlin, which He is, I thought wrong.

I climb off the stool, forcing a smile. "I wish you all the best. For real. You're going across the world. This is a blessing."

Which is how I feel...but...still.

"I should have told you sooner," John says as he steps close to me, wrapping his long arms around me in a warm bear hug.

I grasp his shoulders harder than I should. Squeeze a little tighter than I should. He squeezes me back. Maybe a little tighter than he should. He feels warm and solid and strong, and my nerve endings go off like firecrackers. When he presses his hands into the small of my back, I automatically inch closer to his body, and we hold each other much longer than two friends should.

And this is probably the last thing I'll ever feel from him.

A tiny teardrop runs from the corner of my eye down the side of my nose before I catch it and brush it away with my fingertips. That's enough. I pull myself out of his arms and step backward.

Back to life. Back to reality. Reality is I'm on a plateau and my trainer is leaving on a jet plane and doesn't know when he'll be back again.

"Listen, my weight hasn't moved for a month," I say, blinking fast to clear my eyes.

John wipes a hand over his face and clears his throat. "Uh…are you cheating?"

"No."

"Drinking your water?"

"Of course."

"Chablis?"

"Most of the time."

"Get your water intake back up and cut the starchy carbs out of your meals. No oatmeal or croutons or bread. You'll see the difference in about two weeks."

"You sure?"

"I promise."

"How do I figure out how to change my workouts each week?"

"I'll send you links to some websites to help you build your own workouts. Keep changing your pattern each week so your body doesn't get used to your routine. Plus, you've got Travis and Sheena to help at the gym."

I run out of things to say, except for one.

"I'm gonna miss you."

"I'll miss you, too."

Then I turn away, because I don't want to say anything else.

When I get back to the living room, Terrance, Travis and Sheena all look busy, their hands buried in brown boxes. They probably spent the whole time listening to me and John talk. But who cares? I'm a single chick. He's a single guy. I do like him, and I will miss him, and that's the truth.

It's close to midnight when I get back home. John's stuff is boxed and locked in a U-haul which he'll drive to his brother's house in the Northeast Philly tomorrow. He leaves Monday.

We're still friends and we'll keep in contact. I don't know why he held me so close for so long, but I won't let my imagination run wild this time. Maybe it just felt good for him to hold me.

He told me ditching starchy carbs will get me off my plateau. Well, I gotta do what I gotta do. I've worked too hard to stop now.

I'm exhausted by the time I finally shower and settle down in bed. I pick up my phone to take one last look through my messages. Various texts from Nikki and Felicia. One picture message from my friend Simone, showing her smiling next to baby Najee, who's so plump and scrumptious I could nibble his chocolate face. I'll text everybody back tomorrow.

When I tap to launch Messenger, I see a dozen or so messages. Mostly from my older aunts and cousins who are in love with Facebook and like to send me *have a blessed day* graphics. The kind with teddy bears and red hearts flashing all over them.

Then, there's one message.

All the way at the bottom. From earlier in the day.

I must have been so distracted that I overlooked it when I scanned Messenger this morning. But I needed to skip this one. My hands tremble as I read the sender's name.

Tony Hart.

25

CHABLIS

No. I didn't tap to open the message.

No. I don't want to know what it says.

No. I have no desire to respond.

But I've been texting about it like a madwoman all week long. That and calling my mom. A cell phone tower probably caught fire after I told Charlene Champagne Shields I got a message from Tony. She called him a despicable, muck slurping bottom feeder, and a string of other names only a mother who'd nearly lost her daughter could say.

Mariah, Nikki and Simone all gave me the same advice—don't respond and block him from all my social media accounts. Towanda was the only one who told me to go ahead and reply. She said I should ask for his address, drive to Modell's, buy the biggest Louisville Slugger in the store and then crack him in the back of the head with a six-year return on his investment.

Plainly her opinion is in the minority.

I had to FaceTime Dr. Jerrica four times. Her guidance may be the reason I only had three panic attacks after seeing Tony's message. She reminded me that even though I might feel like I did right after the beating, I'm not at all powerless and I'm not being controlled by someone else's anger.

She's not a person of faith, but she encouraged me to lean hard on my belief in God so I wouldn't start avoiding situations.

So far, so good.

Going to work and attending church hasn't been a problem for me. Actually, I've doubled my prayer and devotions time because I need the presence of the Lord to help calm my soul. I also pasted my meditation scriptures on the front and back of every door in my apartment. Psalms 118:6. Psalms 34:4. Psalms 56:3. It helps.

Those 5:00 a.m. gym visits, though? Um, yeah, the sun's not all the way up at five in the morning, and I'm too tired to fight mental demons at that hour, so that time is a no-go for me. It'll take me a while to feel relaxed enough to strut into the early morning darkness alone and not think Tony's lurking around a corner waiting to jump me.

And I didn't tell John about the message.

What for? He has to navigate a new work team, get used to a foreign country and immerse himself in learning functional German. He did e-mail me pics of famous places in Germany. I printed them out and pinned them to the front wall of my cubicle at work. Right under my Pinterest printout of *Sometimes, We Create Our Own Heartbreaks Through Expectation* and directly above *Slay Your Own Dragons, Princess*.

So, I didn't open the message yet, but I didn't delete it, either. Don't ask me why, because I don't know. I'm staring at Tony's name in my Messenger list when Binky drops her hand over my phone screen. I jerk my head up.

"What?"

She glares at me. "It's your turn to bowl!"

"Oh, yeah." I look around and pull myself back into the moment. Mariah skips back from the lane. She bowled a strike, and her smile is so wide every tooth in her mouth is on display. She looks nice tonight in dark blue capris and a short-sleeved button-down blue plaid shirt. Towanda's here too, but ever since Kim Chase walked in and joined us, she keeps shuffling back and forth to the shoe rental counter because she claims none of the shoes fit her right.

Ladies' night. Yay.

I shove my phone down in my bag as I stand up, then move myself over to grab a bowling ball. I'm happy Kim came out to join us tonight. She's in my life group. She's a Philly cop and mega cool. Mariah started going to her Friday night fellowships, which I don't attend because I'm single and those meetings are for married women.

My cousin is trying to push us all to have a good time. I need to forget that stupid message. Judging from the fact that I've been pre-occupied, Towanda keeps checking out, and Binky is downright sad, I think Mariah and Kim are the only ones having fun.

I take my turn and bowl a strike, as well. My new muscles are good for something.

Kim cheers for me. "Go, Chablis!"

Mariah claps. "Yes! That's what I'm talking about."

"Hoo-ray," Towanda says with her voice low, not sounding the least bit joyful.

I turn around to gaze at her. She stole my seat next to Binky, and she's sucking on a straw inside what has to be the biggest cup of soda I've ever seen.

"T, you wanna bowl now?" I ask.

She slurps. "Nope. Binky can take my turn."

"I don't want it," Binky says without moving one inch, her chin resting in her hands.

"Towanda. Binky. Seriously, y' all?" I say, annoyed.

Towanda is the only person I've ever met who can snarl without making a face. "I told you. My feet hurt."

"I thought you changed your shoes."

"I did. The bigger ones still don't fit. So, I'll sit here and watch, thank you very much."

Binky says nothing. She just stares at me.

This is crazy and I'm not in the mood. I glance at Kim, who has a questioning look on her face. Then I turn to Mariah, whose gorgeous smile has faded. I know she loves us all, but right now it looks as if she wants to knock the hell out of all three of us.

"Maybe this was a bad idea?" she mumbles.

Towanda rolls her eyes and mumbles back. "You said it."

Binky chimes in. "Yup."

I see all of this and…I can't with them. There's too much shade going on, and I don't know why they're dumping on Mariah. Well, Binky's a pain in the butt because that's how teenagers get sometimes. But Towanda? I have no words. I gotta bounce.

I walk to the table where my purse sits, pull a twenty from my wallet and press it into Mariah's hands. "For the games. I know you tried, but I don't know. I guess everybody's tired." I reach over and grab my jacket and slide it on. "Mariah, I'll see you later. Kim, see you at life group next week."

When I nod at Towanda, she gives me a quick nod back. I poke Binky on the shoulder so she'll look up at me, and that's when I mouth, we're gonna talk later, because how she's acting with her mom is not cool.

After I leave, I sit still in my car for a few moments, staring at people walking back and forth across the parking lot.

Why not open the message?

If I need to talk to someone after I see it, my family and friends are right inside Let's Bowl Lanes. Before I stop myself, I pull out my phone, launch Messenger and tap Tony Hart's name in the list.

I FOUND YOU ON INSTAGRAM AND FACEBOOK THROUGH OUR OLD HIGH SCHOOL friend, Andre Cole. You commented on a couple of his posts last week. Anyway, I'll keep this short. In jail, a local minister would visit a couple times a week to teach Bible study and witness to us. He took me under his wing and introduced me to Christ. After my release, I moved to Florida and now I'm in Bible college. When I saw your comments, it was like a sign from God for me. There's so much I could say to you, but only one thing I need to say: I hurt you bad, and I'm sorry for what I did. I'm asking you, from the deepest part of my soul, to forgive me for the pain I caused you.

WHEN I FINISH READING, I'M NOT SHAKING OR GASPING OR ANYTHING.

I.

I'm just.

I need to go home.

On my way there, I have to pass Pizza Hut Express. My brain shuts off when I turn in the parking lot, walk in and order a Meat Lover's pizza, breaded bone-out wings and a HERSHEY'S triple chocolate brownie.

I'm hungry. I'm tired. My eyes hurt from staring at computer screens and my phone all day long.

I'll pray soon. I will. I have to. But not now.

At my kitchen bar, the takeout food sits in front of me. Right now, I'm pushing aside everything messing with my head, but especially a past with a baseball bat that nearly knocked the life out of me.

Right now?

I'm eating.

26

TOWANDA

Towanda climbed into her Range Rover and remained in the parking lot long enough to watch Mariah drive off with Binky looking sad in the back seat.

Waste. Of. Time.

Saturday night out with the girls had been a complete bust. Towanda had been fine during the first twenty minutes — before Kim Chase showed up. What was that about? Mariah getting all chummy with another chick from church? Inviting her to their ladies bowling night? It might have been okay if Mariah had at least mentioned she'd asked the woman to come. Towanda had thought the night would be a chance for the four of them to have fun and bond.

Then, in walked an interloper.

Towanda rolled her eyes after Kim walked in, stepped right past her, gave Mariah a big hug and then proceeded to joke about something that had happened at their Friday fellowship. They both laughed as if they'd been buddies for decades. Since Towanda had zero interest in watching her best friend use all her time joking and laughing with a stranger, she continued rolling her eyes and mumbling snarky comments.

After that, everything went downhill.

But that wasn't her fault either. Why did a slice of pizza which cost five dollars taste like cardboard, ketchup, and paste? Since the food was nasty, the people at the snack bar tried to make up for it by giving her a colossal Barq's root beer. Then none of the cheap bowling shoes fit, and she refused to wear the men's shoes they'd offered her. So what if she needed more substantial sized footwear? Not everyone possessed feet the size of gerbils.

Like Chablis.

Oh, yeah. Chablis. She actually sat there all evening texting her girl-friends about the Facebook message she'd received from her wannabe murderer ex-boyfriend. When Towanda had instructed her to go out and buy her own Louisville Slugger and return the favor, she'd ignored the comment.

"Thank goodness," Towanda muttered when Chablis had finally waved the white flag and left, signaling everyone else to pack up and leave the bowling alley fifteen minutes later.

But Towanda didn't know where to go after that.

Home?

Nope. Too early, and she didn't want to end up working in her home office.

A movie? She picked up her phone and tapped the Fandango app. Nothing good playing.

She could take herself out for a nice dinner, but the crappy bowling alley food had turned her stomach.

What a night.

She needed to go to Nana's.

"Hello. Hello. Hello." Towanda let herself in with her key. Inside, she carefully hung up her bag on the coat rack. Nana hated clutter. No wonder Towanda had ended up being such a neat freak.

"Nan?" She leaned over the wooden railing as she called up the stairs.

"Wanda."

"Yeah, it's me. My night ended early."

Nana called to her. "Come up here."

"There in a second."

Towanda stepped over to the woven mat close to the dining room and placed her shoes there. When she turned around, she noticed a new picture on the wall. An eight by ten in a silver Tiffany frame. Smiling faces.

Towanda recognized the people. Her cousin, Lilianne Waters-Winters, posing with her adoring husband, William Winters, and their four cute-as-buttons children. Two boys and two girls whose names escaped Towanda. They were all dressed in tailored black pants and crisp white button-down shirts, looking like a press photo for the next presidential family.

Lilianne. Auntie Reecie and Uncle Charles' daughter. Towanda hadn't called her since two Christmases ago when everyone on that twig of the family tree had decided they needed Nana to stay at their luxurious home in Prince George's County for the holidays.

Towanda had insisted on coming with Nana as her traveling companion. Lilianne had mumbled something about the guest room only being suitable for one person, which was mainly code for *I want my Nana in the family picture this year, not my giant orphan cousin.*

Lilianne. The cousin who refused to use Towanda as a bridesmaid in her wedding party because, as she told Auntie Reecie, who eventually let it slip to Nana, "Everyone in my bridal party has to be cute." Also, she was the exact same cousin who'd found a reason to avoid being present for Towanda's graduations from U of Penn.

But Towanda wasn't bitter. Lilianne had a precious family. And one day, when Towanda met her six-foot-seven Samson, she'd get married, and then promptly give birth to her team of basketball playing sons who would crush Lilianne's family at the yearly reunion.

"Wonder Woman." Towanda padded into Nana's bedroom, the floorboards squeaking beneath her feet as she stepped toward the bed.

"Stop all that noise." Nana accepted Towanda's cheek kiss. "Can't you see I'm trying to meditate?"

Towanda glanced around. Dim lights. No television. Candles on the dresser. Peaceful piano music flowed from Nana's Bose sound system.

"Meditating? I thought you were getting ready for a hot date."

Nana tapped Towanda's hand, then released it. "Stop all that foolishness."

Nana meditating?

It sure seemed peaceful. Towanda would give it a try.

She climbed onto the empty side of Nana's bed, stretching out her body. Her toes touched the mahogany frame of the four-poster bed. She laid her head back on the pillow and breathed in air which smelled like herbal springtime magic.

This beat bowling any day. She should have come here tonight in the first place.

"You trying to turn this into a new business? Nana's spa? Caters to old folks?" Towanda whispered.

"Hush, before I kick you," Nana whispered back.

Towanda lay flat, her arms at her sides. She breathed in and out. In and out. Soothing music. Soft bed.

And Nana was here.

She reached out for her grandmother's hand and grasped it tight, feeling the delicate bones beneath her skin.

Nana started singing, softly at first.

> Jesus, keep me near the cross,
> There a precious fountain,
> Free to all, a healing stream,
> Flows from Calvry's mountain.

THEN STRONGER...

> In the cross, in the cross,
> Be my glory ever;
> Till my raptured soul shall find,
> Rest beyond the river...

TOWANDA CLOSED HER EYES, AND WITH NANA'S VOICE IN HER EARS, SHE transported. She was no longer a thirty-something, six-foot business-woman. All of a sudden, she was seven years old. A seven-year-old with a head full of unruly curls, too-thick glasses, and the body of a ten-year-old. She still wanted to sleep in Nana's bed. Not that she was scared of the dark or anything, but she'd crept around the upstairs long enough to see her daddy had not come home.

She could knock on Nana's door, and Nana would always tell her to come in. She was always careful to close the door softly, then climb up onto the massive bed with the blankets and cotton pillowcases that smelled of Ajax laundry soap and Estee' Lauder perfume. Nana would wrap her arms around Towanda's shoulders and they would settle down together. Nana would sing, and precious peace would loom so close, Towanda swore she could caress it. She would lie in the darkness, never wondering why her mother left, why her father always seemed to be asleep or away from the house or why it hurt her feelings that kids in her class feared her more than they accepted her.

> In the cross, in the cross,
> Be my glory ever,
> Till my raptured soul shall find,
> Rest beyond the river...

COULD SHE CALL ON THE LORD IN THIS SITUATION? WOULD IT EVEN MAKE a difference? Maybe she should accept losing her best friend, just as she'd feared. Towanda squeezed her eyes shut as an old memory entered her mind.

Angela.

In Towanda's eighth grade year, she and another tall, shapely girl had become close friends. They'd had fun together, and Angela had wanted to try out for the junior girls' basketball team. She'd urged Towanda to try out with her.

Towanda had made the cut. Angela hadn't, and her attitude changed over the next few months. She'd become curt and sour. The younger Towanda hadn't understood what had happened until she talked to Nana about it.

Angela was jealous of Towanda's fast skills on the basketball court. She'd smashed the cup of friendship they had shared, and they never became close again. For Towanda, losing her friend over a game poisoned her interest in hoops. She'd quit the following year.

Towanda shifted to her side. Why'd that memory have to come up now? Where was the peace promised in the song Nana sang beside her?

So now I'm Angela? Now what? How do I put our pieces back together?
She twisted again on the bed. "How?" she whispered.

"How, what?" Nana turned to face her.

She should say it. She should open her mouth and talk with her Nana, and everything would be all right. A more comfortable space on earth did not exist.

"Mariah. She's changed."

"Well, she was supposed to. That's what happens when you lose a lot of weight. What did you expect?"

"I expected her to get smaller, and I knew she'd look different, but tonight at the bowling alley, I don't know. Why can't I just be happy for her?"

"Because you're insecure. Something new is going on with your friend, and you can't stand it because it has nothing to do with you. Afraid you're gonna miss out or lose something. I blame your mother for that, but it's something you need to get over."

Towanda swallowed at the lump in her throat. "Okay, so you may be right."

"Oh, I know I'm right."

"Thank you, blunt grandmother. Got any advice on what I should do?"

"First, don't treat her badly."

"I'm not—"

"Stop it. I know you, granddaughter. You can be as vindictive as the day is long. But everyone isn't in a race with you, and you can't treat your loved ones like the people you competed with during school. Mariah's life is Mariah's life. Let her have it. Celebrate her and thank God for her."

"She's making new friends now."

"Good for her. Now you keep on showing up in her life, and people will get the message she's your sister from another mother."

Towanda's head throbbed. She moved her hand up to rub her forehead, but Nana caught it and held it, whispering to her in the darkness.

"Don't make other people pay for your insecurity." She kissed her hand. "That's not how I raised you."

27

MARIAH

Tears had blurred Mariah's vision as she reached down and removed her rented bowling shoes. When she'd raised her body up, she sat in her chair motionless, shoes in hand. She'd closed her eyes. *Heavenly Father, I need a minute.*

"Hey, you okay?" Kim had leaned down and placed her arm around Mariah's shoulder.

"I'm fine. My family's not usually like this." Mariah had shuddered.

"You think I don't know that?" Kim sat down opposite her. "If they're having a bad night, you can't control that. Trust God with 'em, and leave 'em alone. They'll be all right."

Mariah had placed her shoes back on the floor and then reached in her bag for a tissue to blow her nose. Right after Towanda had dragged her sour self out, Binky had demanded to bail.

For once, she was glad. Everyone was tripping.

"I know. I know." Mariah had wiped her nose. "I don't even know why I'm all emotional about it."

"'Cause you wanted to have a good time and they ruined it. But you're going to forgive and forget and love them anyway, so come on. Let's put these shoes back." Kim had smiled as she gathered up Mariah's shoes with her own. "And listen, your friend was right. The shoes were crap."

Mariah had laughed, happy for the chance to make light of the situation. The more she got to know Kim, the more thankful she was for their friendship. Their relationship had grown from Friday night fellowships and light conversation to leaning on her in moments like these.

Good friends were hard to find. As Mariah's new self slowly sculpted out from her old body, her confidence returned, bringing her long-subdued personality with it. Like a swan from the shadows, she became more attractive to new people as she emerged.

No one stared as she approached a buffet table anymore, true, but more importantly, she didn't care if they did. She'd been courageous and done something different and it had changed her life. For that, she could take a bow. Maybe she'd even open up the Thick Chicks Clique page to other women looking for support for changes in their lives.

Yes. She'd do that. Chablis would love it.

And Towanda?

Mariah didn't care what Towanda thought.

Outside of Let's Bowl Lanes, she'd hugged Kim goodbye. "Thanks for understanding. See you on Friday?"

"Absolutely," Kim had hugged her back. "Now go home and relax, pray for your family and let it go. That's all you have to do."

MARIAH OPENED HER FRONT DOOR AND STEPPED INSIDE. SHE WALKED THE hardwood from the front hall to the living room, traveled through the kitchen to the sun porch and then back around to the living room. Everything was clean, like she'd left it before the bowling outing. Nothing moved or scattered.

She read the signs—empty garage, dark house, porch lit by automatic timers. Oscar had left the house. Maybe he needed some time to himself.

Two weeks earlier, she'd told him she'd call Dr. Seng to discuss pregnancy. She had called her doctor, but she'd never asked about the risks of pregnancy. Instead, she'd asked him when an excellent time would be to schedule body contouring. Later that day, she'd lied, telling Oscar the doctor had said it wouldn't be a good idea so soon because the baby would be malnourished. At the time, Oscar had looked sad, but he hadn't said anything else about it.

Binky was gone, too. She'd shredded Mariah's last nerve back at the bowling alley with her faces and body language, so when she asked to stay overnight at Naomi's, Mariah had grasped at the suggestion like a swimmer for a life vest. She'd dropped her off there on her way home.

"Do you need an overnight bag?" Mariah had asked.

"No, I'll borrow anything I need from Naomi."

"How about we stop past CVS to buy you a toothbrush?"

"Naomi's mom keeps extra toothbrushes in their bathroom, and I'll be back early in the morning, anyway."

"You don't need anything at all?" Mariah had asked when they pulled up to Naomi's house.

"No," she'd said, slamming the car door shut.

Mariah had bit her lip but hadn't done anything else except drive away. Her daughter seemed to be trying hard to make her feel bad about spending a Saturday night with her family. You'd think the girl would realize it was only a few hours and try to have a good time.

But Mariah understood. Once she'd started clamping down on Binky's phone and social media adventures, she'd produced a teen enemy in the house. But if she let Binky do whatever she wanted, and she experimented with drugs, got pregnant or showed up naked on the Internet, everyone would wonder where her mother was.

So, Binky could stay angry all day, every day. In less than four years she would move out into the world and find out life wasn't a free-for-all. Especially when she had to pay her own bills.

Upstairs in her bedroom, Mariah stood next to her bedside and removed every stitch of clothing from her body. Plaid shirt. Sandals. Capris. Bra. Waist trainer. Body Magic girdle. All the clothes she wore made her practically bulletproof.

Nude, she padded over to the full-length mirror. She looked at her feet first, then slowly moved her eyes up. Smooth, curvy calf muscles. Beautiful legs, until upper-thigh level. The horror show started there.

Rippling, dimpling skin folding down into small, then larger waves. Her eyes moved farther up. Handfuls of skin from her abdomen dropped down to touch the top of her thighs. Skin which had fallen down in quick defeat collapsed after losing a war. Where pounds of flesh had vacated, the skin remained, abandoned and hurt after years of stretching.

Even farther up, the surface leveled out, but devastation continued, like an isolated beachhead after soldiers had run for cover. Flat at the rib cage. But right there. Her breast area, formerly plump and nurturing, now flattened and misshapen. The hardest place to view. No more cushion for her husband to rest his head upon. Fast weight loss had claimed the victory, but now the fallout was complete.

Mariah needed to keep looking up, so she did. Lovely shoulder area. Hints of collarbone on both sides. Thinner arms. Amazing neck area.

And then her face.

The smallest she'd seen it in ten years. She smiled with bright teeth, caramel skin and deep dimples. Hazel eyes which more people looked into now because now they saw her completely. People didn't purse their lips when she walked down the aisle at church or in a movie theatre. But those people couldn't see that now her naked body resembled an abandoned war zone.

She turned to talk to the heap of discarded clothing. "You keep me together. Just do your job."

She walked over and picked up her robe from the bedroom chair, wrapping it around her nude frame. Her bag, with her phone inside, remained downstairs on the kitchen table next to her keys. She went to get her cellphone and ended up sitting at the table scrolling through messages.

Nothing from Towanda. Fine. Mariah didn't feel like texting or talking with her right now, anyway.

Nothing from Chablis. Mariah would pray for her and call her later on. That message from her ex-boyfriend seemed to have genuinely stunned her. Mariah could arrange a time to take her out for a spa date or offer to let her stay at the house again if she needed to be close to family.

Two picture messages arrived from Binky's friend Naomi's phone. The messages delivered six pictures featuring Binky, Naomi and their other friend Sasha, all dolled up in bright-colored, contoured makeup. They must have used a photo filter because they all looked like models.

These girls were in high school. And if that blonde streak in the front of Binky's head didn't turn out to be clip-on extensions, Binky would get it when she came home in the morning.

But the picture messages proved one thing—she didn't hate her mother.

The back door opened and shut so quickly, it made Mariah turn around fast. Oscar glared at her with a disturbed look on his face.

"Hi, honey," she said. "Bowling night ended early."

In three long strides, he stood by her side. "Know where I was?"

"No."

"Out driving around, thinking about our marriage, because I emailed Dr. Seng myself this week about pregnancy. He got back to me late this afternoon. Is there something you want to clarify for me before I tell you what he said?"

Mariah swallowed at the lump in her throat. "Um—"

"Let me put it out there. Your specialist told me pregnancy shouldn't be a problem for you at all. The only thing you need to do is keep up your nutritional supplements. He also said malnutrition is extremely uncommon, especially if you're eating healthy whole foods."

"Os—"

"You lied to me. I'm your husband! Here I am thinking you want what I want, but your body isn't ready yet. Now I don't know what to think—"

"Baby, I'm—"

"No! I don't want to hear it." He stalked out of the kitchen.

Mariah followed him down the hallway and up the stairs. "Can you just stop and listen to me for a minute?"

"Whatever you have to say, I don't want to hear it!" He kept moving until he reached their bedroom. "I'm totally disgusted."

"Os—"

He slammed the bedroom door in her face.

At first, she reached for the doorknob, but then she thought better of it and pulled back.

What could she say to him now?

Downstairs in the kitchen, she wrung her hands as she stared at the refrigerator.

Food. Enemy number one. She'd love to have some potato salad or pasta salad, but she could no longer depend on food to comfort her. Her robe felt itchy and heavy. So did the air around her. She could kneel and pray, but when she stood up, she'd feel exactly the same-- sad and tense.

Above their refrigerator was an unused cabinet. Unused for the most part. No one had stored anything in it until last year. Mariah snatched a chair over, climbed up on it and opened it.

There stood the bottles of wine left from their Labor Day party the previous year. Her brother Troy had brought them. White wines. Red wines. She reached in and clutched the neck of a bottle of Merlot, pulled it out and clutched it to her flat chest.

In the kitchen watching Kamau Bell on CNN, she swallowed one glassful. Two. Three. Afterward, she felt heavy, but not checked out enough to forget to put everything away.

She didn't stumble her way back upstairs. Instead, she moved peacefully, her thoughts and worries settled. Oscar could have walked back downstairs at any time, have seen her drinking a bottle of wine and been upset, but at this point in their marriage, it seemed anything she did would upset him.

Granted, she shouldn't have lied to him, but now she had to live with it. The wine helped, at least for now. In bed, she sank into even darkness.

Smooth.

Quiet.

Controlled.

28

TOWANDA

The bowling night massacre, as Towanda considered it, drove her into exile for the remainder of June. But the Fourth of July arrived, which meant Binky's birthday, and Towanda couldn't skip an appearance in the Rodriguez's backyard. Benita Rodriguez had been born fifteen years earlier at eight in the morning.

Fifteen years. Where had the time gone?

Towanda stood in front of her bedroom closet, wrapped in a mint green bath sheet.

What to wear? Backyard barbecue. Hmm.

The boyfriend jeans of course, with the flat brown leather sandals she'd found online at Long Tall Sally. Oh, and that Boss Lady graphic tee she'd bought a week earlier at Lane Bryant.

Why should Mariah be the only one to spruce up her casual wardrobe? Towanda typically dressed with care only for work and church, but that didn't mean she had to slop around in sweats and leggings during her casual hours.

Shower. Dress.

She could wash and condition her hair, massage some mousse through it and then let her strands air dry. The curls would be wild, but it would give her a carefree look. And it was a great time to wear the silver bangles Binky had given her as a Christmas present the previous year. She pushed those up her arms and added diamond studs to her ears.

She added some light makeup and a little peach lip gloss. Then she stepped back and checked her reflection in the mirror.

Not bad at all.

With some extra time left before she needed to leave, she stopped inside her home office and checked on a few issues with her contractors. But before she ended her work session, she launched Facebook to view the Thick Chicks Clique page, just in case Mariah or Chablis decided to ask anything about it. At least she could say she'd checked out some posts, but she just hadn't made any.

"What in the world? Am I on the right page?" Towanda mumbled, scrolling down the words and images.

Women she didn't know were posting all kinds of empowerment links and success stories. She almost exited the page, but then she spied Mariah's posts of her feet on the scale, interspersed with all the other stuff.

This was the Thick Chicks Clique all right, but Mariah had opened the page to others, and people were posting their support for one another. This one lost five pounds. Another lost three. Still another posted a pic of herself in yoga class, doing her first downward dog. There was Chablis up in the mix, looking fitter with every snapshot.

And the further down Towanda scrolled, the worse she felt. Her mouth went dry and her heart actually knocked against her rib cage when she read posts from two women who showed pictures of themselves walking together with their mothers around Fairmount Park.

Everybody happy and doing their thing. And Mariah, putting thumbs up and hearts all over the place. A funny feeling snaked through Towanda's chest and held on for dear life.

"Unbelievable." Towanda squeezed her wireless mouse until the knuckles on her right hand turned white. "Who are these ladies, and how come Mariah didn't tell me about this?"

Towanda slammed her laptop closed and pushed the machine to the side. Time to go see her goddaughter. Why should she trip about a bunch of women with nothing better to do than tell the world about their activities?

She had better things to do.

MARIAH LOOKED *STUNNING*. TOWANDA NOTICED HER THE MOMENT SHE pushed open the side gate to the backyard. She stood on the redwood deck, leaning over and whispering something in Binky's ear. Her hair, skin, nails and everything else appeared as if she'd traveled back in time. She shimmered in a midnight blue, off-the-shoulder summer dress with gold-flecks scattered throughout the sheer fabric overlay. Her slim shoulders were on display. Like Towanda, her curls were popping, but Mariah's dark locks stretched and hung past her shoulders. And it looked as if Binky had struck again, priming and contouring her mother's makeup to perfection.

Towanda couldn't stop staring as she made her way down the wooden pathway leading to the deck.

"The birthday girl's godmother is here, everyone," Mariah announced as Towanda approached.

Binky bounded down the stairs and over to Towanda, wrapping her skinny arms around her waist. "Auntie! You made it."

"Of course, love bug." She kissed Binky's forehead, but her eyes stayed fixed on Mariah. "Wouldn't miss it for the world. Happy birthday, sweetie!"

"What'd you bring me?" Binky kissed her cheek.

"Um...er," Towanda mumbled, looking down to the ground.

"Auntie!"

Towanda brought her face up, laughing as she handed Binky the car keys. "It's in the back of my ride. Go get it."

"Yeah! Thank you, Auntie. You get me the best stuff," Binky said, taking off toward the backyard gate, three female members of her teen squad following her.

"And don't forget to lock it back up again," Towanda called out.

She approached the deck, staring down at her legs and feet as she walked. Jeans? Sandals? A t-shirt. She should have dressed better. After all, this was a special occasion. Here Mariah was all golden glamour mom while Towanda resembled the old spinster aunt. And she wasn't even that old.

Towanda, please put on a happy face. Smile. This is your friend. Heck, this is your family.

"Glad you made it!" Mariah's arms wrapped around her. Her hair and skin smelled like coconut and shea butter.

Towanda hugged her back. "I didn't know this was a red-carpet event."

"Yeah, well." Mariah straightened up. "Binky's friends are here, and more are coming. I think my daughter was more concerned with my look than she was with her own outfit."

"That's so you'll look good next to her in all the Instagram posts."

"Please don't remind me about social media stuff. I'm having a good day."

Oscar was tending the grill, spreading barbecue sauce over rows of ribs and chicken. Towanda called to him. "Hey, Os."

He turned and briefly made eye contact.

"Hey," was his weak response.

"The backyard looks great. Nice decorations."

"My wife," he said, turning back to the grill.

Okay? Not much conversation from Mr. Rodriguez. Towanda turned her gaze back to Mariah, who studied the side yard where a bunch of young people had sequestered themselves. Twenty teenagers sat staring at cellphones. Like Chinese terra-cotta soldiers, waiting for orders, but with less personality. They had each other to talk to. God only knew why they were more concerned with looking at their phone screens.

"You seeing what I'm seeing?" Mariah asked.

Towanda nodded. "Yeah."

"This is a party, right?"

"Yeah."

"Just checking."

As they chatted, Towanda peeked at the reddish-brown stretch marks running across Mariah's shoulders and down into her armpits. Guess the quick weight loss wasn't what it was cracked up to be, not that she would say that to Mariah.

"Where's the music coming from?" Towanda asked.

"The garage. I hired a DJ for the afternoon."

"Is that like smooth jazz or something?"

"We're trying to keep Binky from being so secular, so I asked the DJ to play something mild and summery. We figured it would be nice for a cookout."

"For who? A bunch of fifty-year-olds? Mariah, even I don't like this mess, and I'm grown." Towanda turned to view the scary, depressed teen corner and then turned back. "Binky's fifteen. It's her party. Play her music. Lighten up and she'll thank you later. Trust me."

"Come on," Mariah said.

The two of them marched across the yard, out the gate, and into the garage opening. The DJ stood behind his turntables, headphones on his ears, sunglasses perched on his nose, and about a foot of wild brown dreadlocks sprouting from the top of his scalp. He looked troubled as they approached. "How's the music for you, Ms. Mariah? Not too loud?"

"Jaquarius, this is my friend, Towanda." Mariah sighed. "She thinks we should change the music."

Towanda straightened to her full height, which had her staring down at the DJ by four inches. Time to give instructions.

"Jaquarius, is it? Listen, I'm the godmother. We need to get these kids off their phones. Here's the deal. I need you to play their music, and I know you know what their music is. We have parents and grandparents here, so we'd appreciate only the clean mixes. Run a cable into your phone if you have to find the clean versions online. I have a hundred-dollar bill for you as a bonus if you can coax the birthday girl and her friends to dance a few times."

His eyes lit up. "No problem. No problem at all."

"I'm sure you'll do a fantastic job. Counting on you. Thank you."

Towanda took Mariah's hand and pulled her out of the garage. "He's a professional," she said, reassuring her. "I told him what to do, how to do it, and how he'll be rewarded. Now we walk away and let him do his job. It'll be okay. You know the squeaky-clean versions of those songs have the cursing removed."

Within thirty-seconds, the sleep-inducing music stopped, and the air filled with the sounds of trap beats. Towanda noticed all the adults looked scared for a few moments, until they realized nary a curse or n-word was broadcast.

The teens woke up, leaving their chairs. When Binky returned to the backyard, she placed her pink-ribboned present on the gift table and all Towanda heard from the side yard was *aye, aye, aye.* Kids raised their arms in the air, their bodies moving to the beat.

Towanda smiled and winked. "Told ya."

But Mariah must not have been convinced. Either that, or something else had distracted her, because she only nodded, rubbing the skin on her exposed arms. Towanda watched her eyes. She stared at Oscar, who held the exact same position Towanda had seen him in when she arrived — silent, with his back to everyone as he minded the grill. Something must be going on between the two of them.

Towanda scanned the area. The teens still partied, and Binky appeared to be having the time of her life. Mariah and Oscar's family members sat at picnic tables eating food and playing card games. Kim Chase? Either she hadn't yet arrived or she hadn't been invited, since it was Binky's party.

Where was the food?

Probably set up on the buffet in the dining room to keep the flies away from it. Towanda and Mariah could grab some plates and sit in the house and talk. It had been a while since they'd done that. Towanda was here with her friend, the way things used to be.

"We're leaving." She planted an arm around Mariah's shoulders and steered her around toward the deck. "I didn't come all the way over here to starve. Let's eat something."

"I don't know. I don't want to disappear," Mariah protested.

Climbing the deck stairs, Towanda kept Mariah moving. "You aren't disappearing. You're going inside this house to let your daughter have a good time with her buddies. She's not six anymore."

"Tell me about it." Mariah snorted.

In the dining room, silver roasting pans held pounds of barbecued ribs, sausage, chicken, hot dogs and burgers. Ceramic bowls contained pasta salads, potato salad, chips and rolls. The side buffet held large decanters of pink lemonade, iced tea and silver bowls filled with every type of pink candy.

Towanda pointed at the candy bar before she grabbed a plate from the stack. "Since when do you and Os let Binky have this much candy?"

"Binky told us she had to have a candy bar at her party. Seems all the other girls are doing it at their parties."

Towanda plopped a scoop of potato salad onto her paper plate. "Some things never change, huh?"

"No, they don't."

Towanda glanced at Mariah, who stood with her arms at her sides near the edge of the dining room carpet. "Want me to make you a plate?"

"I'll have something later."

Towanda gripped her plate and frowned. "So, you're going to watch me eat all this, and you won't have anything? At all?"

"It's okay."

"It's not okay." Towanda's voice elevated. "I'm going to be eating alone, looking like a pig in front of you."

"T, listen..." Mariah shook her head, her curls dancing around her shoulders. "You're not a pig, and you know that. I can only have so much food in a day, that's all."

"And you can't have any of it around me?"

"I never said that."

"What're you saying, then?"

Towanda watched Mariah's eyes drift from the wall to the floor, to the window and then finally back up again.

Mariah sighed as she stepped to the dining room table and picked up a plate. "T, if it means that much to you, I'll eat with you."

They stopped talking then. Towanda hovered close to Mariah, watching her hands move from bowl to bowl. While Towanda's plate brimmed with a bit of everything, Mariah's held little in comparison. Three lettuce leaves. A tablespoon of tuna salad. A slice of cantaloupe.

"This is a celebration," Towanda pointed out. "You've come so far, and you look beautiful. Binky just finished her first year of high school.

Why can't you just enjoy yourself and eat. You don't do this every day."

Mariah turned her head toward her friend. Turned back. Then she reached over and added a Hawaiian roll and a slice of lemon cake to her plate before pouring herself a large cup of pink lemonade. "This is enough. Seriously."

Towanda shrugged. "You'll be fine. Let's sit out on the sun porch."

Inside the sunroom, they were Towanda and Mariah. Mariah and Towanda. Sitting side by side on loungers in the sun porch.

Joking. Laughing. Eating.

Just the two of them, and it was just like old times. Two peas in a pod. And the food was so delicious. So filling. So satisfying.

Towanda cracked joke after joke, making Mariah laughed out loud. She talked about their high school memories. She talked about their undergraduate years. They'd had so much fun then, and it felt like heaven to Towanda that they could simply sit and reminisce on the good old days. All of Towanda's food disappeared as they chatted.

At first, a quarter of Mariah's plate was empty. Then half. Then three quarters.

They joked and laughed and ate.

Then Mariah coughed a little. Then she coughed again, this time harder.

Towanda's eyes grew wide and she clutched the sides of her chair as she saw beads of sweat appear atop the glowing makeup on Mariah's forehead. Mariah bolted to her feet and her nearly empty plate hit the floor, food splattering on the wood. Her eyes bulged as she staggered and held her abdomen.

Towanda kept staring, not moving from her seat.

Mariah would be okay. Right? She'd be fine. Of course. She'd stop coughing and sit back down and be fine and healthy and beautiful just like always.

Because too much was never enough.

29

MARIAH

Something was wrong.

The area right under Mariah's rib cage had caught fire, and the pain made her cough hard, while everything beneath her throat shifted into reverse. Nausea arrived in waves as awful abdominal cramps hit her midsection. She'd shot up from her chair, her plate crashing to the floor.

Sweating and dizzy, she coughed hard and tried to get ahold of herself, but the nausea and cramps grew worse. She bent over and vomited, heaving beside the potted snake plant.

Afterward, she felt a little better, but then her stomach twisted in a knot and she threw up again, partially digested food forcing its way out of her throat and landing by her feet. Her palms were wet with sweat as she gasped and gulped in air. Even fresh oxygen didn't stop the sickening, searing feeling spreading across her midsection.

By the time she righted herself and turned around, Towanda had vanished.

My daughter can't see me like this.

Mariah stumbled and lurched from the sun porch, her heart beating like mad.

Where had T gone?

Had she run to get Oscar or to call an ambulance?

Mariah gulped and gasped and coughed. She should get to a bathroom.

Yes. She had to scramble upstairs, away from the noise and the music and the party. Crazy, lazy, trap beats thump, thump, thumped in her ears as she positioned one foot in front of the other.

Hand over her mouth, she moved past the kitchen. *Praise God.* The hallway. *Thank you, Lord.* The staircase. *Bless you, Father.*

In the bathroom, she collapsed onto the white tile. Her whole midsection burned, so who cared that her silky dress was messed up for good.

Good. Yes. Breathing. Good.

Cold tile pressed against her naked shoulders. Everything in her belly was about to explode, and pressure kept building. All the garments under her dress? Could she pull them off? What if she couldn't? She tugged beneath her outfit and winced, feeling the seams of her undergarments rip.

Somebody help me, please.

Her abdomen bubbled and churned. She was going to throw up again.

Pain and fire signaled more than just sickness.

They signaled hell!

T, get someone to help me! Os? Binky? Someone!

Anyone?

PLEASE!

30

CHABLIS

I don't know what I'm seeing.

Inside Mariah's house, there's a crowd in the foyer. A group of young people, some I know and some strangers, standing near the bottom of the staircase, shaking their heads. A few of the girls have their hands over their mouths. Bruno Mars sings in the background as I drop my purse on a side table and jog toward them. I know Mark from Rise and I walk over and tap his shoulder.

"What happened? What's going on?" I holler over the music.

Mark points up the staircase. "Binky's mom. She got sick or something. Bink and her dad ran upstairs and—"

I stop listening and run up those steps, smashing quite a few toes in the process. My heart beats in my ears.

I can tell how dangerous the situation is by the type of people I run into when I reach the second-floor landing. Mariah's brother, my cousin Troy, pleads with people on the staircase, trying to get them to back down and move. He has his arm around Mariah's sister Tamron, whose face is a mix of fright and anger. Aunt Joan stands further down the hall. Her hands cover her mouth, and she looks as if she wants to scream. Uncle Fred holds her, whispering in her ear.

Binky stands right outside the bathroom with tears flowing down her cheeks, making a mess of the colors on her face. She moans, "Mom, Mom, Mom!"

As soon as I reach her, I grab her and hold on, pressing her head into my shoulder. The sound of an ambulance siren fills my ears as I keep squeezing my little cousin.

God gives me the strength to move three inches to my right.

Two more inches.

One more.

I direct my eyes into that bathroom, and as soon as I do, I can't seem to hear anything. All sounds stop for me.

Yellow-orange afternoon sunlight floods the all-white room. Oscar sits on the floor. His face is red, his wavy black hair has fallen into his face and his lips are moving. I squint, staring at his mouth.

What's he saying?

He waves his hand in the air, then points at me.

What? I can't move. I'm sorry. I can only see. And smell. There's a horrible odor in the air. A soiled black girdle lays crumpled beside the toilet and Mariah's body is in front of it. Her dress is up, her thighs are exposed, and rippled, dimpled skin with angry stretch marks streak down to her knees.

She's silent. She looks peaceful. She's reclined on the tile in a pretty, satiny, navy blue dress. Her head rests in Oscar's lap. Vomit covers the front of her dress. Even her hands, which lie on top of her belly, are a mess.

Is she breathing? If she isn't, I'm going to stop, too.

I mean it. I'm done.

I want to cry, even though I still don't know what the heck I'm seeing. I grasp Binky's shoulders so hard I can feel her shuddering. She sheds the tears I can't produce.

And what happened? What happened? What happened?

Then I hear a gasp.

A cough.

Another gasp.

A small moan.

A rush of adrenaline hits me. Technicolor and sounds in stereo all come back to me in full force.

Mariah clutches her belly hard and her bloodshot eyes open. I can tell she's cramping, and the pain has got her good. Oscar's still cradling her head. She's groaning, and he's pointing at me like *get everyone out of here.*

So, I push Binky off me and yell, "Get it together!"

Because her mother's sick. She isn't dead.

But if those EMTs don't move faster up the stairs right now, maybe she could be soon.

"Go to your mom's room and grab her robe. Now!"

"But my Mooooom—" Binky wails.

"Right now!" I smack her cheek—not too hard, but hard, and she touches her face and then runs to do what I told her. I whip around, search the hallway, and see Troy, who uses his body to push everyone out of the way.

I have enough sense to back out of the way and let the EMTs reach the bathroom. Binky's a blur as she passes me on the way back to the bathroom with a robe to cover her mother's exposed body. I sink onto the carpet just inside the door to Binky's messy bedroom.

The music dies as I sit and calm myself. The house becomes lighter and lighter. People retreat as the EMTs load Mariah onto a stretcher and carry her out of the bathroom. They head down the stairs and out of the house. I watch Oscar's feet as he hustles to their bedroom, grabs something and then rushes out again.

I should go. I'm family. But I need to sit here on the carpet until my body stops shaking.

I finally close my eyes when I hear the ambulance roll away from the house.

I don't need to see anything else.

And I don't need my eyesight to show me who's not here.

AT THE HOSPITAL, THE EMERGENCY ROOM IS OVERCROWDED, BUT THAT doesn't matter because Mariah gets rushed right to an examination area. The doctors try to keep everyone out, but my family is pushy, so we stay close by.

I stand by the white curtain, my eyes affixed to Mariah's chest, which is thankfully going up and down. She's alert, with an oxygen tube in her nose and a pulse thingy on her fingertip while medical staff checks her vitals.

Oscar asks the questions. The white-haired doctor states the facts. After a sudden intake of rich food, her body couldn't handle the amount of insulin that had flooded her system and it started dumping.

This is some weird stuff that can happen to people who've had bariatric surgery. Right away, her guts pushed out the undigested food. Stomach pain and anxiety may have overwhelmed her, because she fainted, and that's when Oscar found her on the bathroom floor.

Long story short, the doc tells us she'll be fine. She'll stay in the hospital overnight for observation but will be free to go tomorrow.

Joy fills me, but that's before rage takes over. I start chewing the inside of my cheek until I taste blood. Both my fists are balled up when I turn to talk to Oscar.

"Oscar?"

Weariness colors his face. "Yeah."

"How'd you find out she was in trouble?"

He wipes sweat from his forehead. "I was outside at the grill when Towanda ran out and—"

Towanda!

"Thank you," I say to Oscar right before I turn and walk back out through the curtain. I'm not quite running in the ER, but I'm rushing fast. I know she's here somewhere. The soles of my sandals slap against the linoleum as I turn the corner to the waiting area.

I don't even have to look that hard. All six feet of her sits in the corner, perched at the edge of a gray chair. Her eyes open wide as I run up to her and stop right before barreling into her knees. Her face flushed, she jumps up, pushes me aside and storms toward the glass doors.

I follow her fast and when I reach the sidewalk, I yell her name.

"Towanda!"

She stops and turns around, staring at me.

"What happened, T?"

"To Mariah?"

"Who else would I be talking about?" I try to slow down my words because they're tumbling out of my mouth fast. "Why were you hiding?"

Towanda resembles a tree, swaying back and forth, wringing her hands in front of her. She may be a mighty oak, and I might be a sycamore, but I will take her down if she doesn't start explaining soon.

She stammers. "We...we were eating together. On the sun porch. We were laughing. Just eating and laughing."

"Then what?"

"I don't know. She...uh...she started coughing, then she stood up and coughed harder. She dropped her plate of food on the floor, and she was sick. I thought she'd be okay."

"The woman was having severe abdominal issues. She can't eat like that anymore!"

"I realize that now."

"Well, did you try to help her?"

Something passes behind Towanda's eyes that I can't quite describe. I push my hands to my hips and force them not to move.

"Did. You. Help. Her?"

Towanda shakes her head as she studies the gray pavement beneath her feet. She takes off her glasses and tears fall from her face to the ground. I want to feel for her, but I don't.

And Mariah is her *best friend*?

I should leave. I should stop asking questions and turn around and go.

But I can't.

"Look at me!" I say.

When Towanda turns her face up, she's beet red, her skin slicked with wetness. Her shoulders shake.

"Did you want her to eat all that food?"

"It all happened so fast. At first, she was fine. But I swear, as soon as she threw up, I ran outside to get Oscar."

"But why?"

"What?"

"Why'd you let her—"

"Because I wanted the old Mariah back, okay? I wanted her to eat with me and have fun like we used to, and life could go back to how it was before she had the surgery. I didn't want her to get sick. I just wanted the old Mariah back," Towanda mumbles. "The new one? She's changing so much. She's making new friends...planning a business...doing new things."

"So what? You think she's going leave you behind or something?"

"I don't know." She shrugs. "Why couldn't she stay the same?"

My hands are still planted on my hips and I stand stock still. Whatever's going on inside Towanda's head — it's ugly. Makes me want to yell. So I open my mouth and let rip.

"Are you serious? Normal people try to change for the better. Instead of watching my cousin, you need to do better for yourself. Change your hair. Change your makeup. Do something! Hate being alone so much? Serve in ministry. Get a husband. Make your own family. Get a life, lady! But don't you dare sabotage somebody who's just trying to move forward and be happy!"

I'm done. I push past weeping willow Towanda and head to the parking garage to get in my Focus and drive home.

AT MY APARTMENT, I STEP IN MY FRONT DOOR AND LOOK AROUND MY small and cluttered area. It's nothing like Towanda's interior designed, Center City condo, but I don't envy her one little bit.

I collapse on my couch and stare at the ceiling as I pray out loud.

"Father in heaven, thank you for sparing my cousin. And Lord, I thank you for all that I have and everything you've allowed me to be. My body might not be perfect, but it's strong and healthy, and I move well. I'm grateful for absolutely everything in my life. Help me to use all that I am to glorify you. In Jesus' name, Amen."

When I stop praying, I sit up, just thinking.

Yeah, I yelled at Towanda, but she's not the only one who needs to make some changes. I gained back seven pounds last month stress eating and letting emotions get the best of me.

But I'll lose them again. So, I'm freaked out at the idea of going to

LA Fitness in the mornings. I'll visit in the evening after work. Who cares that the gym will be crowded then? It's not too much for me to wait for equipment while I play "Take Me to the Mardi Gras" through my Beats.

Mariah's alive.

So am I, and I gotta do my best and let the Lord do the rest.

31

MARIAH

Towanda.

Mariah watched her walk through the door on the far side of the atrium. Curly brown hair. Black Calvin Klein suit. Wire-rimmed glasses. She moved through the area with a relaxed confidence.

The nerve.

With all the pain she'd caused the week before, the fact that she even showed up in church this Sunday proved she must be crazy, prideful or both. Who knew what she was trying to do by attending worship service, on time, dressed immaculately and heading straight toward the Rodriguez family.

Uh-uh. Not today.

Mariah tapped Oscar on the shoulder. "You and Binky go into the sanctuary without me. I need to stay here for a minute."

"Are you all right? Your stomach bothering you again?"

"No, I'm feeling fine."

"You sure?"

"Yes. Can you follow Binky, please? I want her to sit with us during the service."

"Okay."

"Thanks."

After watching Oscar plant an arm around Binky's shoulder and guide her through the sanctuary doors, Mariah tucked her purse under her arm, turned around and headed straight toward Towanda. She stopped right in front of her.

Towanda met her gaze. "Mariah, I—"

"No. No way. Uh-uh."

"No, what?"

Mariah shook her head. "No! There's no excuse for what you…I don't care how many times you called or texted. How dare you!"

Towanda's cheeks flushed red. "Can we talk about this quietly, please?"

"No," Mariah said. "What do you think you're doing? I know you're bold, but I didn't think you'd have the audacity to come up in here today."

"Can I explain—"

"Explain what, T? I could have died. Died. In my house. With my family! What's wrong with you?"

"Nothing."

From the looks on people's faces as they passed by, they could hear their argument. This wasn't the best place for Mariah to have a confrontation, but heat and fury had welled up inside of her when she saw Towanda stroll in all confident and self-assured.

Mariah clutched her abdomen as the memory of the embarrassment, pain and mess surged through her. "I know you have issues and you can be downright nasty to people. But why would you let me get sick and leave me? What did I do? All I've ever done is to be your friend."

"I'm still your friend."

"Don't talk to me like I'm an idiot. Friends don't act that way! You evil, scandalous heifer—"

Out of nowhere, Chablis rushed over to them. She grabbed Mariah's hand and held it tight, whispering, "Ladies, I know what this is about, but please, don't do this here."

Towanda stepped even closer. "Mariah, I didn't mean to hurt you. Please believe me."

Her head throbbing, Mariah closed her eyes and clasped her cousin's hand tighter, silently counting to five. No matter how she felt, she couldn't lose it and let her rage spill out right here at church. If it did, security would have to call the police, but that would be after they pried her fingers from around Towanda's throat.

Ten seconds of calm gave way to a minute of quiet before Mariah spoke again. "I don't care what you meant. I don't care anymore about one single thing you do. You stay the heck away from me and my family."

Towanda's face fell. "You don't mean that."

"Oh yeah, I do," Mariah said. "And, when I open my eyes, I don't want to see you in front of me."

"You're my—"

"I'm not anything to you anymore. I'm nothing."

Slowly and silently, Mariah counted again, this time to twenty, still holding Chablis' hand. Chablis rubbed Mariah's back until she opened her eyes again. When she did, she found herself staring at the empty spot on the floor where Towanda used to be.

"She's gone now," Chablis said, releasing Mariah's hand. "And I'm not even going to ask if you're okay because I know you're not. If you want to pray, we can go into the room over there."

"Maybe later."

"Think you'll talk to her again? You know, after you give it some time?"

"Chablis?"

"Yeah."

"It would take a miracle."

PART III

FALL/WINTER/SPRING

32

CHABLIS

P*ray. Run. Lift.*
    That has been my mantra every afternoon, every single day
    since mid-July. The extra seven pounds I gained in June said
bye-bye and they took ten more pounds with them. Oh yes—I crushed
the weight loss plateau I got stuck on in May. And I still have my
curves, they're just more controlled now.

Of all the work I've done this year, July and August meant the most
to me. I went to the gym on my own, I worked hard and I disciplined
myself away from eating comfort foods.

Yay me!

Dr. Houtman will be so proud of me. It's September, and I'm in her
office for my yearly physical. She grins at me when she enters the
examination room.

"Hey, Chablis."

I smile back. "Hey, Dr. Houtman."

She checks my ears, nose, and throat. Once she's done, she listens
to my heart and lungs. After that, she stands back and stares me up
and down. "What on earth have you been doing?"

I flutter my eyelashes, acting like I don't know what she's talking
about. "Come again?"

"My dear, you've been a little dynamo. You're down fifty pounds since last year. Your blood pressure was in the normal range when you checked in here in January and again in July and it's looking amazing today. You definitely don't need medication anymore."

If I could sprout wings, I'd fly up straight up through the ceiling. My blood pressure is normal.

Normal.

Dr. Houtman sits down on her stool and logs into her computer. She scans the screen. "Fasting blood sugar's good. Cholesterol's excellent. I don't have much to say to you today. Whatever you're doing, keep on doing it."

"I will. I still have more weight to lose."

"Maybe, maybe not. I always say, if all your internal numbers look good and remain good I could care less what you weigh. Oh, but there is one more thing."

I open my eyes wide. "What's that?"

She swivels around. "Get your flu shot and get out of my office. You're taking away time from my other patients."

AT MY JOB, THE COMPUTER SCREEN LULLS ME UNTIL I'M NODDING. IT'S Thursday, and my workday is almost over. I'm dreading my evening because I have nothing to do and no one to see.

My options for fun and fellowship are slim to none.

There are a few reasons for that.

Labor Day was last week. Other than catching a glimpse of Towanda in the balcony at Rise from time-to-time, Mariah and I haven't seen her. And I refuse to call or text her.

Mariah isn't the best company right now. Physically, she's fine. She's ninety-five pounds lighter. She seems depressed, though, and I've seen her with a wine glass in her hand several times. Now, I know Christians who drink and Christians who don't, but I don't think she needs a lecture from me. I understand.

I'd be sad too if my BFF ditched me when I got sick.

She told me there's some stuff happening between her and Oscar and it scares her, so I just listen to her and pray with her. I've also asked her to come to LA Fitness with me in the evenings. She says she'll text me about it but she never does.

Some of my boredom is my own doing. To avoid food binges, I had to stop meeting my friends for dinner, fellowships and other celebrations. Last month I skipped going to an engagement party and two baby showers. No Sunday brunches at IHOP. No visiting new restaurants with Nikki and Felicia on Fridays.

Nothing.

But I hate sitting at home alone. Most nights, I spend too much time scrolling through John's Instagram pictures and videos. We keep in touch, and he emails me every week to encourage me. I send him verse images I made in the Bible app, and of course, cool picture quotes I find on Pinterest. We've also had a handful of lengthy phone calls, and those were some truly dope conversations.

The last time I talked to him, he asked me, "What was it like when you gave your heart to the Lord? I want you to give me the full monologue. Go."

And I closed my eyes and talked about salvation and God, and all kinds of spiritual stuff, and he never interrupted, he just listened. Then I asked him the same thing and he spoke even longer than me, telling me how he considers God his permanent father ever since his father passed away, and he's committed to serving the Lord with his mind, body, and spirit. I loved hearing the rhythm and emotion in his words. When he stopped, I opened my eyes, looked at the clock, and saw it was almost two in the morning. We ended the call, but somehow, I heard his baritone voice for the rest of the day.

But I try not to think about how all that makes me feel, because John lives in Berlin, he likes his work team and he's enjoying himself, if his Instagram story tells the truth. What God has for him is for him, and what He has for me is for me.

Some days I wonder exactly what that is.

Yeah. That's enough of that. I push my chair away from my desk and bow my head and pray silently.

Heavenly Father, I trust You to provide for me, because only You know what I truly need. Lord, open my eyes to healthy opportunities. I trust You now and always. In Jesus' name I pray. Amen.

Time to stop letting my brain swim around in la-la land. I have about an hour before I leave the office. Let me go grab some black coffee. I can walk down to the first-floor break room to get some extra steps in.

I'm yawning while placing a pod of Hazelnut in the Keurig machine when someone taps me on the shoulder. My mouth is still open wide when I turn and see Anna Taylor grinning at me.

"You're going to catch flies in there," she tells me.

Anna works in IT, is witty and sharp, and we have marathon conversations whenever I run into her in the building. I hold my Styrofoam cup steady under the running flow of coffee.

"I work in test. Test, Anna. It's a miracle I'm not asleep in my cubicle right now."

"You came down here expecting excitement?"

"No, but you all have the Keurig machine."

"Your team has coffee upstairs."

"Moses was a boy when they bought that decrepit Mr. Coffee." I pick up my cup of hot java and dump one Splenda packet into it. "I'm bored."

"You look it."

"Funny." I take a sip of coffee. "Why are you so happy?"

"This is my night for line dance."

I make a face. Who in the world could be excited about line dance? It's *line dance*. A bunch of middle-agers and senior citizens stepping through the *Electric Slide* and the *Cupid Shuffle* and think they're doing something cool. "So, you're visiting an old folks' home?"

"No. This class is nothing like an old folks' home." She reaches out to make her own cup of French Vanilla. "Our class has teens, college students, people of all ages. It's fun. You should come check it out. It's five dollars and you don't have to register."

I swallow more coffee.

Line dance?

It's dancing the cha-cha. *In lines.* Like at a wedding. But it might be better than sitting home watching TV.

Uh-oh. Anna is staring at me. I should say something.

"What's the name of the dance place?" I ask.

"The Grandstand. Me and my husband like to get there early. We'll save you a seat at our table. You won't sit much, though."

"Your husband line dances?"

"Umm-hmm. Sometimes he teaches."

"There's not a bunch of junk food there?"

"Not unless you bring some with you."

I have nothing to lose, so I nod and tell Anna I'll be there. She gives me the address. Thankfully, it's in Philly, right off of 48th Street. Now I have someplace to go tonight, and I can move my body. Maybe I'll meet more people to talk with, and if I don't like it, I won't go again.

I AM CARRYING VITAMIN WATERS.

How'd I get them? I had positioned my Focus two spots away from Anna and her husband Derrick in The Grandstand lot. They had just parked when Derrick swung his long legs out of their Durango, pointed right at me and asked me to help carry stuff into the building. I obliged, but I didn't know he was going to load my arms with two six-packs of Vitamin Water.

Anna doesn't carry anything. Instead, she holds the door open for us. I'm surprised to see her pay my class fee to a pretty brown-skinned lady with long red braids who sits behind a table with a cash box and clipboard. She points a red fingernail toward the clipboard and hands me a pen.

"First timer? Write your contact information here."

I must have looked at her with a question in my eyes because then she says, "We like to keep a mailing list for our special events."

Special events? This is line dance. I'm here to hang out and keep from calling Pizza Hut tonight. But I keep that comment to myself and scribble down my info. She tells us to have a good time, and when I turn around, Anna is waving me over.

I pick up the bottles I'd set down on the table and then we follow Derrick down a narrow hallway. The bass in the music makes the floors vibrate. Derrick pushes through a set of wooden doors and I find myself standing at the edge of a dance floor.

And there's a party going on right here.

I'm barely listening to Anna as she guides me to a table where two women are sitting. She introduces me and I nod my hello. I'm a little rude, I know, but I'm trying to understand where I am. There are a lot of people here. Men and women. Some folks who look to be my age. I even see three kids. There are a few older ladies and gentlemen on the floor, but they don't seem all that elderly because they are moving fast.

Real fast.

I don't know what the dance is, but it doesn't even remotely resemble the *Electric Slide*. Derrick pulls the drinks out of my arms and places them on the table.

"Derrick," I nod toward the middle of the dance floor. "What's that?"

The music is loud. He leans down to my ear. "*Running Man*. It's a Philly classic."

"They look like they already know it."

"They do. They're just dancing. Sometimes we make requests to the DJ before class starts." He scans my face. "You good?"

"I thought the whole night would be the *Cha-Cha Slide*."

Derrick chuckles, adjusting the baseball cap on his head. "You won't see that unless you request it. You want to dance it? I can tell the DJ."

I roll my eyes. "Uh, no."

"Have a seat and relax. Lessons start in a minute."

I'm in the middle of a conversation with Anna when the music changes and a group of people move out to the dance floor and start dancing to Raheem DeVaughn. They all wear matching black t-shirts and warm-up pants that spell out GRANDSTAND in glittery letters. When the music stops, a raspy female voice comes over the micro-phone, saying, "The name of this dance is *AB2*. Come on, we're going to learn this."

Folks get up to find a spot on the floor. It's crowded and there are people everywhere. I love it. I try to blend into the back, but that's not happening because I can't see over a couple of the big guys who tower over me on the floor. So, I drift toward the front and stay there as the teacher points out each step. Before I know it, twenty minutes have passed. I hear her say, "Let's lock it in."

The music starts, I remember the steps and I'm dancing. I make a few mistakes, but a man next to me in a blue t-shirt calls out the steps for me and I correct my feet and keep moving.

Time flies as we learn three more dances — *Sumthin Simple, Flashin'* and *Cruise Control*. The last two were hard for me, but I love a challenge and it feels so good to move my body.

When lessons are over, the DJ cranks up the music and someone dims the lights. People flood the dance floor and, in my opinion, start showing off. Men dancing up front put extra spins on their moves. Couples off to the side hand dance to the music. Ladies in the middle joke and laugh with their friends as they dance. I bow out to go to the restroom, and when I come back, I hear Jay-Z and see folks doing a dance with fast turns. Then they make a move that looks like they're throwing dice. I run across the room to Anna.

"What's this dance?" I ask her.

"It's called *It's Easy Tho.*"

"Looks hard, though."

"Nah. Our teacher tonight. Jamie? She can teach you that one if you ask."

"Who are the people in the black outfits? The ones in the front?"

"The Grandstand dancers. They're like a volunteer team for this place. Most of 'em are line dance teachers or assistants. I know they performed at Unity Day and Odunde, and half-time at a few Sixers games. They teach free line dance classes at community centers, host back-to-school drives, organize holiday food donations, stuff like that."

"How do you sign up for that?"

"You don't. Joining is kind of secretive."

"Come on. There has to be an application or some sort of process."

"Rumor has it, after they get to know you, if you dance well and you're helpful, the board will mail you an invitation to join." Anna puts her arm around my shoulder. "Thinking of coming back?"

I survey the crowd. Happy people dancing. Beats making the wood vibrate. I've been at The Grandstand for two whole hours and not once did I think about my lack of a promotion, John in Berlin or that mess between Towanda and Mariah. I also didn't take out my phone to check Instagram stories or open Snapchat.

Line dance isn't prayer meeting or Bible study, but I have a funny feeling I need this in my life, if for no other reason than to have a good time.

"Oh, I'll be here early," I say. "And I'll save you and Derrick some seats."

33

MARIAH

The heat and stress of summer hung around a lot longer than Mariah wanted. Hot and heavy days with too many minutes to use. Indoors, the aging central air conditioning kept breaking down. Outdoors, the lawn sprouted crabgrass here, there and everywhere. The grass always needed cutting, and the weeds still needed whacking. And with Oscar spending less and less time at home, Mariah took it upon herself to do the yard work. The extra work kept her mind and body occupied.

She was pulling the electric lawnmower from the garage to the backyard when Oscar surprised her by walking onto the deck. It was early, 6:00 a.m. on Saturday morning. She hadn't asked him to help, but he still stalked down the deck stairs and approached her.

"Why didn't you wake me up?" He asked. "I should be doing this."

Sure, she could have woken him up. Maybe handed him a cup of coffee and pointed out the long-overdue yard work. But she wouldn't. If he couldn't see all the work that needed to be done, why should she lecture him about it? And it was too late to point out that his indifference to her had extended to everything in their home.

She unspooled the orange cord from the top of the lawnmower. "You're here now. If you want to join me, go get the trimmer."

Oscar walked to the garage, his body clad in an old white t-shirt, gray sweatpants and dirty tennis shoes. Mariah watched him as he moved. His habits, conversations and interactions all appeared stiff to her.

"Hey, there are empty wine bottles in the old green tote in here," Oscar called as he returned to the yard. "You know about these?"

Mariah dropped her gaze downward and tightened her grip on the mower handle.

Empty wine bottles in an old plastic container in the far, dark corner of the garage?

Of course, she knew about them. They had become part of her routine.

She bought wine during the day while she did errands. She drank each night while Oscar was either out or downstairs watching TV. She stashed empty bottles in the garage in the morning. Somewhere along the line, she'd intended to place them in her car and drive them to a recycling station but she'd never gotten around to it.

Oscar walked closer, an empty bottle of Riesling resting in his hand. "I want an answer, Mariah," he said.

She started to cross her arms over her flat chest, but then she let them dangle. "I drank the wine. Me. Is that what you want me to say?"

"There are at least three dozen bottles in there."

"I know."

"You drank those by yourself?"

"Yes."

She watched Oscar, who, for some reason looked as if he was moving in slow motion. He returned to the deck stairs, and when he reached the third step, he clutched the rails, then sank down into a sitting position. He stared at her with fire in his eyes.

"So, you're a drunk now?"

"No." She glanced away, then met his eyes again. "No, I'm not."

Mariah knew her husband. He would not drop this or go away. The conversation would not die down. The proof rested in his hands.

Okay, she'd been drinking quite a bit since the beginning of the summer. But she could stop just as quickly as she started. And she didn't drink to get drunk or to party.

She drank to avoid thinking about food or the possibility of gaining weight again. She drank to halt the wheels in her mind from grinding on the lie she'd told him and the fact that he'd been distant ever since he'd found out. She drank to stop hating Towanda, or at least stop wondering what had turned her best friend so sour she was willing to let her suffer.

Unlike food or even prayer, alcohol slid down her throat and acted as an automatic shut-off valve to her nagging thoughts. It reached inside her brain and told everything and everyone to *shut up.*

"What do you call this, Mariah?" Oscar shouted, shaking the empty wine bottle and throwing it to the ground. It bounced once on the grass, then rolled beneath the rose bushes. He opened his mouth, maybe to yell something else, but then his neck and face turned crimson and his lip started quivering.

Mariah rushed to the bottom of the stairs and opened her arms to him, but he swatted her hands away.

"No! You can't control yourself. You never could. You switched from one thing to another, just like that!"

"I can control myself," she said, wiping sweat from her brow.

"No, you can't. I've stayed here and tried to think things were going to get better. This year, I thought we had a real chance."

"We do."

"Really? Will you go look in that garage? You actually think that's a blessing for us?"

Her heart throbbed hard beneath her rib cage. "That's not fair."

"It's the truth." He wiped his face with his t-shirt. "I told you, *take better care of yourself, Mariah. The weight is causing you problems, Mariah.* Then you get so big you have to get an operation. Now you can't eat, but drinking is the new thing?"

"I don't have a problem with—"

"Why should I listen to you? You spent a decade tuning me out."

Mariah pressed her fists against her lips.

Nothing she said would help the situation. Her husband hated everything that entered or exited her mouth.

She glanced around their yard. Overgrown grass, withering bushes and dandelions appeared where the lovely landscaping used to be.

And here she stood with her body slimmed down and covered in new clothing, and still Oscar wasn't satisfied.

His shoulders shook, he cried so hard. She could reach out to him again, but what for?

So he could shoo her away and yell at her? Call her lazy? Give her the cold shoulder for trying to avoid another pregnancy that could destroy her body again? Make another demand?

A chill ran through her as she stepped backward, away from the deck.

Maybe she'd had enough of trying to be better for other people. When could she ever feel comfortable being herself?

"Os," she said softly. "You hated the weight, and now you hate that I drink. Why don't you say it? You hate me."

"This is not you!"

"What if it is? What then? Last year I changed for you and Binky, and I did reverse my diabetes. So I didn't do every single thing you wanted me to do over the years, but I did change. And right now, I like my wine. I like it. Maybe I can find a way to slow down, but I can't do it for you. I'm tired."

Tears dripped from the bottom of Oscar's dark mustache. "You're tired?"

"I'm tired." Her own tears ran down her face and soaked the top of her t-shirt. "I don't know if I have anything left."

He stood then, towering over her from the stairs. "I don't know if I have anything left, either."

A second hung in the air and got caught between the two of them. No one claimed it. Mariah stood still as Oscar turned around and walked up two steps, crossed the deck and opened the back door. He let it slam shut.

She counted to ten before she headed to the garage where the green storage tote sat with the top off. A full container of discarded glass bottles. She would have to pull it to the curb on recycling day.

She had no more use for anything empty.

Period.

34

TOWANDA

"Jerome, I need your work for the Mrs. Brown's Body account right now. You've been overdue for two weeks," Towanda said as she rubbed her temples.

Jerome's sadness and desperation came through in his voice over the speakerphone. "I know. I may need more time. My mother's back in the hospital and it's not looking good."

"I'm truly sorry about your mother, but I'm running a business here. Without your input, our client won't receive the top shelf attention we promised."

"I apologize for that, but clients and jobs will always exist. I only have one mother, and I don't want to leave her side. I'm sorry."

"I'm sorry too. I'll give you until tomorrow to provide your work for the account. If you don't, we'll have to discuss your employment with thinkLARGE. You have a good day."

She pressed the button to end the call. She hadn't wanted to be nasty, but she had their client to consider. If thinkLARGE didn't provide a successful strategy for Mrs. Brown's Body, their company's reputation would be in jeopardy. If she needed to hire another social media strategist, then that's what she would do. She could start looking on LinkedIn and ZipRecruiter today. The show must go on.

Someone knocked on her office door and then opened it. It was Jackie.

"Did you hear me tell you to come in?" Towanda swiveled around.

Jackie sat in the chair opposite Towanda's desk. "I overheard you on the phone with Jerome."

Stupid thin walls. "Yes, and..."

"It's his mother, Towanda. His mother. She's sick."

"I know that, but I have a business to run. A business which pays all of us. Not just Jerome, but you and me and all the thinkLARGE employees and contractors."

"I understand that, but I have to say, I've never seen you like this."

"Like what?"

"Too cold for words. You know, you've been like this since the summer, but we all figured you'd return to normal at some point. Now you're talking about letting Jerome go? Towanda...no..."

So, Towanda wasn't at her best. Ever since July, she'd been troubled. But what could she do about it?

She must have called Mariah at least a hundred times. She'd written her emails. Sent cards and flowers. She even tried to set up a visit through Chablis, but Miss Sunshine and Rainbows refused to help. Chablis flat out told Towanda to leave Mariah alone.

By the Tuesday after Labor Day weekend, it had dawned on Towanda. She'd lost more than her best friend. She'd lost family. No more backyard holiday cookouts sitting amongst Mariah and Oscar and their relatives. No surprise afternoon shopping sprees with Binky. No teasing Chablis about the length of her hair weaves.

All of it. Gone.

"Are you all right?" Jackie asked.

Towanda's eyes blurred with wetness. "No."

Jackie stood up. "I'm blocking your calendar out for the rest of the day. I'll reschedule the afternoon meeting with Mrs. Brown. Take a moment away, please."

"Wait a minute, do I work for you?"

"I run your calendar, and I run the office. So yes, you do," Jackie said before shutting the door.

All morning, Towanda had been trying to get work done. What had she been doing before Jerome called?

Typing an e-mail message. Yes. She'd been typing an email. To whom? For what? Who was she attempting to contact? Or had she been sending a contract through DocuSign for a signature?

That was it. A contract.

For which business? She couldn't recall.

Towanda pushed herself away from her desk and took a few deep breaths. She felt strange, as if she needed more air than the room provided. Jackie had told her to leave, so she would go. She packed her laptop, files and phone inside her bag. She could get work done later after she took a long break.

Outside the thinkLARGE office, the walk down the hall to the elevator seemed to take forever. On the elevator, ten seconds. Twenty seconds. Thirty seconds. Ground floor. The doors opened and she placed one foot in front of the other until she was out of the double doors and onto the sidewalk. Pure warm sunshine bathed her face. She breathed in deep and kept walking.

But oxygen couldn't remove the pain deep in her soul. She'd hurt her best friend. Her sister. And they were past the point of no return.

At the corner of the block, she stumbled forward, almost tripping off the curb. A man in a white Nissan Rogue had his windows down.

He called out, "You okay?"

She caught herself and gave him a short nod. He drove away.

Of course, she wasn't okay, because there was no turning back.

Get a life, lady!

Chablis' words from outside the hospital filtered into Towanda's mind.

Get a life.

Was a career a life? Were awards a life? Degrees? Did church attendance equate to a life? What about her body? How did that affect her life?

Change your hair. Change your makeup. DO SOMETHING!

Towanda was no dummy. Of course, she knew she could do more to spruce up her appearance if she wanted. She didn't have to be so obsessed with Mariah's beauty after she dropped all that weight.

Don't you dare sabotage someone because of what they're doing to move on and be happy.

Towanda didn't hate Mariah, and she shouldn't have pushed her to eat like that.

But what now?

In the past, no matter how terrible any of her life events, Towanda had lived by one motto — move on. She'd have to do that now, as well. She would have to discover a way to fall forward and live her best life.

She stopped walking and looked back. In no time, she'd walked three city blocks and found herself smack dab in the middle of traffic, noise and people in Center City. She'd have to turn around to walk back to the parking garage to get her Range Rover.

Walking had helped her work through her thoughts.

She would have to find something else to help with her heart.

THE NEXT MORNING, TOWANDA HAD A MEETING WITH A NEW CLIENT IN Towson, Maryland. She drove to the office building in record time and still had thirty minutes left before the meeting, which started at 10:00 a.m. Sitting in her Range Rover, she pulled her phone out and tapped to launch Facebook.

The Thick Chicks Clique page was on and popping. And who had the very first post of the day?

Chablis. Who else?

Good. Now would be a great time to text Little Miss Super Body. Even if Chablis was still ticked off, she'd answer the text. She never saw a direct message to which she didn't want to respond.

Towanda texted. *Hey munchkin!*

Chablis' response? *U try to apologize to Mariah for real?*

I told you before, I didn't mean for her to get sick.

Yes, you did.

No, I didn't.

Whatever. Hope u asked God to forgive you.

Their text exchange looked crazy. Towanda tapped Chablis' name, then the phone call icon. She answered immediately.

"Okay, I was as wrong as the day is long. Munchkin, you saw me crying."

"Stop calling me munchkin. I'm praying for you."

"Fine, please do. Look I was a bad friend to Mariah when she was trying to change. Now, I'm trying to see things from her point of view, so please help me out. Do your good deed for the day."

"Good deed?"

Towanda sighed, gripping her steering wheel tight. "I messed up okay, but she's the best friend I ever had, and I don't want another one. What can I do to just start talking to her again?"

"Stop trying to control the situation and get right with God. Talk to Him. Give Him your heart and be patient. It's gonna take some time."

"Okay. What else?"

"That's all I have for now. I gotta go, I have a team meeting in a few minutes. Get right with God, okay, T? Then try to talk to Mariah after that."

After the call ended, Towanda switched her phone to silent and pushed it back in her bag. She'd been on shaky ground contacting Chablis, and she should have known Chablis would mention approaching God.

Give Him her heart? She figured she only needed to show her heart to the person she'd wronged. How could God forgive her when it seemed Mariah wasn't even willing to do that?

Towanda checked the time. She needed to make her way into the building for that meeting. At least Chablis had given her something to think about.

Spiritual food for thought.

35

CHABLIS

This Sunday morning I'm in my kitchen blending a berry protein shake. I'm not running late to church, but I'll still pour the drink into my travel bottle and carry it with me on my way there. Help Squad didn't put me on the schedule this week, so I'm looking forward to a beautiful, leisurely drive to church.

When I get inside, I'll find a good seat, so I can sit back and listen to the message. I'm wearing my favorite long black skirt and a lilac V-neck t-shirt with *Tell Your Mountain About Your God* bedazzled across the front.

I'm living the blessed life. Feeling so good.

While my drink blends, I tap my phone and launch Facebook. What do I want to see first? John's timeline, of course. His page loads. Oh good, it looks like he posted new pictures last night.

The moment the page fully appears, I punch the stop button on the blender. Picture after picture after picture. Five in total. All posted to John's Facebook timeline. He appears his muscular, smiling self.

And he has company.

To his left is a pretty blonde.

To his right is a gorgeous brunette.

Both of them sport bodies thinner than I can imagine having in this lifetime, even with daily hour-long workouts. They have bright white teeth, flawless makeup and slim collarbones peeking out of their identical t-shirts. Their arms are draped around John.

My friend John.

My former trainer John.

My *I'm-trying-to-fight-it-but-I still-have-a-wicked-crush-on-him* buddy John.

I swipe quickly through each pic. Two women with their arms around him. His bearded face nestled close to theirs. God must love me dearly, because my phone doesn't break apart after I drop it on the kitchen floor.

"No, I didn't just see that," I say, squatting down to pick up the device. I double-blink when I scan the screen again.

There's no change to what I saw, only John Gerald and his darlings, hugged up and looking super cozy outdoors. What did they do together after they took these pictures?

My heart starts beating faster than it does after a set of burpees followed by donkey kicks and star jumps. These are only pictures, and I need to relax, but now my stomach hurts and I can't get it to stop. I need to settle down and drive to church.

Once I get in my car, I can listen to *The Baylor Project* CD that Felicia gave me. Their rendition of "Great is Thy Faithfulness" will soothe my soul. Of course, I could call John and demand to know what's going on, but only a girlfriend would do that, and I'm not his girlfriend.

And so, for a few too many seconds, I stand here like an idiot, staring at the floor and squeezing my phone between my fingers. My whole face feels hot, but I don't care that I'm all in my feelings over this man.

I gotta be real. I wanted those arms around *me*, holding *me* close. No matter what he said during the great kitchen hug moment, I guess he really did want something different.

All right. Okay. This is my fault.

Stalking that man on social media every morning and evening? Who does that?

I should ditch Facebook. No, wait. I should unfriend him there and on the Bible app. Done. And stop following him on Instagram and

Twitter. Done and done. And block him in my iPhone contacts. Done. He doesn't do Snapchat, so I won't see his bearded face with his new girlfriends there.

He's not my man. He never was.

But I can get one if I want. I'm cute, stylish, and persevering. I can get out and meet new people. Oh, yes, I can.

My stomach stays balled in a knot, but it's time to get to church. The choir will sing uplifting songs, Pastor Downes will preach a good sermon and I can shift my attention to a God who always cares for me and provides for me.

And in the middle of all that, if I dab my eyes with a tissue, people might see me and think the Lord has touched my soul. No one will ever guess my heart is a little wounded after witnessing a man I desire move to a place in his life that doesn't include me.

AT RISE, I SIT IN A PEW NEAR THE FRONT OF THE SANCTUARY. THIS TIME I'm reading Scripture from the Bible app. This is the app I *should* have been reading this morning.

When Felicia passes by on her way down the aisle to go serve, she stops to sit next to me and leans over to give me a quick hug. Then she whispers to me.

"Did you see John?"

"See him where?"

"Facebook."

Somehow, I conveniently forgot everyone on Help Squad follows everyone else on Instagram and Facebook.

I dodge the question. "I'm too busy to pay attention to everyone's feed."

"Check out his post later. I think he's making new friends now."

"Really?" I open my eyes wide. "Well, good for him. He's a decent brother. He deserves to be happy in life."

She gets a funny look on her face, then she stands up. "We're all heading to Sabrina's Cafe after service. You in?"

I shift my eyes back to the Bible app. "No. I think I'll go run some miles this afternoon."

. . .

MONDAY MORNING. I OVERSLEPT, BECAUSE LAST NIGHT I STAYED UP TOO long brooding about those stupid pictures of John. I also forgot to set my wake-up alarm. By the time I pull myself together and stumble into work, it is a little after nine.

I rush in, clutching my leather backpack over my shoulder. When I pass the receptionist desk, no one's there. I turn the corner and gaze into the fishbowl, and what appears to be our entire company crowds the room. Some guys even sit on the floor. Our CEO stands in the middle addressing everyone.

I creep into the doorframe and wedge myself beneath my co-worker Harry's armpit in time to hear the CEO announce restructuring and layoffs arriving later in the week. After he says it, I see people look at the floor, groan, curse or all three at once.

I raise my eyebrows and shoot a *for real, this is happening* look at Anna, who stands against the wall at the far end of the room. She shrugs and returns a look like, *yeah, I didn't see this coming*.

Twenty minutes later, I'm in my cubicle. I put on my headphones and prepare to work. Worrying never solves anything. Before I launch Outlook, I pull up a browser and review Pinterest quotes. Today my favorite is *Always pray to have eyes that see the best in people, a heart that forgives the worst, a mind that forgets the bad, and a soul that never loses faith in God.*

I print it out and tack it to my cubicle wall, where I study it for a few minutes. Then I turn back to my computer and add a tab to my browser. I know my co-workers are walking back and forth in the aisle beside my cubicle, but I log into my LinkedIn account anyway.

My profile is pretty well updated, but I add a few new skills to it. Sue Ryan has connected with me on LinkedIn. She's still shaking things up in the tech sector. Now is the perfect time to let her know that if she hears of a test position, I'm all ears.

Someone knocks on my cubicle wall. I hate that, but I paste a smile on my face before I turn around.

"Hey, Christopher."

"Did you hear the announcement? I didn't see you there."

"Yeah, well, Harry's a big guy, and I was hidden under his arm. I heard the CEO. WebAbsolute has to scale back next year, and what have you."

He fiddles with his Apple Watch. "You know, if you have any questions—"

"Come see you, right?"

"Right."

"No problem. I'm sure you'll be a big help," I say, turning back to my computer, amazed that I kept the sarcasm out of my voice.

WebAbsolute. Downsizing. Well, I should have left a year ago, so I'll take this as a notice to get moving in the right direction.

Tonight, when I reach home, I'm weary and starving. In my apartment, I go right to my desk and open up my laptop. My fingers move so fast I can't stop them. I open a browser for Pizza Hut delivery. This is a Meat Lovers kind of night for me. I know I shouldn't do this, but I'm a big girl. I know how to get back on track.

So I'm a little down right now. John was partying with cute girls in Germany, and now I'm sure there's no way he's thinking of me as anything other than his friend.

My job may be going away. Who can tell at this point?

I'd dance my cares away, but I can't hit The Grandstand floor until Thursday. But I know what I can do. I can put my Visa debit card number into this web form and get this order going.

There's a knock at my door. I get up, take three long leaps and open it, and there's my neighbor, Song. She stands in the hall with a spatula in one hand and a bulging black envelope in the other.

"Mailman put this in my box by mistake." She thrusts it at me. "For you."

I reach out and take it. My heart flips a little when I read it. It's from The Grandstand.

"Uh. Thank you." I nod toward Song and keep scanning the front of the envelope.

"Welcome," Song says, turning to walk back down to her apartment.

The Grandstand? Two months ago, Anna had said they were kind of secretive. This black envelope proves it. I jog back to my living room and drop to the carpet, tearing open the envelope.

They mailed me seven pages full of information. My college acceptance letters didn't hold this much content. As I shuffle through the pages, gold glitter from the letterhead rains into my lap. Page 1 – Invitation. Page 2 – Contract/Dues. Page 3 – Attendance. Page 4 – Standards. Page 5 - Community Service. Page 6 – Performances. Page 7- Contact Information Form.

The invitation page presents The Grandstand as a performance group/community service organization/social club all wrapped up in one. Anna was right, it wasn't just about the dancing. I'm being invited to join a diverse group of adults interested in setting a good example for youth, promoting health and good welfare for adults and using the spirit of social dance to help unite the community.

I skip to the Standards page. They have actual dress and hair standards, just like dance school. If I join, I have to keep my body, hair and nails well-groomed, yadda, yadda, yadda. I flip back to read the contract and dues. Membership lasts one year before review. Some legalese. Required to assist with community events. More legalese. Required to master all chosen dances. Even more legalese. Yearly dues are two hundred and fifty dollars, covering the cost of a jacket, shirts, warm-up outfit and administration fees.

I scan the Performances page. All members are required to participate in two public performances per year. Some travel may be required. Official Grandstand clothing only. Where payment is involved, all monies will be divided equally among the event performers.

Did they just say I can get paid?

What?

"WHOO HOOO!" I jump up, throwing my papers in the air. Then I dance *Work It Out* all the way to my laptop and close the Pizza Hut order browser window.

Who needs pizza now? I open a new window for Amazon and order myself two pairs of dance socks and one of those headbands that wick moisture away from my hairline, and then I shut down my laptop. I grab a pillow from my couch, place it on the floor and kneel on it. My stomach turns cartwheels, but this time in a good way.

"Father, thank you for this opportunity. Before I sign anything, Lord show me if this is beneficial. Is this something I should pursue? Lead me and guide me, Lord, as written in Psalm 32:8, I will instruct you and teach you in the way you should go. I will counsel you with My eye upon you. I submit myself and my time to You to do with as You see fit. Please show me the wise thing to do in all situations. In Jesus' name I pray. Amen."

It's not all that late by the time I finish reading through the full packet and eat dinner.

What a day, what a day, what a day.

The Grandstand invited me to membership. I'm honored, but I'm also prayed up about it. My head is swimming now. I'm so exhausted, I pad into my bedroom and crash on my bed even though it's only eight-thirty. No need to glance at Instagram or Facebook. The last item of communication I need is the one I just had.

On my knees, with my Father.

36

MARIAH

Reading Scripture helped Mariah keep her emotions in check. As soon as she woke each morning, she put her robe on, traveled downstairs, brewed a pot of coffee and opened her Bible. Her favorite meditation verse? Isaiah 26:3. *You will keep in perfect peace those whose minds are steadfast because they trust in You.*

She rubbed the sand out of her eyes as she flipped through the pages.

What a walking hypocrite. Drinking wine all night and then praying in the morning? How could God bless her when she prayed about how much she drank but still poured three or four glasses of wine each evening, cleaning up the evidence before Binky padded into the kitchen in the morning? She kept flipping through pages, pushing her thoughts aside.

One day things wouldn't be like this.

Good times would return.

In the meantime, she coped with her husband's absence. Oscar had packed up and moved out. For the past month, he'd lived with his mother Alondra over in Norristown.

Who knew if the move would be temporary or permanent? When

Binky asked, Mariah gave her the simple truth — her mom and dad were having a hard time and they needed time away from each other.

Thank God she had Kim and Chablis. Every day at noon, Kim served as Mariah's prayer partner and they prayed together over about her marriage and her health. Kim cheered her on over her continued weight loss and reminded her that all union's hit rough patches.

And when Chablis stopped by on Sunday afternoons, Mariah poured her heart out in earnest, talking about her heartbreak over Oscar moving out. Her cousin never uttered a word about the wine glasses or Mariah's need to drink so much. She only listened and encouraged her to get back in the gym and sweat out her frustrations.

For Mariah and Oscar, their space had grown to four weeks apart. Even though she hurt, sometimes she was grateful for it. Last week, they'd had several screaming matches over the phone which didn't resolve anything. Today, however, for her own peace of mind, she needed to know where they were headed. She repeated her meditation verse in her head when she called Oscar's mobile.

Mariah kept her voice down as she held the phone to her ear. It was early, and even though she sat downstairs in the kitchen, she didn't want the sound to carry and reach Binky's ears.

When he answered, Mariah didn't take time for greetings. "Os, we can't go on like this."

Silence.

"Oscar."

"I'm not sure what you want me to say."

"I just need to know if this is how things are going to be."

"For now, yes, until I can get my head together."

"But you've been gone a month. This has gone on for too long."

"Oh yeah, a lot of things have gone on too long, as far as I'm concerned."

Her stomach quivered. "Um...go on."

"I have to decide if I want to live the rest of my life in these situations with you."

"Situations? What do you mean?"

"Mariah, I don't know, okay. That's all I can offer you right now."

"You still have a family over here. What are we supposed to do?"

"Do what you have to do."

"Do what I have to do?" She asked, sarcasm coloring her voice.

"Yes."

This is only a consultation. It's an information exchange, that's all.

Mariah kept a running monologue going in her head as she drove to the law office. She clutched her purse tightly to her side as she entered the building.

Inside, the receptionist checked her in. Five minutes later, she was shown to a small gray conference room where she sat and waited, staring at the empty walls.

Would she hire Bebb Family Law Services? Probably not. But her conversation with Oscar scared her enough to push her to seek counsel for her side. So, she'd located the law service through an online search, called them and secured an appointment for a week later.

Two minutes turned into five, then five minutes turned into ten. Mariah drummed her fingertips on the conference table and sighed.

Where was the lawyer?

Mariah heard footsteps in the hallway.

Good. The lawyer would arrive in the room any second. She could ask anything she wanted, as long as she didn't insist on counseling, which Mariah wasn't interested in. Both Chablis and Kim had suggested it, but Mariah had vetoed the idea.

When the conference room door opened, a petite lady with a sharp, jet black bob and a stunning forest green business suit walked in and extended her hand. "Mrs. Rodriguez? Good to meet you. I'm Zatia Bebb. We spoke over the phone."

Mariah rose and shook her hand. "Mariah, please. And it's good to meet you, as well."

"I'll shut this door and we can get started."

Mariah returned to her chair, wheeling it around so she could face Zatia, who chose a seat on the opposite side. Zatia placed a legal pad and pencils in front of her. She also pushed a blue box of Kleenex tissues in the middle of the table.

"Mariah, before we begin, I need to reiterate, you are under no obligation to continue with the consultation or to procure our services."

Mariah nodded. "I understand."

"Wonderful. Now here's my most important question of the morning. How are you doing?"

"I'll get better as time goes by, I'm sure."

"Time heals all wounds."

"I sure hope so."

"Things may become harder before they grow easier, but I'll try to make this process as painless as possible." Zatia pulled the legal pad close to her and picked up a sharpened pencil. "I'm going to ask you a series of questions. Some will be quite personal, so understand I'm here to help you, not judge you. Some questions will be financial in nature. For your assets, you can provide ballpark figures if you don't know specific numbers. You'll also tell me about your goals."

"Goals?"

"How do you envision your union ending? If you have children, tell me about how you'd like their care to continue. If your husband is the primary breadwinner, how do you view his support of your current lifestyle? Do you want to share custody? If you haven't thought about those things, we'll work through that today."

So much to consider.

Divorce meant ripping everything apart. The Rodriguezes could move on, but there would be a high cost.

Did Mariah really want to disengage from Oscar that badly?

Zatia pointed her pencil toward the box of tissues between them. "That's for you. Use as many as you need. It's fine and normal to cry or express anger or frustration. The door is closed and you're safe in here. Are you ready?"

"Ready."

"We'll start with your reasons for divorce."

The personal questions were the hardest, but Mariah answered everything.

Who left their home? Oscar.

Why did he go? He was disgusted by her drinking.

Did she think he might be having an affair? No.

Living with another woman? No.

She also talked about her years of obesity, his anger about it and his desire for more children. His lack of intimacy for several years until she dropped most of her excess weight. She even shared her feelings about being rejected and belittled. Her fingers ached as she squeezed her fists into tight balls. Answering Zatia's questions brought out inner emotions Mariah hadn't realized even existed.

By comparison, the financial questions were easy to answer. Oscar's career as a business consultant and Mariah's current work status as a homemaker. The worth of their car, truck, home and furnishings. Their checking, savings, high yield, investment, retirement accounts, Binky's college savings account and finally, their debts and other obligations.

Mariah's face held not a smear of makeup by the time she mentioned her goals for their dissolved union. She'd wiped off all her foundation, lipstick, and mascara with half a box of tissues.

What did she want their ideal outcome to be?

Mariah sat and thought, gazing at the legal pad in front of Zatia. It held pages filled with notes.

"I've made a home for us, so I'd like us to split our assets equally and share custody of our daughter, Benita. I'd also like to continue raising her in our home until she graduates. I'd like Oscar to continue supporting our lifestyle fully until I get a job."

"And when you do?" Zatia asked.

"We can renegotiate the terms of his support. I'm not trying to take him to the cleaners. Despite what we've been through, I still love him. I just want to be free to be me."

TWO WEEKS LATER, MARIAH STOOD ON HER FRONT STEPS. SHE BENT DOWN to fix a lace on her sneaker that had come undone. Time to do an hour of neighborhood walking before Binky came home. Her first trip around the block relaxed her. Her second trip helped clear her head even more. By the time she completed her third trip, she had approached the house and saw a man standing on their walkway. When she stopped on the sidewalk, he trotted over to her.

"Mariah Shields-Rodriguez?"

"Yes."

"May I have your signature here?" He passed her an envelope.

Her sense of relaxation vanished. She didn't even need to ask the man what the envelope held, and she wasn't listening when he spoke again and then left. She wound up sitting on the top step, gazing at the papers in her hands.

Mariah Shields-Rodriguez, you've been served.

Brown, yellow and orange leaves fell all over the front yard. She sat still, but she was falling, too. Her bottom lip trembled as she tightly gripped the papers.

She should call up Mr. Perfect and tell him he'd picked the right time to send divorce papers.

Yeah, she should do that.

Call and tell him she's doing better every day. Inform him about her increased Bible reading and how she feels so much calmer after he started rooming at his mother's house. Yes, she still has those glasses of wine each night, but no, she's not drinking excessively. And next year, she'll go ahead and have the body contouring surgery and she'll look and feel better than ever. She hasn't missed one class at Temple, and she was right on target with her credits.

But Oscar had just filed for divorce.

Divorce.

He hadn't gone for a simple consultation to work things through in his mind.

Oh no—the man actually filed court papers.

So they really couldn't work it out? She couldn't do the right thing or say the right thing to change their situation?

That couldn't be possible.

What about their years together? Yes, he'd tolerated some issues with her, but she'd managed problems with him, as well. That's what you did when you're a family.

This is really happening to me. I can't believe this! What a stupid year. I'm

*supposed to be happy, and now hubby serves me as if he's in control of every-
thing. Lord, You're supposed to be here!*

Amazingly, her eyes remained dry. Confusion consumed her but
she didn't want to cry. Mariah turned her face to the sky, her chest
aching.

And where in the world was Towanda? She wanted to talk to
Towanda.

Once again, Mariah's world had spun out of control, and where
was her bestie? Oh yeah—she'd turned on her and flaked out and
Mariah had pushed her aside.

She dropped the envelope and let her hands rest on the rough
concrete.

She would stay cool. She could at least do that.

Stay calm and know that she had a life without Towanda.

And now, without Oscar.

37

TOWANDA

owanda sat in the last row of the balcony at Rise Church. All the way up in the corner where no one liked to be seated because the spotlights mounted on the ceiling blocked part of the view.

She didn't mind, though. If she wanted to sit in the midst of three thousand people and still be alone, this would be *the* spot. She could lean to the right and view the top of Pastor Downes' clean-shaven head. But she didn't need to see his face for his words to sink in.

"Rely on God, not on your own strength. Stop trying to carry so many issues and life concerns. It's wearing you down, family, it's wearing on you like an old coat you should've donated to Goodwill years ago," Pastor Downes preached.

Towanda closed her eyes for a moment. She'd heard many sermons over the years, but this one? She absorbed the words like a sponge. The old coat analogy? If she glanced down at her own arms, she could probably see the holes in it.

He kept going. "So, when you gonna give it up, sisters, brothers? When? After you've had a heart attack? Maybe after you've signed up for rehab because you tried to drink and smoke your concerns away and it didn't work? When, family? After you've sabotaged every single relationship in your life and now you're finally alone and no one cares?"

That last statement pierced Towanda's heart like a well-targeted arrow. She opened her eyes. Pastor Downes couldn't know about what had happened at Mariah's house on the Fourth of July.

She'd heard the Lord knew the intimate details of your life. Now she believed it.

Yes, she carried a heavy, guilty heart and she'd destroyed a friendship. She'd tried and failed to give an apology, but she had purposed in her heart to treat others better.

What should she do now?

Lord, I think You are talking to me, so show up. Show up and tell me what to do.

Pastor Downes mopped his forehead and face with a white towel. "Family, I can tell you right now some of you are wondering what to do after you've messed things up for so long you don't know which way is up. All because you were trying to control things you couldn't control. I'll bet you someone's told you what to do already. But did you listen? Did you?"

Now that was just plain freaky. When Towanda had talked to Chablis a few weeks back, Chablis had told her to get right with God. But Towanda had figured the petite power lifter only said it because it sounded like something she got from Pinterest.

But maybe she was right. What would happen after she asked God's forgiveness? Leaning on God always seemed like something she should do for a devastating situation like a terminal cancer diagnosis, a parent dying or mortgage foreclosure.

Well, Towanda was healthy. She had enough money in the bank to carry three mortgages because Uncle Charles had wisely counseled her to invest the insurance money Nana had saved for her after her father died. And she'd been diligent enough to earn her own money since before age eighteen. She had her education, talent and her Nana. God made sense to her, but had she ever indeed relied on Him? Relied on Him as if she had no hope other than Him?

Pastor Downes walked toward his lectern. "Family, please, if you do anything today, read these Scriptures. Highlight them in your version of the Bible. Start with Isaiah 41:13, 'For I, the Lord your God, hold your right hand, it is I who say to you, Fear not, I am the one who helps you.' Because He's there to help you. Here's another one, Proverbs 3:5-6, 'Trust in the Lord with all your heart, and do not lean on your own understanding. In all your ways acknowledge Him and He will make your paths straight.' Family, it's there in the Word. Your God is there to help you if you trust in Him. He's there. Yes, He is."

Towanda's eyes grew wet with tears and she wiped them away with the back of her hand. Trust in God.

Here was an immovable situation.

Would God take this? Who knew?

Swiftly, she picked up her bag, stood up and exited out the back of the balcony. In the hallway, she rested her back on the wall for a moment. Out here, she couldn't hear Pastor Downes words anymore, but she didn't want to, anyway.

Impossible situation. Rely on God.

Impossible situation. Rely on God.

Trust Him.

"Ma'am?" An extremely tall, clean-shaven man approached her. He wore a *Need Help?* t-shirt and dark jeans and shoes. "Are you all right? Can I help you with anything?"

Towanda clutched her bag at her side, shaking her head. "No, uh, I'm fine. I'm headed to the restroom."

The man nodded. "It's right around the corner here."

"Thank you," Towanda said, moving quickly down the hall.

Inside the bathroom, which she did not need to use, she stood in front of a sink and leaned against the cool marble. She took a few moments to center herself, jumping with a start when she heard a toilet flush behind her.

Out walked a young woman who couldn't have been more than twenty years old. Towanda moved to the side to let her get to the sink, all the while studying her clothing. She wore cheap discount store sneakers and black leggings. Her black shirt had hot pink flowers printed all over, and it, too, looked like the best thing Family Dollar had to offer. Her short black hair was slicked back with too much brown gel, and her pink plastic hoop earrings held onto her droopy earlobes for dear life.

But the woman whistled and sung to herself as she washed her hands. Something about praising God with a faithful heart, or something like that. When she dried her hands, she glanced over at Towanda and flashed a dazzling smile.

"Good sermon today, right?" she asked.

"Yeah, it's good." Towanda nodded, mumbling back.

She kept talking. "I like your bag. It goes real nice with your outfit. What brand?"

"This? Oh, this is a Fossil bag."

"Oh, I seen the Fossil store before. Out King of Prussia Mall."

"That's right."

"Yeah." The young girl mused. "I saw people buy watches and stuff in there. Real nice stuff. You got good taste."

"I guess." Towanda raised her head up. "You seem happy today. Whistling and all."

The girl shrugged. "I have everything I need to be joyful about. God loves me so much. He's good to me every day and I just gotta praise Him."

Towanda rolled her eyes, but somewhere in the motion her eyes grew wet and she reached in her bag for a tissue, pressing it to her face.

"Hey, you all right? What's wrong?"

For a few moments, Towanda couldn't respond. She looked down at her own expensive shoes, pantsuit and bag. Everything she had on totaled more than four hundred dollars retail.

The young lady in front of her? Her whole outfit probably amounted to twenty-five dollars and some change. But she sang and whistled about praising God, even complimenting Towanda on her bag.

"I'm...I'm..." Towanda stammered, trying to pull herself together. Wait. There was nothing wrong with saying what she needed. She would be bold enough to do that, even with a wet tissue stuck to her palm. "I need someone to pray with me. Can you find someone for me?"

"I can pray with you." The young woman approached her. Reached out for her hand. "I'm Camille. What's your name?"

"I'm Towanda," she said, sniffing. "And we're in a bathroom."

Camille stepped closer. "It don't matter. Let's just pray and God'll hear."

They bowed their heads. Towanda didn't concentrate on the words, but whatever Camille said, it unlocked memories in her head. When she opened her own mouth to pray, she found herself asking for healing from the pain of the past. She even prayed to accept that everyone possessed a different type of beauty.

She grasped Camille's hands tighter, and suddenly it seemed okay to ask for forgiveness for her betrayal against Mariah.

The snide comments. The jealousy. The fear of losing her best friend. She confessed it all and let it go.

When Camille ended their prayer time, Towanda heart felt lighter.

Maybe she would gain her best friend back. Perhaps she wouldn't. But no matter what, she'd given everything in her heart to God.

It would be safe with Him.

"Hey, Wonder Woman." Towanda held her phone by her mouth. She kicked off her shoes and stretched out on the sofa. "How's your Sunday going?"

"My Sunday's great," Nana said. "I'm thinking about what I want to eat tonight. I haven't cooked in days."

"You? Not cooking? Whaaat?"

"Yes, Granddaughter, I do have a life, and I've been out all week long. How does that fix you?"

"Where have you been? Let me guess? Knitting class or crochet class. Or have you found a new boyfriend and introduced him to your meditation room?"

"Fresh mouth. No, but I've gone bowling with my senior's group, then we all went out to eat. And you know I started swimming at the YMCA every Tuesday and Thursday evening."

"You swim?"

"I've always liked swimming. I swam all the time with my daddy growing up in Norfolk. I have the time now, and my new friends all swim, so I get in there. Once you learn, you never forget."

"I see. Glad to know you are getting out and moving about."

"Speaking of moving," Nana sounded as if she'd switched her phone around. When she came back, her voice was louder. "I went down to visit the old place on Monday."

"Why? Did Aunt Reecie take you there?"

"She didn't. I took an Uber. Anyway, Sol from the Sunshine Cleaners next door—you remember him, right? He called me last week and said, 'Maddie, the renters in your old place moved out. It's been empty all year, but they took down their decorations and I can see your old wallpaper in there. I have a key to the front. Come see.' So, I went down to walk through it."

"Empty, huh?"

"Like an abandoned tomb." Nana laughed. "Oh, Wanda, it was so good to walk through it, especially with my old walls showing through. All those memories, you know. Remember when you gave your school bus driver my brownies and sticky buns and he'd drop you off at the bakery even though it wasn't your bus stop?"

"Yeah, I was always the little negotiator."

"Little?"

"You hush, old lady."

"Wanda, drive on over and take a look. The neighborhood is gentrifying. Sol told me if the building owner can't locate a renter for the space, he's thinking about selling the whole building to the highest bidder."

After Nana Cakes closed, the storefront had been a pizza shop, then a deli, and most recently, a breakfast and coffee spot.

"Selling the building? Who would buy it?" Towanda asked.

"I don't know. What would they put in a changing neighborhood? Starbucks? Panera? A fancy vegan food spot?"

"You just said fancy vegan food, Wonder Woman."

"I do read, you know. Some of those restaurants in California, all they sell is chopped up vegetables and toppings for twelve and fifteen dollars a bowl."

Towanda yawned and stretched. "At least it wouldn't be Walmart."

"No, but a Target wouldn't be bad. You know they carry that makeup I like. I looked it up. Makes your skin glow like gold."

What would Towanda do with Nana and her desire to keep acting like a teenager?

"Not enough space for a Target. And you don't need that makeup. You're beautiful the way you are."

"Thank you, baby."

"You're welcome, Nana."

THERE WAS A LOT OF LOVE IN THAT OLD BAKERY. TOWANDA TOOK NANA'S advice and drove to south Philly the next morning. The old block held the Sunshine Cleaners, an Ethiopian food restaurant, a thrift shop, and the storefront where Nana Cakes used to be.

She couldn't resist parking and walking over to the glass window to peek inside. Like Nana had said, it was empty space. Dusty and dark. But Towanda squinted and imagined the wrought iron tables and chairs, shelves that held bags of rolls, cartons of sticky buns and cellophane sleeves of sugar cookies. And the long counter which held tall silver dispensers of fresh coffee.

Concrete crunched beneath her feet as she paced. There was a lot of life in the neighborhood. If the owner sold the building, the people who lived in the apartments above the shop might lose their space. Apartment rents were increasing fast in Philly. But if he could find a renter? Someone who knew what to put in the area. Someone with enough capital to invest.

Towanda would need to do research. Great tasting health food. Vegan dishes. Lean meat dishes. Lots of vegetables and herbs and good-for-you stuff. She'd have to immerse herself in reading.

Healthy food could be hard to find in changing neighborhoods. What if she provided a solution?

More than that. What if she offered a place to meet?

A community table. People could buy their meals as they met with their neighbors. What if once a week there was a small cooking class? She'd have to find an executive chef, but she could search for one. No fancy pedigreed food partners. She wanted someone who needed this opportunity. Someone who wanted to live healthily. They could start small. Create a business plan and strategize together. Work with what they had.

What could they call the place?

Towanda danced around so much she almost dropped her phone to the ground as she pulled it from her jacket pocket. Her fingers trembled when she tapped her phone app, then chose Nana from the contact list.

Nana didn't answer. She was probably at the YMCA or some other place, hanging with her senior gang. Towanda left a message.

"Wonder Woman, I'm going to rent the old Nana Cakes space. No, I'm not crazy. Call me back. I need the number for the building owner. Your fancy vegan food idea might work here. If it doesn't, at least we tried."

She fumbled putting her phone back. She had no idea if she'd be able to find a chef to partner with or if she'd be able to negotiate a reasonable price for the rent.

But she could pray. And what if it worked? A place for great nutrition with colossal taste? Her consulting firm was named thinkLARGE. What about *eatLARGE*?

Yes!

38

CHABLIS

This morning at Macy's I bought some overpriced but on sale interview clothing. Now I'm sitting in the waiting area at Shades of Beauty tallying costs in my head. It's time to redo my weave, and it's clear to me that an unemployed person has no business trying to pay for an expensive hairdo.

Yep, I got downsized, but I received three months' severance pay, so I'm not exactly poor yet. I heard some of the newer workers only received one month's salary. Maybe Christopher finally went to bat for me and pushed for more money, since he likely knew WebAbsolute would cut me from the staff. I've already submitted my resume for a contract software testing position in Center City.

Anna still works at WebAbsolute. We sit together at The Grandstand, so she keeps me up to date with office news. She said she wishes she had been let go, because the company is kind of dead now, but she's in limbo working in the IT department as essential staff. She updated her LinkedIn profile, though.

Quinsara, my hairdresser, whose own hair is electric blue and cut close to her scalp, pokes her head around the corner and gives me an update. "Fifteen more minutes, all right, honey? Sorry for the wait."

"Take all the time you need," I tell her.

This is a numbers game. It will cost me $130 for the hair. I only use virgin non-processed Brazilian, and I want it long. At least eighteen inches in length and a quality brand. Why buy cheap hair that ends up tangled at the nape of my neck in less than two weeks?

That's only the price for the hair, though. I need a deep conditioning treatment for my natural hair. That's another ten bucks. Its Saturday morning and there are no weekday sales I can take advantage of so it'll cost me another $175 for weave installation. Then I have to leave a decent tip because I like Quinsara and she's the reason I have no hair or scalp problems.

By the time I saunter out the front door, I will have shelled out close to $350. If I pay for it in cash, it will make a dent in my budget. I'm generally okay with that when I know money is coming in, but it's not right now.

And it's dumb to tell myself something like *I'll trust God for the increase.* He'd laugh, and say *you foolish, farkle, fool you. The increase is for rent, food or bills, not a hair weave for you to go whipping around in trying to impersonate Beyoncé.*

I sigh and cross my legs.

What are my options?

A relaxer and trim? Out of the question. I'd have to maintain it, and I work out hard every day.

Braids? I don't want micros to destroy my hairline. What to do?

Quinsara pops back around the corner and waves me over. "You can come on back."

I follow her, staring at her blue hair the whole time. The curls are natural and the color is banging. I'm not working now. No one to see me daily. I'll have interviews, but...hmm. Maybe a little color in the front? I could get by with that when I interview. I settle into Quinsara's chair and she runs her long nails through my hair.

"Your usual?" She asks. "Did you buy your hair up front?"

"No. Let's go for a change today." I swivel around until I'm facing her. "How much to cut my hair down short and add some color?"

"Eighty." She says, then her eyes widen. "Hold on. You serious?"

"Yup."

"But you never want short hair. No weave?"

I push myself back around and stare in the mirror. I don't have on makeup right now, and with the weave off instead of covering the side of my cheeks, my scar shows. It has faded over the years, though. When I grin, the scar blends right into the crease in my face where my dimple starts.

I'll smile more. Every day. Smile. Like the Tasha Cobbs Leonard song.

"Wash it, condition it, then go on and cut it down," I tell her.

"Short, natural curls?"

"Short, natural curls. And can you add some hot pink in the front?"

Quinsara rakes her fingers through my hair again. She cocks her head to the side as she looks in the mirror at me. "How bout I leave your hair a little longer at the top and front. I can add color streaks through the tips of those curls and yeah, we can do this girl."

"Let's do this."

Me without the weave. Nothing to pull on to cover my scarred cheek. No more hiding.

Seems like a change for the better. This is what I can afford right now, and it's a better decision than pushing for a weave because that's what I always do.

Besides, this is my life.

Not only will I live it, I'm gonna live it with hot pink streaked across my scalp.

LATE SATURDAY AFTERNOON MEANS CHORES. I WASH CLOTHES, VACUUM, dust, mop and pull together a bag of old clothes I'll drop in a donation box later today. Afterward, I sit at my kitchen counter to write out my food list for the week. I gained two pounds last week, but I won't stress over it. This gain must be muscle because my outfits hang looser than they did a month ago. Let me get out of here and go to the GIANT.

My shopping is simple. Other than my toiletries, my cart holds basic stuff. Lean chicken breast. Eggs. Tuna. Broccoli. Kale. Onions. Avocado. Grapefruit. Apples. Brown rice and black beans. Coconut and olive oil because I'm running out of them. I'm standing in the dairy aisle putting a container of cottage cheese in my cart. My Beats are on my ears, and I'm listening to Dezzie singing "I Can Feel It", and I'm snapping my fingers to the beat.

Yeah, this is all I need for now. My shopping's complete.

When I feel a tap on my shoulder, I turn around. In front of me is a *fiiiine* brother with a texturized mohawk, wiggling his fingers at me, trying to get my attention. He's probably going to tell me I dropped my keys or something, so I pull off my Beats off and rest them around my neck.

"Yes?"

He points to my cart. "That's for you? That cottage cheese? You eat that?"

"I mix it with my Greek yogurt for extra protein."

"And you've got a ton of chicken breast in there. You do fitness training?"

"Yeah."

He steps back and takes his time looking me up and down.

Wait. He's checking me out!

"Oh, my bad. My name's Mike. Mike Roberts," he says with a smile, extending his hand. "Your hairstyle's dope, by the way. So, what's your name?"

I'm kind of giddy and I don't know how to act. I'm wearing my favorite black Old Navy running tights, which means all my lower body curves are on display, and I should've been more modest, but really, who gets hit on going to the GIANT to buy cottage cheese?

I locate my voice and shake his hand. "Chablis," I say.

"Chablis? Like the wine?"

"That's the name my parents gave me. I can't complain."

"You got a man?"

"You're kind of bold."

"Why waste time?" He walks around me in a circle, still checking me out. "So, for real though. You seeing anybody?"

I shift my weight from one foot to the other and think about John. He was never a somebody for me, but he's the main reason I look like I do now. I don't know this guy in front of me from a can of paint, but he's paying me a compliment and I appreciate it, so I answer, "No, no one's in my life right now."

"Aww, you mean no one's keeping that body warm at night?" Mike clucks his tongue. "That's a shame."

And this conversation jumped from complimentary to creepy in three seconds. All right, Mr. Mike Roberts, I have food to prep and church tomorrow. Time to get out of this chat.

"Again, I can't complain. Thanks for the compliment. You take care." I position my cart as if I'm about to roll away any second.

Mike stops me. "Sorry, I didn't mean to be so fresh." He fishes around in his jeans pocket. "It's so good to see smart young women taking care of their diet and exercise. Here's my card." He passes it to me. "I'm a manager at Hot Fire Gym in Manayunk. You want to stop by on a Friday evening, I'm always there 'til seven. Maybe we can hang out or something afterward?"

I read his card. He's a manager and personal trainer by appointment. I don't know anything about his spiritual life, but maybe I'll give him a call and find out later on. Under no circumstances will I give this stranger my number, but he'll probably look me up on Facebook and Instagram anyway because that's what we all do.

"Good meeting you, Mike," I say, clutching his card in my hand. "I gotta get home to do meal prep."

"I see you, cutie. Take it easy."

I will. I already am.

Should I be doing this?

My high-heeled boots click against the concrete steps as I walk into the renovated mill building that houses Hot Fire Gym. I'm here to visit Mr. Mike Roberts. I called him twice during the week to chat, and each time he reminded me he's here until seven on Fridays.

It's close to seven now. If I stroll in and witness a bunch of females hanging around waiting to see him, I'll know he does his *who's keeping that body warm* routine on everyone and I will turn around, exit stage left, dropping his card in the trash on my way out.

I push through the glass doors and climb another half flight of stairs. When I turn to the right, I see Mike standing right outside of an office door at the far end of a room filled with punching bags and exercise equipment. He looks good, too. Strong and healthy and relaxed. He's wearing khakis and a black and red polo shirt with a Hot Fire Gym logo on it.

He grins and waves me over when he sees me. I'm kind of hard to miss with pink streaks in my hair.

I walk over to him. "Hey, Mike."

"What up, Chablis? So, you came to pay me a visit?"

"I figured, why not. You offered." I glance around. "Nice looking place."

"Our team keeps it tight in here. Our clients are worth it. Can you wait here for a moment? I need to take care of something. I'll be right back."

"Sure."

I stand there while he enters the office area, does something with a computer, then comes out and shuts the door behind him.

"I'm starving," he says. "You wanna get something to eat? Manayunk Brewing Company is a couple of blocks away."

"How's the food there?" I say, then I add, "I gotta warn you, I'm not a beer fan."

"You don't have to be. The salads and the grilled salmon are off the chain."

What do I have to lose? Meeting Mike here in his work environment, he's giving off a friendly, professional vibe. Seems like a cool guy. We can hang out, have a meal and talk. I have to get to know other men sometime. Lord knows I need to forget about John, because if his move to Berlin didn't quite shake me, the pictures of him hugging those German chicks certainly did. I'll text Nikki before I get to the restaurant so at least one of my friends knows where I am and who I'm with. It'll be fine.

"My car's right outside," is what I tell Mike. "When you're ready, I'll follow you over to the restaurant. I'll honk at ya when I see you get in your ride."

"You don't want me to drive you?"

"Nah, buddy. This is our first time meeting up. I'll drive myself.

And I pay for my own meal because we've just met, and we don't know each other like that yet. No expectations. Let's just hang out."

Mike laughs. "You know what? I can respect that. I like your style, girl."

"Thanks. Maybe I'll like your style, too."

I MIGHT HAVE BEEN WRONG ABOUT MIKE WHEN WE FIRST MET. TONIGHT, he's nothing but a gentleman. He opens the door for me at the restaurant and pulls out my chair when we reach our table. We order cauliflower bites, salads, grilled salmon, and iced tea. He asks me about myself and listens carefully while I talk. He doesn't flinch when I tell him about my ministry work at Rise Church, and he actually looks interested when I talk about line dance. I leave out the part about John when we discuss fitness training.

"What about you?" I say, spearing my fork into a piece of fish.

"Oh, me? Well, I'm kind of boring," he jokes. Then he tells me he likes riding his motorcycle on the weekends with his friends. He's also working toward becoming a physical therapist. He loves helping clients rehab their bodies. He admits he doesn't attend church much, but he does enjoy visiting Sharon Baptist with his grandmother a few times a year.

His honesty is refreshing, and overall, I can see myself hanging out with him again. He doesn't have to be born again just to be my friend and kick it at the movies or out running every once in a while. But I still ask him, "Why don't you have a significant other?"

He drops his napkin next to his empty plate. "Because sometimes, relationships just don't work out. How come you don't have a man?"

"Same reason," I say.

Mike looks down for a second, then lifts his head and meets my eyes. "When I walked up to you the other day, I thought, now I know this sweetie with the Cardi B. body gotta have a husband around here somewhere. But you didn't have a ring on your finger, and your dimples and smile knocked me out. I had to keep talking to you. I gave you my card because I couldn't let you get away."

"I don't know what to say, but thanks. Know what I told myself when you tapped me?"

"No, what?"

"Now, who is this fine brother in front of me with that fly mohawk? Oh, he's just gonna tell me I dropped my keys or something like that."

Mike chuckles as he leans closer to the table. "I don't think I've ever had a better time getting to know someone before." He reaches across and takes my hand. "I like you. Can we keep this going?"

"Yeah, I'd like to get to know you more."

"Good," he says, winking at me.

After we pay for our meals and step outside, butterflies beat the heck out of my stomach. This isn't a panic sensation though, it's more like plain excitement. Mike holds my hand as he walks me to my car, and it all feels so wonderful. It's early December, but the air is warm, and stars twinkle above.

The type of night when I could let myself fall into something kind of resembling love.

When we reach my Focus, I open the door and drop my purse and keys on the passenger seat. As I turn back around, he stands close enough for me to sense warmth coming off his body in waves. He smells scrumptious, too, like spice and fresh citrus. I haven't experienced something like this in so long the moment seems surreal.

"I had an awesome time," I say.

Mike gently pulls me in for a hug, and I relax in his arms. My mind shuts down, and my body takes control. Stretching my arms over his shoulders, I'm right up against his body. He reaches for my hands, intertwines his fingers with mine, and when we kiss it feels like heaven.

Wicked good.

Phenomenally good.

And I haven't had a good time in a long time.

My eyes are closed and I'm in the moment when I hear clapping behind us. "Whoo. Yeah! That's what I'm talking about!"

I break apart from Mike and turn around to see three couples passing by on the sidewalk, cheering us on. Now I'm so freaked out I could die, but Mike keeps me close to him and rubs my shoulders.

"We must look good together," he whispers. "We sure do feel good together."

True.

"We can keep this going at my place," he says. "Have a private party and get to know each other on another level?"

"I don't know."

He directs his gray eyes at my brown ones. "I just want to spend more time with you, and my place definitely has more privacy than this parking lot."

I reach into my back pocket for my phone. "I'll follow you out. Type your address info in here."

He does and gives me one last hug before he walks over to his car. My heart races as I drop down into my driver's seat. Did I just say okay to a hook up with this man?

No, I didn't.

I agreed to visit his spot so I can stop kissing in public. When I get there, I don't have to go any further than I want to, because *no means no.*

I follow his silver Maxima down the road and I still don't know how I'm not panicking about any of this, but I'm not. With my eyes fixed on his license plate, our cars trace the curves of Lincoln Drive before my conscience kicks me in the head. I just kissed and held a man I barely know because he complimented me. That's not enough. It might have been enough when I was young and carnal, but it's not right now. I've grown up. I know better.

And what about John? Right about now he's probably getting some. Okay, so I don't know that, and this isn't about him anyway.

This battle is about me. The me following Mike Roberts and his Maxima down Lincoln Drive and through the city streets to an apartment in Germantown. Me, with the taut muscles and lethal curves, able to flag a man down while he's shopping for groceries.

God didn't help me transform myself so I could run right back to selfishly using my body because a brother kissed me and made me feel wanted and silky hot inside. But I don't have to hide behind large clothes or big hair just to shield myself from being *that girl.*

That girl with the hourglass shape.

That girl who loved too many guys.

That girl broken and bleeding on the pavement.

"Please, just go on and forgive yourself, girl," I whisper. "Lord, I know You forgive me, and You love me and You always will."

As soon as I turn off Lincoln Drive, I direct my car to the first empty parking lot I see. With my car stopped, I grab my phone and call Mike. He answers on the first ring.

"Chablis, did you get lost? I can stop and wait for you."

I close my eyes, the phone to my ear. "Listen, uh, I'm...I can't do this. You seem really cool and all, and we had a great time, but this isn't me."

He sighs. "I'm disappointed, but I respect you telling me. Like I said, I like your style. Call me when you get home?"

"Will do."

I end the call and sit for a moment in the quiet with my car bathed in yellow streetlight. I had a chance to hook up with a handsome man who was into me and I forfeited. I lost.

So why do I feel like I just won?

39

MARIAH

Mariah couldn't find a reason to be away from the house Wednesday evening. As soon as Oscar walked through the door and she laid eyes on him, she wished she'd had a reason to go shopping, or to a support group meeting, or out with a friend.

Anywhere to avoid speaking to her soon-to-be ex-husband. But she had no excuses when he arrived, so she planted herself on the living room couch and sat there.

"Mariah." Oscar nodded toward her.

"Oscar." She nodded back.

"Where's Benita?"

"In her room."

"Homework?"

"Yeah, it's that time."

"I'm going up to see her, all right?" He gestured up the stairs.

Mariah said nothing further as she watched him walk up the steps and out of sight.

This was the cold they now knew.

Oscar had filed for divorce. She'd responded in kind. He'd worked out a schedule for time with Binky and she'd agreed to it. When he'd retained a lawyer, she'd hired Bebb Family Law Services as her counsel.

He'd stopped attending Rise and started visiting Enon. She'd remained at their home church and attended weekly Bible study and prayer meeting.

Action, response, action, response.

He acted and she responded.

Separation meant they no longer behaved as one. Had fifteen years added up to this? They had joined together with love, excitement and possibility. In the end, they'd drifted apart in disappointment, distance and silence.

One morning in November, Mariah woke up in a cold sweat wondering if Oscar would stop providing for bills and supplies, ignore his daughter, find a girlfriend or otherwise start making her life a living hell.

None of that happened. Their relationship status had changed, but his integrity as a family man remained.

"Get up and stop overthinking things, Mariah," she mumbled.

In the kitchen, she reached inside the freezer, her hands touching a family-sized package of chicken. The other day, Binky had whined about being sick of chicken. Mariah had grown tired of it too, but their meals should always include lean protein.

She peered deeper in the freezer. They could eat shrimp with sautéed vegetables. Binky would probably mix everything together and toss it on top of some ramen noodles with sliced onions, and that was her prerogative. Lately, Mariah found her in the kitchen cooking a lot. She showed a knack for it this season, growing away from her obsessions with hair, makeup and clothing. Culinary arts gave her something to do. Something other than her parents' divorce or her iPhone, which Mariah still held onto.

She turned the tiny kitchen television to CNN and started slicing vegetables. World news and food preparation held her interest to the point where she forgot Oscar was even in the house. She jumped when she heard his voice behind her.

"Benita seems well."

Mariah whirled around, a green pepper in her hands. "Wha...ah...yes. She's doing good. Better grades now. Did she show you?"

Thank God for Binky, because frankly, she didn't know what else to discuss with him now that divorce proceedings were underway. When she stared at him for too long, rage, panic and numbness started to well up inside of her.

Was their marriage really over?

Did he even care that now she was doing this all on her own?

To her surprise, Oscar pulled out a kitchen chair and sat down. "Benita showed me her quarterly grades online. Her math skills are better. She's getting an A this semester."

"See what happens when you take a young lady's phone away? It works wonders."

The corners of his eyes crinkled as they laughed together. Mariah always adored Oscar's smile and the look in his eyes when he was happy. They used to laugh all the time, back when they behaved like buddies, supporting each other in the early years of their marriage. Pain surged through Mariah's heart as she walked over and stirred food on the stove. Busy work for her hands. "There's not so much drama lately with her school or dance team or anything on social media."

"I'm proud of her. And your food smells good. You have shrimp and veggies over there. Any brown rice?"

"No rice. I don't need it. I'm careful with the starchy stuff."

He looked as if he was waiting.

"Uh, you want something to eat?" The words left her mouth before she could stop them. But why not give him dinner? He paid for the kitchen table, the dishes, even the food. He was still her husband.

"You sure?"

"I'm sure."

For the next five minutes, they mimicked their old dinnertime routine. Mariah transferred the food into serving bowls. Oscar stood and carried the dinnerware into the dining room. He set the table for three before calling for Binky.

"Benita! Dinner!" He called up the stairs.

"I'm finishing my English paper. I'll eat later," she called back.

Oscar returned to the kitchen. "Just us for dinner."

"Okay." Mariah held serving bowls in both hands. "Grab the water pitcher, will you?"

He did, and then they sat in the dining room and prayed over their meals. Rewind the tape to last year and it looked like any weekday evening in the Rodriguez household when Oscar wasn't traveling for business.

Except things were different now.

They ate for a few minutes and then Oscar broke the silence.

"Mariah, since it's only the two of us, can we talk? Please."

"We're talking now."

"About the separation. The divorce."

A serious talk could ruin the peace, but he seemed so eager to dive into it. Guess it was inevitable.

"Okay." A ripple moved through her gut. "You go first."

"You filed your divorce response quickly."

"I did."

"You didn't want to talk about it."

"You served me fast. You didn't call to talk to me about it." She folded her arms across her chest. "If you didn't want a divorce, you wouldn't have filed."

"You're still my wife."

"That I am."

"Yesterday, I was sitting at my mom's house and I thought, why am I here? I should be with my family."

Mariah rolled her eyes. What memory should she share with him? The night when she wondered about her future — alone? How about the morning when she struggled about what she should tell their daughter?

And if they really did divorce, would she ever fall in love again or be unable to because bitterness consumed her? Even if she brought that up, he'd probably miss the point. She didn't want him to leave. She only wanted him to stop trying to control her.

"Our home is beautiful," he said. "And I miss being here with you and Benita. I miss the way you take care of both of us. We built all this together."

"Os, do you love me at all?" Melodramatic and emotional, but Mariah had to say it. She needed his answer to hit her ears.

"Of course, I love you. You're my wife."

"You keep saying, *my wife, my wife, my wife!* Like I'm a diamond ring or something you bought. I'm more than just your wife. I'm a person, not a possession."

"I know that."

"Do you?"

"Of course." He stood up and walked to her side. "I don't want this divorce. The drinking is what scared me so bad. When I thought about those bottles, all I saw was a future with a drunk stumbling through the house acting crazy."

Mariah shifted in her chair, crossing her legs and then uncrossing them. Men don't talk about these things easily. But he could have told her about his fears. She would've listened.

Instead, he stuffed clothes in his suitcase and drove to his mother's house. Didn't women do that? Yes, when the man had a drinking problem. This time it was the woman.

She was the woman. Woman with a potential *drinking problem*.

"We should talk more," he said. "Neither of us wants this. You know it and I know it. I've loved you since before I knew I could love anyone this deeply."

Mariah turned her face up so she could see him better. She needed to see his response. "Well, what if I don't change as fast as you want? What then?"

"You're not staying this way."

"Staying what way?"

"Drinking too much. Bottles in the garage?"

"They're gone now."

"You're still drinking though, huh?"

Why should she lie or defend herself?

"Yes," she said.

"When I stop this divorce, you're going straight to Alcoholics Anonymous. I'm not playing with you."

Mariah pushed her chair back. "See, this is what you do, and this is why we fight. All you do is look for ways to change me."

"And all you do is rebel. You did it when I kept after you take better care of yourself, and you did it again when you went against me to get the bypass surgery. Why can't you ever just listen to me? I'm your husband."

"I need love, not constant orders." She stood up then, placing her body toe-to-toe with her husband. "Change has to come from inside of me— when I'm ready and on my own terms."

"Your terms take too long. What about our family?"

Mariah jabbed Oscar's chest with her index finger. "How can we grow a family when you're always mad at me or pushing some agenda!"

"Mom! Dad! Stop it!" Binky called to them from the doorway. Her face reddened and she crossed her arms over her chest. She started toward both of them. "Please!"

Oscar took a step back from Mariah and faced his daughter. "Benita, stay out of this. Go outside or go back to your room."

"You can't keep fighting each other like this," Binky huffed. "I'm not going anywhere until you stop."

This time Mariah stepped back, dropping her gaze to the floor. All of them—they had to calm down.

"Binky," Mariah said, taking a deep breath. "We'll stop, but you have to go. You can't be here right now. Seriously. Outside or upstairs, your choice."

Mariah watched as Binky's eyes bounced from Oscar's face to hers, back again, and then finally over to the doorway. No one said anything else until the girl had left the room, her feet carrying her to the staircase and back upstairs.

"Oh, come off it, Mariah." Oscar spoke first, his voice lower this time. "I never had any agenda. I always wanted a big family, and you knew that since you were twenty and you put your body down on my mattress and told me that's what you wanted, too. So, what? Did you tell me that just so I'd marry you? Got pregnant so you'd get your man? Was that *your* agenda?"

Mariah gritted her teeth, lacing her fingers behind her back. "Apologize for saying that, right now."

"I'm not apologizing for nothing. Are you going to apologize for lying to me about what the doctor said?"

"I needed more time."

"I'm not wasting any more years of my life waiting for you to get it together, woman. Not one more."

Then they stood there breathing for a moment. When he finally backed away, she turned her gaze to the dining room rug. She listened as his footsteps moved from the dining room to the hallway and then to the front door. The sound of keys jingled in his pocket. His feet stopped at the front door. She heard it open, then close.

No slam. Just closed.

Mariah looked around. She could clean up the dining room later. In the hallway, she grabbed her coat and bag from the closet.

"B--Binky," her voice cracked as she yelled up the stairs. "I'm going to Bible study."

At church, she walked straight past the groups of people talking in the atrium. She opened the door to the sanctuary and traveled all the way across to the far side. There in the back pew, between four of her girlfriends, sat Chablis. She looked like a doll, with a knockout makeup job and a colorful scarf tied in a neat bow around her pink-streaked curls. Her blue bedazzled t-shirt read *God's Property*.

As Mariah approached them, she watched Chablis gaze change from joyful to serious. Without words, her cousin stood up and walked out of the row. She grabbed Mariah's hand and led her out of the sanctuary.

In the atrium, they headed right into Prayer Room #1. Once inside, Mariah sat on the bench with Chablis' arms wrapped around her. Her tears fell, soaking her arms and hands. Chablis murmured prayers, softly interceding for her cousin, rocking her as she cried. And Mariah prayed too, repenting for nearly everything her husband had mentioned earlier. The lying. The drinking. Even the comfort food she used to overeat years earlier. By the time she ran out of words, she realized she'd just fulfilled her own prophecy.

Change arrived on its own, on her own terms.

Mariah's marriage?

Over?

Happiness didn't arrive with a smaller body.

Now she understood it didn't show up in a wine bottle, either.

40

TOWANDA

Towanda had watched Mariah from a distance for the past five minutes. There she stood in her driveway that Sunday, right next to her Accord, pulling her black wool coat shut. Then she walked around to get something out of her trunk. She handed an overstuffed plastic bag to Binky, who carried it into the house.

The perfect time to approach her would never arrive. Towanda had to make do with the present. She pulled her blue cashmere scarf closer around her neck as she headed into the Rodriguez family's driveway.

Mariah glanced over at her when she stood about ten feet away from the car. "You can stop right there, all right. I saw you follow us home from Rise. What do you want?"

Towanda tugged at the tips of her leather gloves. "I just came to see...um, how are you doing?"

"I'm well," Mariah said, slamming the car trunk shut. "And yourself?"

"I'm good."

Towanda had no game plan. No idea how to battle the tension between them. All week long she'd thought of how she'd go to Mariah and talk with her in person. When she processed her strategy, she hadn't had to deal with her emotions. But now, with Mariah's gaze on her, shame, guilt and fear washed over her like a wave from a toxic beach.

The Lord had brought her this far. He would have to carry her the rest of the way.

She cleared her throat while taking a baby step forward. "How's Binky?"

"Oh, you came here to visit her? You can ask her yourself." Mariah turned and yelled toward the house. "Binky, your godmother is here—"

"No wait," Towanda said, too late. Binky arrived at the side door and a smile broke out on her face.

"Auntie! Hey." The girl bounded down the stairs and over to Towanda for a hug. "Are you finally finished pushing for business for the year? I haven't seen you in like forever. Mom said you were swamped with work."

Towanda embraced Binky, shifting her eyes over to Mariah's face. She must not have revealed to Binky that Towanda was there when she got sick at her birthday barbecue. "Missed you too, darling. And...we'll catch up...but uh...I really need to talk to your mom alone right now."

Binky kissed her on both cheeks. "Come get me upstairs when you get done. You like noodles? I can make pho from scratch now. I learned on YouTube. I'll make some for you."

Warmth spread through Towanda's chest. This girl with her boundless energy and her growing interests. Towanda missed this so much. "I'll come right up after. I promise."

As soon as Binky headed back in the house, a cold December wind whipped through, almost taking Towanda off her feet.

"It's frigid out here, Mariah. Can I come in?"

Mariah's eyes were icy brown orbs. "The last time you set foot in this house, you pushed me past my limits. I don't know why you did it and I've stopped wondering. Now, I want to hear what you have to say, but pardon me, because you're going to have to give me a minute before I let you come into my home again."

Towanda swallowed hard. She nodded as she shifted her weight from foot to foot. "Will you at least come talk with me in the car? I have a few things to say and then get out of your hair, I promise."

Snowflakes drifted here and there, flurrying from the clouds above. They appeared to mimic the cold look on Mariah's face. Towanda could brace herself from the weather. She'd have to accept the icy reaction from her friend. It was the cold she'd sown into both of their lives.

Mariah sighed. "Let me put my things in the house."

"Thanks." Towanda trudged back down the driveway and over to the sidewalk. Her Range Rover was parked two houses away.

Inside the car, she turned the heat on but kept her sound system off. Who knew if this was going to be the last significant conversation they'd have together? They needed to hear each other clearly.

By the time Mariah climbed into the Range Rover and shut the door, it was fifteen minutes later, and she'd changed out of her church outfit. Now, she wore a white down vest, a Temple University hooded sweatshirt, cherry-colored leggings, thick white socks and running sneakers.

"I forgot to ask. How did your classes go this semester?" Towanda asked.

Mariah faced forward, her gaze on the dashboard. "You didn't come over here to talk about Temple. What do you have to say, T?"

So, she wasn't going to make this easy. But that didn't matter. What mattered? This was Towanda's opportunity to do one of the hardest things she'd ever had to do.

Apologize to her friend and sister in person. And do it from the heart.

Towanda gripped her steering wheel. "Mariah, you know you aren't just my buddy. You've been my sister-from-another-mother for so long, I can't keep track."

"Twenty-one years."

"That long?"

"Yes, but you can go on."

This was the hard part. "I wanted things to stay the same, for you to stay the same. I know I pushed you to eat that plate full of food on Binky's birthday. I should have realized it was too much for you, but I wasn't thinking. I promise I didn't know you'd get sick like that, and—"

Mariah's bottom lip trembled. "My family was here. My daughter's friends. I was so embarrassed, and that pain was unbelievable."

"I'm so sorry. From the bottom of my heart, Mariah. If I could turn back time, I'd change it all. But I can't."

Towanda watched as Mariah sat there for a moment, her chest rising and falling with each breath. She may not have liked what she heard, but at least she'd stayed and listened to the apology.

She turned toward Towanda. "That can't be all you have to say to me. I don't know what you've been to me this year, but you cannot say you've been my friend. Friends don't do what you did. You followed me all the way home today, so I want to know. Why'd you turn on me?"

Towanda moved her gaze to the window. More snow falling. It was starting to cover the lawn, turning the green grass into a blanket of clean and white. She shut her eyes and began to speak.

"I had a hard time seeing you when you dropped the weight, so I just stayed away. You called me on it, and I lied, but you were right. Then, I don't know. I struggled to be happy for you looking better each day, coming out of your shell. Jealous you were changing so fast. Afraid you'd abandon me for your new friends and your new goals."

"Chablis lost weight."

"She's younger, and she's not my best friend. With you, I remember when guys used to brush past me in the hallway at high school so they could rush to your side. I remember when people used to pass me notes to try to beg for your phone number. Anything to get to you."

"That bothered you? You never told me."

Towanda relaxed her head on the headrest. "Sometimes things like that stay locked inside." She sighed. "I hated the idea of being the invisible woman again."

"You? Invisible?"

"Yes, me. Invisible."

They remained silent for at least ten minutes. All Towanda heard was wind and snowflakes hitting the glass.

Finally, Mariah spoke, her voice steady. "Invisible or not, you were my favorite friend and I loved you. You didn't have to be perfect to be my sister."

"I was hurtful—"

Mariah finished the statement. "And rude, mean, nasty and a million other negative things, but you're still my sister. I didn't get to choose Tamron. I chose you. It almost killed me, but I did choose you."

She stopped, a strange look on her face.

"What's the matter?"

She shook her head. "I'm still angry with you...and you have to let me work through that. And—I've got issues with Os. But with you talking to me now, I feel like there's things I have to say to him and—"

"Want to go talk to him now? I don't see his truck. When's he coming home?"

"He's not, and it's a long, depressing story." Mariah reached for the door handle.

"Wait! Can you come with me for a minute? I need to show you something. As a matter of fact, ask Binky to come out here. We can all go together. It won't take away your pain, but it might take your mind off of Oscar, at least for a little while."

Towanda watched while Mariah held on to the door handle, a look of contemplation in her eyes. A few moments later, she nodded. "Okay. I'll get Binky. Be right back."

Oscar had left the house? That couldn't be good. Mariah probably needed someone to talk to or pray with after he vacated, but she hadn't said anything. Towanda couldn't blame her.

Like she'd said, Towanda had been anything but a good friend this year.

But that would change starting today.

Towanda, Mariah, and Binky stood side by side on the sidewalk in South Philly. Binky jogged over, put her hands around her eyes and peered in the glass storefront window.

"There's all this dust in there, and it looks dark. I think I see cobwebs," Binky said.

"The owner said the last renter moved out three months ago. It was a breakfast and coffee spot, but that place closed up shop." Towanda glanced over at Mariah. "The last time Binky was here, she was how old? Four?"

"Four sounds about right. I had to grab her to keep her from climbing up on the stools, trying to get to the cake on top of the display case."

Binky turned around. "This was Nana Cakes?"

"This was Nana Cakes," Towanda said. "Soon to be eatLARGE, my new business. And your Mom can help me. She knows all about good eating now. Your energetic cousin can pitch in, too. You know she can't resist a challenge."

Mariah bit her lip, shaking her head. "Listen, T, like I said, I'm still upset and—"

"Why are you upset, Mom?" Binky asked.

Towanda and Mariah both turned toward her at the same time.

"Never mind," they said simultaneously and then laughed together.

Towanda clasped her gloved hands. "Mariah, I'm not asking you to run the thing on your own, but I'm not going to be able to work full time on this place. I need your help. It's going to be a healthy eating spot. If you help with it, I'll pay you a contractor's fee, unless you fall in love with it and want to join me as a business partner. That's an offer, and there's NO pressure on you, but I can't think of anyone I'd trust more for this."

"I'll think about it and I'll let you know, okay? By the way, what are you going to do with thinkLARGE?"

"ThinkLARGE is my baby and I'm not leaving it. I'll put up the money and we can start small with this. You always said you wanted to be an entrepreneur. Start here. It doesn't matter if we fail or we succeed. What matters is that we give it a try."

Binky jogged back to them. "You know, we should have a group hug. This is like a group hug moment right here, I'd say."

Towanda pulled a tissue from her pocket and wiped her nose. "See, this girl is stealing all my good lines."

Mariah wrapped one arm around Binky's shoulders and the other around Towanda's. "Can you blame her? She's been around you since birth."

"Yeah," Towanda said. "I helped raise her."

BACK AT THE RODRIGUEZ'S HOUSE, MARIAH TURNED AROUND TO FACE Binky, who was sitting in the back seat of Towanda's car. "Here, take my keys and go inside. I'll be there in a minute."

"Don't tell me you're going to sit out here forever?" Binky asked.

"I'll be there in a minute, I promise."

Binky scooted out, slamming the car door behind her.

Mariah turned to Towanda, vulnerability in her eyes. "Os filed for divorce, I've hired a lawyer...and—I might have another problem."

Towanda leaned in and listened.

Like friends do.

41

CHABLIS

With my phone pressed to my ear, I'm on my way into the main branch of the Philadelphia library for a free Tech in Philly seminar, but I stop before going inside. I'm talking to Charlene Champagne Shields. This conversation might take a while.

"Hey, Mom!"

"What happened to your hair?"

I rest my back against the gray concrete ledge on the side of the library. "I cut it."

"I can see that. I'm on Instagram."

"I know its short. You don't like it?"

"Oh, it's real short! Like elementary school boy short. You have no hair at all in the back of your head."

"I know."

"Are you having issues? Broken heart? Something with that John guy?"

"No."

"What about those dance folks you hang out with? They put you up to this, huh? You met somebody there, and now you want to be cool too, so you change your hair?"

I roll my eyes. Why is it if you make a major change to your life, people assume you've lost your mind? Or you're depressed? Or you have a secret boyfriend, or girlfriend, or a drug addiction, or those partying friends are changing your values?

No offense to down and out folks who start changing where they go and what they do, but that's not me. Okay, so I didn't like seeing John snuggling with women in Berlin, but neither that nor my job loss was enough to make me depressed.

The pink curls? My choice all alone.

My mom needs an answer, so I just say, "No."

"Then what?"

"I decided on a change."

"What about work? You planning on being a tattoo artist or a boutique owner?"

"What?"

"I'm trying to think about your job options when the front of your hair looks like a bottle of strawberry lemonade."

That's when the giggle tumbles out of my mouth and keeps going because my mom cracks me up.

"Stop it, Chablis!"

"It's only hair, and I work in software. Some of those engineers wear cut-off shorts and Comic-Con t-shirts to work every day. No one I would work with cares about some pink streaks."

"I've never seen you like this before. You have all these muscles now, and you hang with strangers every week. Now you go and chop off all your hair because you feel like it. What's next? Tattoos all up and down your body?"

"Actually—"

"Chablis!"

"Mom, it's still me." I switch the phone around to my other ear. "I still serve in ministry. I'm in worship service every Sunday, Bible study and prayer meeting on Wednesdays. Yes, I dance with folks you don't know, but these same people teach for free at after-school programs and run book drives."

"Ain't none of that have to do with your hair, pinky."

"You hate my hair that much?"

"No." She sighs. "There's so much going on the world today. You're my only child. I don't want to sit here missing all the signs, thinking you're okay because you never said nothing to me. Three months ago, the daughter of one of my old coworkers ran off to Las Vegas with a man and a woman. She died with meth in her system and no one in her family had a clue what she was into."

I pray silently for that family, then I pray for peace for my mom, since she has the wrong idea.

She's scared. She almost lost me once. I get it.

"Mom, I'm so sorry for those people, but the deceased lady is not me. I'm just a Christian girl who happens to work out a lot. Right now, I can't afford an expensive hairstyle, so I took a shot at a something new. I'm not depressed, on drugs, fallen away from the church or any of that. Trust."

"Thank you for telling me. But does it need to be that short? What if you grew it out some?"

I roll my eyes. "Love you. Bye, Mom."

I end the call and walk into the library because the seminar is about to start and I need to consider what I'm going to grow into next.

AT HOME THIS AFTERNOON, I'M SITTING IN FRONT OF MY LAPTOP STARING at a message from John. Maybe he tried to contact me these past few weeks. I wouldn't know. It's kind of hard for him to get to me after I blacklisted his number on my phone, blocked him from my email, Facebook, Instagram, and stopped following him on Twitter. But I forgot to delete my connection to him on LinkedIn.

So, guess where he messaged me?

MESSAGING

John Gerald • 9:07 AM

Where did you go? I can't reach you anymore. Did you get a new number? I heard you've been crushing it in the gym and everywhere else. Travis told me you plan to enter the Broad Street Run next year. Proud of you, girl! I miss talking to you. Get back to me when you can.

MY HEART BEATS FASTER AS I READ HIS WORDS. WHEN I CLOSE MY EYES, I can see us joking and laughing together after our Saturday runs and my insides melt like hot marshmallow fluff. But then I think of his tattooed arms wrapped around those women and blood rushes to my head. Why wait to respond?

MESSAGING
Chablis C. Shields • 2:35 PM
Hey buddy! I'm job hunting and my time is nuts right now. I wish you well. Glad you are healthy and happy.

AND I MUST HAVE BEEN CRAZY TO THINK HE WAS GOING TO ACCEPT THAT ridiculous Disney-fied answer. I'm staring at my laptop screen while chewing on the tips of my nails when his response shows up twenty minutes later.

MESSAGING
John Gerald • 2:55 PM
Can you please pick up the phone and call me? I need to talk to you. And why are you looking for a job?

HE NEEDS TO SPEAK TO ME? THE SAME MAN WHO TOLD ME HE HAD TO BE really careful about dating anyone and then filled his arms with foreign chicks in Berlin? I'm not falling for it. And since he wants to know what's up with me, I'm gonna let him know.

MESSAGING
Chablis C. Shields • 2:59 PM
My company downsized. Here's everything you need to know about

me that you don't know already: I love Pizza Hut pizza. Sometimes, if I have certain triggers, I'll have a panic attack. That's my burden to bear after the beating. I also have a scar running down my cheek that I disguise with waterproof makeup. That's also from the beating. I am fit and dancing now. I love it. Thank you for training me. You haven't heard from me because I don't want to talk to you anymore. I was crushing on you hard before you left. You and me? We would have made one dope couple. I would have LOVED you. I hope the Lord blesses you good, but right now I don't need reminders of what I'm not going to have. So, you take care, and I pray you make it to American Ninja Warrior or at least the CrossFit Games. I'm still rooting for you!

I SEND THE MESSAGE AND LOG OFF LINKEDIN. AFTER I SHUT MY LAPTOP down, I use my phone to scroll through my schedule for the rest of the day. Job interview at 4:30 p.m. Life group tonight at 7:00 p.m. Bed after that. Tomorrow is another day.

Right now, a quick jog around the block should clear my head. I push myself out of my chair and grab my Nikes from beside the couch. No matter what, I'm thankful for all my opportunities, and for the rest of this day, I'm going to crush it.

TUESDAY MEANS LIFE GROUP OVER AT THE JONES' HOME. THIS TIME IT'S MY turn to serve as a teacher for the kids. Tonight Rev. Alex Robinson serves as my assistant teacher. He is my brother in Christ, but I swear if he asks me to pray for his aspiring actress/singer/gospel play writing former fiancée D'Londa, I'm going to run screaming down the street.

This is our final life group meeting before winter break and I think the kids are happy about that. They're lying around the family room, looking as if they're going to convince us to let them turn on the Play-Station. I see four of them grinning at me expectantly when I step in the room.

"I like your hair, Chablis," Rev. Robinson tells me when he walks in.

"Thanks." I set up two chairs for us at the front of the room. "It was time for a change."

"You know, D'Londa used to wear hers with burgundy streaks all through the front and sides. I loved that style on her."

This brother has problems.

But then again, we all have issues. He's in love with a woman preoccupied with chasing her dreams in life, but he won't give up on her. Is that so bad? I fell hard for my trainer and it wasn't meant to be. We need to show more grace to one another. At the end of the day, we're all just trying to get by.

As soon as he sits down, I turn to him. "Hey, I pray you hear from her soon. And for real, she could sure do worse than to have a good man like you in her corner."

He sighs. "That means a lot to me, especially right now. Thanks."

"No problem, man."

The Jones' eight-year-old daughter, Brianna, Brianna's friend Jada whom she invited to visit Life Group, the Chase's two sons Jarvis and Kinard, and Rev. Robinson's nephew Samson all settle down and open their lesson books. As the kids listen to us lead the lesson and then read through Scripture and talk through their questions and answers, I gaze into their faces and listen to their voices. So innocent at this age. So many possibilities for them. But right now, they're also fidgeting, and I can tell they'd rather do anything but keep reading.

I elbow Rev. Robinson. "You know they want to play, right?"

"Looks like it. Y'all dying to play some games, huh?"

Of course, as they stare up at us, their little bodies are wiggling around and they are nodding at us like *yes, yes, please*. We give the go ahead and they turn on the TV and PlayStation and start fussing about who will take their turn first.

After I stand up, I turn to Rev. Robinson. "Listen, if you want to go to the living room and sit in one of the groups for prayer tonight, I'll keep an eye on the kiddies."

He's gone as soon as I finish the sentence.

Grace. We all need it.

When the kids settle on MarioKart, I get up and drag my chair to the back of the room. My eyes are wet as I sit down and pull out my phone, even though I barely know what I'm doing. I tap Messenger, then scroll down my message list until I see Tony Hart's message. The one for which I never sent a response.

My finger trembles, hovering over his name. Before I tap the name, I take a deep breath and look up and around. I'm here with my life group. The people God provided to love and care for me. I survived to experience this. God never wanted me to be attacked or have panic issues, but He showed up and showed out when I recovered with no lasting brain damage.

I tap the message and enter my response fast.

I AM FINE. I AM DANCING AGAIN. AND YES, I DO FORGIVE YOU.

LATER, ALONE IN MY APARTMENT, I SHOWER AND GET READY TO CRASH. After I say my prayers and stretch out on my comforter, I grab my phone and tap Messenger one last time. There are three messages from different Help Squad members, and right under that, a message from Tony Hart. This time I tap it right away and read his words. There are only two. The only two he needed to say.

THANK YOU.

42

MARIAH

I *need your decision. The position is yours if you want it.*

Mariah put her phone down on the desk and thought for a moment. Towanda wanted her answer as to whether she would take a contract position and manage eatLARGE.

The truth? She still had concerns about working so closely with Towanda, especially on such a big project as a new restaurant. And even though they were talking again daily, Mariah still felt resentment and anger about the pain Towanda had put her through.

Their friendship? They needed to go slow.

I can't commit to a business partnership right now, T. Mariah tapped onto her screen. *I'll help when I can and we can talk about it again after I graduate.*

Towanda's return message appeared a minute later.

I understand. Let me know if you need me for anything.

I will.

But Mariah still needed a job. Finding a job after fifteen years of being a homemaker? Becoming fluent in Japanese in a year might be an easier task. But she wanted to stand on her own two feet financially, because Binky wouldn't be in high school forever.

The sooner she started earning her own money, the better. She'd search for a part-time office position somewhere. She typed returning to the workforce after being a stay-at-home-mom into Google, her eyes widening as the results appeared.

Advice galore. The blog entries seemed helpful, and experts pushed similar tactics regarding considering her strengths and listing those on her new resume.

"Keep hope alive, Mariah, keep hope alive," Mariah chanted to herself when she abandoned her laptop and walked to her closet. More than a hundred pounds down and she didn't own a stitch of professional clothing.

"Clothes. Now, clothes I can fix fast," she said.

She picked up her phone and entered a reminder to go clothes shopping. Macy's and Marshalls would have what she needed but visiting those stores could wait until later.

First, she needed to pick up Binky from school. Binky could ride the school bus home, but Mariah enjoyed picking up her daughter. It gave them a chance to talk and bond.

With the divorce hearing coming soon, the two of them needed to stay close. The girl hadn't been happy to learn about it earlier that morning. Maybe Mariah could cheer her up. It meant going back on her promise, but once she closed her car door, she reached inside her purse for Binky's cell phone. What if she returned it to her on a trial basis? Her daughter could text her friends again.

Mariah turned on the iPhone, entered Binky's passcode, and reviewed her apps. No Instagram, Facebook, or Snapchat apps. She breathed a sigh of relief that her daughter hadn't somehow found the phone and added them back.

Curiosity made her tap the Messages icon and what looked like hundreds of entries appeared on the screen. She scrolled through and tapped a few of them. Lots of group texts and pictures of hairstyles, and several requests for information about homework assignments and grades on test papers. Standard teen stuff.

When she reached the top, she spied an entry from Idris, the boy Binky had a crush on. He'd visited the house for her birthday party, but Mariah never saw them together.

She shouldn't, but she did. She tapped the Idris entry.

Two words: *You there?*

That was it. Nothing further from Mr. Idris.

Farther down on the list was a name Mariah didn't recognize. More like a nickname.

Darkman?

Who was that? Some kid with a comic book obsession? Probably asking for homework information. Mariah tapped the message.

HEY, BENITA. *I HAVE A NEW PHONE NOW, CASE YOU DON'T RECOGNIZE MY number. Holla back.*

HIS NEXT MESSAGE:

MAYBE YOU'RE BUSY. YOU SAID WE COULD MEET UP SOON? WERE YOU ABLE *2 get a key 2 your cousin's apartment close to City Line? I don't work far from there. Your pics have been on my mind all week! I have to see you. Get at me.*

MARIAH CLUTCHED THE PHONE TO HER CHEST.

Binky! Ooh!

She started the car and peeled out of the driveway so fast her tires squealed. She placed the vehicle in drive and zipped down to the end of the block. A stop sign kept her from speeding through the intersection. She rolled down her window and chucked the iPhone out of it, watching it slide across the ground until it disappeared into the sewer opening where it belonged.

On the way to school, she fished her own phone out of her bag.

Oscar. She had to talk to him right away.

He answered after three rings. "Mariah."

"Os! You have time to talk?"

"Yes, I can talk now. Are you all right?"

"I'm fine, listen, it's about Binky."

"Benita? What is it now?"

"I scrolled through her texts. I don't have any proof, but I think she's trying to meet men online. One of them, some guy named Darkman, asked about meeting her at Chablis' apartment."

"Do you know if she did?"

"I don't think so. Chablis doesn't keep secrets like that. But I'm about to ask who Darkman is." Mariah paused to let out loud sigh. "And I don't just need to talk to her. I need to talk to you. Come to the house, please. Not just for Binky. For me, too. We need you."

Mariah kept driving, moving straight ahead as she waited for his reply.

"I'll be there as soon as I can."

MARIAH STOPPED HER ACCORD IN THE NO PARKING ZONE IN FRONT OF Binky's school building. If a policeman drove around, he'd have to ask her to move. She sat on her hands as Binky approached the car and climbed in.

"Hey, Mom." Binky closed the car door and then turned to pull something out of her backpack.

"Benita Rodriguez, you look at me right now!"

Binky moved her eyes upward with a *what now, Mom* expression on her face.

"Have you been talking to men online?" Mariah asked.

"What? No. That's crazy."

"Direct messaging through your apps? Or on Facebook?"

"Mom, you've had my phone for months."

"Yes, I have. So, who's Darkman? Better yet, how does he know Chablis' apartment is close to City Line?"

Binky turned and stared out the window. Her ponytail smacked the side of her cheek as she moved.

Mariah prompted her. "You'd better talk, girl. I'm not going home until you do."

"Darkman? He's a family friend of Naomi's. He was at the house with her brother when I slept over. He thought I was pretty, and I emailed him a few pics of me. I only gave him my phone number because he begged for it. I knew I couldn't talk to him because you had the phone. It's nothing Mom."

"Nothing? Does he know you're only fifteen?"

"I guess. I mean, he knows Naomi and I are in the same class so, yeah. I hadn't thought about it. It's not that deep."

"What about meeting up with him?"

"I was talking trash, I didn't mean it. Just emailing him. Sending selfies. He'd been teasing me about being all scared to see him. I was kind of teasing back, writing him things I didn't mean. Dumb stuff."

"You mean lying?"

She shrugged. Mariah clenched her hands tight to keep from reaching back and shaking her daughter. "According to his message, you said enough for him to think you were serious. How old is he?"

"Mom—"

"How old, Binky?"

"Twenty." Binky looked down at her lap.

This kid kept playing with fire. One of these days, she would get burned. Online accounts. Cell phones. Direct messages. Texts. Photos and videos. Parents shouldn't have it this hard. If a group of parents filed a class-action suit against the technology companies, Mariah would be the first to sign.

"Benita, I'm not moving this car until you tell me why you keep doing these things."

Binky shrugged again, her face red. "I don't know. I want guys to like me. I like to feel wanted, and I want to feel beautiful."

"But you are beautiful."

"I don't feel that way. Girls act jealous, hating on me or saying nasty stuff about me to boys I like. Or, they'll just go further physically than I will and take a guy away that I really like. That's what happened with Idris."

"Why didn't you tell me?"

Binky sniffed, crossing her arms. "Can we just go home, please? I wanna go home."

Mariah turned around. "Oh, we can go home. But we're going to keep talking."

The road in front of her blurred a bit, but she steeled herself to drive home calmly.

Jealousy, huh? Jealous girl or jealous woman, it was all the same—hate. She remembered high school well. The boys liked her just fine, but the girls could be vicious with their eye rolls and attitudes, jealous of Mariah's beauty and grace. Years ago, Chablis used to complain about the girls she had to physically fight off just because she owned a body shaped like a figure eight, and she made their boyfriends' heads turn when she walked down the hallways. No one proved brave enough to battle Towanda, but Mariah had definitely seen shorter women wear sky-high heels trying to imitate her towering height. All of it, swirls of envy projected onto the woman who possessed what the other woman desired.

Dumb. Just plain stupid.

Every woman had something another woman wanted.

When would they all learn to stop staring each other down and just accept themselves for who God made them to be?

WITH BINKY FOLLOWING, MARIAH WALKED INTO THEIR HOME IN A DAZE. How could someone so loved and protected be so darned insecure? Ever since she'd given birth to Binky, she'd made her daughter a priority. She'd been an attentive stay-at-home mother, thinking her presence would be better than a daycare center for her little one.

And after that, she enrolled her daughter in quality schools, made sure she attended Sunday School, youth retreats and dance lessons. And what about the nights when she read Binky bedtime stories and tucked her in at night? What about every home-cooked breakfast, lunch, and dinner, spending hour after hour of quality time with her daughter? All the mornings when she told her God had a plan for her life and she was beyond price? Those investments could not equal a girl with such low self-esteem she needed to tease grown men for attention.

No! No! No! No! NO!

Mariah slammed the front door shut. "Sit your behind down!"

"Can I—"

"I said, sit your behind down!"

Binky trudged to the living room couch and plopped down on it. Mariah sat in the chair across from her but leaned close to her daughter's face.

"Benita. You've gone too far!"

"I know, and I'm sorry, but I…"

"Just shut up!" Mariah clenched her fists in her lap to keep her hands from shaking. "I've spent fifteen years sacrificing time, and love, and God knows what else for you, and for some reason you behave as if life is a game. Darkman? Who cares if Naomi's family knows him? You don't know him! He's a grown man and he wants to meet with a teenager. Do you realize that's like some sick R. Kelly fantasy? My God, Benita!"

"Mom…Mom, please don't cry."

Mariah ignored the water in her eyes. "Do you hear anything the grown folks in your life tell you? Do you?"

"Yes."

"No, you don't. If you did, you would've remembered the story Dr. Blackshear told at the youth summit last year. About that girl in Bucks County who had a fight with her mother and then ran away to a male friend's house. That friend invited a buddy to come over, and even the detectives aren't sure about everything those nuts did to that girl, because her body decayed in a creek for weeks before they found it. Is that what you're going for with all this sneaky stuff you're doing? Is that what you want?"

"No!" Tears stained Binky's cheeks.

"Me, your dad, people from your church—God put us here to love you and protect you. This isn't a game. We're accountable for you, and for more than a year, all you've been doing is hurting our feelings and taking us for granted. I'm sick to death of it, Benita, and I'm not taking it anymore! It's not cute, and it's not funny, and if you can't see from fifteen years' worth of love and support that you're priceless…I…I can't find the words to tell you."

"Mom, I'm sorry. I'll stop. I promise. I'm so sorry." Binky wrapped her arms around her mother's neck and squeezed tight. "I love you. I'm proud of you and I'm sorry."

Mariah felt her daughter's heart beating against her chest. Gushing love mixed with anger and frustration filled her, resulting in a pounding headache. Binky needed to hear more, but those words would have to come from her father.

"Get upstairs. Your dad'll be here soon," Mariah said, pushing Binky aside.

"Mom—"

"Go…"

Binky grabbed her backpack and ran upstairs. Mariah remained in the living room and waited for Oscar. She moved over to the couch and stretched out, looking down the hallway toward the kitchen. A large glass of red wine, maybe two, sure would help her forget the past hour.

She closed her eyes and took a deep breath. Wine might help her stop thinking about it, but it wouldn't take away this pain, or any other, from her life.

Then she must have drifted off for a while. When she opened her eyes, Oscar sat next to her feet, a worried expression on his face.

"Did you talk to Benita?"

"Yes." Mariah sat up. "She's going through some deep stuff — things I didn't know about. Emailing older guys and sending pics of herself. Trying to get attention." She shook her head, grimacing. "I had to throw her phone away for good. I thought maybe she could have it back again, but she won't be able to handle it. Too much of a mess for her to get into. I came back home and lit into her."

"You made a good decision about the phone. She has to live without one, at least until she's old enough live on her own." He rubbed his face with both hands. "I love Benita. I don't know if I have the right words to say to her right now, but I'll figure it out. She's in her room?"

Mariah straightened up and looked at her husband, dressed neatly in his business clothing, with his thick dark hair brushed back and gleaming. Her eyes centered in on his hands. He still wore his wedding band.

"Yes, and she should hear from you, but can you listen to me for a minute first?"

"What do you need?"

Need? She needed to find a way to put the pieces of her world back together, but there seemed to be no solution.

Did she *need* him?

Yes.

Despite all the fighting and pain, deep in her heart, her love for him remained. Hope lived in that love, and she needed to express it. She could be prideful or truthful at this moment.

"Os, I need you. I need you here with Binky and me, and I need you to be my husband. Things have been rough between us, but we married for better or for worse. I chose you almost from the minute I first saw you walk past me. I chose you."

There. She'd said it. No matter what his response, at least she'd told him the truth.

"Mariah, I chose you too."

When his words reached her ears, she found the courage to keep talking.

"We made a life together. We didn't count on all these disappointments, but that's life. You aren't a disappointment, you're the love of my life."

"I know what you're saying."

"Can you explain it to me please, because I'm not totally sure what I said."

"I love you, and I don't know if I'm ready to walk away completely."

He heard her and he understood. Maybe they could start from there.

Mariah stretched her hand out, her wedding band on display. "You remember when I used to wear this on a chain around my neck? Those days are over."

"You've come so far." He sighed, moving his body closer to hers. "I thought we'd have a house filled with kids by now, and then I got bitter when it didn't happen. But I should've taken that to God, not turned it all on you."

"I can't promise I'll be perfect, but what I can say is, fifteen years ago, I chose you to work these things through with."

He wrapped an arm around her shoulders. "We have a lot of work to do."

Mariah recalled Towanda's words from the previous week. "We do. I know. But we need to make an effort. If we fail or if we succeed, what matters most is that we tried."

She closed her eyes and relaxed, feeling the warmth of her husband beside her. If she let herself concentrate only on the moment, that at least, seemed reasonable.

43

TOWANDA

When Towanda told Chablis about the trouble she'd had while trying to locate a chef to partner with for eatLARGE, Chablis had mentioned a Help Squad member who had prayed for his cousin who was trying to find a better chef position. Right away, she asked Chablis to get the man's name and phone number and send it on to her. That Friday, she phoned Gabriel Seay and asked him to stop by the restaurant the next day.

When Saturday afternoon arrived, Towanda opened the storefront door with a smile on her face, grinning at Binky as she walked through the empty space. She'd brought Binky with her to give Mariah some time to herself so she could plan her next school semester.

The idea of bringing a new restaurant to a changing neighborhood juiced up Towanda. She'd stayed up for hours in her home office researching and working on the concept, examining the local competition, making sure the location would work and drafting and redrafting the business plan.

Lots of work. But Towanda was in her element, especially with the research. So many things appeared to be in her favor too, like the restaurant's location close to South Street, the availability of the space and rent negotiation.

What Towanda hadn't counted on was the kitchen area needing so much work. It appeared no one had upgraded anything since Nana Cakes had closed. Reviewing the prices for refrigerators and stoves had given her sticker shock. She hadn't ever heard Nana or her aunts discuss whether they'd leased or bought their ovens. Either way, it was going to cost quite a bit of money to upgrade it all, more than Towanda was willing to invest from her savings. To get up and running, she'd have to apply for a small business loan.

But she definitely had a brand new business and she was steadily building her empire.

"Binky, what are you doing, girl?" Towanda spied her goddaughter sitting in a corner by the window. "Are you crazy, sitting in all that dust?"

"I'll be fine, Auntie. I don't have allergies. This is a good book and I want to finish it."

"What are you reading?"

Binky held up the book so Towanda could see the cover. "It's *Everything, Everything* by Nicola Yoon. About a sick girl whose mother made her live her whole life indoors."

"That could be you right now, or so I hear." Towanda joked.

"Funny, Auntie. Real funny."

Towanda had printed the business plan to show the chef.

Where was he? She'd asked him to be here at one. Maybe she should have met him someplace more professional?

No. If he was the right man for the job, she needed him to see where he'd be working.

When Gabriel walked in the door, he swung it open so fast both Binky and Towanda jumped.

Towanda slid off her stool and walked toward the doorway. Weird. She actually had to tilt her head back to see his whole face. This man was gigantic. Was he looking for a job in the NBA? Did he know this was a restaurant?

"Towanda Mathis?"

"Gabriel Seay?"

"Yes, I'm Gabriel. Nice to meet you." He extended his massive hand to her.

She shook it. "And you…cook?"

"Yes, I am a trained chef. And not for the NBA. I get that a lot."

A sense of humor. Definitely a plus, Towanda thought as she led him away from the door. "The place is dusty and needs furniture, but I set up stools and a table over here. Come on over and have a seat. Would you like a bottle of water?"

"Yes. Thank you."

Nice manners. Another plus. Towanda pulled a bottle of water from the picnic cooler she'd brought and handed it to him. His legs stretched out forever, so it looked as if his body propped up the stool rather than the other way around. She sat on her seat and gave him a once over.

Mustache trimmed and neat. Clean, manicured nails. A starched white button-down shirt and dark gray pants. Even his gray shoes shined. And when he smiled, his teeth were big and white and gorgeous.

Towanda glanced over at Binky. Binky hid her entire face behind her book.

Towanda had brought a list of chef interview questions, but since she'd be partnering with him, she wanted to get to know him first. She pushed her questions to the side of the table. "Where are you from?"

"Originally, Baltimore. I grew up there. I moved to Philadelphia later."

"After culinary school?"

"No. Jail."

Towanda double blinked. No way was she ready for the conversation to take this kind of turn right out of the gate. She took a sip of water and patted her chest. "I'm sorry. Did you just say *jail*?"

"You gave me an interview, so I want to be honest from the start. I've always liked cooking, but I got involved in the drug trade back in the day. No shootings or murders, but I moved product up and down the East Coast. I got arrested the week after my eighteenth birthday — the other two guys in the car and me. We were all sentenced to seven years in prison. I earned an early release and decided to move up here to stay away from the old life. My cousin, Mike Seay, he and his mother let me stay in their home while I get back on my feet. They're good people." Gabriel paused for a sip of water, then continued. "Anyway, I applied to a few programs and managed to get into The Restaurant School. I was successful there and when I graduated, I worked in several hotel kitchens and restaurants in the city. I have my resume with me."

Towanda's eyes darted back over to Binky, who had let her book drop into her lap and was sitting there with her mouth open. Her face mimicked Towanda's thoughts. *What a story!*

She took his resume and held it in her hands without reading it. "So why are you looking for a new chef position, Gabriel?"

"Growth. While I'm grateful for the work I've done so far, I'm getting older, and I'd like to grow into more meaningful chef positions involving some leadership. The type where I can use my creativity daily."

Another good answer. Towanda watched him carefully stared in his face as he spoke. No fidgeting or eyes darting around. His answers seemed honest. "Well, uh, let me take a look at your resume."

Gabriel sat quietly while Towanda read. Everything he mentioned appeared on his resume. Later, she could call these places to confirm the information. Bachelor of Science in Culinary Arts Program at Walnut Hill College. Tour of France. Specialty in freestyle cooking. Work with The Marriott Hotel. The Doubletree Hotel. South. Talula's Garden.

"I see you've worked at Talula's Garden most recently?"

"Yes. Great experience there."

"I heard they're award-winning."

"They are, but I'm looking for the chance to beat them."

Gabriel possessed skill and ambition. So far, so good.

He sounded better and better as the interview continued. Would he be good enough to partner with, though? She placed his resume on the table. "Gabriel, I'll level with you. I'm a businesswoman. I was born and raised here in Philly, and where we sit right now is where I used to sell cake slices and sticky buns with my family when I was a little girl. The space became available again and I want to try something new. I'm great with research, marketing strategy, business plans and hiring people. My family taught me how to cook and bake, but I am not a chef. I'm taking a gamble with this, and I need someone I can trust—"

"Someone organized who can handle setting up a kitchen and running it well, who'll be responsible for all the culinary activities for the restaurant."

"Well, that and—"

"Help you develop the concept, plan the menu, create great food, manage and train the kitchen staff and keep everything clean for the health inspectors."

"I know I'm looking for a little of everything. Frankly, I'm looking for the best, so I also need to know I can communicate well with you and that we can think together for this business."

He stared into her eyes. "In other words, you need more than a cook. You need someone who can lead, think strategically and be thorough. And someone who doesn't mind working long weekend hours?"

What else could she say? "All of that. And if your references check out, do you think you can handle it?"

Gabriel had brought a black bag with him. He stood up from his stool, pulled the bag up to the table and brought out a glass container, which he set before her. Then he handed her a plastic fork. She opened the lid and a heavenly aroma assailed her nose. Warm shredded vegetables with strips of red beets winding throughout. She sampled the food, tasting hints of lemon and ginger and some sort of spice. Not sure what she would call it, but it seemed like what Nana was called fancy vegan food.

"Binky, get out of that corner and come over here," Towanda called out.

"Huh."

"Come taste this." She gestured toward Binky. "Gabriel, this is my goddaughter, Benita Rodriguez."

"Wonderful to meet you, Ms. Benita."

Towanda passed her fork to Binky. "Here, honey."

Binky took a bite and chewed for awhile. Then she smiled and gave a thumbs up as her approval. "Fantastic food! Um, how tall are you?"

"I'm 6'8"."

"Wow." Binky's eyes grew wide.

Towanda placed an arm around her shoulders. "Mind your manners, darling. I think you've just met the executive chef for eatLARGE, Mr. Gabriel Seay."

44

CHABLIS

S ue Ryan, the Bossy Aussie, called me this afternoon. The medical device company she works for in Plymouth Meeting needs a software test engineer. She already told them she wants me for the position. That woman is amazing. I have to think about the offer though, because right now I'm contracting with a company outside of King of Prussia. No benefits, but I'm clocking a high hourly rate and my paychecks are obese.

I'm living my best life, oh yes, I am.

It's a little after nine, and I'm here at The Grandstand. Okay, it's official, I'm addicted, and I haven't missed a week since I accepted their invitation. Tonight I've already danced my current favorites: *DLH Exclusive*, *Nothing to Prove*, *#All Snap*, *Pull Up*, and *N2U*. And I probably sang a little too loud when I moved across the floor during *Watch Your Mouth*, but I don't care because that dance just makes me happy inside.

I tried to do *Some Mo' Ground* and *Unchained*, but I need to practice those more because the footwork is mad tricky.

I'm tying an undone lace on my shoe when the next song starts. It's Luke James singing. This dance is called *Subtle*. Great dance, but it has a lot of wicked body rolls in it. I straighten up and glance around the room real quick. Guess I'll go on and dance it. There's a huge crowd here tonight and I can hide myself behind a bunch of other people and try to keep the rolling to a minimum.

The dancers have already started, but I flow right on in with them. Tap, tap, roll, tap right, and roll, tap left, and step up on the right and one-two-three-four. When I pivot and walk around on the five-six-seven-eight, I see him standing near the edge of the dance floor closest to me.

John Gerald.

My heart thumps so loud I can hear it in my ears, and I stop dancing, because who can dance at a time like this?

Why didn't I keep a towel with me? Sweat is running down the side of my face, but it's too late to worry about that now. I move away from the dancers to stand in front of him, where I flash him a smile and say the first thing that comes to mind.

"Hey, buddy! What brings you back to fair Philadelphia?"

He doesn't laugh at this. Instead, his lips are closed tight. He clutches his coat in his hands, and he wears a short-sleeved black t-shirt. His sword and shield tattoos reach down from the tops of his biceps. I have the urge put my hand out to touch one, but of course, I don't.

"So, this is where you've been hiding?" he finally asks.

"Not hiding, but I have a good time here. I'm still in ministry at Rise. And hey, I switched to the YMCA this year so I could take their Les Mills classes."

"I heard. Sheena told me."

"I guess you can say I've been busy."

A noise comes from his throat that sounds a lot like the hiccup/snort I made when I found out he was leaving for Berlin.

"What dance were you doing?"

"When?"

"Just now, when I caught you rolling your body?"

I swallow hard. My skin tingles and I want to flip a switch in my brain to turn it off. "It's a line dance. It's called *Subtle.*"

A smile finally lights up his face. "Well, if I had to spend ten hours inside a stuffy airplane to come to see you, then that dance was a cool surprise. So is seeing you completely transformed, hair and all."

I laugh a little as I step off the dance floor and onto the carpet. It's still great to see him, even if he does have skinny girlfriends waiting for him in Berlin.

"You came here for me?"

"Well, you didn't answer any of my messages after LinkedIn. I actually flew in real late last night, but I know better than to scare you by showing up at your apartment like I'm stalking you. So, I messaged some Help Squad people this afternoon and Stacey got back to me. She said you dance at this place called The Grandstand on Thursday nights. Tonight, I had dinner with my mom, then as soon as I took her back home, I Googled the Grandstand address and drove over."

Wow. He'd done all that?

"And here I am." I say.

He starts putting on his coat. "Can you come with me? I want to take you where it's a little quieter so we can talk."

"Where are we going?"

"Just a place we used to visit together."

There's a warm vibration in his voice that I've never heard before. He actually went out of his way to locate me. He persevered for me, so I'll go with him. Besides, this isn't like my date with Mike Roberts. This is John. I hung out exercising with him for months. I can trust him.

"Let me get my things. I'll meet you out front." I head over to the table and grab my coat, keys and the bag with my extra t-shirt and sneakers. Waving goodbye to my line dance family, I rush out of The Grandstand.

John pulls up in his Jeep, taking the time to climb out, open my door, and help me inside. Then it's me and him riding along together with the Quiet Storm playing on the radio.

By the time we zoom through West Philly and over the bridge, I smile because I know where he's taking me. We park behind the Art Museum and he leads me to the wooden bench where we've sat and talked before. The wind nips at us, but it's still a beautiful night, with a clear sky and twinkling stars. Couples walk hand-in-hand through the area. John sits down close to me as I button my coat to block out the wind. And since he's right here, not across the ocean somewhere, it's hard to deny I have feelings for him.

I know. I know. I know.

He's not my man, but right now, boy does it feel like he is.

"What happened? I tried to call you and text you and I couldn't get through," he says with hurt in his voice. "You blocked me on Instagram and Facebook. You stopped emailing me. When I finally reach you on LinkedIn, you send me a message telling me all about yourself, but you end it saying you don't want to talk to me anymore? You gotta tell me what the issue is because I'm confused."

"Do Facebook pictures ring a bell?"

"What pictures? I'm busy and hardly on Facebook at all, and I haven't posted any pics to the gram lately, unless you count the shots of famous places in Germany or my workplace."

"For real, John? I saw them, okay. You with those skinny girls? They keep you company over there? I guess they're your type, right?"

"My type?"

"Take out your phone and launch Facebook right now. Scroll through your page."

"All right." He scoots away from me to pull his phone from his pocket and does that swiping, swiping, swiping. Until, "Oh."

"Oh, yeah." I mock his deep voice.

And then he laughs. Loud and strong. Right out of his gut. He even snorts a few times. There's nothing funny about any of this, and I'm glad I brought my phone with me, 'cause I'm about to Uber up outta this jawn.

He passes me his phone. "Will you look at this? Come on now, take a look. Is this what the fuss is about?"

It's those same photos I saw, with his arms around two women. But now I look closer. The shirts those ladies wear have identical red writing across the chest. Some German word that starts with *Scho*. I squint at the post details. He's tagged for the photos, but he didn't post them.

"I went to an outdoor festival with my team and a professional photographer saw me." John says, sliding his phone back in his coat pocket. "He asked if I minded taking a few pictures with his models. I said cool, whatever, and he told me how to pose with them, then he asked me if I was on Facebook and he tagged me. Right now, those photos are a part of some international collage in a drink ad in Germany."

I stare down at my feet. I feel like a fool. "I got it wrong?"

"At least now I know why you turned on me. Please don't do that again." He shifts his body closer to me on the bench. "It bugged me when I stopped hearing from you. I couldn't see what you've been reading in the Bible app. I missed hearing your voice. All that contact I had with you, it really kept me going. When I started calling you but couldn't reach you, it felt like someone took my sunshine away."

Warmth spreads through me and I have a hard time keeping myself from smiling.

He missed me.

That's good to know, because I missed him, too.

Friend zone or no friend zone.

I pat his arm. "Hey buddy, no worries. We're friends again. You want to drive me back now? The Grandstand is open for a few more hours."

He wipes a hand over his face. "How are you not getting this? I want us to be more than buddies. I flew from Germany to Philly because I want you to be my lady."

I stop breathing. "Your what?"

"Do you have room in your life for me?"

"No."

"Really?"

"No."

"Are you serious? You won't even talk it over with me?"

"No." I sigh, fluttering my eyelashes. "My life is kind of busy too, what with my workouts and church. And I have a new contract position and an offer for another job. Sometimes I help with beginner line dance class at Overbrook Arts Center on Saturday mornings. My plate is full, and I don't know if you can handle a pink-haired, line dancing, prayer warrior like myself."

He ignores my silliness and takes my hand. "I tell you what, warrior woman, let me take you out on an official date, and after that you let me know what works for you. I hope I can convince you, because I'm willing to do whatever it takes."

"When you left, you said you weren't sure where you were going to live."

"Germany is all right, but I belong in Philly, with my family and my church, and the Eagles, and this ray of sunshine sitting here next to me. So, I'll be back here for good in April. Until then, I need to hear from you every day. I need you cheering me on when I try out for American Ninja Warrior again and I want you to come with me and try CrossFit."

My mind is a total blank, except I want to text every single contact on my phone for some reason, and what if I can't control myself with him, *and who does this and...and...and.*

But all that comes out of my mouth is, "I can't cook."

"When I get back to the states, we can go to cooking classes together. And I would love to love you, with your panic attacks *and* the Pizza Hut addiction. Do you still want to love me?"

"Yes."

"First, you have to show me something."

I lean away. "What?"

"Where's your scar?"

I trace it with my fingertip. From my right ear all the way down to my dimple.

John cups my face in his hands, then his lips follow the same path my finger just traced. When I smile, he plants a kiss on one dimple, then the other, and then he looks in my eyes.

"That's the last thing I want you to remember about that scar and all that pain," he says.

And his full lips land on mine, and they are warm and soft, and he smells like spearmint close up like I imagined, except now I don't have to dream anymore, because this is real.

John *is* my man, and this *is* my best night ever.

45

MARIAH

Mariah automatically pressed her hands against the seat of the chair, rocking it back and forth against the dirty gray linoleum floor, testing to see if the rickety wooden chair would hold her weight or dump her to the floor. She glanced up and around the room. People milled about, but no one paid much attention.

I'm one hundred pounds lighter. I can sit down just fine in this chair.

She'd chosen this location in Southwest Philly on her own. A forgotten hole in the wall place. Close enough for her to drive to quickly, but far enough away from her house that she wouldn't run into anyone she knew. She settled her bottom on the chair and took three deep cleansing breaths. Old wooden chairs and tables. A long shelf with coffee, tea and powdered sugar donuts lined the wall in the back. Strangers started to take their seats. Different races, ages and genders. No judgmental looks at all.

Alcoholics Anonymous.

Mariah clasped her hands together. Then, she unclasped them and rubbed the back of her arms. Finally, she crossed her arms against her chest and waited. She'd arrived early because the website recommended it. Now she found herself full of nervous energy, not sure how the meeting would go or if she actually needed to be here.

"We're going to get started." A tall man with thick salt and pepper hair and a mustache waved his hands at the crowd. "Everyone, please. Find a seat."

A tiny red-haired lady with leathery skin and a kind smile sat down next to Mariah and offered her hand. "Hi. Good to meet ya. Name's Kelly."

"Hi, Kelly," Mariah shook hands. "I'm Mariah."

"Would you like coffee or anything? We've got donuts today, but if you want chips or a soda or something, I can run next door to the store for ya. Won't take but a second."

Mariah shook her head. "No, thank you. But thanks for the offer."

"No problem. Let me know if ya change your mind," Kelly said, settling back in her chair.

Max, the tall man with the salt and pepper hair, served as the leader or *chairperson* for the meeting. He asked everyone to silence their phones. Mariah muted hers and slid it in the front of her purse. If an emergency happened with Binky at school, her phone would still buzz. As everyone settled, more strangers waved to her or reached over and offered their hands to shake. They all seemed to know one another. She was the only new person.

Max opened the discussion, and Mariah sat back and listened with an open mind. People from all walks of life discussed their week.

Kelly shared that she was alcoholic, and in the past few days, she had a hard time, missing her grandkids who lived in Alabama with their mother, her daughter, who refused to speak to her.

Steve, a shy-looking man in a Phillies baseball cap, was on leave from his job as a ninth-grade biology teacher. He said he struggled with drinking more because of the time on his hands.

Max had been clean and sober for five years, but with his wife suffering from complications of multiple sclerosis, he'd thought about drinking this past weekend again.

Stephanie, a curvy waitress with a fiery voice, said she didn't appreciate her friends coming up to her job at night offering Xanax and Percocet to help her make it through her shift easier.

Peter, with his sandy brown hair, vintage KISS t-shirt, dusty blue jeans and construction worker boots, appreciated two years sober.

Chubby Destiny smiled wide, showing two missing front teeth. She had not taken a drink in six months and shared about studying for her GED.

Tim, who wore a sharp, navy-blue three-piece suit, had tears streaming down his cheeks while sharing. His wife had taken their two grade school children and year-old baby and moved them to Florida to stay with their grandparents after she grew tired of his drunken rages. The people closest to him patted him on the back and offered him tissues. He'd thanked them.

Story after story. People admitted they were alcoholics. No one interrupted anyone. Everyone respected the other person's right to share their words. Mariah remained still throughout, her arms crossed, listening. Not quite sure if she should share. Did her story even compare to theirs?

After Tim calmed down, Mariah heard her own voice before she realized she was speaking.

"My name is Mariah," she said.

Various greetings arrived from the group, then all eyes rested on her. She unfolded her arms, sitting up straight.

"The truth is, I don't have a clue if I'm an alcoholic." She glanced toward Max, who nodded his encouragement. "But this week I felt like maybe I should get some help. I lost a lot of weight last year, and I stopped eating a lot of my favorite foods because I couldn't do that anymore. Somewhere along the line, I started drinking wine to soothe myself. And it did, but I don't want to keep going down this road. I'm in the middle of a tense time in my marriage. My best friend caused me a lot of pain last year and we're trying to mend fences now, but it still hurts. My daughter is a teenager and, I have to say, she's been in rare form. Oh, and I'm back at college trying to finish my degree. Now I'm sipping every night to relax. Sometimes it's a lot. My husband moved out after he found out. I just can't make life any worse for myself." She sniffed. "So, I'm here. That's it."

Max passed her the box of tissues. "Thank you for sharing with us, Mariah. It helps."

She wiped her nose and took a few more cleansing breaths. She'd shared. Kind of felt good to get it all off her chest. Between support groups for weight loss surgery and AA, would she spend the rest of her life sitting in chairs sharing and crying?

God willing, she wouldn't.

She filled her lungs with air and then breathed out again. This wasn't so bad after all. Whether food-dependent or alcohol dependent, a community of people existed who were willing to lend a hand.

Sure, things were bleak, but she was far from alone.

With the hour nearly up, Kelly passed around a donation basket. Max asked if anyone was celebrating an anniversary and then passed out a chip to Peter whose face turned red.

Two years sober. Everyone cheered for him.

Afterward, Max closed the meeting in prayer.

That was it. Mariah's first AA meeting. Over.

At the back of the room near the coffee machine, Kelly gave her a hug and offered her phone number. "Sorry to hear about your family trouble, darling. Such a beautiful lady you are. Listen, you go on and give me a call if you're having a hard time this week. I'll listen anytime."

Then Stephanie walked over and offered Mariah a hug and some reassurance. "It gets better. Let me tell you, girl, I used to drink and get high on the regular. AA saved my life. Facts."

Mariah hugged, shook hands, and said thank you to everyone who gathered around her. She was a little overwhelmed by it all, but grateful.

In the car on the way home, she kept the radio turned off, preferring to ride in silence and reflect on the previous hour. There were so many places she could visit on the ride back home. Fast-food drive-thrus. Restaurants. Liquor stores. Any of them would take her money.

But the cost was too high.

On the phone, Mariah spoke as soon as she heard her husband answer.

"Os?"

"Yes, Mariah. How are you doing?"

"Good." She put the car in park. Home again. "I...uh..took myself to AA today for the first time."

"Really?"

"It wasn't too bad. Just wanted you to know."

"You said you would do it when you were ready, and I support you. I have some news for you too."

"You do?"

"Today, I went to the courthouse and filed the form to stop the divorce. All I had to say was that I'm voluntarily dismissing my own case. I didn't have to give a reason. Is that okay with you?"

"That's better than okay with me."

"I spent the past week fasting and praying for us. Our home. Our daughter. We've invested too much and cared for each other too long to let it all go."

"Does this mean—are you coming home?"

"Let's keep talking and try to hear each other out. If we can do that for a while, then yes, I'll be back home."

"Can you do me a favor?"

"Okay."

She clutched her phone tight in her hand. "When we talk, can you please stop blaming me? I'm not perfect, and I never have been, no matter what you saw in me when we first met."

"I hear you, and I want to tell you I'm sorry. Resenting you because of your health issues and body changes? I should have apologized a long time ago. You are so beautiful to me, wife."

Mariah opened her car door but stopped before she stepped out. "Forget how I look, because I'm not an ideal, I'm a person. From now on, please just see me as Mariah. That's all I ever was."

"Mariah."

"Yes."

"Forgive me. I love you."

46

TOWANDA

Together, Towanda and Gabriel put in three months of hard work preparing eatLARGE for the masses. Towanda took care of the funding, licensing, inspections and city paperwork. She also hired the thinkLARGE contractors to create the logo, tagline and develop all the marketing and branding.

Gabriel took control of the menu offerings and put his imagination to work creating low-calorie dishes with high nutritional impact. He also hired an excellent support staff for the restaurant. Mariah even managed to lend a hand, using her eye for detail with the restaurant interior design and helping with the community restaurant concept.

Whenever Towanda walked up to the restaurant, she wanted to pinch herself. The hunter-green-and-white eatLARGE sign hung over the front door and their hours were posted in white lettering on the front window. The glass door opened to a large room with hardwood floors. The huge community table sat right in the middle with seating for twenty at a time. Decorative strings of lights hung around the perimeter of the room and leafy green plants took up residence in the windows. A small green and white sign reading CASH ONLY / BYOB sat on the counter. Gabriel came up with the idea of placing a large silver bowl filled with water out front on the bottom step — a courtesy for the dog walkers in the neighborhood. Last but not least, tall sunflowers stood in pots on either side of the front door. Sunny and friendly.

By the time eatLARGE opened, they barely needed to advertise. Who needed a promotional team when Towanda had Chablis Shields? Chablis handed grand opening postcards to every person she knew. All her buddies in her exercise classes at the gym. Ministry leaders at Rise Church. Walkers and runners she passed while training on Saturday mornings. Every single line dancer in the tri-state area. On the night two local running clubs visited the restaurant, Towanda almost passed out. They joked and ate their way through first and second helpings, paid well and said they would return soon.

Thank God for Gabriel. In the kitchen, he sang—badly—while he cooked. But the meals he made tasted fresh and scrumptious. His dishes entranced Towanda — she brought food home every weekend now. She'd also started parking her Range Rover first two, then three, then four blocks away from the restaurant. She enjoyed walking outdoors more now, especially with a new project to think about and a brand-new friend in her life.

Baby steps.

Small, consistent, baby steps.

"WANDA!" GABRIEL CALLED FROM THE KITCHEN DOORWAY.

"Yeah?" She had her head down one early Saturday afternoon, focusing on Inventory Center in QuickBooks Premier. The restaurant seemed to run out of some supplies faster than expected. No complaints, though. eatLARGE was catching on.

"There's a phone call for you."

"I'm coming right now."

He held the wall phone receiver against his chest until she reached him.

"And since when have you started calling me Wanda?" she asked, taking the receiver.

"Since Nana visited and she said I could, and what Nana says goes," he teased her, grinning as he stepped back toward the kitchen.

"Oh, really, now?"

"Yes, and you should know Nana is in love with my food and we're going to be good friends. Your Nana knows what's up."

Towanda raised the phone to her ear, flashing him an annoyed look. If he didn't loom over her or mention Nana, she'd probably say something about him calling her Wanda.

"Yes, this is eatLARGE. How can I help you?"

"Hello. My name is David Stein. I recently read a Philadelphia Tribune online article about your restaurant. I'm trying to locate Towanda Mathis."

David Stein? Never heard of him. This must be a press call. Great! More publicity. Towanda could provide him with the next steps for starting his article and they could schedule an interview.

"Hello there, David. I am Towanda Mathis and I'm honored you've called eatLARGE. If you visit our website, you'll find a downloadable media kit to start your article. Please read the press release. Give us a call back and you can schedule an interview with me and my business partner, Executive Chef Gabriel Seay. We'll be happy to tell you all about eatLARGE. We are a proud part of the South Philly restaurant scene."

"Did you just say you are Towanda Mathis?"

"Yes, I am."

"Did you grow up in Philadelphia?"

"Yes."

"And…" The man's voice broke for a second and then recovered. "Is Rodney Mathis your father?"

Why was he asking about her father? Journalists usually didn't ask such personal questions for business articles.

"Who is this, again?" She asked.

"Your mother? Who is your mother?"

"Her name was Miriam, but she's been gone since I was three. My grandmother, aunts and uncles raised me. Are you interested in writing a deeper feature article? I can provide better answers if we schedule an interview time."

"If you're indeed Towanda, you need to sit down. Right now."

Towanda whipped around, looking across the kitchen. Gabriel

caught her eye. He stopped rinsing a sink full of kale and shut off the water.

"This talk is becoming too personal," she said, raising her voice. "I don't know you, but now I think I had better disconnect from this call. It sounds like you're setting me up for identity theft."

"Don't hang up, please!"

"Who are you again?"

"I'm David Stein. Towanda, I'm...I think...I'm your brother."

TOWANDA AND GABRIEL HAD ONLY BEEN BUSINESS PARTNERS FOR A FEW months, but none of that mattered now. She desperately needed him there for that phone call. He brought her the chair she sat on, trembling, as she listened to David Stein. And he remained by her side as she heard details that squeezed her heart so tight that she had trouble breathing.

David Stein. Twenty-four years old.

Brother of Shayna Stein. Twenty-three years old.

Both of them, children of Miriam Stein. Towanda's mother, previously Miriam Levin of southern New Jersey. The Miriam Levin who had enrolled as a student at LaSalle University, who'd met and befriended a tall, charming jazz guitarist named Rodney Mathis, a college dropout who liked to visit the campus.

Rodney Mathis, Towanda's father, loved a good party, so much so he kept a celebration going on with Miriam when they set up in an apartment in North Philly. The details were fuzzy about their relationship, but eventually, Towanda was born. Miriam and Rodney broke up. She moved to California, leaving Towanda behind with her father and grandmother.

Towanda's hands shook. "So...uh...my God...uh...is my mother...?"

"I'm sorry, but Mom has passed on."

Her lungs emptied. Gabriel's strong arm around her shoulders reminded her to take in oxygen again.

David continued. "But that's how we found you. Shayna and I, we don't even know if our father knew about you before he passed away ten years ago. When we cleaned out Mom's closet, we found an old wooden box at the top. We broke the latch, thinking it might contain old love letters and possibly some keepsakes from her childhood. We opened it and found you."

Tears rolled down Towanda's face. She couldn't find the strength to stop them, but she managed to nod toward Gabriel when he gestured to the speakerphone button. She kept sobbing as David's voice filled the room.

"Mom saved a lock of your hair in a plastic baggie. Several baby pictures. But it was the picture of Mom holding you on her lap, with your name and hers and the year 1983 written on the back that let us know you were probably her daughter. She also kept a few letters and torn journal pages which told us about her relationship with your father, Rodney. She collected articles, too. Clippings about your awards from Penn. Entrepreneurship articles about your business, think-LARGE. She even had a full printout of your website. Towanda, she used to visit the public library every week, and I think she followed you all over the Internet. She may have been planning to visit you. I took all the information and Googled you. eatLARGE appeared in the latest search results."

Towanda's mother remembered her. Her mother had followed her. "My mother? Miriam? What happened to her?"

"She battled breast cancer these last two years. Shayna took time off from school to help care for her. She passed three months ago."

So much to take in. Towanda couldn't stand it. She stood up and paced in circles on the kitchen floor, sobbing, then cleaning her face off with a dish towel, then sobbing again. Gabriel wrote down David's contact information and then hung up the phone. Towanda didn't ask him to, but she was thankful when he wrapped his arms around her and let her cry for the next hour.

Towanda never found her family.

Her family found her.

47

ONE YEAR LATER

Everything needed to be on point for the evening.

Towanda must have circled the eatLARGE dining room a hundred times that Saturday afternoon. The restaurant didn't open until six, which gave her plenty of time to double-check everything behind her staff. She made sure the floor shined, the chairs were dust-free, fresh daisies adorned the middle of the big community table and the glass door and windows were so clear the entire front of the restaurant smelled like Windex.

Nana arrived via Uber right before six and Towanda led her to her favorite big comfy brown chair in the corner by the window. Nana had become quite a fixture at eatLARGE. Several return customers even asked Towanda what time her grandmother would be there on the weekends so they could talk with her.

Once settled in her chair, she reached out and gripped Towanda's hand, halting her from taking another loop around the room.

"I can tell you're nervous. You stop being anxious, you hear." Nana squeezed her fingers. "This is for you."

"What if they don't like visiting here? What if they hate the restaurant?"

Nana waved her away. "You hush. They'll love it, just like I do."

Towanda straightened up to her full height but still glanced down to make sure she hadn't wrinkled her outfit. She made one more trip around the big table and the plush brown chairs in the front and then looked over toward the doorway.

There they were.

David and Shayna Stein.

Months earlier, Towanda had flown to San Luis Obispo to meet her siblings officially. Amazingly, it took the rest of the year to coordinate their schedules so they could spend time in Philly, but now, with her siblings finally inside her business, she stepped over to them and welcomed them into her world. Her brother and sister. The son and daughter of Miriam Levin-Stein. Her mother. A lady who'd never once forgotten about her.

She approached them. "I'm so glad you came."

David reached for her. "There's no way we would miss seeing you again."

They drew her into their arms and she hugged them tightly. She didn't want to cry, but tears still dripped from her face. Inside the doorway of eatLARGE, they stood holding one another until Towanda broke the embrace.

"I'm sorry. Where are my manners? I was raised right." Towanda took Shayna's hand, then David's. "Come over here and meet my grandmother. Her name is Madeline Mathis. Her friends call her Maddie. I call her Nana."

Towanda stood back and watched as Shayna and David greeted her grandmother, and then she offered them seats at the community table. "Sit here. Chef Gabriel, my business partner, has prepared a special menu for us tonight and the food will be out soon."

"Towanda, come on, you must sit with us for dinner," Shayna said, as she pulled out the chair next to her. "Please."

Towanda looked up, and suddenly there stood Gabriel, right next to her. He placed a paw-like hand on her shoulder. "Are you okay?"

"I'm going to be just fine. I've been picturing this day all year. Now I'm trying to figure out how to handle everything."

"Who says you have to? I'm right here, so have a seat," he reassured her, gesturing toward the community table. "Me and the staff, we've got this tonight. Enjoy time with your family."

With that, for the first time, she took a seat in her own restaurant. And each time she glanced around, it seemed Gabriel appeared, serving them personally. First with icy cold bottles of Pellegrino, and then with white, rectangular plates of chocolate balsamic red beets. They ate their appetizers and chatted. She found it fascinating. The more they talked and enjoyed one another, the more David and Shayna actually felt like family to her.

"Tomorrow, let me drive you both around this town. Philly is a lot more than cheesesteaks, Rocky and the Liberty Bell. Your sister grew up here, so you have to learn this place," she told them.

Later, when Mariah and Oscar arrived with Binky trailing behind, Towanda introduced them to her brother and sister. The Rodriquez family sat down on the opposite side of the community table while the eatLARGE staff served them water and brought Towanda and her siblings the next course--bowls of avocado gazpacho.

"Whoa. That is bright green, Mom!" Binky said.

"And it's healthy and good, and you'll eat it." Mariah winked at Towanda from across the table.

Towanda winked back, pleased to see Oscar with his arm draped around Mariah's shoulder, and Binky without a cell phone in her hands.

Chef Gabriel pulled out all the stops with a delicious mushroom and cheese lasagna so wonderful Towanda wondered how he came up with the recipe. By then, other customers had arrived. Without hesitation, Mariah stood up and helped them find seats around the table. She explained how the restaurant worked and what Gabriel had prepared for the evening meal, talking with them about the community table concept.

By the time Chablis strolled through the door holding her boyfriend John's hand, Towanda and her siblings were sharing fresh homemade berry water ice. Chablis walked right over and greeted David and Shayna like old friends, hugging them and introducing them to John.

"You are way late, but my, you look happy." Towanda stood to embrace Chablis and John. When she stepped back, she looked down at Chablis, who, with her gleaming smile and bright eyes, seemed happier than usual.

"Munchkin, you want to turn that smile down a little? You're burning people's retinas," Towanda joked.

John's grin spread across his face. "My bad, Towanda. I think I had something to do with that. We just came back from her parent's house and she's still a little in shock."

Towanda glanced from Chablis to John and then back to Chablis. "Wait. What?"

Chablis put out her hand and flashed a diamond solitaire. "And let me tell ya, I don't care how many weights I have to lift, I'm never taking this bad boy off."

Mariah walked over and took Chablis' hand. "Lemme see that ring! Last month at church, John told us he was going to propose, we just didn't know the day. Congratulations, cousin."

Oscar placed an arm around Mariah's shoulder. "Yeah, we told him, don't worry about being perfect with it, just make sure her parents give their blessing."

"Well, you could have told me," Towanda said. "I would have had a cake here or something. Let's turn on some music and make this a party. Congratulations!"

"Save the cake for the wedding." Chablis turned toward Nana, who was still seated in her big comfy chair. "And I want Nana to make us a big old-fashioned one if she doesn't mind."

"You all are making me cry. Acting like you haven't seen each other for months," Nana fussed. "You all went to church together last Sunday. Now stop all that sweet stuff."

They all laughed, stopping when the front door creaked open. A family of four peeked inside and a man called to them. "You're open tonight, right? Is this a private party?"

Towanda opened her arms wide as she stepped towards the doorway. "I'm Towanda Mathis and welcome to eatLARGE. We are definitely open, and you are right on time. We're about to turn on some great music, and just wait until you taste the food Chef Gabriel prepared tonight. All low calorie, but big on taste. One price for four courses. Hang your coats on the hooks on the wall and have a seat at the big table. You're all welcome!"

Come.

Share.

Enjoy.

LETTER TO MY READER

Hi! I hope you enjoyed *Thick Chicks*. This book was all about friend-ship, health, family, marriage, divorce, rebellious teens, jealousy, deception, abandonment, addiction, fitness training, falling in love, fear, and forgiveness. And just for fun, I threw in some line dancing.

I'm a little exhausted right now.

Chablis, Mariah, and Towanda lived in my head for three years before I finished the first draft. First, Chablis came to me, telling me she'd been beaten as a teenager, and she didn't mind keeping her weight on because she felt it slowed her down and protected her from herself. Then Towanda arrived, tall and strong and unafraid of anything except being abandoned by the people she loved the most. Last but not least, I heard from Mariah, and she told me she'd never lost her pregnancy pounds. She kept gaining weight and requested prayer about her marriage and family issues. The other characters — Oscar, Binky, John, Gabriel, Mrs. Brown, Jackie, Nana, and the others filtered in as I started writing the story. Dr. Brian Jones, Tracey Jones, and Pastor David Downes first appeared in *Broken Together*.

The opening scenes of the novel were difficult to write, but I needed to include them. Unfortunately, when a woman is curvy or plus-sized, people tend to think her most significant issue is her weight. But what about her heart? Her aspirations? Her past? She has all those too, and people need to understand that.

Are you ready for another adventure? I just finished writing *Engaged,* a humorous novel describing the six months of full-on crazy before John Gerald and Chablis Shields wedding. I hope you'll join me on the journey.

One last thing. If you liked *Thick Chicks: A Novel,* please consider leaving an online review wherever you purchased the book. I would truly appreciate it.

Thanks again for reading.

May the Lord bless you and keep you,
   Until next time,
   K.L. Gilchrist

ACKNOWLEDGMENTS

This is the best part of the trip.

Thank you, Father, for allowing me to seek a closer walk with you while I wrote this novel. When I do not know what to do, my eyes are upon you.

To my family, Chris, Howard, Sweetie, and Crazy — thanks for accepting my apologies for shooing you away whenever the writing started to flow. It's a cliché to say that I couldn't have done it without you, but I couldn't have.

Much love to Christian Stronghold Church, where I sat in a pew with my MacBook and typed the first draft of this novel while the Junior Choir practiced. Thank you, Sister Patricia Richardson and women of Stronghold, for supporting me so much with *Broken Together*. Rest in heavenly peace to my cherished friend and sister in Christ, Deaconess Barbara Jean Keller — I named the Barbara Jean Brown character in her honor.

Many blessings to Pastor Paul James and Pastor Christine James of CareView Community Church. Thanks for your prayers and support as I entered the final stages with this book.

There's a bunch of people who directly encouraged me after I released *Broken Together*. Their support helped me sit down to write and finish *Thick Chicks*. Thank you to: Kim Colbert, Yolanda Perkins,

Samantha Alexander, Tonja Belo, Stacey Strickler, Orielle Jeffries, Linda Brooks, Aja Gunning, Miriam Richards, Nikki Brown, Trina Singleton, Tashajuanna Muhammad, Tracy Ferguson, Lanee' Daniels, Theresa White, Shakira Coleman, Pamela Henley, and Ken and Penny Getchell. Charles "Tank" Harris — I wouldn't have completed the first draft of this story if you hadn't talked about the book *The One Thing* — thanks so much.

Thank you, authors of American Christian Fiction Writers (ACFW), for every suggestion you provided for this work. Special appreciation to Caryn Hoang, Susan Karsten, Megan Kinney, Christine Noble, Caroline Powers, and Cameron Walker.

My beta readers! Bless you for your insight and every mistake you caught: Stacey Strickler, Krista Strickland, Tashajuanna Muhammad, Lynn White, Hunter Kimble, and Jemiscoe Chambers-Black.

I can't drop the mic before I shout to my urban line dance family — when the writing gets tough, you all make life a lot more fun. Hugs and kisses to the ladies I've laughed with the most: Judith Wagner, Kathy Thomas, Sharon Peterson-Coleman, and Trina Watson. Blessings to my instructors: Gloria Kingcade, Ronnie Williams, Christopher "DJ Chris Blues" Torres, Devonte' Normand, David and Selena Earley, and Theresa Brown. Much love to EVERYBODY who danced at Eastwick Community Center, Overbrook Arts Center, Rose Hill Community Center, Mill Creek Community Center, and We Dancin' Over Here/The Parkside Experience. *Who's teaching? It's your OTHER left! Let's lock it in!*

Note: The Grandstand Dance Hall scenes are loosely based on *We Dancin' Over Here/The Parkside Experience* in Philadelphia, PA.

ABOUT THE AUTHOR

K.L. Gilchrist is the author of *Broken Together*, *Holding On*, and the upcoming novel, *Engaged*. She lives with her husband and two bright and funny daughters outside of Philadelphia, PA. You can visit her online at www.klgilchrist.com.

 facebook.com/402435140151793

 twitter.com/KL_Gilchrist

instagram.com/KLGilchrist

BROKEN TOGETHER

by K.L. Gilchrist

A story of marriage, betrayal, commitment and faith.

Tracey Jones life is picture-perfect. She's crazy in love with her attractive doctor husband. Her only job is raising two healthy children in their stunning home. However, looks can be deceiving. When Tracey discovers her husband's involvement with a young nurse at his private practice, it becomes a challenge to hold everything together. As Tracey's household falls apart, and the full extent of Dr. Jones secrets come to light, a series of events leads her to do the unthinkable. In order to heal in her marriage, she must face a painful past that forces her to offer grace and empathy to someone who may need it more than she does.

Get your copy here: http://www.klgilchrist.com/books/

HOLDING ON

by K.L. Gilchrist

Tracey's story continues...

Tracey and Brian Jones have much to celebrate. They've been married for more than twelve years, their son is doing well in college, and a new baby is on the way. However, small resentments still exist beneath the surface in their relationship. When Tracey betrays Brian's trust in order to provide emotional support to a family who helped her in the past, battle lines are drawn in their household. Will Tracey be able to hold on to her marriage and family when her past and present collide?

Get your copy here: http://www.klgilchrist.com/books/

SIGN UP

Please take a moment to sign up for newsletter updates. You'll be the first to know about my book releases, free stories, special deals, and giveaways. My emails are short, I won't stuff your mailbox, and you can opt-out at any time. Go to www.klgilchrist.com to subscribe.